Healer

Shadows of the past

Magdalena Kułaga

From the editor

A fantasy novel set in an alternative world, in a time close to ours. The story of a man with the power of healing, kidnapped by force to the royal castle in order to protect the life of the king, his family and the nearest court from a deadly plague that decimates the kingdom.

A healer named Vivan is a very sensitive man. He has the gift of feeling moods. This is called the gift of compassion. Too much evil and meanness around him makes his strength weak, draining his will to live. He is destined to save others, give them hope, and lift them up from their fall. In the castle, he is overwhelmed by the darkness of evil, intrigues and hidden murders. His stepbrother comes to help him. Due to the coincidence of various, sometimes quite dramatic circumstances, the mission of saving the most important man in the kingdom at that time is undertaken by people whom no one would have suspected before. In this rescue act, the author involved people from… House of Pleasure, a local brothel.

Life outside the castle is the darkest scenario for mankind. The plague takes away the feeling of humanity. Mentally weak individuals become bandits and murderers. They do not hesitate to sacrifice others to save their lives. The worst instincts are revealed: bestiality, the pursuit of satisfying one's desires. It is not easy to survive this hell while maintaining self-esteem. The heroes find nobility, bravery and friendship where they least expect it…

For Agnieszka

Sam and Frodo as one…

Prolog

He was a healer of unprecedented power in the kingdom, even though he was only twenty years old.

Now he was being led to his death.

"What are you actually planning?" he asked the viceroy, "you will not give me back my freedom. So, why didn't you kill me sooner?"

"Blot my hands with the healer's blood?" the king's brother played indignation perfectly, "my future subjects would not love me for it," he put his hand on his shoulder in a gesture that was too familiar, as if he was revealing a great secret. "I want to gain their love and favor, my dear. You see, power over the people is mightiness! A good ruler wins the grace of his subjects by deception. Sometimes he uses love for this. Don't you know about it?"

"Everyone will know about your accession to the throne, Tenchryz!"

"Yes, it will. Probably soon after the attack. Some of the subjects will be indignant, yes. The more implicit and too troublesome will be welcomed by our Mother Earth. Most, however, will be grateful for you and the overthrow of the tyrant. Of course, I also foresaw the possibility that, under certain favorable circumstances for you, you might be able to get out of your present situation. I hope you will appreciate my grace towards you, your family and, of course, the inhabitants of your small, godforsaken mountain town, because then I will be especially mindful of," he leaned towards the convict so close that Vivan could smell his breath, "the good of you all. Especially any of those dear to you who are still alive."

The words disturbed Vivan. Before he could reflect on them, the viceroy added:

"My dear, no one will blame me for removing my brother and his family from the throne. A king whom the people had begged in vain to give them a healer and save the lives of his subjects. Who cares about the truth? And having an army, I will shut the mouth of the rebellious."

"You'll be an ordinary murderer..." Vivan looked into his eyes with clear contempt. "He had at least one rule - he cared for his loved ones. You will have no one, because you will always be afraid that someone will kill you, just like you did with your brother. You will curse this day!"

Terlan, the king's brother who had just led to the bloody coup, stared at the young healer seriously, as if he had just discovered something in the young man that he had not expected in him, and gained his appreciation. Indeed, although Vivan had entertained him in the last few weeks with his clumsy attempt to prevent the attack, probably as a result of his disease progressing in him, associated with his legendary special sensitivity, he now had to admit that he had never lacked courage.

"Get him out!" he ordered. But there was no earlier verve in his voice, as if he was still hesitating with the decision.

It was just like that.

"Vivan!" He called after a moment.

The healer struggled to glare at him without concealing contempt.

The viceroy waited silently for a moment, observing his behavior. He could not see the fear in his eyes, although, as he was sure, the young man was aware of what was about to happen to him.

"This is your final decision?" he asked him finally. "You have a choice. It is a pity to waste such great talent! You know very well that the Court Medic is no match for you. Consider! Life in my service or death?"

Vivan looked away. Out of the corner of his eye, he noticed several of the closest guards looking at him with growing hope, hoping that he would change his mind. They would be fools to think otherwise during the raging plague.

But he had to disappoint their hopes.

In mourning silence, the soldiers took Vivan from the guard quarters. This time it was not easy for them to obey the order.

They knew that they were helping to kill a man whose healing power and big heart were almost legendary. His hands might be needed by their families and themselves in the future. However, their relatives could pay with their lives for disobedience.

They had no choice.

Vivan didn't resist. As the gates of the wall surrounding the castle began to open, he was seized with a cold that had nothing to do with the ambient temperature. Fear and despair had usually been the source of this chill, and now they tightened his heart with an iron band. They wanted to push him out, perhaps thus venting his growing frustration, but one look of him, full of dignity, which he still tried to keep, thwarted his intention. They pulled back, letting him pass like a ruler himself, and their bodies involuntarily straightened in a salute.

They bid farewell to him, the mighty healer, the savior of the kingdom, and the hero in the only way available to them, showing him respect.

The crowd outside, seeing the gate open, fell silent in anticipation.

Vivan, aware that he had little time left before people understood who they had in front of them, closed his eyes for a moment. He tried to gather strength for what lay ahead.

There was no way out. No turning back.

And no hope.

The gates of the castle walls closed with a piercing crash like the gates of a tomb...

CHAPTER 1 — Last moments

For a moment the crowd conferred with a soft murmur, venting their disbelief. However, it quickly began to give way to cries of joy. "Yes, it's him! I recognize him!" People cried. "He helped my mother!"... "He saved my wife!"... "My brother was rescued from the clutches of death!"

Fear seized his soul as the buzz grew and euphoria seemed to sweep through the crowd like a tide.

It will happen soon. The nightmare that awakened him at night has just begun to materialize. He will pray for death that will not come soon.

The end was near.

The chill penetrated his body. Helplessness. It is a pity that he cannot prevent anything, change anything. It was causing him almost physical pain.

The crowd around him argued furiously as they approached him. Vivan tried to flee his mind elsewhere to keep from succumbing to his mounting dread. He thought of the queen who had a long and painful road to death. Her beauty aroused in her brother a desire that had been hidden so far. It released a primal nature devoid of any warm feelings. In him she awakened a monster of inexpressible cruelty, eager to destroy. These feelings were contrary to the nature of a healer who was sensitive to someone else's harm, to frighten him. And disgust.

The viceroy confidently carries out his plan, whereby the queen's sons will be cruel and immediately killed. He will order that Meron, the eldest, always suspicious of him, be dealt with very brutally. Then he would rape the queen as he always wanted, and would continue to do so until he quenched her will to fight and live.

Within the walls of the castle Vivan could sense the emotions of the viceroy, very well masked from others, but by him as a healer sensitive to a whole range of different feelings, readable like an open book. More than once, the strength of these feelings and a rich, demonic imagination forced into Vivan's mind visions of torturing the queen in front of her helpless husband. The scent of the viceroy changed then for the affectionate Vivan as well. The man's heart was accelerating beyond measure and beating louder, and sweat poured over his body for the viceroy was slightly obese, unlike his brother. But the worst thing was the excitement several times in the presence of Vivan, ending with an erection. The feelings that caused it, and the very fact that they did so, made the healer feel sick and defiled. In his subconscious, they also built an inappropriate and disgusting image of erotic behavior, aided also by the behavior of men and women in the castle. For the royal court enjoyed all pleasures, as if death were not raging outside the walls. Or maybe because she was still there. They joyfully vented their desires, which only a few seemed to refuse.

He warned Meron about his uncle several times, but since the latter was cunning in concealing his feelings and plans, Meron failed to approach him. When Terlan began to be confident of his success, his suspicions that the young healer would reveal his plots before time vanished. On their last dinner together, the viceroy's erection again filled Vivan with disgust. He hasn't eaten anything. Others were then occupied with an empty and meaningless discussion about the plague raging around. They felt safe in the castle, under the touch of the healer, energized and free. As always, Terlan made him sit close to him under the guise of showing respect for his extraordinary abilities. The truth was quite different. The viceroy wanted him close to him so as not to lose sight of him during public meetings. With disgust, Vivan remembered the moments in his mind as the other had reached discreetly into his pants, and then, savoring the healer's disgust, slowly and carefully rubbed his hand into the young man's straitjacket. To complete the work, deliberate and knowingly, he took his hand and squeezed it tightly. The smell of that hand made Vivan nauseous. He could hardly control himself.

"Thanks for the entertainment you give me," Terlan leaned in to his ear.

Vivan's world suddenly spun. Uninvited stimuli reached him from everywhere, radiating from the tainted hand. He saw a vision of disgracing the queen. He felt the pressing feelings that caused the viceroy's hatred and lust. The queen would be his wife, not his brother, if he were to sit on the throne. The one whose hair is like fire and eyes like green pastures will be his. She will writhe under his touch. She will scream, grunt like a whore under him. He would plead and he would enjoy her helplessness and feed her eyes with the despair of the brother he genuinely hated. Jealousy clouded his mind. Anger filled him with lust and murder. He relished these visions. He liked them like a juicy fruit. He fed on them.

Now, with Vivan standing in front of the crowd, he must be carrying out his monstrous plan...

"Fascinating." The healer still had echoes of yesterday's landmark events. "I find your extraordinary capacity for compassion extremely exciting right now."

Vivan felt contaminated. Dirty in every imaginable sense he could imagine. He was surrounded by foul thoughts, gestures, touches, behaviors, the whole world had forgotten that there was also a place for more delicate feelings in making love, that often people at least like each other, if they do not love, and do not mate like wild animals. There was no warmth in it, too much bloated heat.

"The sensations are stronger when touched directly," the viceroy noted calmly, still watching him.

He jumped up to bring his mouth back to his ear. Vivan remembered the gesture suddenly catching Meron's attention as he was talking to his aunt on the other side of the table. He frowned anxiously at the pale face of the healer.

"You see it, right?" Terlan's breath stank of garlic. "You feel it. It will come soon. Then I will fuck her and you will only have a rich imagination. Have fun..." He patted him on the shoulder, which was supposed to be a friendly gesture, but it did not fully calm Meron, who was watching them from a distance. However, the prevailing noise did not allow him to hear their conversation.

Suppressing the urge to punch the king's brother for fear of the dire consequences of the act, Vivan forced himself to contain his anger. He looked at the queen. After a moment she caught his evocative gaze. At first she misinterpreted it. Since he appeared at the castle under rather dramatic circumstances, taken by force from the house at the behest of her husband, she looked after him like a mother. At first, a terrible thought crossed her mind, but inconsistent with what she had heard so far of the viceroy's exploits, that in some way the healer had been disgraced by him. But when Vivan understood what the queen was thinking, he shook his head, then looked at the wine drinker, the smug viceroy now engrossed in talking to the chancellor. She understood what he meant. The agitation rushed blood to her head. Yes, it coincided with her suspicions now. Her husband, always sensitive to her presence, sensed the change in her mood. In a gesture of concern, although he was not yet aware of the cause of her anxiety, he interrupted the conversation with the minister to take her hand. She didn't have to explain anything to him. He was angry as he guessed the cause. The veins in the forehead and neck were clearly visible. If he had only obtained real evidence, not merely the guess that his brother had just humiliated his beloved wife, he probably wouldn't even have waited for trial. Their mutual fraternal dislike, over the years had grown into hatred, intensified by the appearance of Konstancja in their lives. But there was no reason to remove Terlan from the court. He was too cunning for that and knew too many things. Against his will, Vivan thought a little warmer of him, seeing how devoted he was to his wife. King Heron regarded his brother with a mysterious gaze with blue iris and thick dark eyelashes. People were afraid of that look, seemingly impassive, with a cold fury hidden deep within the soul. It did not bode well for the viceroy. But how far was his brother willing to go?

This Vivan had no time to find out.

"Look for your end. It's close," he whispered, looking into his tormentor's eyes.

"Depends on what the end will be," Terlan smirked mysteriously, raising his goblet in a soft toast. He took a sip, ending the conversation.

"I should have known that," thought the healer. "Depends on what the end will be..."

Time slowed down. The sounds muffled from afar. A strange heaviness, as if he were falling asleep in the snow, slowed his reactions. The last picture of his mother he remembered was the mark on her face from being hit with the open hand by Captain Gereme. Tears in her eyes. Her despair...

They must still be alive... He must believe it! There are traces of his presence everywhere in the town. After all, he has great power...

It had to be enough.

He looked calmly at the people around him.

The crowd started toward him, arms outstretched and screamed for help, as if waiting for the move. They touched his face, his hair. They grabbed his hands, stroking his clothes tenderly. They placed kisses on his hands and cheeks.

They pressed on from all sides, surrounding him tightly. Everyone wanted to get to him. Everyone wanted to be close to a healer, so despite the chill of the morning it soon got as hot as if it was noon on another summer's day.

At first they all seemed kind and devoted to him, but Vivan knew otherwise thanks to the nightmares that had haunted him before. He knew the end of these events.

He waited when it would come.

The pressure of people wanting to be close to him was too overwhelming. He could hardly take a deep breath. There were several cases of fainting in the crowd. Half strangled, they were dragged outside the crowd to let others pass, and in many cases left to their own fate.

The bustle was like the busiest day in the marketplace. With every gesture, moment or detail, further, much more dramatic events would start like an avalanche.

He waited for worship to turn into a nightmare vision.

He was sure it would happen soon.

He was fed up with unceremoniously feeling his whole body under the guise of wanting to contact the healer. Pretty hot and stuffy.

But he couldn't get out.

He couldn't even move from his seat.

Not even to raise his hand freely.

It was then that a well-dressed young man with eyes like gray stones, clearly distinguished from the crowd by ruthlessness and stubbornness, got to him. It was the stone-colored eyes that made the closest man move away from him as much as possible, respecting his presence without murmuring. The man appraised

Vivan with the gaze of a knowledgeable slave trader. In his ruthless and calculating eyes, Vivan saw the preview of a nightmare coming true.

He was the ignition link.

The dark, almost black hair of the other, contrasting with the unusual color of his eyes, intensified the mesmerizing gaze of the serpent. He may have been only three or four years older than the healer, but his coolness and movements testified to experience he had already acquired. This man has already killed. Those who had a remnant of decency in their hearts and those who recognized him hastily tried to withdraw. But there were those who did not see him well. They weren't going to quit. The precious healer could not slip out of their hands.

The gray-eyed man looked down to where the precious family mementoes hung on chains on Vivan's chest: a cross and hands embracing a ruby. The decision was made immediately. He lunged forward, and before Vivan could prevent it in any way, he grabbed the jewels shining in the morning sun and pulled, ripping one of them from the young man's neck. By a strange twist of fate, Vivan was only pushed away by someone during the commotion that left only a chain with the hands embracing a ruby in the thief's hands. The cross slipped from his hand. The thief took a quick glance at his prey and got out of the crowd as quickly as possible before anyone could recover from this act of audacity. Vivan, on the other hand, desperately tore his hand from someone else's and, in a desperate defensive gesture, clenched his fist on the cross.

He did it just in time...

Another man was evidently about to take the cross, impudent by the deed of his predecessor, but Vivan's gesture thwarted his plans. The lust for anything that belonged to a healer still shone in his eyes. It had to be satisfied! With a quick, greedy glance, he scanned the healer's clothes for new prey, until his worn hands found one of the buttons on the caftan that Vivan had put on, along with the rest of his clothes, in the morning. It was the garment he was wearing yesterday as well, still bearing the stains of the viceroy's feat, for subsequent events made the servants no longer resume their duties. The thief's long fingers quickly grasped the prey and pulled with such force that the healer, with his pulled hand, almost tore the chain from his neck. Old eyes sparkled with excitement, and the gray-haired man vanished with his prey as quickly as he could. Even the jerked one did not allow to take what he had won.

Now the hands of former worshipers stretched out ominously, with destructive force. He was searched meticulously and neatly stripped of any buttons, belt, or the few things in pockets, not to mention any part of his body. Maybe outside the legs - from an obvious lack of space.

The crackle of the material being torn made the people freeze for a moment in their robbery...

A piece of a healer's shirt was in the hand of a fat veggie seller.

For a moment, this act woke people from their trance.

Suddenly they realized what they were actually doing and where it was going.

Many of those who had not hesitated to plunder and grope the healer unceremoniously looked at the woman with sudden indignation as if her act was worse than anything they had done before. She squeezed the torn piece in her hand, looking around fearlessly. "Yes, I did it," her eyes said. "What about you? Are you better?"

Then her eyes met that of the young healer...

Sensing that her gesture would be the true beginning of a long and suffering end, Vivan, having no more strength for anything else, looked at her, his face wet with sweat, wishing his gaze would convey to this woman everything he had just felt.

She understood what she had done to him with that gesture all too well.

In a defensive gesture she hugged the shred of his shirt against her, as if to say, "I didn't mean anything wrong." But she knew.

Now he will die...

With this gesture she contributed to his undoing.

A tear ran down Vivan's face. His gaze became unbearable to her. Someone, taking advantage of her dilemma, tore a shred of shirt from her hand. She groaned in silent protest, still shaken and stunned by the magnitude of her act. She didn't even think to defend herself.

Moments later, the crowd lunged at Vivan.

People tugged at him like angry wolves. They ripped clothes apart with their hands and knives. They were pulling his hair out. He began to scream in terrible agony, wounded on all sides by fingernails and uncontrolled, chaotic knife cuts. His blood made people mad. The woman was pushed to the ground, where she was literally trampled on along with several other people, and soon died. They licked his blood off their fingers and reached for more, as if suddenly he was a loaf of bread from which to pick out the dough. He was bitten. The chain of the cross broke under the pressure, but the people failed to take it from the healer's clenched fist. He screamed while he had enough strength and air. Then the world in chaos and pain began to spin, and the crowd around them screamed or merged into one endless rumble. He was losing strength. "Enough already", he wanted to plead, but he didn't even know if he had even opened his mouth. His eyes were red. He felt that some bottomless abyss was gathering inside him, a terrible despair tearing at his soul and heart, which he could not bear.

Suddenly, in the midst of terrible suffering, wanting to end this torment, he took a breath like drowning in the last gust of despair and the will to survive...

In the next moment the hearts of the next ten people stopped...

After a while they began to turn blue, as if they were suddenly cut off from the air with great force. They felt pressure in their chests.

Then one by one they began to die...

Vivan slumped to the ground, not held by anyone at the moment. Everywhere, except pain, he was surrounded by the feelings of the dying and the living. Fear, pain, and helplessness weren't just his anymore. Horror, awareness of imminent death, surprise. Their suffering literally burst into his mind.

They raped his soul.

A terrible, piercing scream would have burst from his chest, if he still had the strength to scream.

There was a deafening silence.

The crowd was paralyzed by fear.

Among the dead and dying ones, a bloodied, mortally wounded healer lay before the eyes of the living who suddenly witnessed things beyond their comprehension. Here is a man, treated almost like the incarnation of gods through his gift, previously famous for bringing back life to the dying, revealed a new power that paralyzed their dull minds with primal fear.

He killed those who raised their hand against him!

And at first the crowd stood in fear of the next punishment, ready to run.

But then nothing happened anymore.

The healer lay among the dead bodies, bleeding out before their eyes. So he wasn't dangerous. It didn't take long for them to figure it out.

He was dying. He saw the fear in their eyes begin to give way to animal greed and rage, before torment prevailed and mercifully knocked him out.

They circled him slowly, somewhat timidly, but with a clear intention - like a horde of wolves. Deprived of humanity by an act they have already committed, stained with his blood and ready to murder. The woman spoke first. With a ragged dress and almost no teeth, she aimed the blunt knife. Then an arrow suddenly shot through her, hitting her neck. Her horrible death took the others by surprise. There was total chaos in their minds.

Immediately afterward, other arrows reached their targets...

CHAPTER 2 — Deal with the devil

Oliver became a thief by necessity. His father was a royal goldsmith, his mother secretly sold her paintings under a male name. When the plague broke out in Verdom, people began to die en masse. The most necessary things have become the most sought-after commodity. And the dearest. The goldsmith and his son felt more and more anxious about their family. The customers were scared away by the death lurking on their doorstep. The best were taken by the king to his castle with the guards, turning it into a real fortress. Every day, bodies were taken from the streets and burned at the stake outside the city. Sometimes the wind blew the ash onto the dormant, depopulating streets, covering everything like snow with it. The dirt of the city, previously famous for its cleanliness, slowly surrounded the still living.

The street where Oliver lived with his family was one of the streets that belonged to artisans and artists. Fate spared almost no one. The closest neighbor of the goldsmith Nilas, the confectioner, until recently took orders even from the end of the city. One day he and his spouse were found dead under the table, surrounded by untasted food. In filth and vomit.

It was only at night that their son Moren saw their bodies, returning from another of his adventurous trips. They were still in their nightgowns. The mother's already graying blond hair was still loose, instead of her usual braid, wrapped at the top of her head.

Moren had long wanted to subdue Oliver. At first it ended in a struggle, which left slim Oliver coming home with the traces of fighting and numerous bruises. Once, running away again, the goldsmith's little son managed to climb the wall to the roof. And so it started. From then on, he never let himself be captured by Moren and his men. It was said that he could even climb a bare wall, because he could cling to it like a spider. It was said that he would jump down from the highest tower without doing anything to himself and squeeze himself into every hole. There was much exaggeration, but one thing has come true. Oliver has become an unsurpassed champion in such feats. He had built up a pretty silhouette as well, which made many women's eyes look longingly after him. But he wasn't the wooer type. In fact, he was rather a recluse, though it was more of a necessity. The Morena's gang, although constantly changing their numbers, always persecuted him, following the example of their leader. This was especially worsened after the outbreak of the plague. It included the closest neighbors of the goldsmith's family, a once-tight pack of rascals now the terror of the living. Outside of Artisans Street, Oliver had few fellows, and almost no friends. For good reason. He was a recluse and did not make friends for fear that Moren would take revenge on those who dared to deal with him. Consequently, he seemed to be silent and weird, and even somewhat limited mentally to avoid deeper acquaintances. He relied only on his twin sister - Julien. And parents.

There was only one exception. The only person who knew about Oliver's true nature enjoyed genuine respect from Moren, and more than once stood up for his other friend. It was Selarion - terminally ill with heart disease, Moren's closest and only true friend. And Oliver himself at the same time. Selarion, whom everyone called Sel on a daily basis, surpassed his friend and his buddies in intelligence and resourcefulness. He was the son of a respected silk merchant in the city and his wife, still famous for her extraordinary beauty and as cold as ice heart. He inherited from his parents what was best in them, except for health, and, for a reason not entirely clear, he himself, already in his childhood, established himself as the guardian of Moren. It was said that this happened because Moren had saved his life during his childhood. Though Moren had repeatedly given him a reason to make Sel lose his trust, he never let him down in times of need. He often inhibited his attempts to start fights. Moren got into fights, drank too much, but Sel's rebukes finally did their job. He calmed down. This care finally resulted in graduation from the castle's school named after the previous queen, which also accepted the children of rich merchants. He had no talent for it. It was only thanks to Sel that he learned to write and read, although count went smoothly. It was said that maybe thanks to a friend's devotion, he would eventually turn out to be human. But as the plague took hold of the city and took his family, Moren changed enormously, though Sel continued to influence him. Most often in defense of already frightened city residents. Darkness seemed to slowly sweep Moren's soul, and madness was in his eyes. Sel warned Oliver to avoid meeting the leader of a gang of bad guys who were slowly gaining influence in a city abandoned by law. He sensed a serious danger in this.

It was because of an incident at Queen Constance's costume party the year before the plague for all the townspeople that Moren, if at all possible, hated Oliver more and was willing to do something completely unpredictable. More than just to kill. At least that's how Sel imagined it.

The Queen organized a fancy dress party, reportedly to celebrate the extraordinary harvest that summer. However, it was whispered among themselves that the main goal was that the queen and her sons, under discreet guard, could blend in with the crowd in order to get to know their subjects better. On this occasion, the Queen made an agreement with merchants of cotton, linen and silk to lower the prices of the brightest colors a month before the ball, and in return received discounts on the purchase of other goods. Drinks at the ball were not free to prevent excessive drunkenness and its consequences. The food was cheap. The music was provided by the best from all over the kingdom and even further regions, attracted by the promise of a reward for their skills. In the middle of the market, which had been cleared, there was a huge platform for musicians and dancers.

Everyone who came to the ball surprised the guards with their behavior. Although there were of course the inherent fights and theft, everything was admirably calm. The opportunity to meet in the crowd the adored Queen and the future heir to the throne and his brother apparently worked on the people.

Oliver then disguised himself as a woman - a lady in a gown given to her mother by some baroness. His dark hair, usually spiky and unruly, reaching half an ear, was smoothed by his sister and, with the help of Julien's closest friend - Milera, pinned up in a beautiful dark hair piece of curly, waist-length hair. Milera was a simple girl from a village near the city of Adelaine, on the road leading to the healer's homeland. Even then, she was the secret bride of Selarion, although this fact was then hidden for safety, because of her work as a peaceful, in one of the largest houses of debauchery in the district known as the Pleasure Corner. She had access, thanks to the owner of the house, to a large selection of wigs, buns for pinning, hairpieces and other such accessories. The fake woman's outfit was complemented by cheap but beautifully made jewelery and shoes and gloves matching the color of the dress. The effect made the women speechless, and their masculine costumes and carefully selected wigs and mustaches seemed completely devoid of the desired effect. Oliver looked so perfect as a woman that if they had not transformed him themselves, they would have been fooled along with the others. Maybe the makeup was too strong to hide the slight stubble that was just emerging, but the whole thing was captivating. In addition, the movements like a cat acquired by Oliver thanks to his daring climbs, gave him a feminine charm.

This nearly contributed to his undoing.

There was no man who would not look after him that evening, nor a woman who was concerned about his beauty. He was not recognized in any known family. His parents, however, were amazed. He could read many contradictory feelings from his mother's face, from anxiety to obvious concern, as if she had already sensed that her son might be in trouble because of her unusual beauty.

Moren didn't recognize him.

Not right away, at least. He saw his family and friends. Thanks to Selarion's presence at Milera's side, he recognized Julien. He knew the friend was dating Oliver's sister's best friend. For a long time he searched for Oliver near the family of the goldsmith Rysever, confident that he would find him in a male disguise. It took two hours for him to realize that the siblings had perversely changed roles at the ball. And a woman of eye-catching beauty is not some family relatives unknown to him...

Now the veil had finally fallen from Moren's eyes. It was Oliver! How amazing he looked in this outfit! Oh yes, there was something of a woman about him. His beauty was always so ambiguous. His face did not want to cover with stubble for a long time. It was just a soft down, probably as soft as silk. His body was both soft and springy. He was always fastuous, never succumbed to him. Moren never managed to break it.

Oliver paled under Moren's gaze. He was afraid to even glance again in the direction where Moren had been sitting with his companions since the beginning of the ball. And Moren continued to watch him intently, like a cat that had just spotted its prey.

There was something dark in his eyes. As if a cold fury or a lust for murder with difficulty, combined with a dark promise of a long and painful death.

Oliver concluded that it was on that very night that Moren had decided to kill him. He just waits until they are alone. He won't stop until he does it.

He was very wrong.

A shiver went through him. It was worse than the hate so far. This was pure uncontrolled obstinacy. Outrageous that Oliver is just walking around in this world.

He was absolutely sure of it.

When he came back in the company of his sister, her friend and Sela, taking advantage of the fact that Moren had just disappeared somewhere, he was suddenly dragged into a house and the door was closed. He was sure he was going to die. Heard them looking for him when he was gone so unexpectedly. It was so dark that he could barely see the outlines of the figures in front of him. But he would never mistake it for someone else.

"So you would like to be a woman?" He heard Moren's voice.

"It's a disguise, idiot!" He growled, trying in vain to free himself.

He might as well try to take a great weight off his shoulders. Until now, he had avoided such direct clashes at all costs. He knew well that his chances were slim then. What Moren did in the next moment he would never have expected. It certainly would never have occurred to him. Even as a passing thought.

With a delicacy so extraordinary about his meetings with Oliver so far, Moren ran his rough hand over the outline of his chin.

"I wasn't wrong," he whispered to himself, "like silk."

Oliver stiffened with amazement, but then it all became clear to him. He felt nauseous with fear and disgust.

"What are you doing?!" He asked softly, afraid his voice would fail him.

This couldn't be happening!

"I imagine the rope rubbing that delicate chin," Moren said in a strange, warm tone.

"I already know what you are imagining!" Oliver shouted, regaining his courage.

The shock he felt at the suddenly hidden intentions of Moren made him tremble with anger.

"Smart guy," Moren squeezed his shoulders, leaning closer. "You wanna be a woman? So, feel it like a woman! We'll see if you'll still be so haughty..."

A fight in which Oliver's chances were never high could only have one end. Slender Oliver could not beat the fight-hardened, strong as a giant, overwhelmed with unrestrained lust, adventurer.

A few blows made no impression on Moren.

The skillful kicks stunned him, but for too little time. Moren took Oliver's head and struck it with his. Oliver nearly passed out from the force of the blow. He felt himself fall, and Moren, overcome with frenzy, turned him onto his stomach. Desperately struggling with the enemy's overwhelming weakness and strength, he tried to throw him off. Moren twisted his right arm, using too much force for his real intentions. Involuntarily, Oliver screamed as he crunched painfully a joint in his hand. The bandit froze for a moment, crushing him with his weight. Oliver closed his eyes, silently praying to Mother Earth that help would come. He felt he was close to crying because he had no strength left, and if Moren broke his arm, he couldn't defend himself either. He wouldn't want to live after Moren had managed to achieve his goal. He couldn't bear even the thought of it.

Even now, feeling the attacker's penis sticking into him, for now through his clothes, he was filled with disgust and something he had never felt before, and it was a feeling worse than terror. Although nothing has happened yet, Moren has already burst into his intimacy and soul, marking his presence there forever. Having learned to dodge for years, unconsciously at that moment he began to run away in his head from what Moren was going to do to him. He defended himself against being aware of and fully participating in what was about to happen, because it was beyond his usual endurance. He hoped that this way he would survive the worst.

Suddenly Moren stood up and yanked him to his feet. He felt his sore hand with a quick movement.

"You're lucky," he muttered softly. "It's not broken."

Then he quickly took his shoulders and leaned forward. Oliver felt his breath and the warmth of his sweating body. He could smell his strong scent. He could almost taste it. The thug's mouth was touching his neck as he said:

"Say a word and I'll take care of your sister, Oliver. She really looks VERY like you."

Only now Oliver managed to hear, through the rush of his own blood, someone violently trying to reach them. The pounding and warning slam of the wooden door grew louder. Help was near!

Moren released him abruptly and swiftly opened the door. Behind them stood the guards accompanied by the Rysever and Andilo families - Sel's family.

"What's up, ladies and gentlemen? What's the noise? Mistake! I took him for a woman!" He exclaimed in a seemingly careless tone, while the royal guards circled him in a circle, "See for yourself! A man can go wrong with this goddamn ball today!"

"It's a lie!" Julien shouted, rubbing her right hand and ahead of the guards. "You knew very well who he was!"

Moren sized her up with a short, ice cold glance and laughed with apparent glee at the benefit of the assembled onlookers.

Oliver had to show up. Despite the unfortunate state of the dress and hairstyle, it was still easy to understand Moren's supposed mistake. In addition, due to the apparent gaiety of the bandit and the general mood that prevailed that evening, the feelings of the crowd changed in favor of the adventurer. Probably the sight of the deplorable condition of the young man dressed in a dress also helped. And his tousled hair. The event, due to the circumstances, immediately caused general merriment, much to the outrage of the Rysever family and their friends. After all, it was night, a costume party, people drank a lot. It was easy for such situations. After a few unequivocal comments from the crowd, a few taunts from the guards that Moren laughed at politely, each walked away.

Oliver saw Sel's face staring at his wayward friend. The insincere smile disappeared suddenly from Moren's face, turning into a strange grimace of both stubbornness and fear at the same time, as if the other deeply regretted his act, not wanting the friend to know the truth about his desires.

***

Moren had so far been afraid of more than just revealing the truth to Sel.

He did not want his four dodgy companions to find out about it, for whom he was a genuine leader. At least not now that he has not yet consolidated his leadership enough. So, whenever they were seeing Oliver somewhere, Moren made it clear that his threat was not a joke. He made no attempt to touch him in any way, he even avoided it like fire, but his constant presence quickly began to tear Oliver's nerves more than his earlier taunts, because now he knew what was behind it. He felt constantly being watched. In public places, he could feel his eyes on him. At night he saw Moren standing by the house window. He was afraid for his sister, and Julien was more and more afraid for him. He couldn't talk to anyone but her about it, fearing that the truth would come out by accident and Sel didn't want to get involved.

Moren's obsessive interest was taken by his companions as a new display of hostility in the name of old and new scores. After all, Oliver had a hard time with Moren. There was nothing unusual about it.

When the plague killed Moren's parents, he first moved in with Sel, but mounting anger and paranoia soon made him rarely there. His company was exhausting, especially when, faced with the still-looming death, Sel's parents accepted Milera's love for their only son and took her under their roof. Sel looked after his orphaned friend as best he could. He offered him further hospitality also after his hasty wedding at which Moren was the only witness apart from the groom's family. The servants left the house in the first days of the plague, and it did not allow anything to be delayed. The next day, even the next moment, could be the last ones. Milera's parents were to find out about the wedding when couriers were to be delivering letters again.

The world seemed to tighten strangely, like a noose around a neck. Sel's father learned to do various household chores by himself and to smoke in fireplaces. He even appreciated some of the innovations his son had made in their home, such as the water drain, though he used these ideas surreptitiously so that neither son nor wife would see. The discovery of this secret was a source of bitterness for Sel, which both Milera and Moren, still devoted to him, tried to suppress. But each of them realized that it was something they could not mitigate in any way, not because they tried too little, but because of the way Sel was treated by his family. Even though nothing was certain anymore, the way the mother treated her son and her father's submission to her had changed only slightly.

One day, on Artisans Street, the baker, Ileon, sold bread at an exorbitant price and bought flour. His bakery was watched over by well-paid people, volunteers from the city, who grouped into something like a town guard after the royal guard locked themselves with the king in the castle. The next day the baker died of the plague, his bakery has been robbed, and the volunteer guards were killed.

Oliver was forced to participate in the distribution of the loot. Officially, theft could risk cutting off your hand, but no one enforced it. He and his family needed flour and bread to survive the days that followed. The royal guard did not move away from the safe walls of the castle, fearing the growing anger of the subjects moved by the betrayal of their king.

Since the healer was brought in, the number of those who waited for help in the devastated market square near the castle had grown steadily. Every day there were more and more people who had already lost almost everything. The lack of food and supplies in the city soon made fights for scraps of food frequent, as did house break-ins. And more and more brutal.

Life was dying out in other parts of the capital. People started to hide in their homes like rats in their hideouts.

Though Moren and his gang tried to catch him looting to collect the loot, Oliver was always ahead of them. He always managed to steal something right in front of their noses. The remnants of Sel's scruples and vigilance prevented Moren from attacking the house of the goldsmith's family, because Sel's parents spoke well of Oliver's family, the old goldsmith himself was considered an honest and good man, and his wife still delighted with her beauty and warmth. Moren simply liked them, though he didn't admit it to anyone. Sel evoked remorse in his friend with his thoughtful gaze. There was also a secret that was hard to admit in the end, even for fear of himself. Moren still wasn't sure if, following Sel's example, who had done just that, he wanted to touch the man. He tried it a bit, but he knew it still wasn't what he expected.

Bandits reigned not only on Artisans Street. Nobody dared to oppose them. Whoever tried it disappeared or his body was found, most often hung on the gate of some house. They divided territories among similar bands throughout the city and took them under their control. They were ruthless. They took anything of value from families who had just lost a loved one. They collected their loot in various parts of the city. Oliver saw Sel in secret helping those who had been threatened by his recent friend, and now someone more and more alien and distant, who by his behavior terrified even his heart. Moren couldn't and didn't want to do anything to him. From birth, Sel had a heart disease. His days could pass at any moment. He did not dare raise his hand against him. Or his relatives.

It was said that Moren had obtained the healer's belongings, so his men and he had not yet fallen ill.

The city gates were open. The carts with the cadavers ran smoothly and returned for new ones. Soon the families of the goldsmith and the silk merchant were the only ones on the first Artisans Street that had not yet lost their loved ones. This brought them closer to each other, thus distancing them from others, suspecting the actions of Moren and his gang. Acting discreetly, fearing Moren's madness, the family fathers decided to leave the city.

"Son," Alea Rysever, after whom the children inherited their beauty, chose the moment when they could talk without witnesses, "if something happened to us, you will take your sister to Aunt Semeralda, to the city of healer."

"Mom, you'll be fine," he said softly, hugging her.

The sight of fear on her face made fear squeeze him by the throat. She always knew what to do. She was always sure of her actions. It was the father who sometimes forgot himself and was distracted. Never her.

And now he could see her fear.

It made him feel less confident.

Secret preparations for departure, fear and haste intensified his anxiety. He was afraid Moren would do something to prevent him from leaving. He might even be preparing an ambush now. Although the mother did not fully know the true causes of her son's fear, she guessed that he had a lot to do with the life he was leading now.

"Semeralda has part of our property," she avoided his gaze, not wanting to reveal the rising tears. "Enough for a while. If you couldn't find an honest job," she glanced at him meaningfully, "seek help from the healer family. Remember how your father made for a healer mother this necklace with hands holding a ruby?"

Of course he remembered. Father was so happy to do something for a healer. He valued him very much for what he had already done and how many people he had helped. It was over two years ago. It also brought them further business successes.

"Yes," he whispered.

She smiled at the memory. Then they became very friends with the countess. So much so that she stayed with them while waiting. She was open to people, just like her son. She did not try to exalt herself.

"Then father made two pendants. He gave one to Vivan's mother and hid the other. I couldn't be angry with him about that. Such an event may be unique in your entire life. The pendant is hidden where time has always passed the best for us. I don't mean the bedroom, Oliver." She smiled.

"Mom!" He scolded her gently, even though a smile also appeared on his face.

He loved her for this defiance. As with a young woman, not a mature lady.

She looked at him with a playful sparkle in her sparkling eyes.

"Aren't you and I supposed to talk about something?"

"Would you like a few lessons from me?" He easily fell into her mood, guessing what the conversation would be about.

"You're incorrect!"

He tilted his head to look at her urgent. She sighed, abandoning the topic.

"You're..."

"Lady," Silva, the cook in the goldsmith's house, one of the two servants who remained in the house after the remaining servants had escaped, peered into the room. "Your husband is calling you urgently. Can't find tools."

"That's him all over," she shook her head and winked knowingly at her son. "I'll tell you later."

He saw her smile again, this time hiding this uneasiness and she was gone...

Two hours later, she was dead. She lied on the threshold of the house facing the garden. The plague caught her as she was climbing the stairs. At their peak she suddenly felt unwell and fell, smashing her head, which was the direct cause of her death. The disease killed her husband. At one point, when the preparations for departure were almost completed, he stood by the window, looking as if he was looking for help. She saw him fall. She ran to save him.

She realized too late.

As in a terrible dream, he watched what happened, cradling his sister in his arms.

Moaning Silva and even now peaceful, valet Ner helped to lift the bodies of their employers. They were already old. They spent their lives serving the Rysever family. Death as a result of infection did not impress them. The life they knew was ending. They loved the family with which they worked their entire lives, and they treated the hosts' children almost as their own. If the worst came to worst, they would at least die where they had spent their lives in peace.

Two skinny gravediggers came for the bodies. They took them without exchanging a word with anyone. At the sight of the wagon, Julien nestled her face in her brother's shoulder, terrified by the number of bodies. It was full of them. The nameless corpses lay in simple costumes, and sometimes even without them at all. On this ghastly pile, without sentiment or delicacy, with the skill of a laborer doing his job, the gravediggers dumped the bodies of Oliver and Julien's parents. These people, like ghostly shadows, wandered the streets every day looking for bodies to burn. Often they robbed them of valuables. The gravedigger who barely gave them a glimpse, smelling heavily of booze, wore a diamond necklace around his neck. Oliver saw the glint of diamonds in the sunlight. If he had been able to think clearly right now, he would have been indignant at such an audacious theft. But now he glanced only briefly at the precious jewelery, barely embracing it by his head. Moments later, his sister's cries and her grief permeating him made the undertaker to forget his immoral behavior.

Until the wagon was completely out of sight, he watched it in anguish, cradling his sister in silence.

They stood in an abandoned street for a long time. No sound broke the silence around them. Even the wind fell silent. The world was dying around in this deathly silence. You couldn't even hear the usual city noises: creaking shutters or even a cat meowing. It was there, on this deserted street, almost in the heart of a deserted city, together with their mother and father, more than they could have imagined. There was no grave for them to cry over. There was no funeral. There was no longer any support that gave them strength against harm and the dictates of fate. They had no one else here, for although Silva and Nar were still at home, they could not, with all their goodness, replace their loved ones.

He didn't know how long it was before he suddenly heard a familiar voice:

"Oliver," Sel's hand gently rested on his shoulder. "I'm so sorry, really... Listen..." He took a breath, taken in by the sight of siblings' tearful faces. "We," he looked quickly at Milera who was accompanying him, who embraced the sympathetically quiet Julien, "are leaving at dawn. Come with us. Nothing keeps you here anymore. If you are left alone, Moren..." he said sadly the name of his old friend. "He's not the man I knew anymore. For a long time. The plague gives him power. If you stay... You may not be as lucky as you did then... at the ball..." he finished quietly.

Oliver met his eyes. Sel wasn't a fool. What he did not say remained silent between them.

He guessed the truth.

"Yes," he told him forcefully, driven by despair, "We'll leave at dawn."

For the first time since they had known each other, Sel came over and hugged him tightly. Grief-filled, devastated, Oliver hesitantly, though with a gratitude that had brought tears back to his eyes, returned the embrace. The weight of loneliness ceased to overwhelm him. Finally, he had the right, and undeniably, to have a friend. He was leaving this town and his old life.

He could finally change something.

There could be something good in his life.

Moren watched them secretly.

Anger at Sel, whom he still considered a friend in his thoughts, even though their paths temporarily (in his opinion) parted, she fought confusion in his soul when he heard their conversation. Sel already knew! And Milera, that harlot who marked the beginning of the end of their friendship, entering their lives, as he thought mistakenly, stood beside, supporting her naive husband. A deceitful dirty bitch! The slut who took it from him, probably hoping for a fortune after he died! And that Julien whose friend pulled Selarion away from him! And finally the heat! The heat that burns his soul at the news that Oliver is leaving tomorrow! Madness and lust for Oliver, whom he blamed for destroying his life with his existence! Now he is going to leave?! When he, Moren, finally knew what he wanted from him?!! He will go away and be gone forever?! Oh no! He wasn't going to let him do that. It will cost them all!

The night darkened the streets. Nobody lit the lamps anymore. The streetlights were not lit. Only in Selarion's house was the faint glow of the candles visible. Julien forgot about light, food, past and future problems. Leaning against the wall, her thoughts suspended in time, staring at that faint, only visible light across the street from her friend's house.

The silence was broken only by the sounds of bustle downstairs, where Silva, sniffing in a soft sob, tried to prepare something, clean up, put away...

Somewhere far away there was a scream, a soft cry. Rats scuttled down the street, hitting trash. Soon they will take over the empty house. They will eat what's left. They will live in abandoned beds or looters will come here to steal what else can be stolen.

She had a glimpse of the royal castle visible from here, towering over the city. At night it was not visible how many colors it was painted. During the day it looked almost comical. Torches were burning on the walls and in front of the gates. There were many lights in the windows. The people living there were doing well. Their bodies among the nameless corpses would not be carried outside the city, and they would not be burned on the great, undying pyre. They had a healer!

"You think we'll die soon too?" She asked her brother sitting at the table.

Oliver looked up from his bleak thoughts.

"Perhaps," he replied softly.

Just like that. Without any attempt to mitigate the brutal truth. He was always honest. She loved him and for that too.

"And if we get there... What next?"

Now even the prospect of going to the healer Town did not seem interesting. He got it.

"We're gonna live. That's all."

"There is no healer there now."

"They'll release him eventually."

"Have you ever seen him?"

"Two, maybe three times. It's a boy about our age. Calm, kind to people, firm when necessary. He has such eyes..." he thought for a moment, "like a child's. No one would have guessed that he had probably seen many things by the time," Oliver's soft voice was thick with sadness.

"Would he help us if he was free?" She looked at the castle.

"If he had time..." she heard the answer. "Yes. For sure."

Uninvited tears ran down Julien's face. She didn't rub them. She didn't want to.

"She wanted to leave all her paintings," she whispered. "We couldn't even..."

"Bury them properly," Oliver finished mentally as he heard his sister sigh.

He shuddered again at the memory of the car full of dead bodies. So many... The mother lay with her head smashed in the dress she wore during her daily duties. He had time to close her eyes. He couldn't close his heart. He was filled with so many different feelings, memories, last images and moments. And it's a terrible illusion. Nothing seemed to have changed. As if they were still alive. There, in their bedroom. It was enough to leave the room, knock, open the door and see them again. Such as they were that morning...

Heart refused to believe what reason was telling.

"Oliver?" Julien whispered.

She didn't have the strength to say anything more aloud. She looked at him. Her sadness was breaking his heart. He got up to hug her and hide his face in her long hair. They didn't have to speak. It was enough that they both felt the same, forever connected with their souls. Words were not needed.

The violent opening of the door to the room snapped them out of their grief, as if a lightning struck suddenly nearby. Moren stood on the threshold, followed by several of his men. Julien held her breath for a moment. Oliver instinctively hugged her tighter, trying to protect her, though he knew he shouldn't be worried about her in the first place. Moren's face changed expression. He must have fallen into the Rysever Estate, ready to crush everything in his path if they put up any resistance. With difficulty he managed to act on the now unnecessary caution by stealthily stealing himself. Inhabitants of the house did not care for their safety that day, they were mired in grief. Quietly and quickly, his man slit the throats of two old servants. The rest of them searched and looted the room.

He wanted to find siblings.

At the sight of their tearful faces, especially Oliver, he hesitated. For one brief moment he stared at the couple standing by the window. They had the same looks, the same eyes. The same tears on their faces.

And the same instinct to protect each other. From him.

Julien, knowing Moren's intentions towards her brother, embraced Oliver, clutching his clothes tightly, determined to defend him. Oliver did likewise.

Their world, their former lives so far preserved in mutual respect and love, their innocence, in desires and dreams, ended brutally and suddenly. They were not even allowed to feel sorry.

For the first time since Moren had become obsessed with Oliver, there was more to the adventurer's heart than just a desire to satisfy his own desires. Understanding. He, too, recently lost his family. He knew what that meant. Though he was never a very good son, he knew the pain of such a loss.

He looked at the face of the man who had become an involuntary source of his anxiety, and seeing him try to protect his sister from the coming evil, seeing his tears hesitated. Doing what he planned he will destroy his life. There will be no turning back. It will not undo or change anything. He will become a source of suffering for the person he cares about, without gaining reciprocity and understanding. He was sure of that.

Suddenly, however, the world around him ceased to exist.

He walked over to them and looked into the blue eyes that fascinated him in contrast to the dark hair. He examined him closely. His grief was touching. The courage of the suffering filled his wormy heart with pride. He reached out to gently wipe the tear that ran down Oliver's face.

Julien moved violently, filled with disgust and anger.

"Don't touch him!" She screamed.

The world came alive again. The sounds of bustling and looting muffled for a moment - came back. Moren's companions' voices became audible. Julien raised her hand to give the bandit a luscious cheek, but he gripped it quickly and firmly. Only the echo of the recent feelings he had felt at the sight of Oliver kept him from striking the cast. The veins in his neck and temples swelled with mounting anger.

"Let her go!" Oliver ordered him softly, in an unnaturally calm voice, seeing that Moren was barely in control.

There was clearly a threat in that tone.

He looked into his eyes and noticed a shadow of those feelings that in a moment will stay in his soul forever. But that must happen...

"Tenan!" He summoned his best in the gang, who had become his right-hand man after Sel left.

"Yes," he called out.

If there was anyone worse than Moren, it would be him. He was said to have no feelings. Tenan was well built, well dressed, and the complete opposite of the nervous Moren. He had never been seen to upset him before.

His eyes were gray stones and as cold as they were. He was in charge of the corpses of Moren's opponents floating in the sewers. There was blood on the sleeve of his white shirt now, and a dagger was clearly visible under his belt. Julien's hands tightened on Oliver's shirt, staring at the killer.

Oliver paled. The deaths of two devoted servants whom he had known from childhood took a heavy toll on his heart. Ultimately, he realized that there was no chance of any resistance. To keep Julien safe, he must agree to all conditions and pray that it will be enough to save her. His fate was doomed...

"Sel's here?" Moren stood before his assistant with the confidence of a man who was in control of the situation at all times and should not be forgotten. Tenan didn't seem to have forgotten who was in charge, and since he felt even a hint of respect for Moren, there were reasons why it would be foolish to underestimate him. Even a weakness for Oliver could be a dangerous weapon in the hands of a moody leader - unpredictable, formidable - for both Oliver and Tenan. His authority was no longer in doubt. He achieved complete power over his people.

"He's waiting downstairs."

"Get him," Moren growled shortly.

Tenan backed away to the stairs without a word.

"May death come quickly," Julien whispered softly. "I'll get the knife. I'll kill myself or let them kill me," she whispered straight into his ear. "I will not help him torment my brother..."

"Stop it!" He replied quickly, hearing that a group of people was approaching them.

"You have to let him kill you," she said softly. "Otherwise, you will leave me no choice!"

For the first time in his life, Oliver began to ponder the thought fearlessly.

Moren stepped back to let a few people in. Tenan brought the bound Sel and Milera, led by men of the gang. Milera wore only white embroidered underwear and Sel only pants. Despite the fact that they had apparently been ripped from their bed, it was not entirely possible to drag them here without a fight. Moren's men, stiff in anger, had the marks from blows on their faces, and they treated Sel fairly roughly. One of Milera's guards had a clear mark of fingernails ripping his skin on his left cheek.

Julien noticed Milera. The two young women were united by fear.

"You've outdone yourself," Sel yanked forward to meet his old friend's eyes. "Free us!"

"So you can leave, yeah?" Moren stretched his words a little. "You're just going to leave the city in my hands?"

"It's a city of dead bodies. You fit it."

Moren looked into the eyes of his former friend. Sel would never voluntarily stand by his side again. He had a life of his own, and he hated what Moren was leading now. But he won't have a choice. Moren was not going to give up any of his beloved toys.

"I brought you here," he began the speech he had prepared earlier, "to set an example for others. Because from now on you will stay with me."

He nodded to Tenan. He pulled out a rope that had been prepared in advance, which had not been noticed before. He swiftly wrapped the surprised Milera around her neck, then yanked her towards the window where siblings were shaken by the sight.

Moren without a word drew his sword and pointed it at Julien. Sel screamed, held back by Moren's men. Without hesitating, Tenan pushed the defenceless, tied girl out the window, one hand gripping the rope. Two bandits who had been guarding Milera so far ran up to help hold him.

Julien hid her face in the excited Oliver's shirt, trembling all over her body. Sel knelt on the floor in silent suffering, pale as death. Tenan handed the rope to the accompanying murderers and leaned out to assess the situation with uninterrupted calm. Then he nodded briefly.

Finished.

They let go of the body.

After a while, all they heard was a click.

Moren waited until Julien looked back at those present to meet her gaze. For a moment he filled her eyes with disgust and fear. This allowed him to turn his mind away from the suffering Sel, at the same time preparing for further conversation with him. Slowly he lowered his sword and turned away.

"Sel," he called to the kneeling man, with apparent ease, "You're a bachelor again!"

His companions laughed shortly at these words. Everyone except Tenan, whose face was expressionless like a mask. He slowly returned to his place, straightening his shirt. Above the wrist of one hand, something flashed for a moment, but Julien didn't want to know what it was now.

She couldn't look at him. And at the same time, she couldn't stop.

Sel continued on his knees in silence, trying his best to contain the grief that swelled within him. Oliver would have given a lot to approach him, but he had to quickly forget his friend's despair. Moren approached him again. He felt Julien's hands tighten on his shirt again.

"As for you," Moren said in a low but firm voice, "I have other plans."

Oliver waited silently. He had expected it from the beginning of this brutal visit. In fact - since that ball... He could feel the warmth emanating from him then.

"From now on," Moren did not take his eyes off him as he said it, "you must obey me completely. If you object to anything - I will put your sister in the hands of my people."

It only confirmed Oliver's forebodings.

"If you even look at me in a way I don't like," Moren continued, and Oliver closed his eyes for a moment in silent anguish, "I'll hand her over to my men. You know what that means, don't you?

And if you wanted to be noble and deprive yourself of life - she will die, yes, but I will make sure that she die long and in torment. Believe me, I will not be in a rush. Neither I. Neither my people." He waited a moment for the weight of these words to weigh on Oliver's mind to ask, "Got it?"

The answer that sealed this monstrous system did not want Oliver to pass through a lump in his throat. He had to agree, but he couldn't do it. Each of the outputs proposed to him by Moren with a smirk full of satisfaction was for him a future full of suffering and unimaginable anguish.

"Answer me!" Moren ordered.

Oliver mentally made the final decision without looking at anyone. He will be lost, but he will do anything to keep Julien safe. Until he finds a way to escape for her.

"Understood," he replied quietly, confidently looking into the eyes of his pursuer.

"You'll never really have me," he passed to him in his mind with contemptuous mixed with despair. "Never."

He looked away just as Sel slowly rose to his feet.

Suddenly he was struck by the way the man looked at his old friend. The anguish on his face was not just due to a recent loss and a cruel betrayal.

Only a brokenhearted man could see this way...

He forced himself to look the other way. The irony of fate was that Moren wanted so much a man who would never share his feelings and only hate him, while he had true love at his fingertips almost all the time. Certainly the thought had never crossed his mind. And now he trampled the feeling just like that. Still painful for Sel, unaware of what he really did to him. Instead, he relished Oliver's confusion, misreading the reasons for his feelings. He was already looking forward to the suffering he would cause him and the pleasure he would feel when he would break his will. This was what he had been missing until now as he grappled with his decision. The helplessness and despair of the victim. He'd love to have Oliver in his hands. There was only darkness in his eyes, so pale blue they were almost transparent. A chill ran down Oliver's spine as he thought about the future. Moren watched him like a hawk at his prey before speaking again in a calm, seemingly dispassionate tone.

"Oli," Oliver had hated this diminutive for as long as he could remember. Apart from Moren, no one called him that, "I have your first assignment for you."

Oliver's heart began to beat restlessly driven by fear.

"You see, we are, as they say, in possession of certain things that the healer had," Moren smiled at his companions, who replied the same. Everyone except Tenan, whose expression did not change. "It cost us a bit of trouble and a few dead bodies," Moren continued, "but the power of these things turned out to be insufficient. We need something that has belonged a long time to the healer. Something more durable than clothes," Oliver felt himself relaxing a bit, apparently it was more pressing than having Moren's needs satisfied. "In the city they call you a cat because of your climbing. Prove yourself worthy of the nickname. You will enter the castle and steal one of the pendants for me, which the healer always carries with him and never, even in the bath, part with them. It is about..."

"Hands embracing a ruby..." Oliver recalled as Moren spoke the words.

"...apparently made by your father. And... Tenan... remind me..."

"Cross," Oliver spoke first before the other opened his mouth. "I know about it. Everyone has heard of it."

Moren nodded.

"Yeah. A testimony of some wird religion not from our world." He grimaced. "Get me any of these pendants." He put a hand on his shoulder, and Oliver twitched nervously. "And we both benefit from it. Everyone will benefit from this. Understand?"

He nodded as agreement. At the same time, he thought of the fountain in the back garden. As a memento of the healer's mother's stay at their home, the mother asked his father to erect a statue of a long-haired girl with water pouring out of a jug. The girl had the face of a healer's mother, still youthfully beautiful - perhaps thanks to the power of her extraordinary son. Her other hand was raised and slightly clenched, as if she had just caught something.

In this hand rested an exact copy of the ruby necklace. He remembered it now. This was what his mother wanted to tell him before Silva arrived. He saw his father at night hiding a copy of the necklace there. In a small, leaf-shaped box. He was so proud to be given such an important assignment. He wanted to keep a memento of this event. He thought it would bring him luck.

The healer's mother was a nice, kind woman with eyes radiating a child's curiosity about the world and sensual, feminine movements. She came with her younger son, Vivan's half-brother, who inherited his cloudy beauty and dark, shoulder-length hair from his father. The somewhat reticent Paphian did not resemble his open-minded brother.

"Hands..." could be replaced...

Let the plague hit him if Moren gets the pendant that really belongs to a healer. That one must fall into Julien's hands! He just needs to come up with an appropriate plan. It was clear that Moren would see to it that Oliver was at the castle.

That doesn't mean he'll get what he asked for...

CHAPTER 3 — Maid

Morning

The wagon rolled loudly on the cobblestones, surrounded by guards. Four royal guards on horseback and six on foot. It had no windows, only an iron-clad kennel with small openings for air or defense. A well-protected crossbowman could kill someone from within. Only the place on the coach-box remained uncovered, which was not to the taste of the elderly man accompanying Oliver. He bit his pipe nervously and looked uncertainly from side to side at the people gathered in the marketplace. From time to time he also looked at Oliver with a mixture of admiration and apprehension for his lady companion. So brave that she decided to go with him to replace her sister in the castle service, after her mysterious death, to which the viceroy himself could have contributed. That's what he was told when the girl was brought to him. That was enough for him. Moren's gang and their leader could not be questioned.

It was more or less confirmed information, and the events coincided with reality, except for one detail: the unfortunate woman whose story had served Moren's intentions never had a sister. But the coachman did not have to know about this. However, if it were a time and a place to talk about it, he would advise against a slim pretty girl with dark long hair from working in the castle after her sister had finished there. Oliver even had a prepared answer to the question of why he had decided, or rather, for such a fate. From poverty and hunger. It was a credible and brutal truth for many women who would not hesitate to take his place on the coach-box next to the coachman. The plague did not give much choice.

Oliver's disguise, whom the coachman had never met before, was impeccable, and the wig held perfectly. The delicate beauty did not even require any special retouching. Oliver still had no stubble, only a slight fluff, even though he was nineteen, and the girl's disguise was still taking his years off him. It was necessary to adjust to the conditions as soon as possible, although he was not entirely sure why Moren would want him to leave the castle with the spoils on the same day.

Something was in the air. Was Moren impatient because he wanted to enslave him as soon as possible, driven by lust? Perhaps. But there was a bottom line to it, much more important, and Oliver, trained to be vigilant, could sense it clearly. Was it related to the rapidly growing number of people gathered in the ruined and dirty marketplace? There were as many of them as there were only on special occasions and festivals. They surrounded a wagon with a supply of fresh food, because the rich, trusting in the power of the healer, indulged their whims at the castle, regardless of the cost. It's as if the world would cease to exist tomorrow. Only the presence of armed guards kept the hungry, desperate people from attacking. Instead, they alternately held out their hands in pleading or threatened the coachmen and the royal guards. Mothers were dragging their skinny children to Oliver, crying. The old women wailed pleadingly. However, when the car went by, the black-haired girl was threatened more than the others, spat after her and called the worst words.

It wasn't easy for Oliver to ignore their behavior. He couldn't help but stare at misfortune and hostility. He couldn't pretend he couldn't hear them. But he was helpless. The car and its contents were now worth a fortune. Stopping to give away even a small amount would not help anyone, and could even be harmful. The coachman, an experienced man in life, finally took his hand and squeezed him vigorously for comfort. The gesture towards the girl overwhelmed by misfortune aroused the young man's sympathy for the old man.

Yes, Oliver saw it too.

If he had given even a little to these crying mothers, the others would have rushed to them and ripped the food away without scruples. If they stopped the cart, the crowd could pounce on them and they wouldn't get away with their lives...

It was so close that the crowd was overwhelmed by emotions.

And then this man in ragged clothes appeared, like a harbinger of impending disaster. Surprised, Oliver saw a flash of a dagger flying towards them. He dodged before he fully thought of it...

The coachman, whose name he had no time to learn, was not so quick. The dagger lodged in his heart.

"Take the reins..." he croaked a moment before his end. "Run away or you'll die too, girl..."

The madman who stood in their way, said goodbye to his life almost immediately, shot down by an archer from the castle walls. The security of the small convoy responded immediately. The scraping of steel that reached Oliver's ears was a clear signal that the swords had been drawn.

"Go!" The commander snarled briefly, giving him a cursory glance, apparently ready to send one of his men or himself to the coach-box.

Oliver, however, made his decision at the same time the commander approached him. He stood up, and a sudden gust of wind, as if to help, wrapped a cold gust around his face and tossed back his long, dark, tightly attached wigs. He yanked the reins with a loud cry and lapped his whip over the ears of the agitated horses. The threat of being trampled by animals caused many to run sideways in a hurry. Another crackle of the whip removed the lazy ones. Oliver was fully aware that if the crowd decided to pounce on them now, even the best armor of the guards and all their weapons would not be able to save the convoy. There were just too many people.

He swung his horses sideways to avoid the madman's body, quickly returning to the road leading to the king's gate. The wagon lurched forward, escorted by two riders. The others, along with the commander, covered the rear. A few bolts, screams of the wounded and blood from blows with the sword of the more insistent forced the agitated crowd to stop their intentions. Before thinking about the tactics, the royal escort drove off behind the speeding food cart. Few on the way to the castle fled in panic from the speeding cart.

From the walls, a frantic ride was watched with shouts of encouragement. A few shots almost missed the disguised girl, and one was stuck in the body of the unfortunate, dead coachman, now lying on the coach-box. Several bolts were fired from the crowd in the marketplace towards the zealous archer, but it was the commander of the unit, famous for his bravery and accuracy, which was supposed to result in his promotion in the near future, who killed the archer with one shot from the crossbow given to him by the elves. The entry behind the gate of a small convoy was met with shouts of appreciation and applause from the service and guards who were observing the event. Oliver took the tribute with a messy feeling, as did the guards escorting him. After all, those people were just desperate and hungry. It won't be easy to forget their pleading faces.

After a short greeting, they quickly resumed their activities. With such a large royal court hosting the castle, there was no shortage of tasks to be performed, and the penalties for the alleged sluggishness on the part of some lords were sometimes severe.

"Pretty good," the escort commander, who was already approaching his thirties, nodded his head appreciatively. "Pity old Ramoz," he looked at the dead coachman. "He has provided food here for years. Miraculously, his family had survived the plague so far. I'll see that the body is given back to them. As for you, my dear..." He smiled, and it was a mischievous smile, more of a boy than a brave soldier. "Good start to the service! I'm Delen." He held out his hand both to greet and courteously help Oliver off the wagon. "Delen Serne, King's Guard Commander. Future commander," smirked again. "They say."

"Selena Calis," Oliver smiled unforgivingly at the amiable soldier. "Celina's sister, helpers to the cook. I came to replace her."

The mischievous smile vanished instantly from Delen's face. Anxiety replaced him.

"In your position," he said with a strange look on his face, "I wouldn't say too much about it."

"You know...?" the fate of the unfortunate woman, whose sister he was impersonating, should not really concern him, but as if sensing something greater in it, he became alert.

He sensed that the commander was even more than kind to him. He saw his interest in Selena's beauty. He became even oversensitive about the excessive interest on the part of Moren, which is why Delen's behavior, although undoubtedly completely innocent in this respect, immediately aroused his vigilance. He would have preferred not to catch his eye, but it was clearly too late for that. So he decided to rely on improvisation. Nothing bad is happening yet. He must not be paranoid whenever someone looks at him. Such nervous behavior, given the circumstances of his arrival, would only do him harm.

"Not here. Not now," Delen replied quickly, "The royal medic will be here soon," he took his hand gently. "For now, you have a friend here. And beware the viceroy!"

Oliver looked into his eyes without a word. "What have I not been told?" He thought silently, "Will the circumstances of this woman's death be a serious obstacle to my task? To Moren, I am valuable as a future prey, he would not put me at risk. My story is credible. But... What if some things were not foreseen?"

"Forgive me for leaving you with this secret now," Delen whispered, stepping back at the sound of footsteps approaching.

"Celina's sister is not lacking in courage as I hear," a tall, slender man with a narrow face and dark, almost black eyes hurriedly approached them.

Oliver, who had lived his entire life in Verdom, had no trouble recognizing court medic, Sedon. He curtseyed, imitating his sister and mother as they greeted the great ladies. It came out quite naturally. He cursed silently. No wonder Moren got interested in him, since he has such girlish talents!

"Lord," he bowed his head, changing the key of his voice to be polite but not humble. He had no intention of groveling and humiliating to anyone, now or in the future. He did not bow to Moren, and despite his bleak future, he was not going to give up. Neither him nor anyone else who thought he could rule him.

The medic regarded him with a faint amusement. Delen, meanwhile, bowed and went back to his men. When the order was given, several of his men dealt with the dead coachman.

"Are you surprised I know who you are?" The Medic asked. "Knowledge is a powerful tool today. It helps to get ahead of the facts, to guess the future. But sometimes it also leads... nowhere," he smirked. "In your case, I can see that my help will not be needed here. You seem like a healthy woman to me, although nowadays appearances can be deceptive. Fortunately, there is a healer in the castle, who can correct my possible mistake. His presence here might suggest that my humble person is unnecessary in a royal court, right? But anyone who would dare to think so would be wrong. Only a fool would now deprive himself of all defense. After all, the healer himself cannot be everywhere. Have you ever been to the castle?"

"No, sir," Oliver lied without stammering, feeling better and better with his role.

Half a year earlier he had been at the castle and was led into the audience hall with his father, who made an intricate necklace for Queen Constance. It was another great commission after making a pendant for a healer. Proof of starting a new, truly prosperous life for the whole family. Until now, they had not received orders from the royal family, only from a few noble ones. This sudden turn was a dream come true for his father. Apparently, the queen had heard of an elaborate gift made by the skillful hands of his father. He really had a talent for it. Half a year later, shortly after the outbreak of the plague, they were robbed by strange coincidence, and the son of a respected goldsmith became a thief to support the family. Moren certainly contributed to it...

A slightly balding man with a nervous, probably reflexive movement, acquired during his internship, began to roll up the sleeves of his shirt as they entered the service entrance.

"Well, we'll see what task they assign you to," he smiled sympathetically. "Although after such a loud entrance, I would rather see you as one of the guards than the cook's assistant, for example."

"I'm supposed to clean the rooms," Oliver replied.

The medic looked at him quickly, too quickly for Oliver to make sense of the look. He opened his mouth to say something, but changed his mind, and instead of the original words that must have touched his lips, he said:

"Then you will probably meet a healer. He's a really good boy. Among others here, he is like a rose that grew on dung, for example."

Oliver looked at the medic, surprised by his comparison, but said nothing. Apparently the medic used to make such comparisons.

"There is Purser Kanel now. Go to him," the medic showed him one of the service corridors. "I hope that we will meet during our duties."

"It will be a real pleasure," Oliver bowed slightly, taking the bow as his own, not like your typical obedient maid. Sedon noticed it right away.

"Considerately, but without too much servitude," he muttered, neither to himself nor to him, seeing the movement. "May your courage never leave you, girl," he bowed politely and walked away to the stairs that led to the upper floors.

Oliver watched him for a moment, alone in the corridor, which, despite being intended for servants, was as offensive as the entire castle, and at the same time delighted with a multitude of decorations and colors so varied as if an architect could not decide what style to choose.

"Time to start," he thought. "The game has started. And I can't escape..."

* * *

Purser Kanel turned out to be a nervous man, equal to Oliver's height. First, he assigned him the duties of cleaning certain floors in the castle, he allocated a room in the cottage for the castle servants, located under the walls. Then he instructed the location of the changing rooms, where Oliver was to change immediately into appropriate clothes, laundry, drying rooms and other important utility rooms. He explained it all in a hurry and almost without a break. After constantly complaining about how much health it cost to organize all this with so many powerful people, and how much weight it put him at risk, he finally assigned him the first task. As a precaution, Oliver was to go to the healer's chambers and check that everything was in order and that nothing was missing. The real reason was that new maid Selena is one of the few newcomers. In order to avoid unnecessary trouble and bring a plague to the royal court, for which the purser could even lose his head, she had to be allowed to contact the healer immediately, and if it did not happen immediately, at least with his things, which are famous for the power of their owner. All this the purser blurted out in a stream of words, hastily gesturing and introducing an atmosphere of nervousness. So Oliver was finally grateful to his fate when he was finally released with an order to go to work, because he was already getting a headache from the talk. With his heart pounding, he changed into the modest clothes of the maid, tied his hair into a bun and put on a cap.

He nervously checked the effect in the mirror.

The ease with which he changed from a slender son of a goldsmith into a girl of overcast beauty amazed even him. He studied his reflection in exasperation. More than one girl could envy him complexion. He could be calm about the disguise. It masked him perfectly.

His fate was sealed...

Quickly, lest dangerous thoughts take over him, he took a deep breath and headed for the healer's chambers, following the directions of the purser. He wasn't going to stay here any longer than necessary. If he is lucky, he will get at least one of the pendants and escape the castle along the paths of Cat, as he was already called in the city. He was prepared for that too. In the pockets of his long skirt he hid his beloved slingshot and a pouch of stones, and around his belt he hid his most precious treasure in the thief industry - a thin, extremely strong rope of elves that Sel had once stealthily given him. His father had contacts with mountain elves. As a silk merchant, he often did business with them. It was only thanks to the elves that Sel was still alive. However, they could not cure him completely without taking him out of the house, and his mother did not allow that. Maybe she was afraid that death would take her son when he set out? It was hard to guess. Perhaps she just thought it was a pity to waste time on it. Sel said so in moments of bitterness.

Oliver was sure the friend would try to save his sister, even if it did endanger his own life. Not one word of Moren could be believed anymore...

It was almost eight o'clock by the Sun Clock in the castle tower, visible from the windows, as Oliver entered the healer's chamber.

What he saw was beyond his imagination. Above his head, the ceiling swayed almost with ornate arches, carved heads with different expressions: sad, gloomy, mad, mysterious, with the tongue hanging out or without teeth. Carved vines or some other vegetation filled almost every place. The walls of the chambers were rich in ornaments and elaborate decorations. Heavy candelabra completed the overwhelming impression. There were figurines or miniatures of ships on tables and cabinets. The bed, sofa, and armchairs were all crimson. Everywhere it shimmered and glistened in the sunlight. Only the corner by the window in the sleeping chamber was not overwhelming. There was an armchair in which the healer was probably reading, and near the window stood a modest telescope, compared to the splendor surrounding it. Outside the window, you could see the city and the nearby sea. He could even make out the white manes of the waves.

Oliver was sure he had never seen such an accumulation of furniture and ornaments before. At first glance, the room was stunning with its splendor. After a while, however, in a person who was used to the simplicity and interior design full of harmony, it caused a feeling of breathlessness. It was as if there was not enough air left in the chambers after the interiors were full. The enormity of it all was overwhelming, and though Oliver had only seen the healer once or twice in his life, he was sure he certainly didn't feel comfortable here. It was clear that the interior was not being arranged with the healer's comfort in mind. Here Oliver saw no bookshelf that the healer was said to have liked. Even a small one. Only on the window table in the bedroom he noticed one entitled "The First Kings." The cover was richly decorated and the interior contained intricate, careful writing on handmade paper. As if it was the property of at least the heir to the throne or the queen. So she was still here, not sharing the fate of the healer's belongings, the lion's share of which was owned by Moren. Anger seized him.

Both were exploited and imprisoned for the pleasure of other people. It was getting harder and harder for him to come to terms with the idea that he had to rob this man.

The entrance door to the adjoining chamber opened softly.

"Lord Count," Oliver heard a soft woman's voice. "The brightest lord has ordered me to notify you, my lord, that the morning audience has been postponed by two hours. Therefore, the king invites you to a modest breakfast with his family in half an hour before the audience."

"Tell King, Alena, I will come," the healer replied kindly, and Oliver's remembered voice from the past was melodic and pleasantly soothing.

Hurriedly he stood in the bedroom doorway to be seen by anyone entering. The maid nodded and walked away.

A young thief dressed as a girl with a pounding heart looked into the healer's unusually blue eyes.

"My lord," he bowed lightly, "I am ordered to check that you are not missing anything."

He hid his surprise at the sight of his condition. When he and his mother visited Aunt Semeralda in Barnica, a town of healer in the mountains, over a year ago, he saw him helping several people. The Count was then a young man with a clearly defined belly and a rounded face, kind and full of joy in life. He was slim now, as if he had been starving for a long time, and there were shadows under his eyes. The joy of life was replaced by determination, like a fire that ignites his gaze. There was a certain tension in all his attitude, as if staying in the castle had taught him to be careful. It was a shocking change in the human being, so far open to people, after such a short period of staying at this court. So he wasn't treated very well here...

"I can see," Oliver continued a little nervously, shocked by the change, "that the water jug is almost full but the cup is missing."

Actually, he shouldn't comment on that. But Oliver knew that he might feel more comfortable with the healer.

"It was still here this morning," the healer remarked, looking towards the bedroom where the aforementioned water jug stood on the nightstand. "They disappear every day," he finished, without a trace of irony, but with a strange note in his voice.

They both fell silent, aware of the meaning of these words.

"You're the girl everyone's talking about right now, aren't you?" the healer noticed quietly after a long silence. "Hero... You saved our food."

"Yes, my lord."

"They say you're Celina's sister, the kitchen assistant?" The healer noted softly.

"Yes, my lord."

Oliver silently congratulated himself on his composure. For his first instinct was to deny this whole masquerade.

"They say you're Celina's sister, the kitchen assistant?" The healer remarked.

He was so quiet and calm. So different from himself a year ago. Oliver watched the change sadly.

"Yes, my lord."

"Tell the purser there's nothing wrong with you. You are healthy boy," a slight smile appeared on the healer's lips for a moment.

Oliver opened his mouth to answer. However, the sense of the last words quickly closed them. It might have been a slip of the tongue, though it was unlikely.

"I'll get another cup," he decided to ignore it for the moment, though the healer's words upset him a little. He cursed.

He waited silently for the briefing, though his heart continued to pound with anxiety. The healer looked at him thoughtfully.

"Tell me," his gentle tone of voice almost immediately muffled Oliver's anxiety. "You were told not to talk to me?"

The purser had apparently forgotten it. Anyway, Oliver decided from the beginning not to stick too closely to the instructions.

"No, Count," he replied truthfully.

"I will not reveal your secret..." Vivan approached him, lowering his voice. "Do not worry. Nothing reveals this. This is my special sensitivity. I can sense a mood, a smell, even a taste or someone else's thoughts. Just tell me: do you know anything about my family? Have you heard of them? Do you know if they are alive?"

The pain from the recent loss gripped Oliver's heart. And anger at people who remain silent about such an important matter for the prisoner.

"I'm sorry, my lord. I don't know," he really regretted it.

There was something about this man that made him immediately like him.

The disappointment on the healer's face genuinely saddened him. However, as Vivan approached, the young thief's eyes, as if by instinct, automatically rested on his neck. Both pendants were still there. It was enough to come up and break the chain...

It had to be a survival instinct.

Oliver's pulse sped up again, this time for a completely different reason.

Hands. They were right there.

Vivan looked into his eyes. Oliver realized that the healer sensed a change in his mood. He commanded himself restraint with difficulty.

"And the plague?" Seemingly in the same neutral tone the count continued, "Many died?"

The thoughts of it apparently tormented him as well. Julien would certainly like him.

"The death toll is terrifying," he whispered softly, overwhelmed with memories of the departing wagon full of dead bodies, with the bodies of his mother and father.

Thoughts about what happened and what would happen, especially about what might have happened began to overwhelm him like a burden. He felt the lively emotions choke him again.

Suddenly he wished it was a different place, a different time. So that all that has happened so far has not happened. He wanted to tell the healer about everything, a man he didn't even know, but he felt there was no falsehood in him. But he couldn't do it.

Not if he did what he intended. He was to steal the pendant and save Julien from disgrace, and at the same time destroy everything that was part of his good memories of his family. His mother and the healer's mother became friends, hosted her in their home, and his father proudly made the pendant he would now steal. Why did fate make him do this? Why did it have to be this way now?

"What's bothering you?" The healer asked softly.

He looked at him. He must. He just must to do it! There was no other way out!

For the sake of Julien...

Suddenly, raised voices from behind the wall snapped him out of his gloomy thoughts. Both instinctively looked towards the bedroom, behind the wall of which a quick, nervous female voice and a low, angry male voice could be heard.

"The viceroy and countess of Weren," explained the healer, "again..."

There was reluctance and weariness in his voice. Oliver gratefully welcomed the event. It allowed him to cool down a bit. He glanced at the healer. The countess's meetings with the viceroy certainly did not allow him to fall asleep at night. They must have been a fairly noisy couple. The anger stung him again. He felt a strange bond form between them, as if he had met someone very close to him. He didn't know if Vivan was influencing him or if it were his own feelings, but now he knew for sure that he would treasure his friendship with this man. It was getting harder and harder for him to fulfill his intention.

But he couldn't give up...

The couple behind the wall, after a brief argument, began to groan and grunt as they paired violently. Vivan's gaze grew strangely distant, as if he was mentally trying to escape the noises. Probably not the first time.

"You can go," he said, still not raising his voice.

Oliver has been dismissed. He should be gone now.

Next move. You have to bow your head. Cut off thoughts. Focus on the task at hand. Steal it walking away...

He moved.

At that moment, he felt the skin on his right cheek begin to sting, and a moment later it burned like fire. The sudden pain brought tears to his eyes. He groaned reflexively, and the amazed healer looked at him. Oliver put a hand to his cheek, burning with pain, and felt a distinct blow against it. In sudden fear, he realized that if the pain was so intense for him, then...

"Show me." The healer's hands gently took his hand away from his face. As he put his hand on the spot, Oliver recoiled instinctively. "Relax," the healer's soothing voice held him in place. "Hit," he whispered, "Do you have a twin brother?"

Oliver froze.

"A sister," he replied, his heart beating anxiously.

"All twins have a spiritually connected heart. You're hiding it, of course," Vivan said calmly, while Oliver felt a soothing warmth spread across his face like circles in water under his hand.

"I've already seen it."

The voices still coming from behind the wall grew more violent, but now the healer ignored them. He focused his attention only on him.

"You may not believe me, but this way I will help your sister too. What are you feeling..."

"Thank you..." Oliver only managed to whisper.

The pain passed quickly, and the smacked cheek returned to its appearance. Warmth spread over Oliver's body, making him feel calm, and the tense muscles visibly relaxed. He felt a sudden surge of strength. And remorse.

The viceroy's voice, angry and impetuous, suddenly broke into the silence. They clearly heard the words:

"Do what I want, you dirty bitch!"

"I must go now," the healer's voice turned colorless again. "I'd rather go than listen to it."

The viceroy's puffing made Oliver nauseous. He grunted with effort, cursed, and that slowly shaped Oliver's mind into a future he didn't want to be part of. He would rather hide in the disguise of a woman than come back. He would rather help the healer escape this nightmare than steal from him. Moren did not keep his word. It is very likely that he was the one who hit Julien, and if not even him, then he allowed it to be done. Rage seized him and a sense of terrible harm. Is he supposed to rob a good man for a bandit who wants to fuck him until he breaks him and kills him? Is she supposed to let him do what he wants, lavish Julien's life, and eventually die in shame and humiliation under any pretext? What was he counting on?! To keep the word? He put his future and Julien at stake for the sake of an empty promise. He expected Moren to be dishonest. But he hoped that because of the pendant he cared so much, he would keep his promise until Oliver returned and finished his job.

No. Now he certainly won't get what he wants so badly.

The plan was simple in principle. Oliver was to steal the "hands" and go home unnoticed, where he would change pendants in the garden. The right one was to get Julien, who was to be allowed to escape at the earliest opportunity. The pendant was to help her wade safely through the plague lands to reach Aunt Semeralda. He believed he could manage to confuse the chase and not get caught by anyone. He had great hopes that she would be able to take Sel with her. Sel has always been practical. Unfortunately, his illness could thwart all plans at any moment. He did not care about his fate. The fake pendant, deprived of a healer, was to be returned to Moren, and then to make sure that there was nothing within his reach that belonged to the healer. With luck, Moren would fall ill. And if not him, then Oliver himself, sending the plague on Moren and his people and praying to all the good spirits that as many as possible would die.

He wouldn't be able to live after... And such a death by disease wouldn't hurt like a violent death would... He'd heard about it before.

"Help!!!" A desperate scream broke through the walls.

It chilled the blood in his veins.

"Is that part of their sick fun too? Sounds..."

"No," the healer interrupted quickly, "she usually likes violence, that's true. Just a moment ago it was as always. Now she really suffers. He's causing her pain. He rapes her. He made her pretend..." He stopped suddenly, not wanting to reveal too much, and then quickly said: "You have to go get the royal guard! Find Lieutenant Delen! Enter the Countess' chambers without waiting for permission. Go!"

"And you?" when the moment came when the master and servant became allies in the game, it didn't matter anymore.

The healer winced slightly, not indignant at the familiarity. It was supposed to be like that. From the very first moments of the meeting, he knew that they would communicate quickly.

"I'm going to them!" He said sharply as he left. "Run for help!"

Behind the doors of the healer's chambers they dispersed in a hurry. Oliver looked back. Determined, Vivan briefly dismissed the guards who were trying to stop him quite sluggishly, and stormed into the Countess Weren's chambers. The guards, torn between loyalty to the king's brother and respect for the healer, simply stood behind him...

Oliver started running.

Meanwhile, Vivan burst into the sleeping-chamber. Without further ado, he grabbed the viceroy struggling with the crying woman by the tuft of hair on his head and pulled. This forced the man to let go of his victim and stand up. With unbelievable strength for such an emaciated man, Vivan turned the half-naked viceroy face to face, pushed him onto the bed with a hard kick, and jumped. Countess Weren - young, pretty, in a now tattered red dress and red hair, slipped hastily from the bed, holding her dress with trembling hands and looked at her savior with gratitude and amazement. Of all the people she knew in the castle, she expected him the least. Not only because her chambers were often visited by the viceroy and other men, which was probably disgusting her neighbor. She had been trying to seduce him ever since he arrived, curious to know what unusual attributes the healer hides under his clothes. After a week she wanted him so much, he made her so passionate about his presence, his apparent inexperience in these matters, his innocence and kindness towards women, unusual in this place that she became possessive of him. She wanted to get him to caress him whenever possible. Finally, when he firmly demanded that she leave him alone, she came to her senses as if a bucket of cold water had been poured over her. Perhaps it was the tone of his voice, perhaps a long-dormant morality that opened her eyes then. She realized she was tormenting him. And when, with that new gaze, she saw other women, sometimes as old as Queen Lizetta's court lady, as old as the world itself, and even some men, intrusively approach him, she felt sorry for him. Although he did not know it, she discreetly spoiled the ranks of the intruders. Seemingly no big deal, some laxative drops at dinner or a closed door unexpectedly. Celina, a kitchen assistant, initiated this, and sometimes she added this or that to the dishes and drinks of selected people. She was especially eager to do this when the countess explained to the skillful girl that it was about the good of the healer. Unfortunately, Celina was murdered...

It was whispered that the viceroy had his fingers in it, who did not miss the opportunity to accost young girls. She was inclined to believe these rumors. If he hadn't given her what she liked so much, a pleasure bordering on cruelty, she wouldn't have easily let the story go by. She was going to get the truth out of him for her private use.

She got up, determined to help and suffer the consequences together for the attack on the king's brother himself. She had done many bad things in her life, but for once she wanted to be loyal to the man who had come to her aid selflessly. He deserved it. For him, she could do a lot...

Only for him.

Just like that. Though she didn't quite understand it herself.

But before she came, the viceroy grasped Vivan's hands with an angry cry, and despite his great body, managed to immobilize him. From the moment the healer stepped in, the fight had gone quickly, and even now that Vivan was struggling with the king's brother, it could have ended in death. The beautiful countess jumped on the viceroy and bit his hand. Terlan jerked suddenly with a loud scream and slapped her in the face with all his might. As she fell, she hit the bedside table with her head and froze.

"Wolf pup!" He grabbed the weakened healer by the skirts of his doublet. "If you weren't so important...!"

"Viceroy!" Suddenly they heard a firm voice. "By your brother's order I am to take you to the royal chambers. In case of resistance, I must use force!"

Lieutenant Delen was standing in the chamber, with several of his men with him. He was accompanied by a dark-haired girl whom the viceroy had not yet seen, and from behind his guards, one could see the curious faces of the castle's inhabitants and servants, drawn here by the sounds of fighting and the lust for sensation.

Delen took an expectant posture. Under other circumstances, the viceroy would have taken it as an insult, but now that he was so close to his plans, it was not time for the show. The healer yanked out of his grip angrily. They looked at each other for a moment.

"Dinner tonight," Terlan drawled to him. "I want you close to me. Otherwise I'll finish my conversation with your ginger friend."

He climbed rather awkwardly from the bed, being watched by a healer who was visibly exhausted by the brief skirmish, but anger gleamed in his unusual eyes. The viceroy made his gaze dismissive as he stared into the lieutenant's eyes, without a trace of embarrassment tipping on his trousers. His confidence, even in such an awkward situation, was so great that no one dared say a word or even smile. Calmly, first looking into Delen's eyes, and then focusing his eyes on the girl, he dressed and fastened with a truly royal dignity, showing open disregard for both of them. Oliver began to tremble slightly. The interest in him did not go unnoticed. He could feel those looks, curious and burning. Viewers now watched his reaction, eager to continue. Although the viceroy had challenged him as a woman, Oliver, remembering his future, stared back proudly, wishing with all his soul that no fear would be seen in him. Delen stepped forward as if trying to shield him. He took an expectant posture again, saying, "Come on. Enough of this show!" After Terlan smirked at it all, Oliver realized he could expect to acquaintance the viceroy. And in the condition of the countess, which the healer had now gently taken care of, he could easily imagine how the acquaintance would have ended for him if he had been a woman, and the thought made him involuntarily blush.

Why he must also always enjoy the interest of such scoundrels?

The viceroy looked briefly at his two men, seemingly with a look of little importance. They failed him. Soon, if nothing changed, they could expect significant changes in their résumé. They paled slightly under that gaze, but behind his back their eyes met the lieutenant's. Now Oliver fully understood their passivity towards the viceroy. They only seemed to be subordinate to Delen.

So he didn't understand why they hadn't helped the healer then. Apparently, Delen didn't like their behavior either. He noticed his watchful gaze.

Careful with your own skin.

He remembered their faces well.

"So I will find out what my dear brother wants from me," smiled the viceroy dismissively, completely sure of his impunity.

The crowd passed him in silence. Delen looked questioningly at Oliver, whom he treated as his new acquaintance. Oliver tried to find a comforting smile for his use. "I can handle it," he made him understand, actually thinking so. Why not? There is no need to worry about the whole situation any longer. He won't be here soon.

He led the marauders out and closed the door. When he entered the chamber, the Countess was conscious. The trace of the hit slowly disappeared before his eyes. Vivan touched her head gently with one hand. On the other, the young woman clenched her hands. She stared at the healer in silence, never taking her eyes off even as Oliver entered. She was so calm and beautiful right now. So different than he expected. The sight of her suddenly aroused feelings in Oliver that he had never suspected before. These were thoughts he didn't allow himself to do, fearing Moren wouldn't forgive him even a moment of happiness. Desires that he had pushed into oblivion by focusing on protecting his beloved sister.

The Countess took a deep breath, her eyes sparkled with vigor.

"Much better," she whispered, as if answering a silent question.

Vivan got up and helped her too.

Then he suddenly staggered and turned pale. Both women - real and fake - grabbed him at the same time.

"I'll be fine," he tried to calm them down.

"Yes. Especially looking at how much you've been eating lately," said the Countess sarcastically. "Girl," she said to Oliver. "What's your name?"

"Selena, Countess."

"Take the count to his chamber and let him rest," the countess instructed. "And make sure he has dinner tonight. I can handle. I'm already a big girl." She smiled, trying to make this smile playful.

Of course, neither of the men believed that she was doing great.

"Nilan..." the healer began, but she covered his mouth with her hand.

Oliver suddenly envied him at this touch.

"No need," she said calmly, and in the tone of her voice they heard a certain maturity, the fruit of experiences from the past life.

Even her eyes took that special expression.

A discreet knock on the door made all three of them freeze. Oliver helped Vivan sit on the bed. He mechanically adjusted the tightly pinned hair of his wig.

The lieutenant and two of his men were standing outside the door.

He bowed politely, paying close attention to Selena.

"Lady Countess, Lord Count. I have been instructed to inform you that you are to remain in these chambers until the King's visit. The King wants to hear your version."

After these words, he politely saluted and set people out in front of the door of the chamber.

"Great," Oliver thought wryly as he closed the door.

As Vivan clearly felt worse on the bed, Oliver, remembering his earlier words about particular sensitivity and glancing at the matted sheets, made a guess at the reason for this condition. He discreetly offered an armchair and a glass of water, then opened the window. The smell of sweat and sperm was perfectly palpable. He calmly suggested leaving nothing to be done until the king arrived.

"Are you holding on?" He asked the healer's with quiet concern, taking advantage of the fact that the countess had gone to refresh herself.

"It'll be better when I finally get out of here," Vivan replied grimly.

"You should eat... my lord," he stammered, feeling the countess's gaze upon him.

"I just wanted to say the same," she interjected. "Vivan, a hunger strike won't give you freedom," she sat down next to him.

"I'm not starving myself," he told her. "Since I'm here, I can't eat or sleep in peace. Just like that."

He looked at her.

She considered it.

"Are we so horrible?" She asked.

It was the right question.

Vivan didn't answer. She was for him a symbol of so many things that happened from the beginning of his forced stay at the castle.

The Countess looked at him thoughtfully. After a long moment, Vivan took her hand and squeezed lightly. She smiled a really soft, girlish smile that probably hadn't been on her lips in a long time. It was an innocence of old age. A trace of a completely different life.

Even knowing a little about her, Oliver felt he was beginning to like her. The healer undoubtedly felt a weakness for her as well.

"Sorry," she whispered softly with tears in her eyes.

Vivan smiled warmly, a shadow of that old smile Oliver remembered.

The Countess hesitated.

"Haven't seen you here before." She slipped her hand from the healer's hand, as if to correct a muted gown. She needed to change the topic of conversation, she was not used to honesty in feelings. "Here and especially now, in these times the service rarely changes. We have a healer, so nobody gets sick, and so far I've been served by Alena. Has something happened to her?" She asked anxiously.

"No, Countess," he replied calmly. "I only came this morning. I was ordered to go to a healer to check if I was healthy. By coincidence... I'm here now."

"I understand," muttered the Countess. "You got someone here?"

"My sister worked here as a kitchen assistant."

"She worked?"

"She's dead," he replied, pretending sadness.

The countess's expression changed.

"Was her name Celina?" She asked, seemingly calm.

Oliver looked at her in amazement. The healer did the same.

"Did you know Celina?" He was surprised.

"You too?" She replied, surprised.

"I know everyone in this castle." The healer's quiet words were a bit scolding. "I'm surprised you knew her."

"I..." She was slightly perplexed under their gaze. "Once I went down to the kitchen... Stop it Vivan, I sometimes pay attention to others..."

"Sometimes…"

"I needed something."

"So much so that you remember the name. You must have needed often."

She didn't know what to say to that. Oliver rushed to help her.

"Lady Countess," he felt compelled to ask. "What do you know about her death?"

She looked at them both.

"Just what they say, girl," she replied.

"What do they say?"

"That the viceroy is behind it," the healer replied, and he saw a silent warning in his eyes, a little different from the one the countess had spoken aloud.

"I saw how he was looking at you, Selena" she looked into his eyes. "He's a cruel, dangerous man. It isn't and won't be good. Runaway. Run while you can!"

"Has he… disgraced her?" if he was to pretend to be the sister of that girl with whom he was beginning to have a peculiar bond, suddenly making him her instrument of justice, then he had to ask about it. Was it really a coincidence that he was going to pretend to be her sister? Of all the possibilities Moren probably had here, one could choose a completely different story. But he chose it. As if Celina herself wanted it.

"I don't know for sure," she replied. "But that sounds like him."

"She hit something she shouldn't have found out," the healer said suddenly. "She died for that knowledge. You chose the wrong time to find out the truth. You can end up like her." He looked into his eyes.

"She thinks I'm her brother," Oliver looked back calmly. "A brother who has a twin sister and came to find out the truth." If he knew how different it was from his guesses.

"What do you know, Vivan?" Asked the Countess. "What do you want to tell us?"

But at that moment the sentries opened the door and the king entered the chambers with his wife, sons and escort.

The time was now for other explanations...

CHAPTER 4 — Dance with death

The same time...

Sel stared in awe at the disappearance of the slap on Julien's smooth cheek. After a while it wouldn't be there anymore.

Oliver met a healer.

Some unnamed thought flashed through Sel's mind, stabbing him with a faint feeling of jealousy. He once dreamed of this meeting. He dreamed that the healer would heal him, and then he would gain strength and take over the family business, or finally completely change his life. The father will stop treating him like a burden he has to bear. The mother would stop looking at him with regret and gloomy anticipation. He was her only child alive, which she did not want to notice, even though she had already lost three children. The first one was born dead. The second one died a week after birth.

The third one died tragically.

Without any special emotions or regrets, convinced that this and nothing else had done her fate, she waited for his heart to finally give up and stop beating.

Sel's sister Noela was two years old when her mother decided to give fate a chance and became pregnant again. Noela was her mother's beloved child, the apple of her father's eye. They poured out on her all unfulfilled love. Sel grew up in the womb surrounded by this love. Expected with hope. The future looked brighter, and the composition of the silk merchant was gaining more and more recognition and customers. Everything was on good track. Noela ran around and played around with care. Sel moved in the womb of his mother, finally smiling, carefully allowing herself moments of happiness and hope.

Noela, like most children her age, wasn't very obedient. She was everywhere. She held out her hands confidently for almost everything.

Many people came to see her father. Middlemen and clients. One of them brought a dog with him.

Dogs often accompanied their owners, and there was nothing unusual about it. This one was taught to hunt. And his ears picked up the squeaky sounds of the little creature.

He left his master, left the warehouse located on the ground floor of the house where Andilo's family lived, and found himself in the yard where Sel's mother was talking to Moren's mother, her closest friend at the time. Noela, bored and waiting, circled nearby, saying something in her own way. They were about to go to the garden.

The dog attacked a trusting girl who only wanted to stroke him. He bit her head, digging his teeth into the skull. In the blink of an eye, he was separated from the girl and beaten to death. However, the evil has already happened...

The child died in the arms of the shocked mother.

Rina, Selarion's mother, never recovered. Regret, loss and despair broke her heart. The tragedy hastened childbirth.

His father, wanting to save his suffering wife and child in her womb, turned to the elves for help.

Sel was born ahead of time. He was not given great hopes and yet he survived. Mother, overwhelmed by grief, could not enjoy it or fight for it. She moved away from him, convinced that fate would soon take him too.

He was close to death several times in the following years.

And she was waiting for this death.

She accepted that it had to be so. That she would never have children with her. If he was going to die anyway - why get attached, why connect with him hopes that will never come true?

Why ask a healer for help, when a perverse fate will probably take the child away from them, anyway?

Why enjoy every moment spent with your only child, when it may die any moment?

And finally... Why love him?

However, the years passed and Selarion did not die. Despite everything, he clung to life, although it was often not easy for him. More than once he saw his father's uncertain gaze, as if he were saying: "Make up your mind - are you staying with us or going to the afterlife?"

They both treated him well, although his father paid more attention to his needs. Sel felt that if he wanted to, they would have given him almost anything. These were gestures towards the one sentenced to the ax. He could become a very spoiled child. Instead, he made a character for himself. He was resourceful, knew how to take care of himself, and he studied well. He grew up to be a young man who took what was given to him from life, demanding no more. His mother continued to look at him with this strange sadness, so he stopped talking to her about his dreams as a child. She already condemned him. Father acted as if he was holding back from something with difficulty, pressed his lips together and looked as if he were pondering something, fought against the feeling that wanted to flow from his heart. Several times Sel had caught him with a proud look of fatherly appreciation when he had done something really good. Like when he clandestinely devised a way to bring running water to the kitchen and a drain. With the help of two servants, he put it on when his parents were visiting another merchant they knew.

The father looked at him then, then glanced at his mother.

And she left silently, barely glancing at what he had constructed.

They cared for him because decency dictated that. The persuasions of Oliver's mother and the confectioner's wife did not help. The scolding glances did not help. Mother shut herself up in her world, and father loved her so blindly that he was loyal to her decisions.

They never went with him to a healer.

When Sel was ten years old, while playing the battle in the square behind the confectioners' house, he fainted and did not have the strength to get up. He felt very badly. The royal medic, shaking his head in disbelief, it is not known whether he was surprised that he was still alive or the stupidity of his family, told his father that this time it might be the end. The leaky heart Sel was born with will eventually give up. Of course, he couldn't have known what condition and what was actually wrong with Sel's heart. He made a hole in the heart just after his birth, adding that his condition was probably caused by the fact that at the time of Noela's death, the mother's heart was pierced by a dagger of pain, the blade of which reached the heart of the unborn child. It didn't kill them, but it killed the love in mother's heart and hurt the baby because she stopped loving them. Father would only nod his head then, but later, when everyone was asleep, convinced that no one could hear him, he cried softly by the window in the corridor.

Sel heard the cry. Then he clutched and desperately grabbed the hand of the only person who was watching over his bed. Moren, the playmate, was snoring in the chair, but at least he was there. Not only that, from the day he appeared about Sel's illness, he hadn't been dismissed. He took a permanent place with him, brought him water, tried to feed him, and even a bit awkwardly, but still with the same vigor, wiped his forehead with a damp handkerchief. And he spoke. He spoke almost constantly. About everything he did, what he was going to do, and about others. Even every close of Sel's eyes would raise an alarm in Moren. He immediately put the house on its feet. He was dragging an adult whom he only met and had him judge if Sel was getting worse and if he needed a medic. His nerve and confidence moved the whole house. He had a habit of speaking loudly and quickly, and was very, very aggressive if he wanted something done immediately.

"When is dinner because Sel is already hungry and I'd eat something too?" He was asking.

"And where are the other pillows because the ones Sel has are sweaty?"

"Sel would like to pee, where's the potty, ma'am?"

"Sel just fell asleep, so please don't come now."

Although Sel had to endure the sometimes tiring presence of his best friend for the next few days, he was grateful to him. Without him, he would be allowed to die in peace. Meanwhile, he, with each time his breath came out with difficulty, fought to continue to be with his friend. Because Moren started fights, so he had to be reassured. He still could not read well, and he would not practice without help. And because he had promised him that he would be the general of his army. Generals don't always have to fight in person, Moren explained to him. He himself will be an undefeated hero, alongside his general, and together they will conquer the world.

Because he is with him.

Childish dreams, but they and friendship were Sel's only strength.

It was then that Sel became attached to Moren with all his longing for warmth, which in time seemed to him love. And Moren, active, impatient, always feverish, clung for good to his calm and strong-in-spirit friend.

He doesn't even know how much pain he has caused him now...

He's not that kid anymore, so overwhelmingly caring and faithful, ready to jump into the fire to save his friend. He is greedy, quick-tempered and unpredictable. He wants to keep everything he has and everything he wants to have with him at all costs. Before that, he was not a bad person. He fought with Oliver to subdue him, for he was impressed by his dexterity. As a matter of fact, he would like to have him in his gang if they recognized his authority. Perhaps he had secretly thought that it would turn into something deeper over time? The drastic change, caused by his sick desire, surprised not only Sel but, as Sel noticed right away, Moren himself. Something dark about him turned the usual rivalry of kids into psychopathic lust.

People don't change without a reason.

With Moren it was a disease of the mind... That Sel was almost sure. For many points to these changes. The heart would not accept any other explanation. He couldn't accept it if Moren were just that bad! After all, it was Moren, the same one who cared so much for him! Moren, who had listened to his advice so far. This can not be true! He can't be a bad person - just like that! And that thing with Oliver! This is all twisted and sick! Moren full of lust?! Moren - Milera's murderer - out of jealousy?!

It had to be a disease. There must be an explanation for that! He would have noticed sooner, he guessed! He would know!

Or maybe he didn't want to know...

He was determined to protect him at first. He calmed him down, convinced him, influenced his ambition, put his own way. But then Moren picked his current four buddies. It was the beginning of the end. Each of them incited him to evil in a different way. Everyone had a detrimental effect on him. Sel, dealt with them patiently at first. Moren, even if they quarreled a lot, never allowed them to insult him. And woe to one who would try to ridicule Selarion, mock his illness. Once Moren had beaten

Rosten, one of four, so that he was locked in a dungeon for three days. Because he called Sel a weakling. Sel appreciated his devotion, but was then terrified by the magnitude of the feeling. There was some grim bitterness about it... Like the story with Oliver that grew into a lust for destruction. Or when he wrecked the brothel room they both went to because his favorite courtesan wasn't there, and then he got drunk and threatened everyone he messed with - for words and deeds old and new. Sel passed out once more, stopping Moren, with drunken stubbornness late into the night trying to beat Oliver. His condition then worsened so much that he had to stay at the confectioners' house for several days. Moren then apologized to him for everything when he finally sobered up. According to Sel, however, it didn't sound sincere then.

Then all those people with whom the friend also began to surround himself. This whole bunch.

They only increased aggression in him.

And finally the plague. Getting loot.

Death of parents.

He didn't want to leave him. They still had their own affairs. Own plans. Like flashes of peace in a life full of quarrels. But Sel was losing. It not only exhausted him mentally. He was aware that the fight for a friend was almost lost.

He felt physically worse and worse, he suffered frequently, weakened and could not keep up.

Milera.

A good girl he was seeing in a brothel. In search of work, she came to Verdom. By chance, Julien met her at the marketplace, and a minor incident soured their friendship.

She left her parents and many siblings stranded with life.

They were both looking for an escape from their fate. Sel rested among the inhabitants of the House of Pleasure, feeling accepted there and cared for more than he experienced at home. She only wanted to improve the well-being of her family. To really do this, she would have to sell herself. Sel didn't let her do it. He made a deal with her. Marriage and a decent life for taking care of him. A good, respected name instead of a bad opinion.

Time could make what was meant to be just a union of sympathetic two lonely people, maybe turned into shy love.

Moren killed her.

At twenty, Selarion became a widower thanks to a recent best friend who had previously trampled his heart...

Valeriea, an elderly courtesan in her fifties, still with a perfect figure and vivid eyes, applied the powder to Julien's face with skill. Sel had never seen a friend like this. Julien never painted her eyes with a thick black line, never put shadows on her eyelids. It wasn't her style. It couldn't be. This was the picture of the women of the House of Pleasure on Pleasure Street, the largest and most populated building in the plague-ravaged area now that Moren had taken over. They both always came here.

Valeriea spun Julien's long black hair hurriedly. Nobody knew they were here. They fled the room that Moren had locked them in, forgetting that each room of the tabernacle had a secret door, hidden behind a wealth of paintings and carpets. Sel didn't wait for a moment for his memory to come back. Moren flushed at the sight of Julien's face, which he had left in the next room for a moment to talk to his friend. But Tenan was no longer with her. And now Moren, consumed with rage, was probably looking for him all over the house. He wasn't afraid that they would run away, he probably didn't even think about it in anger. The House of Pleasure was full of his people, and as he entered, he set up guards at the door. Most of the bandits hung out with female and male courtesans as they pleased or simply went about their duties. Almost everyone knew Sel as a friend of the leader, and as Ross said, the young man Sel turned to for help, everyone knew about Moren's intentions today. Sel couldn't leave unnoticed, though Ross insisted he would. Hence, he was washing his hands quickly after he had slightly blackened Sel's knotted, sweaty hair. The rest was completed with the make-up that was obligatory for all men of different orientations in the brothel to distinguish them from the "macks" as the others were called. He turned the exhausted Sel's face into a mask of an angel of death. Strongly underlined eyes made him look wild.

"Ross," Valeriea bit her lip nervously, now helping Julien to tie the corset of a red - black dress adorned with sparkling pebbles. "How are you doing? You know what will happen if Moren finds us here?"

Both were turned away because of their respect for Julien, innocent in so many cases.

"We're done," said shortly, dressed in provocatively tight black pants and a black vest, the man whose makeup was identical to Sel's makeup, "Sel, try to smile a little," he looked at him with concern. "You look like death."

As if a smile after what he heard was even possible...

"You already know, don't you?" Ross knelt beside him, taking the initiative wordlessly and buttoning up the buttons on his ribbed black shirt.

Sel lowered his hands, trembling like an old man's, and, sitting silently, allowed himself to help. He felt the elven elixir slowly spread through his body and warm his heart. Ross had it always in his room where they were now, in case Sel came to see him. Although he knew about his marriage, he did not give up on this habit.

Perhaps Sel would be dead if it weren't for his memory.

Because Ross was not only his friend.

The first… and the only… Probably forever, considering how often Sel felt bad lately.

"Hurry up," Valeriea said nervously.

Ross could read everything he wanted to know on his face. Better not to push.

"You look brilliant," he said quietly, with apparent calmness, although inside despair torn his heart when he saw in what state it is. "Nobody will recognize you. You never looked like this. But honey…" He looked above him at Julien turning away. "You must leave this place as soon as possible! It's all about to start draining off him."

Julien froze as she saw a changed friend. A skinny boy with dark blond hair, long eyelashes that would be envied by many a girl and eyes brown as coffee, always shiny, as if he was constantly consumed by a fever, turned into a dark-haired male whore. Defiant makeup, clothing that concealed his sickly thinness, disturbing gaze. It was some other nature of Sel. As different as night from day. She didn't like what she saw in his eyes...

"You have to go," Valeriea said what Ross, concerned about Sel, couldn't bring himself to do.

Sel wasn't looking at the women. He couldn't look at Julien's face, fearing that everything was about to fall apart. The elven potion calmed his breathing, restored some strength. His action grew shorter and shorter as his life grew faster and faster, but he no longer cared about it. Not any more. The most important thing he had to do was get Julien out of here, take Oliver and help them get out of town.

The agony and suffering, however, prevented him from thinking clearly. They had to find some outlet, relief for a while. Otherwise, his soul would break in two... Time mattered, and so did escape, but if he can't find the strength to move now, he won't help his friends. A bit more. Just a few more hours.

Otherwise everything will be lost. Oliver, independent, skillful Oliver will eventually die in humiliation, probably tortured one day by Moren, and Julien... Not only will she look like she does now. She will be the embodiment of Milera's nightmare. As long as she lives long enough...

"Sel," Ross whispered softly, "it's time..."

When Moren pulled them out of the goldsmith's house, Julien prudently covered Sel's eyes as they went outside and didn't discover them until they were far enough away. So he didn't see Milera's body...

"This is not how you want to remember her," she whispered in his ear.

He felt a tear as she brushed her cheek, her tear. She refrained from giving Moren any satisfaction.

Oliver was led alongside Moren to the House of Pleasure. Then he disappeared somewhere in the building. He only managed to give them one farewell glance. Moren had them taken to the room of his favorite courtesan, Reniel. Reniel herself, a young girl whose beauty was strikingly similar to Oliver's, ordered her to get out, simply throwing her out the door. Reniel was badly beaten. She left meekly, half dazed, as if she had turned into a puppet pulled by strings. Sel's heart squeezed at this yet another cruel act.

On Moren's orders, Tenan then led Julien out and they were left alone.

He never expected their conversation to be like this one day. It all - the assault, Oliver's humiliation, Milera's death - still seemed like one great nightmare from which he could not wake up. A very real nightmare.

"How do you like the place I chose?" Moren asked clearly relaxed. "Much better than the confectioner's house, isn't it?"

As if nothing special happened.

"Come on, say something." He put a hand on his shoulder. Sel budged. "Stop belaboring the point anymore. It's a new life, Sel. From now on there will be you and me as in the old days." Sel remembered the number of times Moren had let him decide, but remained silent. "And Oliver. Maybe with time it all gets stuck together somehow."

Sel glared at him, shaking his head in disbelief.

"You don't believe it yourself."

"Why not? Everything changes. You can too," Moren replied quickly. Too nervous. And fast.

He knew it was impossible. He was trying to deceive himself.

"Free them," Sel said calmly, as he always did when he saw Moren in this state, so agitated but indulgent toward him.

"And you will stay?" Moren faced him, tensed his muscles. "You're gonna stay, right? Won't you try to run away? Won't you leave me? Will you never even try?"

Sel found it hard to breathe, his heart beating restlessly.

"Look," Moren pointed out the door they had entered. "I have everything I need there. I will soon rule this place..."

"The city of the dead," Sel thought.

"You can't leave me. Not now." Moren put his hands on his shoulders. "If you try to escape or help them escape, I will have to punish you, for example. You know that, right?"

Sel silently told himself to be calm. Just not now.

"Even if it were only ten lashes, it could kill you. And I cannot do otherwise. You know how it is. Eat them or they will eat you. Tenan is just waiting. He already thinks he has something on me because of Oliver. I see it! I am putting myself at risk for you to protect your skins!"

Moren's twisted logic as he spoke the words terrified Selarion. There was no way to distinguish between what was right and what was wrong. Moren completely lost it. After so many years, when Sel tried to instill in Moren honesty and respect towards others, his efforts were simply wasted. Moren only saw what was good for him. But the worst part was that his eyes continued to stare at him as they did in the old days, seeking approval for his actions. Sel was about to say, "Yes, you are right. I appreciate what you do." It was just unbelievable! Moren, depending on the situation, treated people as means to fulfill his insidious plans. If anyone got in his way, they just removed him. Like Milera. He asked softly:

"Moren, what did you do with my parents?"

Moren's expression changed as if he felt confused, guilty about something. Cold sweat poured over Sel before he spoke. Pain pierced his heart in sudden dread.

"What do you mean?" Moren asked, clearly wanting to gain time.

Tears filled Sel's eyes. Anger and despair almost clouded his mind. He could feel it. It felt like it was within his hand! The aura of death...

"What did you do to them?" He asked, heavily emphasizing each word.

His heart pounded violently and quickly. He felt a warning pain.

"I set them free," Moren replied quickly, not meeting his eyes.

"You're lying!!" the emotions he had suppressed so far finally found an outlet. "What did you do with them?!"

He heard a buzzing noise in his head.

"Sel." He saw fear across Moren's face for the first time since they had seen each other. "Listen," he embraced him suddenly, hugging him tightly as if to comfort him, at the same time, unaware of it, taking his breath away. "They didn't care about you anyway," he tried to convince him, gently stroking his back. "I killed the mother. They slept. I stabbed her in the heart. She didn't even feel it. I mean..." he corrected himself quickly, and the shocked Sel could only stand in his embrace, shivering. "Maybe she felt, but briefly, because she didn't have a heart anyway. Tenan killed your father as I told him. He is fast and knows what he is doing. It's good for you, isn't it? It's over now. They will no longer be there. They won't torment you anymore."

Sel listened. Thoughts chased wildly, emotions swept over him. Why wasn't he carrying a dagger? Why was he allowing himself to be hugged by this murderer? Why didn't he have the strength to pull himself out of this embrace, not to listen to this calm tone, as if Moren was explaining to him the most ordinary thing in the world. Why is there no strength to move away from his touch?

"Sel." Moren took advantage of his agitation. "We'll start over. We will be together from now on. I'll take care of you." Sel tightened his hands on Moren's shirt in silent anguish, tears streaming down his face. "Come on. It's all water over the dam. I'll get a healer. I will free Julien. It's gonna be okay, right?"

He was unable to answer him.

In one moment he stood embraced by him...

The next moment Reniel was lying on the bed and Julien was sitting next to him. He saw fear on her face. Fear for him. Fear of being left alone here.

"Where's Tenan?" He heard Moren's scream furiously.

It was like that then.

He looked more closely at Julien. He saw purple on her face. Hit. Strong one.

"You passed out," she whispered.

"Is that Tenan?" He asked softly, feeling a twinge of anger.

She nodded.

Sel's heart twitched in warning. He felt pressure. Not now! He has to control it. He has to endure it somehow.

"He said I'd be his whore soon. I kicked him in the groin."

She looked at him anxiously. He must have looked really bad.

"I'm opening a can..." he whispered softly to himself. "I put a rusty spoon one after another, a broken stick, a stone from a river..." he quietly exchanged the first things that came to his mind, starting his unusual habit of dealing with violent emotions.

"What are you doing?" She asked, wiping the sweat off his forehead with a handkerchief.

"I turn thoughts into objects and put them in a can," he replied. "It's my way when things really get bad."

"It works?"

He was close enough to scream in despair...

"It must," he struggled to sit up.

He won't help anyone if he gives up now.

The breathing slowly calmed down.

His heart slowed down. Inside his chest he thought he had a burned hole, but he was still alive. After all...

"We're getting out of here. You have to get out of here!"

"You can barely walk!"

"I can handle. I always make it."

This is how they ended up in Ross's room. And now Sel was getting ready to go, but the suffering kept him from moving. Everyone noticed it.

Finally he looked, overwhelmed by all this, into the eyes of his first lover...

Ross didn't wait for more. He jumped up to him and hugged him gently, unlike Moren, whispering soothing words in his ear. Julien stared at it, confused, shocked by this Selarion's mystery. The tenderness of this embrace left no doubt. Milera had told her that Sel was often at the House of Pleasure. That he liked the company of both women and men. She had hoped to win his love someday, and it seemed that everything was going in that direction, because Sel hadn't been anywhere after the wedding.

Ross was the other side of Sel. And it happened in his life. They had something in common.

She couldn't blame Sel for it. Marrying Milera was a deal. It was time to show what their future would be.

"Ross," she said softly, feeling her friend wouldn't hold it against her. She certainly wouldn't want Sel to be alone right now. "Come with us."

Ross slowly let go of Selarion, checking how he was holding up. It seemed better now.

He looked at her. She knew what he was thinking about now. He wondered how much she knew about the past. And what, she really thinks about it. He hesitated.

"Come with us." She also looked at Valeriea, wanting to show him that she really has good faith.

They looked at each other knowingly. Valeriea hesitated too. They did not expect such an offer. Though Julien had too little experience in this matter, her intuition told her why it had surprised them so much. In their world, full of corruption, no one would have thought of them.

"And what would an old whore do out there?" She asked softly, glaring at Julien with warmth in her eyes, "Go, kids. Far away from here. Don't look back."

She looked at Ross expectantly. So did Sel.

"Maybe I'll come visit you sometime," he smiled mischievously, although it was clearly difficult for him. "But not yet. Not yet."

So outside the room they split up. Nobody recognized Sel and Julien among many similar people. Nobody tied Valeriea and Ross to them when they went each other way. Before they split up, Ross touched Julien lightly on the shoulder.

"Take care of him, please," he whispered.

She looked up at him, still shocked at the disclosure of her friend's second nature. He noticed her confusion.

She stepped outside without looking sideways at the hugging couples, right behind Ross who was making sure she wasn't harassed by anyone. Sel and Valeriea were not seen. They disappeared in the crowd. She even passed Moren, still looking for Tenan. He didn't recognize her. This was not what he had expected. The House of Pleasure has never had any walls, gates or even fences. The guards looked for the same people who had come with Moren. Not a courtesan and her counterpart. People went in and out confident, full of power and convinced that a few things that belonged to the healer would save them from everything. Or simply because they had nowhere to go and, working for Moren, they had at least something to live on. The House of Pleasure, a magnificent structure, the largest building on Pleasure Street, with rich carpets and all luxuries, became the headquarters of Moren's gang. There were thieves and murderers. Several other thugs and their men, as agile as Moren, apparently shared quarters with him. As she walked, she recognized one of the wanted posters in town. They were here unchastised. She doubted that Red Rebecca, the owner of the brothel, was satisfied with this turn of events. Probably she was already dead.

The House has always enjoyed a certain reputation here. Even she had heard a little about it. They weren't forced to do anything here, they weren't offered children. As long as they did what they were supposed to do here, Rebecca's people were placed under protection. Fights were unacceptable. Dirty and sick customers were not allowed in. Violence against one's will - was not allowed.

It all gave the place an atmosphere. Pure entertainment, only pleasure, uninterrupted fun. The mood is like a never-ending festival. It was a fair now. As disgustingly noisy and hideous as the worst brothel. Everything that the inhabitants of the House tried to achieve, giving it a certain style, fell into ruin. They were in the hands of people who did not want to follow any rules here. Julien saw tired, scared women trying to get away from the intruders. And the battered faces of the men of the House, probably getting hit more than once in their defense. Before her eyes, in one of the rooms, she saw two bandits beating one of these unfortunates. Ross hurriedly took her away from the sight.

Favorite habitat of plague. It was only a matter of time.

She looked at him. She felt a sudden sympathy for him. She regretted now that he had turned down her offer. The place he seemed to be clinging to was no longer safe. By protecting her from intrusions, he risked that it was him who might start beating in a moment. She could see the fear in his eyes as he noticed the incident. He was ready to come to the rescue. Only her presence and sense of duty stopped him.

Her attitude to him and his past with Sel has softened. This was not the man she had expected to meet here. It was the same with his older lady friend.

Ross stood against the wall outside and lit a cigar. She passed him without a single gesture, as had been arranged before. She didn't even glance. They were to avoid such gestures. She was about to leave, mingling with the people who were going in and out of the driveway.

When she suddenly noticed her.

She could not mistake Reniel with anyone. She was as much like her and Oliver as if they were related. With a strange, half-insane smile, she pulled a dirty scarf stained with white stains of vomit from her pocket. She put it around her neck with a calm gesture.

Coming to terms with fate.

The scarf was contaminated. She went out to get what belonged to those who had died of the plague. She decided to infect Moren.

She will kill everyone.

Julien let out a muffled groan and looked back in horror. Ross met her gaze and beyond her he saw Reniel coming.

"Run," she whispered silently, stepping out of the way of the unfortunate girl. "As far as possible!"

She shivered with concern. Unhappy inhabitants of the House! Poor desperate girl! So similar to Oliver...

Harbinger of his nightmare.

She looked around.

Ross was gone... He entered the building.

Reniel walked calmly past the people talking outside, unconsciously rubbing against a few people in the doorway.

Julien clenched into a fist. Sel will be worried. She can't tell him about it.

Ross must have gone to warn the others.

He preferred to warn his friends about the dangers than to save lives.

"Good luck," she thought, wishing happiness for both the wronged girl and him.

She will meet Sel at the appointed place and together they will do everything possible to prevent Oliver from returning to Moren. The rest must remain silent. At least for now.

* * *

"Goddamn it all!" Moren slapped the table angrily.

The cup of wine rocked and overturned. Red the color of blood slowly trickled from the table to the floor. He hardly noticed it.

Tenan took the outburst calmly. As always, anyway.

"He seized the opportunity," Moren began pacing nervously around the room.

"I told you it wouldn't work." Tenan casually pulled back the curtain to peer out the window. "You killed his wife. You want to destroy his friends. You could at least leave his old ones. But you wanted otherwise. As usual, you listened to yourself. And only yourself."

"I wanted to start over..."

Tenan looked at him with faint amusement, revealing feelings other than cold indifference. He only allowed himself to do this when they were alone. Like now.

"You didn't ask for his opinion."

"How did he do it?! After all, he was weakened!"

"Someone was helping him. Should I ask?"

"What will that change?" Moren asked hollowly, looking straight ahead with an unseeing eye.

"You wanted it, right?" Tenan asked calmly, looking at him. "But you wanted him to leave."

Moren's eyesight turned glum, his eyes gleaming suspiciously.

"In fact, if Oliver had escaped as well..." Tenan began, but at these words Moren suddenly jumped up and grabbed his shirt.

"If Oliver had escaped," he said ominously, his eyes turning into a maddened expression, anxious and unbelievably inhuman. "I'd get him where he hid, drag him out of his hiding place, and fuck him until he begs to die. And then I would have prepared it for him, but one that would be told throughout the kingdom."

"Why such stubbornness?" Tenan asked with apparent composure, though even he felt uneasy about the look.

"Because he stood up to me," Moren unexpectedly patted Tenan on the cheek, to which the other jerked angrily. "You want to do it too, I know it." He smiled madly at him. "You're not listening to me anymore. What was I saying about Julien, ha?" He tried to grab him by the chin with his free hand, but Tenan was not one of those who allowed someone to make such gestures with impunity.

He jerked out of his grip.

"I told you later, right? I told you. You have no idea what you did. Oliver knows you hit her. If you raped her, he would know too. They are twins. They are connected, you dumb vagrant! We were supposed to do it simultaneously. That was the plan. And you broke it. He's not coming back. I have to look for him. You must look for him. Lots of work and work. And what was it for?"

This time, Tenan was unable to break free from his grip.

"Here's what you will do," Moren looked him in the eye. "You will go to the castle, find him and bring him here. Together with what he will take with him. He'll want to run away from town. He will take the pendant for protection. Take as many people as you want. Sel and Julien will probably want to let him know they are free. Maybe you won't screw it up and bring them back too. And remember! If you're planning a voluntary plan, me and my people will find you. You can't get your ass out of town. And if even... You have no idea how much I love to hunt. I love feeling fear. People are shaking with fear, crying, shitting their pants, and I love watching them do it. And to break you," he pressed with his whole body, "it will be a pleasure. Because I know how much you want to be free. You hear, Tenan? I know about your secret. About the bracelet. And the curse."

"You're insane," Tenan whispered softly, losing his carefully placed mask of indifference.

Moren watched him coolly as Oliver had done before, glad to get the fear out of him. He was saturated with it.

"Sel wasn't afraid of me," he said, seemingly calm. "Do you know why?"

"Because he had nothing to lose," Tenan replied softly.

Moren whistled in admiration as he released his grip.

"Each day could be his last," he added. "He could stand up to me, argue, even beat me up, if he had the strength to do so. And what would I do the worst to him? If I started beating him - he would have died before I started well. I couldn't rule him. Even scare him. I had nothing on him. Death was still close. You know why I didn't get him an appointment with a healer so far? Because then he would start to care. On life, on all these things. Even you care. And I wanted him to remain independent, to have his own opinion. I wanted a friend, not another helper."

"He won't allow our plan. He'll want to stop you."

"And for the all demons sake!!!" Moren screamed excitedly and madly happy about it. "Let him want it. I WANT IT!"

Tenan stared at him until the meaning of the words fully penetrated his consciousness.

Moren was insane.

Tenan considered the options. He put together a plan of action.

Then he nodded and started for the exit without saying a word.

In the doorway, he almost collided with Reniel, who looked at him with a strange calmness. He glanced at Moren.

"Let her in," said Moren, still excited by his plans. "I want entertainment."

He let her pass, again putting on his mask of indifference and calculation.

CHAPTER 5 - In the footsteps of a conspiracy

On the eastern side, on the corner of the castle building, two windows in the healer's chambers overlooked the marketplace behind the castle wall and the streets of Verdom.

Vivan stood by the window, watching the market crowd swirling below. There were many more people than the day before. They constantly flocked to wait. The morning incident with the cart and the unusual girl only made them brash. They couldn't see him hidden behind the curtain, but their eyes still followed the windows. If he opened them, which he couldn't do (there were bars in them and the windows themselves were nailed down), he might have heard them.

He struggled with the feeling of being trapped and growing weakness. He still felt everything that popped into his mind after the viceroy touched him at dinner. Unfortunate Queen Constance... A scream. Cry. Pain. Violence. Cruelty...

He hated this place.

He hated how it poisoned his thoughts, spoiled the image of the world he preferred to remember. He was more sensitive to others than an ordinary person. His feelings were heightened. It was called female nature. They tried to ridicule it. It was so until Vivan proved by his actions and behavior that what others took for weakness, a sign of unmanliness, was in fact his strength. His nature was to be affection, the ability to empathize. Without it, he would not be the most powerful healer in the kingdom, but a simple, profitable miracle trader. Love for others heightened his gift. It couldn't be different. If he had lost this sensitivity and indifferent, he would have lost the gift that sometimes, like now, became a burden for him, but at the same time was the essence of his existence.

Meanwhile, everything was done here to suck the last drop of life out of him. Like a wild bird, he was caught and sentenced to a golden cage. Everything that gave him strength was torn away: from the people who loved him and those who surely needed his help now. He was ordered to heal minor ailments, to lay hands on the privileged. His gift was changed into change and he was treated like an exotic toy. He faded with longing, despair and a sense of helplessness. He was killed by omnipresent lust, anger, conspiracies, lies, distrust, insecurity, negligible concern for others and, above all, the insensitivity that was common in the castle. The world may perish, but I must have veal for dinner, or a dress ready for the evening. Where's my maid? She's gone? Fled? She died? So what? Let them send for another soon. Have you been hurt? Then get out of my sight. Are you worried about your people outside the castle? We will make you find a reason why you will fall out of favor with the king and lose everything...

He was sure he could handle even that. But the constant anxiety about his loved ones deprived him of his strength. If he had any news... Everyone was silent, even the young prince. So what was he to hold onto? What to hope for? What to bet against all of them?

And this monstrous man... Viceroy. His intrigues that he still couldn't prove. Too many things were distracting him here. So is his deteriorating well-being.

All of this cannot happen!

* * *

"You bitch!" Moren yelled. "You thought you were gonna infect me?!"

Reniel was lying on the floor. She was only half clothed, but she still held the scarf in her hand, like a knife. Blood flowed from her head wound. Moren slapped her several times in the face in a fit of rage, and then she fell, hitting the edge of the table. She felt pain and a strange numbness. As if something had been taken from her that will never come back. Some part of her self, an important part, but she couldn't name what it was. She lost her mind. But the scarf was still the most important thing. It was important. She remembered.

"Look," he reached out and yanked her unceremoniously off the floor. "See for yourself." He reached her hand over his chest to touch his shirt. "It's a healer shirt."

She touched the silk material in a daze. It was so nice to touch! But then she whispered softly, from the depths of dull awareness:

"It's your shirt."

"Are you deaf?" He pushed her to the floor "It's a healer shirt!" I told you before.

"It's your shirt now," she smiled, or so she thought. "You wear it all the time. Your sweat. Your stench. There was nothing else left."

She looked into his eyes with effort, curious about his reaction to the words.

Moren paled.

This time she was sure she was smiling.

* * *

"They're expecting us there, you know that?" Sel asked Julien, trying to somehow distract from his gloomy thoughts.

"So what?" She muttered. "I'm not going to get caught."

"I can't," he thought bitterly. "I don't have enough strength. She is in greater danger because of me. I'm good for nothing at times like this."

He cursed his own weakness once again in his life. If he were healthy...

But speculate couldn't help them now.

"Wait," he said, stopping her somewhere at the gate. "I need a drink."

He leaned against the wall, fighting the temptation to slide to the ground over it and stay that way for a long time.

She pulled a potion bottle from the bag Ross had given her.

They were two streets from the marketplace. It was empty and dull all around, as if Verdom had never been a bustling city before. Somewhere the wagon's wheels creaked ominously. They could be gravediggers. The thought of them gave rise to sad memories. She focused on Sel, who strained to drink some of the potion. After a while his eyes brightened visibly. He straightened up.

"It works shorter and shorter," he whispered.

"You just need to rest," she pulled a handkerchief from a hidden pocket in her dress to wipe his sweaty brow.

Eyes framed by black crayon looked at her seriously.

She understood that look.

"No," she replied at his words before they were spoken. "No. It's not true!"

"I'm just get in your's way."

"Stop it!" She covered his mouth with her hand. "Stop now! Think better what we can do about it."

He waited for her to remove hand, still determined by the unspoken thought.

"I just thought," he replied calmly.

She shook a finger at him nervously and vigorously, in a manner typical of the temperamental women living here. Her dress gave even more energy to these movements. He mellowed as he struggled to hold back from yelling at him. He hadn't seen her like this in a while. It was the Julien he knew.

"We just," she said finally, "we'll look for horses or a cart, hide somewhere and go get Oliver. Or I'll go get him and you'll stay with the horses."

"Is that your plan?"

"Yes."

"And the guards? There is a healer in the castle. Guards are all around."

"I'll figure something out," she said, trying to be confident.

"It's a lame plan."

"Do you have another one?"

He shook his head. No idea was coming to him now. Maybe indeed, when they get close to the castle...

"What about Moren's people?" He wondered.

He looked at Julien carefully. She was unrecognizable in this outfit, it is true, but at the same time her red dress was very noticeable. He himself was dressed better, given the circumstances. Unfortunately, this camouflage was insufficient. He was physically weak and tired too easily. He closed his eyes in annoyance. He was as useful as a broken wheel. Which meant a lot would depend on Julien. Everything, actually.

"Did Ross give you any clothes?" He asked.

"Yes. For you and me."

He looked at her critically.

"It will fit..." he said to himself after a brief discernment.

She looked at him questioningly.

"You need to change..." he started to say, but she cut him off.

"I know. It's a whore outfit."

He raised his eyebrows in surprise at the remark, but continued calmly:

"You'll put on Ross's clothes..."

She looked at him in amazement.

"...and you will get your horses," he finished. "Or a cart. Whatever you want. And then we'll see..."

* * *

Ross opened the door to Valeriea's room. They had become friends when he first appeared in her life - a streeter, father unknown, mother always drunk and in company, among whom there was no room for a sensitive kid. Valeriea took him into care after he showed up to her, beaten by another of her mother's lover, she got him a job at the House of Pleasure. She never had children, he never had a real home.

They cared for each other.

"Valeriea," he said deliberately with a western accent. "It's time for us."

Valeriea adjusted her makeup in front of the mirror, more out of habit than out of real need.

She was putting off the moment to return to the Great Hall, where she would entertain customers.

She looked at him with a faint amusement.

"You changed your mind so quickly?"

He hurried over to her, taking her hand gently.

"There is a plague in the House. Reniel brought it."

She worried, the smile faded immediately on her face.

"Poor girl..." she whispered, sympathetic to her sincerely, then asked quickly. "Everyone knows?"

"No. Nobody noticed."

"We have to tell them, Ross."

"Of course. Tell them. I'll go get the horses."

"Stop!" She stopped him before he returned to the aisle. "Two horses are not enough! Take Rebecca's carriage!"

"Valeriea..." he wanted to protest, but they both knew they couldn't have done otherwise.

The House of Pleasure was like one family. Maybe not everyone liked each other, but they certainly stuck together in front of the world it gladly took from them, giving hardly anything in return.

"I'll take care of the rest."

"Be careful."

She ruffled his hair with a maternal gesture.

"I've been doing this my whole life, honey. You don't know if she was walking around the House?"

"She came straight from town to her room."

She thought for a moment.

"Before you go to the stables, take some provisions from the kitchen. There is great confusion after lunch. Nobody will pay attention to what you are doing."

"We don't have time..."

"Ross, get what's at hand. Go now! Go."

She watched him as he closed the door of the secret passage. The carpet covering it completely masked it...

* * *

"Evidence!" The prince who came to visit the healer clenched his fists in anger. "You know very well we need evidence, Vivan!"

"I know," replied the healer. "Then get them. Watch him closely!"

"You think I'm not trying?!" The future heir to the throne began to circulate nervously around the room. "I have nothing sure. Only Celina was so close then..."

Suddenly he fell silent as they both realized. how the unfortunate girl finished.

"She was talking about a conspiracy..." Vivan whispered.

"Delen is to get evidence today. His people are working on it."

"You know what you're exposing him to?"

"Do you see any other way out? Besides..." the prince sighed, sitting down in the chair, "He has volunteered. Maybe he felt something for this girl."

"She was very brave," the Healer said softly, walking to the window.

The crowd in the marketplace increased even more.

"And your father?"

"Father works on his own," Meron snorted. "He's not telling me anything. But he's furious."

"You asked if he knows?" Vivan couldn't help himself.

He asked this question almost every day.

"He says there is no time for this," the prince shrugged, not concealing a slight annoyance. I have to tell you to stop making the show and start eating normally, otherwise he will assign people to force you to feed you. You worry my mother and my father cannot bear that. And it worries him in its own way."

"I'm risking his life," Vivan remarked ironically.

"I'm not starving myself to force him to release." Vivan couldn't tear his eyes away from the marketplace, drawn to him by a strange, disturbing force.

"What is it?" Meron stood beside him. "You won't get anything with this. Not with him. In fact, while I do not support the way he did it..." he hesitated, "...I think it was a wise move."

Vivan looked at him in disbelief.

"It is the good of the kingdom," continued the prince hesitantly. "I can understand that. But I'd bring your family here too. It was cruel. Monstrous. And I'm sorry for that. On our behalf."

Vivan thought to himself, "What about the others?! With my friends, neighbors? They don't count?! They don't deserve to live because they are less important?!".

It would be unwise to offend one of his sympathizers, the future king. Maybe even too emotional, childish.

Wanting to protect everyone who mattered in his life, who treated him kindly, without desire for profit, would be childish?! He couldn't understand it. Not him.

So, he was silent, and Meron took that silence for a silent rebellion.

"See these people?" He pointed to the marketplace seriously. "What do you think would happen if I released you now? They attacked a food cart today. After that, my father stopped deliveries and reduced the ration. We have to deal with ourselves. And if you left the castle... Think! They are desperate, without hope. Capable of anything! They'd tear you apart," he whispered softly.

The words, however, did not soften with a whisper, but weighed down like a stone in the healer's heart.

They aroused memories of the nightmares he had dreamed of in the last few days.

* * *

Delen was hoping to meet Selena in the castle kitchen. He was not mistaken. She was just leaving after she had already brought the last batch of plates. Due to the limited number of places, some of the nobles had to do without personal service, including the countess Weren. This, of course, applied to the less significant. In return, they were offered royal service. Considering how many were refused shelter in the castle for lack of places or a suitable position in the company, the honored people preferred not to argue with it, although it obviously spoiled their habits.

Selena and two other servants served the guests during the day. Others watched at night, in case their help was needed. There were times when someone disappeared or left, though the latter was even less common than the former. The king officially ordered the service to be treated well due to the prevailing circumstances, but there were occasions when not everyone obeyed this order.

Selena aroused interest through the morning events and ambiguous, intriguing beauty. She was well aware that today she was given special attention by everyone. She treated the meeting with Delen with clear relief and confusion at the same time, knowing about the constant curious glances from the numerous servants in this place." "Will you talk to me?" He asked gently.

"But not here," she said.

To his amazement, she gestured to the window through which she stepped onto the wide roof.

In the evening, people often went out like this to get some air. He noticed some meaningful smiles as he followed her lead. However, he said silently that at the moment such suspicions were even convenient for him.

Selena stood as far away from the windows as possible and leaned against the wall.

He saw weariness on her face and shadows under her eyes. He cursed silently. He didn't know she would be tired.

He looked around. Several guards, including two of his men, circled on the roof. Too far for them to hear the conversation.

"You look tired," he observed.

"I didn't sleep that night," she explained quietly. "Did you want something from me?"

She looked at him. From under the dark fringe of her hair, the blue eyes were as beautiful as the sapphires.

Celina was brown. Maybe Selena had them after her mother?

He could see the alert in that look, despite the weariness.

"You're Celina's sister," he said to her. "You know how to keep a secret like she?"

She looked at him carefully.

"If that helps expose the murderer..."

He was mentally surprised, but it also reassured him that he had a good feeling. He knew he could trust her.

"I will need your help for this, too," he said. "Tonight, the viceroy will give orders to his men."

"What?"

"About the assassination of the king."

He let the words hang in the air between them, drawing closer as if he were just complimenting her. Their faces are very close together. He smelled the faint scent of her skin, the scent of soap. No sign of perfume. He found himself unable to take his eyes off her startled gaze.

Oliver's heart began to beat quickly.

He understood in an instant what he had gotten himself into.

"Are you sure?" He asked, his throat dry.

Delen nodded briefly in confirmation.

"Orders will probably be in writing."

"So, we have to intercept them!"

"All Celina," Delen whispered appreciatively, smiling slightly. "Ready to walk with both feet into the dunghill for the cause."

"It will be evidence for the king and help stop them at the same time. Without orders, the soldiers won't do anything."

Oliver thought frantically, cursing Moren silently about what the world was standing on.

"You said," he finally said with apparent composure, "in that too I need your help." In what else?"

He smiled again.

"Actually, I'd like you to take care of our unexpected guest as well," he said, his eye twinkling.

"A guest?"

"A certain man entered the castle, probably taking advantage of our unfortunate arrival, asking for trouble. He's in your room now. I figured you wouldn't mind."

"Talk finally!" Oliver sounded impatient, "As if I didn't have enough surprises for today!"

"Who is it? Who is he?"

"This is Count Paphian Beckert. Healer brother. I suppose he didn't come here to visit."

Oliver felt all his weariness leaving him for good...

* * *

Julien walked out of the next yard. The stables were already empty. In two of the five gates she entered, she encountered the dead of the plague. Well, she has already made her way to her own home.

What if she gets her?

Better not to think about it. Who will save Oliver then?

She would know if he got sick. As he would know about her.

He knew she had been hit. He must have been furious. She hoped it hadn't happened at the wrong time for him. No, after all... She touched her cheek. The heat still spread pleasantly over her skin. The mark from the impact was gone, but the feeling was left as if the healer's hand was still on her brother's cheek and hers at the same time. She felt his touch. When she was little, her mother would sometimes take her face in both hands, slender, gentle hands, and then playfully kiss her on the nose, drawing to her.

She will be gone... The touch of the healer's hand was so much like it, so much like other things - yesterday's events, unwanted images. It aroused suppressed regret.

And at the same time, this still perceptible touch gave her strength and uplifted her spirit.

She must be strong now. It wasn't time for tears. She must get her brother back, she must be sure that she is with her, that she got him out of this nightmare, safe and sound. Nobody has a right to it.

Only he was left with her. She wasn't worried about herself. She was safe for now. But he...

"Oliver," she whispered, touching his healed cheek, warming it with her hand.

She wished he would feel the warmth of her touch on his face as before she had felt the soothing touch of a healer. She wanted to tell him that she thought about him, that she was fine. She wanted to cheer him up. He felt just like her, weary and exhausted by the experiences. She felt it.

"I'm thinking of you," she whispered.

* * *

Oliver touched his cheek. Delen left him on the roof, rushing to his assignment. He, too, should hurry up. But now, for one moment, nothing was more important than a tender sisterly touch. Her touch, her love and warmth, inseparably connected with him, always close and familiar, always evoking the same feelings in him.

Twins.

They were not alike, but they always knew about each other, bound by an invisible bond. The bonds of these identical twins were said to be stronger. So indissoluble that one thought about the other. They even shared the same dreams.

They were glad that they were weaker, although it still held them tightly together.

He kept his hand on his cheek, conveying the same thoughts to her.

He smiled.

Suddenly, unexpectedly for him, her gesture opened the gates of the feelings he had so bravely tried to suppress. Hidden in the shade from the hot early summer sun, away from the guards who did not intrude into his privacy, presumably due to Delen's earlier appearance, respected among them despite his young age, he had a moment to breathe before the next events.

What will happen next? If he miraculously saves himself and fulfills his mission, he must return to Julien.

He must go back to Moren...

He deliberately did not think about it, pushed the unwanted thoughts into his mind. But suddenly he felt that he didn't have the strength to do it any longer. Torment swept over him like a choppy wave, sweeping away all other feelings.

Whether it helped Julien or not, and he felt Moren's word could no longer be trusted, he would be humiliated. Eventually Moren would get his way, and when that happened, he would keep him alive as long as Oliver had the will not to be broken. And it won't take long. He might cheer himself up, take comfort in the thought that it might help him leave his sister alone, but the truth was... he wouldn't be able to bear it.

He slumped on the roof and covered his face to hide his tears. He had to do it now. After that, he won't even have a moment.

And in the distant future, in the darkest future, he would do everything not to beg, with all the willpower he would then be able to do, not to beg, not to entice this bastard to spare him. He won't give him that satisfaction. He knew Moren was expecting this fortitude, but it didn't matter. He will not do otherwise.

His anguish and fear echoed in Julien's heart, though she did not recognize the meaning of these feelings. Oliver was suffering. He suffered in quiet despair; she knew.

Unwittingly, tears ran down her face as well, caused by her brother's anguish. A sense of loss was awakened, previously pushed into the shadows. Grief for the parents. Fear for a brother, now tormented by gloomy thoughts, who is alone among strangers.

"Oliver," she whispered softly touching her cheek. "Shhh..."

She sensed the change in his mood as if he had heard it. She felt a rush of warmth on her cheek, previously touched by the healer. Oliver also placed his hand there in a comforting gesture.

Soothing warmth spread from under their invisibly joined hands, and like a balm, it enveloped her heart and calmed her mind. The healer's touch worked once more.

And it gave them strength.

She looked around. She felt that Oliver had calmed down as well, their bond weakening to its usual limits when they were not tormented by strong emotions. They moved away from each other, though it was like being apart at arm's length. Nearby, but not too close.

She had almost left Sel in one of the abandoned houses an hour ago to look for horses. She still hasn't found anything, and yet Sel won't be able to leave town without it. With the pursuit of Moren's men sent after them, they would need mounts.

Sel, however, will not stay in the saddle. All the recent experiences worsened his condition even more, despite the elven elixir. She pushed aside the loathsome thought that perhaps she should have listened to him.

No!

Sel always helped them. Moren went into a frenzy of jealousy when he saw Sel talking to Oliver and then bonding with Milera, but Sel refused to be intimidated. He had the steadfastness of a man with the specter of death still looming over him. Moren knew there was not much he could do. Sometimes he managed to hit Oliver a couple of times. Most often, however, her brother slipped out of his hands like a cat, because of his sister. He can climb, jump off or jump over from any place. As for her and Milera... Moren was merely making threats. Sel knew Moren cared deeply about him as a true friend with whom he could always talk honestly. He knew that he was influenced to some extent, but this should not be abused. When it came to Julien and Milera, Moren let himself be calmed down, he didn't care about tormenting them. On the other hand, Oliver... aroused such extreme feelings in him that sometimes it was better to be silent, because it intensified his emotions. Even so, not once Sel did his efforts to separate them, to distract Moren. Especially recently, when it turned out that Oliver had been competing with his people for food. Sel let Moren's anger focus on him, for he was still living on the verge of life and death anyway.

He won't leave him here, because Moren's rage might kill him this time.

The city was dead. Sometimes you could only hear the squeals of rats, the sound of the wind in empty houses. Entire families have recently lived on this street. In the narrow streets, the boys played rag ball. After a hot day, the neighbors would sit at tables outside, eating and talking.

It has never been so quiet.

Now the silence seemed to press in on all sides.

There is nothing else here. She would have to walk all the streets of Verdom, hoping that there would be horses somewhere. Or to steal them from what they dared to stay.

She never had to steal before. It's always been Oliver's.

She checked that the hair was well hidden under the cap. Ross' male attire was quite plain, not what she had seen him wearing. He probably came out in it when he just wanted to blend in with the crowd. It was definitely more comfortable than the dress she had left for Sel. She was going to take it. She has never had something so beautiful, although she probably won't be able to wear it.

She started searching again.

She dared to look not far from the House of Pleasure. She was separated by two streets from this place. Nobody would expect her here. Not that close. She will be careful.

Then she heard the thud of hooves. A strange carriage rode down a dusty street. It was more of a hut on wheels, painted white, with dragons by the coachman's coach-box and rich paintings on the sides.

She had seen a similar hut once, though not so rich looking. It was owned by a family from the Wandering People - a certain tribe that did not stay occupied anywhere, lived off horses, elaborate ornaments and fortune-telling. Father then bought gold from them. The car then seemed beautiful and mysterious to them. The family stayed with them overnight, and she and Oliver became acquainted with two children about their age who were traveling in the vehicle. She remembered how much they both liked the wanderers' beauty. They were especially fascinated by Oliver. The sibling's mother even wanted to read fortunes from him, but Oliver was always afraid of fortune-telling, so he refused. They were about twelve at the time.

She didn't know there were such carts here. But what surprised her even more was that Ross was the driver. There were a few more people inside.

She couldn't see Moren and his men behind them. Her heart leapt with joy. Sel would be pleased, and she was glad Ross took her advice so quickly.

She ran to meet him.

"Ross!!" She cried. "Stop!"

Surprised Ross stopped the horses. Valeriea peeked out from behind him.

"Mother Earth!" She shouted. "Is that Oliver's sister? What are you still doing here, girl?"

"Sel needs help," Julien ran to them, at the same time full of fear, "Moren is with you?"

"He can only dream about it," Ross replied, jumping to the ground. "Where's Sel? We have to get out of here."

"I'll show you," she said, "Ross..." Suddenly she felt that she had to do it, without the help of these people she wouldn't go far. "We need your help."

"I was hoping to find you," he said. "Do you want us to get Sel out of here?"

"I want much more," she replied significantly.

He smiled as if she had just told him about some great fun in the neighborhood. He glanced knowingly at the people inside the carriage.

"Get in!" He wanted to help her, but she did just fine.

"Where then?" He asked, taking the reins in his hands.

She turned to see the others. Valeriea, a big bastard, two girls, two young guys who smiled significantly at her. She blushed and looked quickly at Ross, who didn't bother her.

"To the castle," she replied.

"Aye!" He whipped a short whip in the air, away from the horse's rumps.

She couldn't help herself with happiness. She hugged him happily, until tears of emotion sparkled in her eyes like stars. He laughed in surprise, and his laughter broke the deathly silence around him.

"You look good in my stuff," he said jokingly.

She gave him a sidelong glance but said nothing.

He lightly, gently touched her hand to give her a squeeze. She returned it tightly in excess of emotion. He didn't want to disturb her delicate balance, so he didn't say a word. With an expression of his eyes, he stopped Valeriea from approaching the girl. She understood.

He felt great relief. He would see Sel again. And maybe they will leave together...

* * *

Oliver sighed resignedly.

"Why is this happening," he whispered, a bit harshly, standing at the door to the old "sister's" room, in the words of Alena, the maid who served with him on the floor with the healer's chambers. Alena, a young blonde in a dark mourning dress, walked with a small smile to Viscount Marden's chambers, opposite the Countess Weren's rooms. The Viscount was expecting the Countess before supper. So, Alena was to tidy up his room. He liked perfect order. All the way from the kitchen to the servants' rooms, where the worried Alena had led Selena, seeing her condition, they talked about the wealthy guests of the castle. Actually, Alena was speaking, and Oliver listened silently, gratefully finding something to distract him from his gloomy thoughts. Then Alena hugged him and walked away. Oliver could smell her pleasant scent, a delicate perfume she must have sprinkled on some rich lady in the castle. Her touch was so nice.

Well, you had to go inside.

In a modestly furnished and small room, the healer's brother sat on the bed. At the sight of the man entering, he stood up, instinctively pulling the sword from its scabbard with a quick, practiced for years movement. Oliver cursed himself for the way he came in. But he couldn't knock on his own room without arousing suspicion. Paphian sheathed his sword when he saw the woman.

After a while, however, he regarded Oliver with an expression of surprise.

"Julien?" He wondered, coming closer. "Julien Rysever? I was expecting…" He broke off suddenly, staring at him.

Oliver waited for the inevitable. If the Count remembered Julien so well since his visit to their home...

"Wait a minute," Paphian looked at him suspiciously, and his dark, long hair, which had grown from the time he had come to the goldsmith's house with his mother, tied in a ponytail, flowed smoothly from his shoulder to his back. "You're not Julien. You are not Selena. What's that supposed to mean, for the demons?"

"Could you speak your thoughts more quietly?" Oliver said sarcastically. "We are not on Artisans Street."

Paphian's eyes widened in astonishment at the sound of his voice, and then he quickly became amused.

"I'll be damned..." he whispered, eyeing him up and down.

"Be careful, it will come true!" Oliver threatened, who didn't like the amusement at all.

"You always looked like a woman," Paphian, even speaking in a whisper, did not stop smiling cheekily, and Oliver gave him a murderous glare. "Well, but now..."

He fell silent as Oliver raised his hand in warning.

"I came for my brother," he changed the subject quickly, though his eyes still sparkled with glee.

"Undoubtedly."

Paphian pulled him from under the door, wrapping his arm around him.

"Will you lead me to him at night?"

"A lot can happen at night," Oliver removed his arm, a wig tied to his hair ruthlessly tugging on it.

"This is your own hair?" asked Paphian, "they look like real."

"Because they are," Oliver replied. "But they're not mine. And back to the question..."

"You don't have hands like a girl," Paphian remarked. "Actually, they are a bit too..."

"Are you finished yet?" Oliver had had enough of these remarks.

Paphian grinned, revealing his white teeth.

"You know, I could do it for a long time," he snorted, seeing Oliver's menacing gaze. "What's all this for?" He asked, finally becoming serious. "What have you gotten yourself into?"

"I would have to talk a long time," Oliver said softly.

On his face, Paphian saw clear traces of recent experiences.

"Is it that bad?" He asked with concern. "Is something threatening you? And Julien? Your family? Say."

Oliver looked at him grimly. Paphian looked gloomy. When he was here last year with his mother, who wanted to visit the family, where she had a good time waiting for Vivan's gift, things were not going very well between Oliver and his neighbor, the pastry chef's son. People without bad intentions don't stand outside your house every night with a strange expression on their face. The other didn't seem in love either. More like a man overwhelmed with some strange, abnormal obsession. There was something in the air, but Paphian had been there too briefly to interfere further. Anyway, in the presence of such guests in the goldsmith's house, the bloody neighbor wisely would not lean out of anything. It is a pity, because Paphian would gladly look for an opportunity to talk to this man.

Paphian liked the Rysever siblings. Taught by his brother to be sensitive to others, he could not stand it when something bad happened to the people he liked. He was immediately ready to step into the middle and inquire about the causes by any means. Was it from this neighbor that Oliver was hiding in Castle in that outfit and under a different name? Was it something else?

"I guess I really need to tell you," Oliver said finally.

As he began to talk about the death of his parents, about Moren and his intentions, and finally about the viceroy's conspiracy, Paphian felt the dread rise in his heart, and the hair on the back of his neck stood on end.

Oliver also hesitantly told him why he had been sent by Moren. And although he hadn't done anything so far, he felt like a thief in his heart.

"I know my brother," said Paphian after a long silence. "When you have the opportunity to go to him again, just tell him what you told me. He will give you the pendant back without hesitation, because he just is like that. If it is to help, he will do it. And at night you will lead me to him and we'll run away before the lark starts."

"And the king?"

"You and Delen will let know who needs it by then."

"How do you know Delen? You were lucky his people caught you."

"True," agreed Paphian. "Beginner's luck," he smiled mischievously. "I stayed at his house when I attended Queen Constance's school with his brother, who also serves here. It was Kirian who found me, or rather I made him find me."

"Will you show me where it brought you here?"

Paphian smiled again.

"It's for nothing. Now it's full of guards."

"So, we use my exit?"

"You already have one?"

"I had time to look around while walking around the castle. I have a few exits."

"A few?!"

For the first time since Paphian had seen him, Oliver managed a smile. It was the same smug smile as the cat which Paphian had seen when Oliver first showed him how to climb. He already sensed what he was going to hear.

"Some are not for you," confirmed his suspicions. "But we can all take advantage of two."

"What if the ensuing chaos makes those exits compromised?"

"There are always doors that can be opened."

Someone knocked.

He was silently pleased that so far, they had been whispering the entire conversation. He carefully lifted them.

"Fine?" He saw the concerned face of petite Alena. "Better already?"

"Much better," he replied truthfully.

When he could finally confide in someone, he felt real relief. He was no longer alone.

"I'm glad," said Alena. "Listen, I have to help the Countess before supper..." She smiled significantly, and Oliver mentally marveled at the woman's changeability - to improve her appearance and change her dress. You will go to the count and ask what he wishes for dinner. Apparently, he will eat at home. Tell him you are to tell the Court Medic if he has eaten at the king's orders. It's a pity the Countess got me involved. I'd love to go myself. Will you do it?"

"Of course," he smiled sympathetically at the pretty girl.

"You have a nice voice," she noted. "A few of the guys have a few more commands to follow before you go to the Count. Maybe we'll do this... When I go..."

He silently listened to Alena sharing their duties, sometimes nodding slightly, until the girl was about to leave with a heavy sigh.

"Is it cold or am I the only one that freezes this way today?" She remarked, suddenly trembling.

Oliver was surprised. It was hot on the roof, even in the shade, and the castle was stuffy.

But too engrossed in what was about to happen, he only remarked calmly:

"Maybe you caught a cold?"

"Maybe," she mused, then said goodbye and left.

Paphian waited for Oliver to close the door again.

"You have your opportunity."

The latter smiled at his guest.

CHAPTER 6 — Gravediggers

Each of Moren's words, as he reached the carriage house, was definitely not suitable to elegant ears. The House of Pleasure was one big chaos. Someone had spread the word that Reniel had brought the plague. Many have already left in extraordinary haste. Moren realized they were just looking for an excuse to leave. After all, house was the only place they had. When he and the Red Guard leader Ramoz, and with them a few other lesser thugs, took over the place a week ago, killing the Mother, everyone called Red Rebecca - from the wine-colored dress she had liked to wear since her youth - they both knew the whores living here would stir up they will soon revolt or run away. Not a day went by without some or any one being taught humility, but when one was finished with one, the others already looked up.

Like Reniel. She was fed up with his practices. Recently, he hardly let her out of the room. Finally, she stood up to him the day before yesterday, so he beat her up. If the bitch hadn't done that plague thing today, it would've ended up with another hosing. But she did, and before that, Sel thwarted his plans by an unexpected escape.

So Moren went astray.

He had to finish her off. After the beating, she was now useless. One of the blows seemed to have messed her head. Stupid whore!

He was staring now at the empty interior of the coach house, furious with her and Sel for having led to this situation. Because of them, he lost control. When he gets Sel, he won't fail to remind him.

"Who the fuck took Rebecca's carriage, Sheron?" He asked with a twinkle in the eye of one of his four confidants who had been in his gang from the beginning.

Sheron dealt with the supply and it was he who sent Oliver with the coachman Ramoz to the castle.

Fynn led the spy network.

Tenan killed and intimidated.

Rosten, whom Moren once beaten, collaborated with Tenan. He loved to beat others.

"I've seen Big Len, Sai and Lena, those whores who always go together, old Valeriea, two little macks, one is probably Alesei or something, and the other I don't remember. And Ross. Do you remember? It was the twat that had punched Ramoz's man when he started beating Valeriea for being slow. I seriously thought it would be the end of this male doll, but Ramoz liked his chivalry."

Ross!

Moren thought frantically. While he was hanging out with Reniel or another whore, Sel sought companionship among those who weren't busy. He wasn't to go home. It was too gloomy in the house, and it was always moody here, the music played subtly - although Moren paid little attention to it - you could drink and dance. The house always had a good-toned fun atmosphere, not just a dive. Sel knew everyone here thanks to these visits, because he treated everyone kindly, and the inhabitants of the House of Pleasure felt sorry for him for his sad life. He could have any whore with that sympathy, but he didn't take advantage of it. Moren never figured it out, whether he wanted to or not, because there were times when Sel felt pretty good. Instead, he slept where he could. In Big Len's small room, making sure that the girls working in the House do not get hurt. At Sai and Lena's, who would always lie down on both sides of Sel after work, and that's how Moren found them when he came to take his friend home. At Valeriea's - most often - because she gave him the key for the whole night and went to pour champagne, massage, serve and earn less with her body. Even with Red Rebecca, who usually chuckled loudly and wiggled those big tits and played cards until dawn.

And with a few others.

Finally, Ross. This male...

He already knew who had helped Sel and Julien.

Ross took the white carriage. He was behind it, Moren was almost sure of that. He probably wanted to take Sel, who reportedly not only slept with him. Julien... and Oliver! After all, a worried sister would not have left her brother in need! They won't let him come back here. Oliver will meet Julien and will not be coming again!

He won't see him again.

He wouldn't even taste his fear. He won't touch his skin anymore...

"Damn it!" he struck in anger at the door of the coach house.

Sheron thought it was time to gather his gear and get Moren out of sight for now. For the first time since it had happened, he missed Sel a little too. Sel had always been able to control Moren's moods.

"Where's Tenan?" Moren asked furiously, the veins in his neck and forehead swollen with anger.

"You sent him," Sheron reminded him, not feeling very confident at the moment, despite the fact that he was taller than Moren and just as strong as he was. Everyone knew how erratic Moren could be in anger. Reniel has already found out about it.

"Change of plans. We will join him. Gather those who remained..."

"There'll only be a few. The rest of them ran away for fear of the plague," Sheron said, eyeing him pointedly.

The news that the girl had entered the room with a contaminated part of her clothes spread quickly. But despite this, Sheron still believed in the protective power of the healer shirt the leader wore, and he believed in the girdle and tuft of hair from the brush he carried in his pocket.

"If so..." Moren wondered, but preoccupied with the will to act, immediately downplayed it. "We'll find Tenan and get Oliver, the pendant, Sel, Julien and the carriage. Anyway, you will do what you like with others.

"I was about to tell you," Sheron sighed heavily and wiped his face nervously with his hand, "The rumor is that they will release the healer from the castle at dawn tomorrow. Tenan was there when it was passed on to me. We probably won't see him again. He will pick up the pendant himself, or the healer's blood or a piece of his skin and run away."

"What are you talking about?" Moren was surprised.

These words changed the course of his thoughts. A piece of skin? Blood?!

"Because you see," Sheron, who was starting to take a toll on the prevailing heat and the commotion around, pulled the sweaty handkerchief from his neck and wiped his bald head with it, "the healer is to be alone. No guard. And no protection. People will tear him to pieces..."

* * *

He thought he only closed his eyes for a moment, waiting for Julien. It was hot and silent everywhere. There was a shadow in the gate. He preferred to wait here. The dead were hiding in their houses.

When he opened his eyes, he saw two thin men with greedy, anxious eyes. One of them had a shimmering gold on the neck, a strangely out of place diamond necklace. It seemed utterly absurd to wear something like this openly in the street and it was extra ironic that it was done by a man. Well, now times and the world had completely changed, which gave the whole situation a completely different dimension and completely stripped it of its ridiculousness.

The man leaned over him as he slept. He saw his face right in front of his. He would have flinched if he had the strength to do so.

"This one is still alive!" He shouted to his companion. "And I don't think he's dying of the plague here!"

"Anything?" The other inquired.

Sel's eyes widened and he focused. Behind the man with the necklace, he saw a cart. It was full of bodies.

Gravediggers!

"He has a gold ring on his finger, but he's going to be struggling against it," the man replied expertly, studying Sel and the gold ring.

"Are we waiting?"

The question hung over them like an ax. Sel felt his broken heart begin to beat hard, sweat pouring through his body. He didn't even have the strength to get up. He knew his time might end that day. His heart was giving up.

The gravedigger with the necklace thought about it.

"Hit him in his head and into the car!" he decided briefly. "And then for the others. I don't want to come back here today. Nobody will notice the difference."

He held his breath, but then a strange calm overtook him.

"What's the difference, after all?" He thought bitterly. "At least it will be fast. Only Julien will have to do without me."

In fact, he preferred it to be over now. He was fed up with his life, filled with illness and suffering, which he could never fully enjoy. He was tired of this fight.

The gravedigger reached for a shovel. He took it out of habit. He hadn't buried anyone for a long time, but had burned. Sometimes, like now, it was necessary to kill someone, because suddenly the alleged corpses would revive when they were transferred to a wagon or even on a burning stake! The shovel was good. As he held it in his hand, his strength seemed to grow in his hands. He didn't even wash off the blood.

Sel stared at it, still fearless.

"I should be scared," he thought, "but I don't want to. It doesn't matter anymore...".

The gravedigger walked over to him while the other eyed the situation with interest.

Without further ado, the executioner of the dead raised his shovel to the blow. He didn't even meet the eyes of the man he was about to kill. He just wondered where to hit the right punch to keep it good. He hated the trouble his companion happened on the job. The blow usually turned out to be too weak and had to be corrected so that they would stop moving...

Sel smiled ironically at his murderer...

The other gravedigger, seeing this, opened his mouth in amazement. Suddenly he felt something like a twitch in his heart. Something he hasn't felt since he killed the first man...

Respect for the courage of the dying.

"Stop!" Suddenly they heard a voice.

A white, ornate carriage, drawn by two white horses, rode down the street. Seeing their intentions, the coachman whipped his whip, and before the carriage flattened it with the gravediggers' wagon, he jumped to the ground. Behind him, a girl in men's clothes jumped off, and a huge swarthy guy quickly stood nearby.

"Ross, just don't touch them!" The woman with dark hair, no longer young, shouted to the coachman.

Ross wanted to lash the gravedigger with the shovel with his whip until he was drowning in blood. He could barely make himself hit him just once. Julien, on the other hand, pushed against the seated Sel. His condition gripped her heart in fear.

"Get out of here!" Ross shouted at the gravediggers, shocked and furious.

They did not resist. They preferred to protect their lifes, to hide their dark intentions. The gravedigger with a shovel crumpled from the impact and looked with an evil hateful look at the young man who had hurt him. His drunken face twisted into a sullen smile.

Before he got on the cart, he pointed his finger at Ross as if marking him.

Ross felt a superstitious fear. He regained his composure and lapped the whip once more, urging them to hurry.

The last thing he saw was a dead man lying on the wagon with his eyes open. He had no clothes on, only a death mark. Nobody cared anymore. It became a garbage that had to be thrown away or burned to cleanse the city. Ross thought that his body, so warm and alive, might soon, as the gravedigger wished, end up on that wagon, just as nameless, cold and without dignity. Robbed of clothes and soul. Nobody needs anymore...

Len, for that was the gorilla's name, lifted the surprisingly light Sel, and carried him fainted to the carriage. Julien, full of concern, followed them and saw for the first time the interior of the vehicle in purple, with a large bed full of cushions. They arranged Sel on the satin sheets, and then hurried instructions were given quickly. Windows were opened and water and elixirs were brought. Julien wiped his forehead with concern while the women, Len and Ross stood beside him equally concerned. Each of them liked Sel and saw how serious his condition was. The two young men sat in front and the carriage continued on.

"Sel," Ross whispered softly, desperately trying to pretend he didn't see the deterioration in Sel's health since they broke up. "Listen. Oliver is in trouble. There are rumors that a lot will be going on in the castle tomorrow. The healer will be taken out at dawn without escort. Do you know what people can do to him then?" - "Does he still care about this?" he thought despairingly. "We want to help him. He will help you. Just hold on. Please…"

He was unable to control his voice for the last words. Everyone heard the tremor in him. Julien looked at him with a mixture of surprise, disbelief, and dislike. He noticed it out of the corner of his eye. He didn't care at all now. Only Sel mattered. That's why he had an elven potion! He hoped Sel would come back someday…

Julien stared at him like an exotic bird. She had never seen him before, or after Sel started dating Milera. He wasn't in Sel's daily life. As if he felt his place was only in the House of Pleasure. He probably has never revealed his feelings before. Everyone, especially Sel, would know that. Now they were looking at him as surprised as she was. He met their stares, ignoring them. The time has long passed when the watchful gaze of others made him feel ashamed or shy. He was used to such looks.

Sel looked at him unreadable. He had been through so much that he wasn't even sure if he could feel anything else. He felt empty. That feelings flowed from his leaky heart and there is nothing left. But he made an effort to lift the spirits of his friends gathered around him.

"How could I have missed such a row," he said to them, making a heroic effort to bring a smile to his face.

They gave him a forced smile, not being deceived. Len squeezed his hand.

Ross, however, looked at Valeriea as she put her hand on his shoulder.

She understood him without words.

CHAPTER 7 — Blood and fear

Evening

"My vixen," the Viscount said with a wry smile when he finished dressing. "As always, you are unmatched."

The young Countess Weren, with her back to him, smiled at her thoughts. Oh yeah, this sex was like a refreshing bath after being brutally treated by the viceroy. In addition, the healing power after Vivan's touch stimulated her. The joyful mood almost burst it. The Viscount was young, well built, and playful in bed. This was what she needed. Pleasantly tired, she stretched delightfully and looked at him. He drank the wine, looking at her with a strange mixture of desire and regret.

"I will miss it," he said with unexpected seriousness.

He walked over to her. There was no wine for her, she noticed. What an indiscretion! The words he said sounded strangely ominous. She became concerned but did not show it to him.

Slowly his eyes moved over her body. Despite a sting of anger at the wine, she gave him her warm smile, meant for the best lovers, so innocent looking, so different from what she did in bed. Seemingly carelessly, she ran her hand through her waist-length, flaming hair, cascades running down her back and down her slender neck, as if stretching a little. His eyes followed the movement of that hand. Then he looked at her bare breasts and shapely hips. There was a hesitation in his eyes that she mistook for heralds of desire.

A moment later she saw it.

Dagger!

Blood from the cut throat ran down her neck and breasts. She grabbed herself defensively, wanting to stop the wound. In a flash of terror, she realized that the gift of a healer would not save her. Only his direct touch could do it, but you'd have to get out of here first and cross the corridor! She wanted to get up, she really wanted to. She was choking. She was desperately fighting for her young, so energetic life that she had enjoyed a moment ago. But all she could hear was the quick, nervous voice of the Viscount amid the enveloping red:

"The viceroy demanded your death from me as a loyalty. Apparently, your services are no longer needed. The queen will replace you. It's a pity, but as they say: 'There are no irreplaceable people.' You've gotten too burdensome, vixen. So is Count Beckert, your protector."

Each of those words filled her with fear. But it was too late. She died in a pool of her own blood on the floor.

With a trembling hand, he raised his goblet to finish his wine. The bloody dagger dropped from his hand as if suddenly weighing heavily on him. He silently watched as her hair darkened where the blood touched it.

This price was necessary.

The moments passed slowly, one by one, in complete silence.

Suddenly he heard a knock. He shuddered nervously before walking to the door.

"Lord Viscount," he saw the pale maid behind them. "The Countess told me to come for her an hour before supper."

Carefully covering the interior of the room with himself and masking his shaking hands, he replied with forced courtesy:

"The Countess is staying with me today. We'll have dinner here."

Showing no surprise at this decision, the girl bowed. The whole time her face was very serious, as if she was barely in control. Truth be told, he didn't care. He was about to close the door.

"Yes, Viscount," she told him, and walked away.

He closed the door and rested his forehead against it, calming his pounding heart.

It's time to call the viceroy's soldiers.

* * *

Oliver saw Queen Constance this close for the first time. Living in Verdom all his life, he had the opportunity to see her often in a carriage or even when she spoke to a crowd of subjects at important ceremonies. But he had never been so close that he could clearly see the green color of her eyes. She and the Duchess of Redan and several mansions now sat on the castle terrace, out of sight of her subjects. At this hour, the terrace was shrouded in shadow, but the prevailing heat and steamy air made the gathered women irritable and drowsy. This time Selena's task was to provide refreshing drinks and make sure that there was no shortage of them. There was still a large supply of pitchers when he arrived, and the servants were fanning the women now busy embroidering and reading books. Queen Constance, seeing the maid with a new, cold drink - as she thought (and rightly so, because the drinks were kept in the cold water of the stream that had recently broken its way through the floor of the corridor connecting the two castle wings, and was now enthralled by the court architect in the form of a fountain, in which the drinks were cooled) - asked for it. Worried about the unexpected meeting, Oliver moved close to her. Up close, her hair was fiery red, her complexion had lovely freckles hidden under a thin layer of powder, and her face... was one of the most beautiful he had ever seen. She smiled and thanked him politely, looking at him, which was rare in this place. Most of the nobles paid no attention to who served them.

He couldn't remember if he said anything.

He quickly found himself outside the door. Was his rush suspicious? He did not know. All he knew was that he had to go out, because the pants hidden under the dress were starting to hurt him painfully, and he really understood now why men spoke with such admiration about her beauty, and why the king was crazy about her. It was also apparently true that she was not vain.

It was the last assignment before going to the Count Beckert, whom his brother had locked in his room to wait until dusk. He would come back soon for him.

He wondered if the masculine and feminine incarnations he had within himself would eventually drive him crazy. On the one hand, he was clearly feeling his senses awakening, maybe because of the healer, or maybe because of himself - and on the other hand, he had to subdue them in order to play the role. He didn't know why being here was so confusing to him, but he was starting to get concerned. He had more serious matters ahead of him, he shouldn't be distracted because it was easy to make a mistake. As he walked down the corridor, he forced himself to be calm. Especially when he saw Alena on the other side. She was just talking to the Viscount about Countess Weren. Holding an armful of fresh clothes in case the healer wanted to change to dinner, he nodded to the sentries and knocked.

The Count smiled when he saw him again. However, he seemed to be absorbed in something.

"Haven't you seen anything suspicious now?" He asked anxiously as they were further away from the door.

He shook his head truthfully as he put his clothes on the table.

"Something happened," whispered the Healer. "Something bad... But my senses... I'm beginning to feel like I'm at the bottom of a well..."

"Can I get a medic?" Oliver worried.

The healer smiled slightly.

"He can't help me."

"And who can?"

"Someone who cares about me, cares about my well-being."

"Really?!"

"Listen... What's your real name?"

"Oliver."

The healer looked at him sympathetically.

"If something happens to me," he began seriously, "If I start dying..."

"Dying?!"

The healer gestured for him to be silent.

"They don't get it. This is not some fad of mine. This castle is full of corruption. It poisons me. It destroys me. I need kindness and love. I need it like air."

"Can't you control this mood somehow?" Oliver wondered. "But this bondage will not last forever. And it's not that bad here."

"I'm sensitive to moods," the healer tried to calmly explain. "It's not my invention. This is how I was created. I draw strength from love. She's hardly here."

But he knew that he would not convince the boy with these words. It would be hard to convince anyone if he has never experienced it. And perhaps he will never experience...

"It's just some..."

He had expected such a reaction.

He touched his arm gently. Oliver felt the tension ease away from him and his thoughts softened. It was reminiscent of the good times as a child when his mother would come at night and cover him with the quilt he had shed in his sleep. It's soothing warmth, her touch as she stroked his head before she left. The peace he wanted so much overwhelmed him. It was a great feeling.

"Look," the healer said calmly. "My touch was enough and you feel better. You feel more confident, you are calm, right? What am

I supposed to draw strength from? Maybe there are a few people here that I care a bit about, but for them and for others, I'm just a useful item. I could change the moods of them all, soothe their disputes. But there are many of them. And I am alone here..."

He fell silent, not wanting to tire his interlocutor with further explanations. He treated his gift with utmost seriousness, even if in the eyes of others his approach to the world seemed a bit naive. His friends and loved ones took it for granted. That was usually enough for him.

Oliver was beginning to understand.

On an impulse, he embraced him and squeezed him tightly, wholeheartedly wishing it would help.

"Listen," he whispered in his ear, "this will be over soon. Hold on!" Then, after a moment's thought, he added, choosing his words carefully, "You are not alone here."

He was afraid to say more. If he had revealed that his brother was here, and something would have happened... As he embraced Vivan, he could even feel through his clothes that Vivan was strangely cold despite the unusually heat around him.

Suddenly he felt that it was changing. After those few whispered words, a soothing and warmth radiated from the healer's body. It crossed his mind that how much more with his presence he would have had if he had been cared for properly. His touch brought to mind the best moments in life. Oliver hadn't felt so well in a very long time.

Vivan slowly slipped out of his grasp. In his eyes, Oliver could see what he had seen when he first saw him among people. Sparks of life. There were no other words for it. Just like then, Vivan stood in front of him with the same energy, he stopped slouching a little, and above all, now he felt an extraordinary strength that he had never seen in this place before.

"See for yourself what your gesture and words give me," whispered the healer. "It is because they are sincere. Think what will happen when I get back to mine?"

At that moment, though he'd never suspected it before, Oliver realized something extraordinary. He had never imagined that a stranger would become close to his heart as quickly and as closely as his own family. Now he suddenly realized that he would do anything to protect him. Vivan can't stay in this place any longer! It will kill him!

"Listen," he said seriously, aware of the unusual change in his heart, "I'm ready to help you on your escape. But I also have to do something. My sister's dignity and life depend on it! I came here to take something..."

Without further ado, he told him about Moren and his task. He just didn't mention what would happen to him when he returned. As long as he was in the castle, he could see it from a distance. But he thought he saw a hint of suspicion in the healer's eyes. As if the other knew there was something else behind this story. However, Vivan didn't say a word about it.

"So that was it?" He asked. "About my pendant?"

Oliver groaned inwardly. In this way, the words took his story to a completely different course. A thief deluding the healer with promises to obtain the desired item!

The thought depressed him so much that he wanted to leave immediately. Or even give up completely.

"I believe you," Vivan assured him, sensing his mood. "Of course, I will give it to you."

"I'll give you back!"

"I know," the Healer smiled brightly at the sincere assurance. Oliver certainly didn't want to cheat him. He could sense it.

With him, he finally felt better than the last few days. Finally. He was beginning to choke in this atmosphere, and that, as he knew perfectly well, did not bode well for him.

According to his brother's predictions, he reached out without hesitating to the chain on his neck.

Then the door swung open...

Captain Gereme and some of his men stood on the threshold.

"Lord Count!" He said shortly. "The plague is in the castle! One of the servants fell in the kitchen. You have to hurry!"

In the blink of an eye, everything else was forgotten. Vivan had seen how quickly death stretched out its hands for the sick.

"Come with me!" He said quickly to Oliver.

"The girl had a lot of work today in connection with the prevailing heat," said the gray-haired captain on the way, while his men rushed through the corridors. "My people, thanks to the instructions of the purser, will find those she visited today and gather them in the dining room."

"Excellent, Captain," Vivan replied shortly. He hated this man. It was Gereme who brutally dragged him to the castle. So, he kept the conversation with this man to a minimum.

The captain had so far not apologized to him for his mistreatment, and he did not even feel guilty in any way. He believed that he had done everything he had to do and as the sovereignty expected him. The order was to bring the healer to the castle at any cost, no matter what the consequences. This meant that, for the sake of the king and his family, he could even murder those who tried to resist. It almost happens.

Vivan, though not usually unforgiving, was not going to forget it this time, especially since Gereme was not going to apologize to him for having followed orders diligently. It was not a matter of blind obedience to the king, but fanatical loyalty and discipline. The order had to be carried out. And even blood and tears won't change that. Their few meetings were therefore based on the exchange of necessary information. Gereme believed in the viceroy's bad intentions because he thwarted several plots on his part on his brother's life. However, there has never been a direct link between the viceroy and the assassins. The latter ones died quickly and the tracks were lost. So, having a particular concern for the welfare of the royal family, the captain did not ignore the healer's words on this one important point for him.

"Lieutenant Delen is investigating one disturbing case right now," the captain added once they were in the corridor leading to the kitchen. "Nobody knows where the Countess Weren is, Count. Supposedly, she was supposed to go to Viscount Marden for a meeting, but he suddenly claims he hasn't seen her."

Vivan stopped abruptly.

That feeling…

Oliver's arrival distracted him. The echo of feelings that suddenly hit his soul was as faint as a needle prick, and just as quickly faded into nothingness. He only sensed someone's fear.

Now it's gone. He wasn't feeling well when it appeared, and now he couldn't define them anymore. Gone...

But it meant something very bad. And it wasn't far away.

Could it be Nilan?!

"Lord Count?" The captain looked at him questioningly.

Vivan looked at Oliver, witness of the morning riots with the viceroy. Oliver understood the anxiety on his face. He also made a connection between the facts. But time was pressing. They couldn't wait any longer. They ran anxiously into the kitchen.

A girl was lying in the middle of the floor. All those present here earlier fled in panic, only the court physician and the assistant fought for her life. The medic was washing her mouth with water while the young helper rubbed her pale legs and stomach with all his might. Her black skirt was raised up. Blue threads of veins were visible on the almost white skin.

"Great Mother, it's about time!!" Exclaimed the nervous medic. "Vivan, it couldn't have happened in a worse place!"

Vivan fell on his knees to them, without delay. He put his hand on the sick belly. He put the other one on the girl's forehead, as if to measure the temperature.

"Alena," Oliver whispered in shock.

"Get some clean rags, sweetheart," the medic said. "And put some wood in the fireplace. Quick girl!"

Hastily he obeyed orders, glancing over his shoulder.

Alena looked at Vivan, conscious. Shaken by convulsions, unable to speak, she tightened her hand on her belly.

"I know," he said gently to her. "It'll be over soon. Only the body will cleanse itself. Just one more time, Alena. I'm already here."

Dirt stained her underwear, a white paste, like rice gruel, flowed from her mouth. Alena groaned desperately, humiliated by her condition. Oliver froze, devastated by the sight, full of pain and gloomy memories. Vivan lightly stroked the girl's head.

"Okay," he said, still in the same calm, melodious tone, "It's over now. It will be over soon. Do you feel warm? It'll be okay, you'll see."

For a moment there was no expression of disgust on his face. Oliver saw the young assistant medic back away uneasily at the sight of the impurity, but medic Sedon watched the healer in action carefully and with admiration. Oliver noticed something else as well. Taking advantage of this unusual situation, Sedon looked at Vivan with concern. The latter did not take his hand from the girl's hand, although her grip must have hurt him. All the while, when her belly was slowly returning to its normal color and her legs were no longer marble-colored, he spoke to her calmly. Her breathing slowly calmed down and her tremors stopped.

Finally, there were tears of relief and exhaustion.

At the medic's signal, Oliver reached for the clean linen cloths from the sideboard. He smiled reassuringly before starting to wash her. Without a word, but as gently as he could, concerned with what he saw now. Sedon gestured for the helper to leave and remove the rags that had been used earlier. Vivan touched the boy's forehead before they left. The medic shook his arm in silent thanks. Only then Vivan managed a soft sigh of relief.

Oliver stayed with him alone with the cured girl. Alena stared into the healer's eyes. He understood. She didn't want him to look where Oliver was washing her now, still convinced like the others he was Selena. She was clenching her hand, although the grip was clearly weakening. Oliver blotted out all meaning of what he had just seen. He concentrated on washing gently without thinking about the woman's thighs and body. He took off her dirty underwear. When he was done, he made makeshift diapers out of clean cloths and put them on. Without a trace of thoughts, he had with the Queen or Countess Weren, without disgust. As if he had been doing it all his life. He just made sure that everything went neatly and quickly. He straightened his dress. He washed the face of Alena, looking at him now with gratitude. She smiled weakly at both of them before falling asleep.

Vivan touched Oliver's forehead, which beaded with sweat.

"For protection," he explained.

"I noticed."

"You must be very hot in all this."

"This is definitely an understatement," Oliver replied sarcastically. "Will we carry her to her room?"

"I'll call Sedon. You are a girl and I don't have the strength for it. Just stay with her to disguise her from this dress. She'll be fine by morning. She just needs to rest."

"And you? You look tired."

"I had a hard day," they smiled knowingly to each other. "I will sleep like a dead man until dawn and I will be like a newborn."

Oliver looked closely at the healer. Despite his exhaustion, Vivan looked better than the morning he'd seen him for the first time. I think he did help him. It amazed him, but at the same time it made him feel proud.

Vivan looked once more at the sleeping woman and finally released his hand, which showed a distinct red mark...

He got up to call a medic.

Sedon began giving orders immediately. One of the cooks, who evidently had a special affection for Alena, carried her to the room assigned to her. With him, Oliver left as requested by Vivan, and arranged everything.

It was only when he left that he realized what seemed suspicious to him from the very beginning about the disappearance of the countess.

Captain Gereme conveyed the words of the Viscount. The latter claimed that Countess Weren did not come to him. Meanwhile, he, Oliver, saw Alena talking to the Viscount through the ajar door. Except he couldn't hear the words, still thrilled by his recent meeting with the Queen and the plea he had made to Vivan.

But now he remembered the conversation with Alena.

Alena said she had to go get the Countess before dinner...

Vivan asked him as soon as he arrived if he had seen anything suspicious. He must have sensed something...

Oliver felt a start to dread him.

A nice, though debauched countess.

Incident with the viceroy.

A blatant lie of the Viscount. The healer's strange premonitions.

Alena might have repeated what the viscount had told her, but now she was too exhausted for that.

He was sure that something had happened to the Countess. Maybe she's still in the Viscount's room?

He would have to meet with Delen and investigate it. He can't go there himself. It's too dangerous. He could not, if only for the sake of his bond, put himself at such a risk.

Was he going to take care of it? Should leave everything and run with the Beckert brothers from the castle as planned?

Stay or go?!

What if something happened to this lovely woman? If she need help?

Could meet Vivan's eyes knowing he had left her? Anyone?

He would take Paphian and look for Delen together.

He hurried back to his room.

"What about my brother?" Paphian asked immediately

"He went to sleep. He just saved the girl from death. Give me a moment…" He sat down, tired with tension and anxiety. He had to focus. "It's time to get out of here and get your brother. Just check something else first."

"As for the family," said Paphian, taking a scrap of parchment from his pocket. "Someone slipped it under the door when I was blooming out here of boredom."

Surprised, Oliver took the parchment, thinking that Delen was probably giving him a sign. On the sheet of paper, a cryptic text was crossed out in neat writing: "Don't go home. We are waiting here for you. Your family".

He stared at the writing in amazement. Undoubtedly, the handwriting belonged to Julien. The content was a bit strange, but under the circumstances it is understandable. There was no fear or compulsion in it.

So, she was free! She escaped Moren and was waiting for him somewhere here. Someone helped her. Probably Sel. He thought gratefully of his sick friend. It was only moments later that another thought struck him, full of ineffable relief.

He didn't have to go back to Moren...

He sat down to cool down. Too much was happening at once, and he felt it was far from over today. But at least it was... He doesn't have to... He doesn't have to...

"I give you a few moments for delight and we move," said Paphian matter-of-factly, enjoying in his spirit his joy. "More and more guards are here."

Hearing the word "guard," Oliver looked at Paphian somewhat distractedly.

And then he understood the subconscious thoughts...

* * *

The royal gardens occupied an enormous space, most of them extending beyond the castle. In front of the castle there was an avenue among the few palm and mixed trees. The garden was arranged on small hills like a delicate carpet shimmering with a rainbow of colors. Streams meandered among the alleys, paths, and bridges, sparkled with little ponds, and flowers and shrubs of all varieties and shades bloomed all year round. It was easy to hide in the thicket that prevailed here. Even if the white, decorated wagon was also to be hidden. Or a bunch of thugs.

Sel avoided each of the landmarks in the garden. He knew perfectly well that Moren knew every arbor, ornate tower or statue in this place and that he would look for them in the first place. As he suspected, they found one of the groups near the characteristic trunks of a large sequoia. One of the two trunks formed a gentle arc just above the ground, next to which a few members of the gang stopped, sending two out for reconnaissance.

The problem was that they were Ramoz's people...

"How many are there, Alesei?" Sel walked over to the window like an old man. He was still recovering his strength.

A young man who, not long ago, before the outbreak of the plague, with a friend entertained wealthy clients at the House of Pleasure, sat next to him on a dresser. He was one of those people who, like Ross, did not wear harsh makeup to stand out. His dark hair was plaited in a braid, and well-trained muscles played under his skin.

"Ten. Including Ramoz. Two are searching the neighborhood."

"He doesn't have many followers left," Sel smiled in satisfaction.

"This plague thinned them a little," Alesei crossed his arms over his chest. "They'll find us quickly."

"They don't mean us. Just for a healer."

"I also hope."

Sel looked back. Julien slept in the bed, covered with a colorful bedspread. He took care of it himself. She was very tired.

"You think the friend of Sai and Lena's guard delivered the letter to Oliver?" He asked.

"Selena," Alesei smiled, imagining the boy he had seen a few times as the son of a goldsmith, in women's clothes. "Good thing Darmon was there when the youngster was taught this story before he left. Apparently, Oliver was unrecognizable." He shook his head with a smile. "Of course, the guard delivered the message. He told Sai that he missed the next meeting."

Sel smiled too, though sadly. He unexpectedly remembered Milera. His throat tightened with regret.

"What's up?!" Alesei asked immediately, seeing the change in his face.

He had once seen Sel choke, gasping for breath. He couldn't forget that sight. Nor his helplessness then.

"I thought about Milera," Sel explained to him.

Alesei breathed a sigh of relief, although he felt deeply sorry for him. He liked Milera.

"Where's Darmon?" Sel asked, breaking the silence after a while "He should be back by now."

Alesei looked out the window anxiously. Outside were the others enjoying the fragrant air of the garden while Ross washed quickly in a basin of water. He was taking off his makeup. Alesei glanced at Selarion, which was still painted. The dark eye pencil smudged into a thick line. He looked like some kind of death ghost. Maybe the girls could handle this. Or Ross. It looked ghastly.

"May it not be where I thought it was," he replied softly.

He saw the same anxiety in his eyes that tormented him.

* * *

Julien opened her sleepy eyes. Sel was standing by the window with one of those young men whose professional smiles were a little annoying to her. She felt naked under their gaze, as if they could guess all her hidden desires and thoughts.

"Sel," she said softly, surprising both men with the sudden sound of her voice. "You should rest."

"I can't lie down," he told her truthfully.

She got up and walked over to them, avoiding Alesei's eyes.

"You let me sleep too long."

"You needed this. You must have strength."

She put her hand on his shoulder.

"Are you ok?" She asked with concern.

Ross told her about Sel's parents when he fell asleep. She never liked them. They seemed polite, Sel's father was even nice, but the most important thing for her was that they were waiting for their son to die. Seemingly they cared for him, he was cared for, he was always well-groomed as it should be as a person bearing a name that has been respected for generations. But they didn't love him. Her mother wiped his tears away more often, comforted him, talked to him more than his own.

He didn't answer, but his eyes revealed hidden suffering.

Ross went inside.

She stared at him in amazement. He looked as ordinary, but at the same time as unusual as he was. A nice boy with a warm look was hiding under the makeup. Now his damp hair twisted slightly. All rapaciousness, defiant gaze, even provocative movements disappeared. She felt a pang of regret as she watched Sel's reaction, and it genuinely surprised her. Ross has changed his appearance, true, but he hasn't changed his liking. For unknown reasons, she now felt hurt and disappointed. As if suddenly, she saw him with different eyes...

Sel looked as if he had just actually noticed him now. There was something else in it, too, something Alesei noticed with his trained eye. Ross noticed it too.

"Do you have any shirt?" Alesei asked with apparent ease, as if he saw nothing.

"I just came in to see if Valeriea took anything for me."

"I'll give you mine," Alesei said quickly, almost breaking his word. After Sel's face he could see what was coming, "I have a backpack in the back of the car."

Then he gave Julien a meaningful look at the reasons for his behavior and left.

The three of them stayed.

Only now did Julien feel uncomfortable. There was clearly something going on. Ross, who knew what it was about, felt uncomfortable with Sel's gaze. Only a few days ago, he would have been grateful for this renewed interest. Now he was starting to feel more and more humiliated by it. It won't do him any good.

Sel walked over to him slowly, straightening up. He took a sip of the potion he was still holding with him and discarded the empty bottle. Ross felt regret building up. Sel had never approached him like that, never started that way. This was done by clients who only wanted to satisfy quickly...

Julien looked down to hide any unexpected tears. But she couldn't take her eyes off both of them for long.

Sel took Ross's face and kissed him. It wasn't a gentle kiss. He was violent, hot-tempered, as if there was some strength in him seeking an outlet. He began to kiss him furiously, struggle and caress him, and there was no trace of restraint or self-control in his movements. There was no delicacy.

Suddenly he was overcome by the urge to let go of all the built-up tension at once, rapidly, without inhibitions. Drown out suffering, turn off thoughts. Satisfy yourself.

Julien, touched by his behavior, decided to leave. He, a friend, not long ago her best friend's husband, intends now to...?

It was beyond her mind.

She couldn't understand it.

And Ross... The boy she liked. True, she knew who he was, but did not know that he would be...

That right here and now...

"Sel," Ross whispered. "Sel, stop it!"

He felt worse and worse in this situation. Julien's presence at his humiliation was even more embarrassing. She was just walking by, wanting to leave them, and then Sel would get his way because Ross wouldn't be able to say no to him. So, he gripped her hand desperately in a defensive reaction with his free hand, trying to push the feverish Sel away from him. She looked up at him in surprise, disturbed by their behavior. She saw a silent plea for help.

She understood what Ross was feeling now. How much Sel's behavior hurt his feelings.

"Sel," she grabbed him immediately and began to gently pull him away. "Leave him. Can't you see how you're hurting him? Ross is not the whore you paid for. He cares about you."

Sel looked at her with anguish. She felt regret seeing his pain. Slowly he sank to his knees and hid his face in his hands.

In the remaining silence, you could hear the horses screeching outside and soft voices. Ross closed his eyes. Suddenly he felt Julien gently hug him and hold him in that embrace. He hugged her back, grateful for the unexpectedly warm gesture. And understanding.

He knelt after a moment, gently slipping out of her arms to comfort Sel, devastated by misfortune.

* * *

"I can't find Vivan," Kirian said to them as Oliver sneaked him into his room. "I looked for him everywhere except the queen's chambers and the dining room. Maybe that's where he is. The doors are closed. The king ordered to double the guards, Geron goes crazy. I need to go back. They will notice my absence."

"Thanks for that," said Paphian, taking the package from Oliver's hands. "Although... you know my aversion to uniforms."

Kirian smiled. He resembled his older brother in many ways. Same dark hair, same eyes, same posture. Clear parental characteristics. However, the smile was completely different. Mild. With warmth in his eyes.

"Your brother helped me last week," he said to Paphian, "Nils, one of the viceroy's bodyguards, thought I was hitting on his girlfriend who works here. He slashed a dagger across my face." He indicated the direction of the incision from left cheek to chin. "He said neither would look at me now. Instead, he spent three days in the dungeons. Vivan healed me. We chatted. We laughed. Nothing has changed as far as the approach to people is concerned. Just…" he continued, while Paphian changed his clothes in a hurry. "He really wants to go home. Apparently, he hardly eats anything. And he became terribly sad. This place is bad for him."

Paphian's jaw clenched in grief and anger. At home, he had seen Vivan depressed very rarely, when he treated someone for the consequences of exceptional cruelty or had not managed to help. He knew his brother almost as well as he knew himself. Vivan was two years older than him and was not his father's child, but that never mattered to them. He was his model. Maybe not in all things, because sometimes Vivan was too emotional about life. An energetic Paphian, who could not sit still since childhood, solved problems in his life in a completely different way. But the brother was always an authority for him. He taught him to listen to others, to consider his actions also from the point of view of the other side. It is true that it was most useful in combat to predict the opponent's movements, but still.

He shifted the chain with a small bottle behind his shirt and began buttoning his uniform. All this he did quickly and effortlessly. Kirian watched this with some amazement:

"You weren't hurt when Geron was taking Vivan?!" I was told yes."

"I've been wounded," Paphian grimaced as he remembered the sword thrust in the arm by one of Captain Gereme's troops. "But

Vivan always leaves us with security wherever he goes. Everyone in our family wears it," he pulled out a bottle.

Kirian and Oliver stared at the item. Inside, he saw a ruby-colored liquid.

"Is that his blood?" Oliver asked softly.

The Paphian nodded.

"It helps with everything," he added.

"A precious gift," said Kirian admiringly, without a trace of greed.

"Are we going?" Oliver asked a little impatiently.

"Wherever you like, my lady," the Paphian smirked.

Oliver stared him down.

* * *

"And so?" Paphian asked as they stopped at the fork in the corridors, just below the tall clock tower. "What now?"

"The sun has just set," Oliver said. "I'll go outside through the window, and from there, after a short climb over the rocks and walls, I'll peer into the Viscount's room. You don't even have to try. You stand on watch."

"Not bad," Paphian nodded. "I have one question?"

"Yes?" Oliver opened a window behind the bend in the wall, out of sight to the sentries outside the healer's chambers.

"Are you going to do all this in this dress?" The Paphian pointed with amusement to the maid's dress.

Oliver began to lift the hem of the dress.

"Please, spare me this," Paphian feigned scandal.

Oliver looked at him wryly.

"I have pants," he said dryly. "And besides, I'll leave the dress downstairs. I can't move around the castle without it."

"Fine, I'm relieved," Paphian said in an amused whisper. "Go before they notice I'm walking alone."

The two uninitiated guards had been disposed of moments earlier. Oliver distracted them with a well-aimed slingshot, and Paphian put them to sleep with a stronger blow. They both landed outside the window in a small hollow in the rock, and the bushes masked their bodies. From there, they could only bruise themselves. The whole castle was set on a rock and similar depressions, and there was no lack of unevenness around it.

"What would you say...?" Oliver asked him.

"That I'm patrolling the corridor as ordered."

"I'm going," the boy said shortly and jumped off.

The dark hair of the wig and the gown fused together in the faint glow of the ending day. Paphian looked out to see if anyone had noticed their maneuvers. It seemed not. He glanced at the panorama of Verdom below, the sparse lights and the beauty of the buildings and guard towers. In the distance he could see the walls surrounding the city, and beyond them, the valleys and mountains.

"Lord Count," he heard a voice suddenly approaching from the corridor, which he could not see well in this place, "we know the cause of this maid's illness. The coachman who accompanied this girl, Celina's sister today, had symptoms of it, in the words of the Court Medic. Supposedly, it was only a matter of time before an attack like that of the unfortunate Alena would occur. The food probably came from a contaminated harvest or he himself contaminated it. We burned everything."

Paphian looked around frantically. Vivan could not see him now, because with his affection, he could expose him. He closed the window and walked slowly forward. After a while, he saw the sentries outside his brother's chambers. Vivan, meanwhile, was approaching the fork, and the talkative purser, as usual, continued nervously:

"That's why I took the liberty of bringing Lieutenant Delen's squad to the dining room. You've met this brave girl before, haven't you, Count? I sent her to you this morning."

"I saw Selena," the Healer replied calmly.

"The Court Medic has instructed me to tell you that dinner will, understandably, be long delayed. They still wash and scrub everything there. Did I bring you a cook who carried Alena to her room?"

"I'm not sure," Vivan replied wearily.

"Well, I'll ask him if he was there," the purser muttered under his breath.

At this point, they reached the window that Paphian had looked through before, and Vivan stopped suddenly in surprise. He felt a familiar scent and the pulsing energy of a few people he knew. He sensed Oliver. There was someone else in the place besides him, but his presence mixed with the smell of another person. Unfortunately, there weren't many smells, although maybe he should have been there after a month's stay. He was too distracted by other things to remember.

The pulsating aura was so remarkably similar to that of the Paphian. But this smell...

"Lord Count?" The purser asked in surprise, and the guards accompanying them looked at the healer with mild surprise.

Vivan sighed. He was so exhausted that he could barely keep his feet. He had just left the dining room, where he had placed his hands on every person who had come into contact with Alena this morning, not counting Oliver, Sedon, and his assistant. As of today, he was fed up and it was starting to care whether he would eat anything now. He still felt comforted, but his body was already failing to obey. His eyes were literally closing on their own. He barely noticed that a guard was walking ahead, who did not look back. Usually, he was always greeted. The guards at the door of his rooms straightened at the sight of him, and one of them politely opened the door for him. He must have looked ghastly.

"Marcus," Vivan smiled at the chatty purser, "tell everyone I'm going to sleep. I will not eat. I only dream of a dream."

"Fine, Count," replied the purser understandingly, seeing his weariness. "And in the morning, I will order a solid breakfast delivered to the room."

A dozen or so meters away Paphian, whose corridor was beginning to end, heard the door close behind his brother, and the purser returns with the guards to the fork of the corridors, from where he will probably go to the kitchen. It was then that he dared to turn around and slowly began walking to his position by the window. Oliver should be back by now.

* * *

Oliver pressed himself against the wall, soaked in sweat, feeling terror tighten his throat.

He saw her...

He slid into the darkness of the rock adjoining the building, trying to calm his breathing.

The Viscount's room was empty except for the body of a woman laid on a bed and covered with a sheet.

Her hair, beautiful, twisting red strands - spilled, lay on the sheets. The right hand was hanging limply. It could have become a beautiful picture of death if the throat was not blemished and the bloodstain was clearly visible on the sheets.

The Countess was murdered.

And the murderer must have gone to the dining room, where Vivan was also supposed to go before going to bed. After all, he was talking to Alena...

Was the countess dead then?

The viceroy was probably also involved in her death, as in Celina's death. She became uncomfortable, and the Viscount would probably get something for it.

Oliver remembered her smile, her suddenly sympathetic advice to Selena to stay away from the viceroy. Even with her tattered dress and messy hair, she was beautiful.

She was like that even now.

She and Vivan stood up to the viceroy. Did he also order to kill the healer?

No, it's definitely not. It would be crazy!

Shaken, trembling hands, he put his dress back on and returned to his seat by the window, noting the still unconscious guards lying nearby in the bushes. He lifted the gown and unwrapped the elven cord around his waist...

* * *

Purser Kanel was just leaving with the guards briskly, muttering something under his breath. After a while Paphian appeared.

"What did you find out?" He asked.

Before they came here, Oliver had also told him about the incident with the viceroy without going into the details.

"The Countess has been murdered," he whispered. "Let's get out of here. As soon as possible!"

"You don't have to persuade me to do so," replied Paphian, without a trace of a smile on his face. "I like this place less and less. How are we going to take Vivan?"

"Maybe we can lure him out of the room on some pretext?"

"No. He just told everyone he was going to sleep."

"Have you met him?!"

"Fortunately, I was far away. He didn't recognize me."

Oliver thought for a moment.

"Maybe an emergency..." he muttered.

"You try it," Paphian whispered to him. "The sentries at the door saw me. I'm surprised they haven't started to suspect anything yet. If I..."

"I know," Oliver broke in.

"They woke up?" Paphian glanced out the window.

"They're tied and gagged anyway. I had a rope."

Paphian looked at him with sparkle in his eyes.

"I'm afraid to ask what else you hide under your skirt."

"I think you have to go," Oliver remarked coldly, who hasn't jokes in his head right now. "They haven't seen you there for a long time."

"And they probably already started to miss you," Paphian smiled mischievously, but after a while he prepared himself, pretending to be serious at the sight of the scowling Oliver, and slowly walked back to the corridor with his brother's rooms. As he passed, he nodded politely.

And only now did he understand why the sentries hadn't approached him the first time. They belonged to Delen's squad and were like Kirian, who stayed with some of the people in the castle for his own safety, which was, unfortunately, the idea of the older brother. He met with him upon arrival. Delen's squad could be trusted. They winked at him.

What a fine stroke of luck.

"Want to see your brother now?" One of them asked with a smile. "Do you prefer to take a walk?"

"You gave the boys pacifiers and made them go to sleep?" Said the other.

The guards patrolling the corridor belonged to the king's troops. Both sentries knew the Paphian would not kill them unless he had to defend life.

"And the pillows for the head," replied Paphian.

Everyone was smiling now.

"Wait," he said to them, and quickly followed Oliver, who must have walked farther down the hall to prepare for a moment. Their early plan was no longer needed. Another corridor from behind that with the window they used led to the kitchen and to the part occupied by the most important guests, royal advisers, the royal chancellor, and then into the royal chambers with a tangle of smaller corridors. At its exit, Paphian saw Oliver disappearing...

* * *

Oliver reached the next corridor and saw several guards. He cursed silently. Fools had harassed him a couple of times today with dirty jokes. He will have to put up with them again...?

Weird. There was a great stir at the sight of him. And in the middle of the corridor, he saw clearly several of the viceroy's men, including two from the incident that morning with the countess whom he did not trust. One of them pointed his finger at him.

"That's her! Get her!"

At first Oliver froze in amazement. What is going on? They hadn't exposed him, otherwise the two-faced guard wouldn't have screamed like that.

So only one thing remained.

They are the viceroy's people...

He immediately understood the danger.

He turned on his heel and began to run away. He was close to the end of the corridor. But he might not have made it. Side exits led to kitchens, servants' rooms, and other aisles. There he could try his luck. Better not to risk Paphian. One alone wouldn't do anything here. He lunged to the side. He only foresaw one thing. The betrayals of several of the king's guards. On the stairs, one of those who treated him with unrefined jokes during the day caught up with him. He wrapped his arms around his waist and held him down.

He did not know, however, that he was not dealing with a woman. Oliver has defended himself many times in his life. And the many years of climbing have built up his muscles. He delivered the punch right in the guard's face, causing the guard to release his grip. He managed to break his nose open, which he hadn't expected. The guard was not a seasoned soldier, or else he might not have been easily snatched from his victim's grasp. Glancing back, Oliver saw the pursuit approach.

He started running up the spiral staircase again, but it was too late. Two of the viceroy's men gained time with this brief struggle. They grabbed him and started dragging him upstairs. If he ran downstairs, maybe someone would see what was happening. But he couldn't. They dragged him struggling upstairs, back to the same corridor.

"She's a strong girl!" One noticed.

"I'll kill this bitch!" The one with the broken nose screamed, trying to stop the blood.

"You better get it together!" The one who pointed Oliver commanded him. "Where to now?"

"We're going down the hidden corridor. We'll go out past the royal rooms and make sure they don't chase us, and then to the viceroy," the other guard, known to Oliver, nervously twisting his mustache. "But fast! Someone can come here!"

"Lucky everyone who lives here are still sitting in the dining room," noted another, looking around nervously.

Oliver, held in the firm, tickly grip of one of the men, couldn't even scream. His mouth was covered with a hand. The guard was strong enough to break his neck easily. The taut wig hair painfully pulled his hair by all the pins and pins that one of the courtesans had pinned on him as he was disguised. He worried about the plethora sticking tightly, so far. So far it was most definitely so. He might still have serious concerns that his wig and hair would be torn off, and judging by the pain, perhaps even his skin.

A group of guards in the colors of the viceroy approached one wall. A secret mechanism was activated and everyone, along with the struggling Oliver, found themselves in the narrow corridor. The passage was carefully closed behind him.

Several of the king's other bribed guards returned to their places undetected.

As if nothing had happened...

At the end of the corridor, torn by terror and uncertainty as to what to do, stood a Paphian, hidden from the eyes of the king's traitors.

Vivan and Delen's two men were nearby.

But the brother was so tired that his help was of little use. And for what was he supposed to expose the sentries? They might have found out about Oliver's fraud, which they probably had no idea. For the sake of his plan, it's better to leave Vivan under their custody than to put him at risk now. And do not initiate anyone.

Not even Kirian.

He has to do it himself.

He has to free a friend.

CHAPTER 8 — Kiss of love

Night

Luck favored the kidnappers. The viceroy's rooms were remote from the others and in a side corridor. Now it remains to travel a short distance from the hidden exit to the door. One of the viceroy's men decided to create effective confusion, distracting the king's guards. He killed one of the guards, then broke a window and escaped through a window overlooking the garden into the darkness of the falling night. Directing attention to the act allowed the kidnappers to slip past before being noticed.

"Now listen, bitch!" The excitable, two-faced guard grabbed Oliver by the throat while another held him in a grip. "The viceroy has other things on his mind now, but he'll be here in a minute. Before spending time with the queen, he wants to fuck you first. You cannot resist him, and from what we see you will. We must teach you humility."

The others, and there were three of them in total, because the one with the broken nose had to leave them as well, smiled ominously.

Then the first blow fell on the cheek.

Aimed at by an open hand so as not to disturb the bones, it stung painfully.

Another one followed immediately.

And another one.

After a fourth hard cheek, the brutal soldiers released Oliver, who fell to the floor with a buzzing noise in his head. He cringed instinctively for the next blow, but he didn't even groan as the soldiers stared at him for a moment, waiting for the woman's expected reaction to such treatment. Unfortunately, this behavior did not work in his favor.

"She didn't even scream," said one.

"And she doesn't cry. You must have hit her too weakly," the other asked his companion.

The utterance of such a remark caused a dangerous aggression in the guard who was only looking for his own interests. It violated his sick ambition.

He pushed his companion away with cold fury. He fell to the huddled figure and grabbed her by the hair.

Oliver's entire head ached as if from sticking a hundred pins. Although the guard only grabbed a handful, the wig on which it was worn made it hurt not only at the place of capture. Oliver got up quickly to avoid more agony, and then the guard pushed him and knocked him over onto the viceroy's bed. He straddled him, then began slapping his face over and over. Sulfurous cheeks, from which involuntary tears finally appeared on Oliver's face, fell one after the other.

"Sten," the second of the two-faced guards finally broke in, seeing that his comrade had obviously lost it. "Stop it! The viceroy will order to kill you for smacking her mouth! You hear?!"

Sten stopped as abruptly as he had begun and, gasping angrily, studied Oliver's face. He clearly wanted more, and the too calm, dignity-filled demeanor of the woman beneath him aroused dark desires in him. He mastered himself with effort. He was so strong with an aura of fury that not only Oliver was afraid to move. Even Sten's companions felt uneasy.

Sten hated women behaving dignified in the face of danger. He believed that they were prancing and the easiest way to unlearn them was to strong push into the vagina. It could have been brutal rape or the use of a dagger. He was considering the possibility at the moment, and only the viceroy's express command had stopped his aspirations.

"The important thing is that it worked," he judged finally, seeing the tear fall, to which even his companions responded with some relief, and he slowly stood up, finally relieving the victim of his weight.

Oliver felt like a real girl in his place would feel right now. Battered, humiliated, knowing that in a few moments he will face an even worse fate. His face burned with a living fire of pain, the skin on his head ached as if it had been torn off.

He knew exactly what was going to happen. If he were a girl, the viceroy would finish the work of an unpredictable guard, and then he would probably order to kill. As an impostor who had inadvertently ridiculed the viceroy, attracted attention with his perfect disguise, and had driven the passion of the impetuous guardian, he could be sure that death would not come soon, but would subject him to endless torture.

Then suddenly his despair broke loose. A terrible sense of injustice and humiliation. They had no right to do this to him. Moren couldn't just drag him to the bed because he wanted to. He couldn't hurt him or his loved ones for his own satisfaction. Everything he had gone through this bastard so far - alienation, humiliation, attempted rape, punches - and now a perverted fat viceroy who would most gladly do the same to him if he were the girl who's gasping and groans he could still hear in his head he had ordered the beautiful woman killed, for she was defending the only man she believed to be devoid of all corruption. Death of his parents, Milera, and a slap aimed at Julien finally filled the cup.

It aroused hatred towards all those who had contributed to his suffering so far.

Oliver lost his temper.

* * *

"You!!" Captain Gereme appeared at the end of the corridor leading to the royal rooms. "You're coming with me!"

He quickly pointed at Paphian, who froze for a fraction of a moment for fear of being exposed. Anger seized him. He didn't have time to wander the castle with the guards now. Oliver was in danger. Fortunately, the captain, preoccupied with his own thoughts, did not look even more closely at him. Otherwise, he would have recognized him. But his abrupt departure now would have aroused suspicion.

The captain thus brought in a few people and found himself in front of the murdered royal guard, eager to report on the event. There was a hearing of witnesses, a description of the incident.

Time passed.

Paphian felt a cold sweat begin to pour over him. Not only was he in danger of being exposed at any moment. He felt somewhere in his soul that something was wrong nearby. An irresistible force pulled him towards the corridor that led to the viceroy's chambers. He was still looking there, helpless in the face of the gathering squad. Finally, the royal family appeared and the captain's attention turned to them. Personal security joined. There was a bit of confusion. He slowly began to withdraw from the crowd.

Then he met the young prince's gaze.

Meron looked at him, clearly recognizing him. He opened his mouth to say something. When he heard the killer escaped, his face softened, but he still looked as if he were deeply struggling with the decision whether to reveal to his father the presence of his healer brother among them.

The queen calmly placed her hand on his lips and with a slight nod of her head signaled to Paphian to go away. He gave her his cheeky smile a little smile, a slight bow, and walked slowly away with relief. The son and mother quickly looked back at the captain and his men as if nothing had happened. Faced with a threat they had heard rumors of, they agreed that the healer should already leave Verdom.

However, Paphian encountered a more serious problem on his way. The king's brother has already appeared in the corridor.

He intended to go straight to his rooms, but seeing the congregation, his brother, and his wife, he felt he couldn't do it just like that. His dissatisfaction was visible to everyone. A pleasant surprise awaited him in the room, which he was forced to discover later. He could barely pretend to be interested in the situation, all the more so as he was less and less willing to keep up appearances. He and his men were just approaching those gathered by the dead guard, passing Paphian watching him, when suddenly the door to his chambers opened with a roar resembling a thunderclap.

There was a silence.

From their place, Paphian and the viceroy saw a hand grasp the carved doorframe, and then the rest of the bloody, tattered little figure appeared, dark hair matted with sweat and blood.

Paphian ran over to catch Oliver before he fell.

* * *

"What we do?" Ross asked softly as he finally managed to lead Sel to the big bed. "Sel? Darmon will not come back. He's probably dead by now," he said with quiet regret.

He liked Darmon. He chose him to run away with them, because Darmon did not condemn anyone, he liked everyone. He had such charisma that he was able to win over everyone. He should be doing some business in the capital rather than serving his wealthy clients. He even had some ideas on how to get started. He was also such a womanizer that he accepted clients for two or three in one night. And he laughed a lot. Ross liked his laugh. He got everyone on their feet. Rebecca said that the laughter warms her heart. Valeriea had a soft spot for him. She dreamed of such a man in her life. Of course, at her age. She was probably despair in secret now. He should go to her.

And he should also be here. It was the first time that he had felt so internally torn.

They lay down with Julien on either side of the sick man, listening for his heavy breathing. The grief he felt in his heart caused him almost physical pain. He felt that death was about to take his lover.

"Get it going," Sel whispered softly. "Tell them to drive as close to the castle gate as possible, but not to leave the shadows of the garden."

Julien gently stroked Sel's pale hair.

"Ross," Sel whispered softly, "I'm sorry... I was..."

Ross smiled weakly, shaking his apology away. His heart has already forgotten.

Julien sprang up abruptly, pale as linen, interrupting their moment.

"Oliver!" She whispered.

She felt his fear. Then a choking in the throat. When they were tormented by strong emotions, one always felt what the other was happening at that moment. She felt her own fear begin to choke her. She looked at Sel, mentally pleading for him to help her. He forced himself to sit up, though it was dangerous for him now, and opened his arms. No matter how bad he felt, he was always ready to come to the rescue as much as he could. The sight touched her. But when the guard in the viceroy's chamber gave Oliver the first hard slap, she felt the blow against her skin. Everything else ceased to count...

Surprised by the unexpected behavior of Julien, Ross saw the convulsions shaking her body. She bit her lip in sudden pain, and her eyes filled with tears. The terrifying jolts of each punch to the face made the hearts of both men grapple with an inexplicable fear of an unexpected phenomenon. Ross sat down next to the sufferer.

Finally, Julien, as Oliver, shocked by the blows, lay on the bed, freed her helplessness and clung to Sel desperately. She was sobbing from the sudden shock, and purple blows began to appear on her face.

"What happened?" Ross asked, devastated to see it. "Is it about the bond?" He made sure, not knowing the siblings very well so far. "They're twins, right?"

Sel nodded his head in agreement, stroking her with a trembling hand. Whenever he happened to witness how their bond worked, when one of them felt pain, he was angered by Moren's own helplessness and the deliberate action of Moren, which usually caused suffering. How could he punch and tug Oliver, how could he think about what he had now revealed himself with for good, knowing Julien would feel it too?! Why had he, Sel, had not seen before and deep down in his heart still refused to see what kind of man his recent friend was? Moren... A monster and a friend. He harmed people without hesitation, and then almost looked after his terminally ill friend. Who was this man?! Why was he so deceived?! These thoughts aroused great bitterness in him, the world turned gray in their reflection.

Julien screamed out loud and broke free from his embrace. She began to convulsions as if she had been possessed by a demon, which terrified both men.

And then she started screaming again.

Her screams were quieter, sometimes louder, but frequent and desperate. They made the other escapees from the House of Pleasure quickly show up.

"Can't you be a little quieter while having fun? "Alesei asked nervously, not knowing what was going on "We'll have all of them soon...

He froze as he saw Julien, the words stuck in his throat. Sel and Ross tried in vain to help somehow the hapless girl who was throwing herself on the bed and screaming.

It was evident that something inconceivable was happening here. Although it was not a surprise for everyone. The three people looked at each other knowingly.

"Sai, remember?" Lena asked.

"The Raven twins," the other said softly, and Lena clung to her at the memory.

But their expressions now, as they watched Julien's anguish, expressed fear and relief that they weren't that close after all.

"Poor girl," Lena whispered, watching in horror as the red marks from the blows appeared on Julien's body.

"Poor Oliver," Valeriea corrected her, "it'll pass her by. But her brother…" She shook her head in concern.

They all stood shocked at the sight of it until Ross, tearfully, said:

"Lena, Alesei get out of here! Come on! As close to the gate as possible!"

"She'll alarm everybody," said Alesei, trying to be businesslike as gently as he could. "Sel, forgive me, but her scream..."

Sel put Julien down slowly. She was squeezing his hand with all her strength, so he pulled out the other one and before anyone could stop him, he put it to the girl's mouth. To keep from screaming, she gritted her teeth on his hand like a gag. The teeth pierced the skin and stabbed the flesh. Sel gasped and pressed his lips together. Ross tried in vain to free him from that embrace. In Julien's bout of extraordinary suffering, there was no question of any force that could open her mouth.

Valeriea, seeing that something had to be done on her own, sent Alesei to drive out of the ravine elsewhere in case Moren could discover their hiding place, though she doubted Darmon would reveal anything. She believed he would not. Darmon did not lack valor. He would sooner die than betray his friends, although his appearance might have appeared differently. Lena and Sai tried to pass Julien a makeshift gag. While Len was vigilantly checking that no one heard them.

Sel suddenly felt a completely different pain. Inside, the strong, searing pressure took his air out of him, overwhelming him so that after a while he saw dark spots in his eyes. It had never been this bad before, and he knew what it might mean for him.

When the women finally managed to get Julien to let go of him, leaving a bloody mark on his hand, Ross caught Sel's losing consciousness.

It was quickly realized that something bad was happening again. Sel was choking. Valeriea rested her head on the sick man's chest, listening to his heart, while at the same time Julien was silent, and now she was just crying soundlessly from exhaustion, unable to do anything else, and the girls comforted her and rubbed her face with a cold compress, applying cold compresses to her battered body. Ross took her battered hand in a gesture of affection, but the rest of his body pressed against the dying Sel, cradling him in his arms. Valeriea dressed her hand. She stroked Sel's thin hair with concern and kissed her eager friend's forehead with motherly tenderness. They didn't have a potion. No drugs or potions to help him. It could only mean one thing.

Julien froze after a moment, her eyes fixed somewhere outside where she was, crushed by her and her brother's pain and suffering. Still, like a drowning man, she held the hand tightly grasping her hand, as if she still wanted to fight for her senses and awareness with the last of her strength. She did not hear or see anyone, or rather heard and saw, but the meaning of it disappeared somewhere in her consciousness.

"He's still alive. Death, it seems, is in no hurry. He's starting to breathe," Valeriea whispered softly to Ross. "But you know... it's all just a matter of time."

He didn't answer her. He couldn't find any words for what he was going through. Not only because of his love, but also because of what he saw. Julien's suffering was part of her brother's suffering, who now lies somewhere even more brutalize than she is. And Sel was dying... That one gloomy thought contained everything he lived through, all past and future. Sel was only moments from death, and he was from dark despair. That was all that mattered...

* * *

"Sorry," Paphian whispered to the semiconscious Oliver, taking him in his arms. "That bloody captain made me late to help."

Oliver whispered only one word softly, expressing the whole state of his soul:

"Julien..."

"You'll see her. I promise," said Paphian.

Unable to walk through the crowd with weight in his arms, he laid him gently on the floor and quickly reached for the vial hidden under his uniform. Oliver was beaten and cut. There was blood wherever he was looked at. It flowed from a broken head. Of the knife-notched grazes on the arms uncovered by the torn gown, extraordinarily delicate for a young man, but utterly natural in a woman whom everyone but Paphian still saw in him. Judging by his symptoms, blood in his mouth and shallow breathing, at least a few of his ribs were broken and internally injured. His face was clearly red from blows. So Paphian did not hesitate, although he knew that they were in real danger. He poured a few drops of his brother's blood, carefully hidden from others, more precious than any gold or the treasures of this kingdom, into the mouth of a mortally wounded friend and hid the rest, though after the movement he realized he had been recognized.

"Brother of the healer," Captain Gereme said shortly to the king, sounded like a bark.

Queen Constance froze, terrified of the consequences of the unmasking's that were about to come, while Viscount Marden, the murderer of the red-haired countess, ran to the viceroy's rooms along with several guards. At the sight of the massacre, he froze in terror and amazement, then looked fearfully at the wounded girl in the arms of the healer brother, wondering what strength and determination she had to win her freedom by defeating three soldiers. The comrades of the dead watched them incredulously for signs of life, but it soon became clear that their hope was in vain. Sten looked with no longer seeing eyes at their behavior, the visible brain after cutting his head presented the horror of its end. His companions presented themselves even worse, as if a demon had passed through the room. There were even traces of blood on the walls.

Slowly many approached to examine the inside of the ruined room, where the traces of fighting were visible everywhere. Some, however, including the royal family, remained with the wounded girl, curious about the effects of the blood, which they had not had the opportunity to observe before.

Oliver's face changed from puffy to delicate in its beauty. The cuts disappeared. The body was healing in the eyes.

The first of a hypnotic view of this unusual phenomenon was the viceroy, and with him his brother.

"What did you have to do with this?" The king asked his brother.

"How do you think?" He heard the hard answer.

At the same moment the fate of the kingdom was on the edge of the knife, and the viceroy lost his patience with any further concealment of his intentions, having taken away a foretaste of the pleasure he had promised himself. He was disappointed and furious with the girl that she was able to defend herself and upset his applecart. He gave his brother a sudden grimace of disgust and anger, finally removing his mask of hypocrisy.

"This whore's place was soon to be taken by your wife!" he uttered the meaningful words.

Like a pre-arranged signal, both sides drew their swords. Above the wounded Oliver, who was slowly recovering, and surprised by the turn of events, Paphian blades ominously shone.

Meron instinctively stood at his father's side, pawning his mother and younger brother. Captain Gereme stood beside them, with the small troop assembled, ready to repel the attack. Queen Constance touched her hand to the dagger hidden in the secret pocket of her dress. In the blink of an eye, from a cheerful, kind-hearted woman, she turned into a warrior ready to fight for herself and her relatives, which was an even more attractive sight for the viceroy.

"The throne will be mine!" he concluded briefly.

But when Captain Gereme gave the order to defend the king, the viceroy unexpectedly withdrew for his people, leaving them to fight. He pulled the accompanying Viscount by the arm:

"Give a signal," he ordered. "Time to start!"

The Viscount pulled out the horn slung over his shoulder and blew it.

Everyone was surprised by the sound of the horn. It was the beginning. A commotion could be heard from the side corridor. From other parts of the castle, similar horn sounds came after a moment. Paphian realized that Delen and Oliver had sought in vain for letters ordering the attack. The horn was a signal. While the royal family undoubtedly expected an attack and at least had a weapon with them, it quickly became clear that the most important one had not been able to find out in time due to an unfortunate coincidence. With no evidence they could not have stopped the viceroy sooner, and it was clear now that they had not prepared a proper defense.

"We're backing out!" The king ordered. "Captain! Summon your people!"

"I see some of these traitors here," the captain replied grimly.

The king looked at his devoted servant, showing no fear. These words were confirmed by the hostile faces surrounding them. And he had a family to save.

"So, we have to defend ourselves!" He replied firmly.

The small squad of the viceroy who had helped him move away towards the growing sounds were killed by the sword blows of faithful guards and members of the royal family. Only Aron did not kill anyone then. Meron did not allow his younger brother, who was only fourteen, to face direct confrontation with the viceroy's soldier. He killed him himself in defense. He allowed himself only a brief moment of fear and grief after killing a human for the first time in his life. He knew he would probably do it more than once that night, and the thought made his throat bitter. But nothing could have made the evil avoidable. Most importantly, his family should be able to count on him right now. He was not just a prince who would one day take the throne after his father defends his legacy. He was the protector of his family, and that was now much more important than the title. His father shook his arm in appreciation and comfort at the same time, and his mother gave him a sad smile. Only Aron seemed disappointed that he did not fight directly and bit his lip. Meron waited only a moment for his brother's anger to explode, certain that he would have done the same if he were in that situation again. It was still a kid. It seemed inconceivable to see him killing a man after seeing him enjoying the sports events held at the castle. Suddenly he felt much older than him, as if the murder had given him years.

He went to Paphian, who retreated with the wounded girl to the viceroy's rooms during the skirmish. Already with a different look, which he had not yet had a few moments ago, he examined the interior. Even in his heart, now numb with terror, the shambles made him uneasy. While his father consulted the captain in a hurry, he crouched down next to the healed woman. Oliver was lying on the floor as a guard with his head cut open was sitting on the bed. The terror of what had happened in the bedroom slowly seeped into Meron's mind like a stench poisoning the air. Was it really possible that this girl who was now battered next door was a part of it all?! He became concerned.

"Paphian," he said. "You have to come with us."

"It's a suicide," Paphian replied calmly. "Get out. They are already coming back."

Judging by the sounds, it had to be true.

"Get your brother out of here," Meron ordered him. "And forgive us for dragging you into this."

That said, he looked at them one last time and left quickly to join his relatives as they departed with the captain from the dangerous part of the castle - the same hidden passage that had drawn Oliver here. After a while, more soldiers appeared in the corridor, but without the viceroy. Paphian did not even have time to consider what strategy the other chose, since he did not fight immediately. Maybe it was really just that the unexpected turn of events with Oliver had mixed it up. Soldiers, some of which were already fighting among themselves, had just noticed them. Several others started down the hidden corridor.

Oliver groaned. He was already recovering. In addition to better and better well-being and returning strength, he felt as if some strange power was forced into his veins, which began to burst him, penetrate his limbs, pump blood, painlessly adjust his bones and make him feel as if he was about to explode. There was something incredibly exciting that he had never experienced before with such force, and it made his face flush with embarrassment when his body, awakened by this extraordinary power, wanted to get rid of the delightful, though at the same time somewhat painful, tension.

Paphian closed the door in front of the guards, who he did not know who was who, because the king's and his brother's men often fought in the same colors and now he was putting a heavy chest of drawers against them. Then he looked at his friend. With a faint surprise, he saw his body begin to tense and his breathing quicken, as if he had been straining.

He quickly understood the cause of this state, and despite the confusion around him and the uninteresting view of the interior, he could hardly hold back a smile.

He knelt beside Oliver and, striving for a serious tone, which he could hardly think of what the other was going through at that moment, said in a rather composed voice:

"I should have warned you. My brother's blood has a very stimulating effect on many people. For example, the best night of your life with a woman."

Oliver looked at him uncertainly, from which Paphian immediately understood that neither the best nor any night with a woman so far had happened in his life. So, he smiled understandingly.

"You'll understand what I'm talking about in a minute."

After a while, they both heard someone trying to break down the door.

"Fortunately, it won't take long," he added gently, completely making no noise at all. "At least you will die happy," he added, smiling, taking his sword just in case.

Hearing his explanation, Oliver tried in vain to stop the overwhelming feeling of utter, bliss overwhelming him. He might as well try to stop the wind.

He realized it very quickly...

* * *

Julien felt the saving power of the healer's blood. And the warmth of Ross' hand holding her. Slowly, but much faster than ever before, her injuries disappeared and healed. Just as quickly her consciousness awoke as if from a dream, not only aided by her brother's obvious concern and anxiety. She tightened her hand on Ross's, her bond with the real other human. She felt her brother's love within her, pulsed in her heart. He mentally apologized to her for the suffering he had caused her. She felt a tear roll down her cheek. He had sacrificed so much time to keep her safe, knowing with cruel awareness what would happen if she did not yield, would run away like a coward, would not put her pride in her pocket, as was said. He risked a loss of honor and mockery for her. Also, for loneliness, because would any girl want a boy who avoided fighting? Because of her, he was partly alone. He was always worried about her because of what was going on in his life. Now too, though he was barely alive himself.

Once, a few years earlier, she had a crush on a boy. Finally, the moment came that they wanted to kiss each other. And since she had been connected to Oliver always and forever, she knew the pleasure of those kisses would fill him too. She was glad about it, because she hoped that a substitute for these feelings would bring him some relief in solitude. Though at the same time she was afraid of hurting him. Peer's kiss was a fulfillment. The most beautiful memory. After that, she had no one left, for she had promised herself that until Oliver was free of Moren, she would not be seeing anyone. She broke off an affair that had no chance of surviving anyway. Oliver, though he tried his best to hide it, he was suffering. The kiss aroused hidden longings in his heart. But there was Moren and his persecution. There were constant skirmishes between the two families who stopped living in harmony with each other because of their children. There was Sel who risked his life to reconcile both sides. A mother who was afraid something bad would happen in the end. In this situation, how was it possible to have a relationship with someone, even for a short time? Any girl that Moren would notice with Oliver would be in danger.

It was the kiss that made the twins realize for the first time that the bond could be a curse, not the pain from the blows they took for granted in their connection.

Now, however, Julien felt the warmth of extraordinary sensations and feelings, which made the elation after the kiss only a weak glow. An unusual fever began to seize her, the source of which was in the heart of her femininity, where she had never felt like this before. The body throbbed and trembled, breaking into something she hadn't known. Likewise, she felt her brother, though she sensed fear and shame in his feelings as well. If she knew where Oliver was now, she would understand a little of his fears, but their gift was limited in that respect. All she felt was a growing, painfully demanding bliss, almost as strongly as her brother. Like a coming storm.

Thunder must have hit...

She looked down at the hand she was still holding, a thud of blood in her ears. She could see the line of the veins, felt a slight roughness inside. Ross didn't just move from bed to bed, as she dared to imagine, not allowing himself, and not yet able to imagine any more with his little experience in these matters. He also worked physically or just kept in shape. His body was harmoniously shaped. It was a real pleasure for the eye. He had a gentle look and a wonderful laugh. He was the embodiment of a woman's desires.

In fact, in her present situation, she didn't care of his taste...

So, when he looked at her, interested in her movement, with concern in her eyes mixed with sadness, she succumbed to this gaze immensely. Ignoring the surprised glances of the others, or of the boy himself, she grabbed him by the shirt with unexpected force, pulled him to her and kissed him. Gently and possessively at the same time. He tried to resist, but there was something about the healer's blood imparted to her, some aura and power that gave him no chance to defend himself. Ross, in spite of his whole life, succumbed to the kiss of a young girl. Helpless in the face of the unusual element in this kiss, he slowly laid Sel down, barely realizing it. He kissed her back. He couldn't resist. Subtly and sensually, as if just getting to know the taste of a woman's lips. The astonished observers of this event were shocked by the passion of this kiss. Ross kissed Julien like the embodiment of their desires. As if they were not separated by a gulf in life experiences and choices. Valeriea has never seen Ross with a woman. His kiss was a double surprise to her. She smiled warmly as, with so much emotion, Ross was embraced by Julien.

She doubted that, when this extraordinary moment had passed, he would be truly delighted with it. She knew the strength of his feelings for Sel. What she saw now could be nothing more than a spell cast, or at least something completely inconceivable and impossible. It wouldn't change that fast. And not when Sel was dying.

Julien released Ross with a soft sigh, letting him simply collapse onto the bed, stunned and devastated by the experience.

Ross couldn't explain to himself what made him do it.

And it quickly turned out that the kiss also had other effects than inexpressible pleasure.

He felt an ubiquitous, unusual heat, not caused by excitement, of which he was sure. His body was overwhelmed by the warmth that came from his stomach and legs. He was almost on fire with a sudden fever. He pulled himself up from the bed, staring at no one, feeling nauseated and dizzy. He was sure it wasn't because he hated Julien. The kiss was wonderful, though he was afraid to admit it to himself. Something much worse was happening with him. Something that filled his thoughts with fear and his body trembling.

"Ross," Valeriea, concerned about his condition, quickly stepped back beside him, helping him to stand his feet. "What's wrong?!"

Sai and Lena looked at him surprised by his reaction, though they could have sworn they hadn't seen him resist earlier. But above him, at the same time, they saw Julien bending over the deathly pale Sel. This made them no longer know what to really think about it all. The air seemed almost to sparkle with extraordinary power.

Len helped Valeriea lead the trembling Ross outside, where he immediately vomited. The vortices shook him again and again, as if the body were demanding a rapid cleansing of the effects of a strange poison.

"You think it's a plague?" She asked worriedly to her companion as Ross shaken up and shook everything he ate.

"I don't know," Len nodded negatively. "Actually, I think a healer worked here," he summed up his thoughts, and it was one of the few times when he said so many words in a short time.

"Healer? Through Oliver to Julien?! And to Ross?"

"They're twins bound together."

She wondered.

"But if Ross felt it like that, then he was sick..."

They froze, stunned by this statement. From the small balcony they could barely see the escaping road. After a while, the car stopped.

Alesei has arrived.

"You must see this!" Sai suddenly called them, "Sel is recovering from her kiss!"

Ross sat up, weakened by the nausea and the force of the unusual heat that had now cooled at last. Sai's words made him stand up and as soon as possible he returned to the bed, though he staggered as if drunk. Len and Valeriea were there moments later, and Alesei looked on the other side.

Watching Ross sit down next to her lover and Julien, Valeriea felt both relieved and joyful.

Her young friend, whom she had always treated a bit like her son because of his age difference, had escaped death. She was pretty sure it was the plague. She saw the gravedigger's sinister gesture, and so did Ross. And then she felt almost this immense fear.

It must have been the plague.

* * *

The pounding on the door stopped suddenly and there was silence. From outside you could hear raised voices, short orders, hasty consultations. Paphian listened, tactfully trying not to look at Oliver, who was almost writhing with his overwhelming emotions. He knew a way to ease him, he just didn't know if he could really suggest it. Oliver was rather secretive about such emotions as he thought.

He was worried about his brother. Is he still safe? After all, it wouldn't be in the interest of the viceroy in the time of the plague to kill a healer?!

"Paphian?" He suddenly heard the familiar voice of Delen, the lieutenant of the guard "Are you still there? The captain said you took Selena here. Talk to me. Are you alive? Is she healthy?"

"Oh no," Oliver whispered at that. "Not him. I don't need it..."

"We are safe and sound!" Paphian shouted back.

"Open up! We have to get you out of here!"

Paphian glanced at Oliver.

"What have you got to him?" he became interested.

"Nothing," Oliver forced himself not to shout it.

He felt his soul tearing with desire, and at the same time, like a blow, the desire to fulfill a secret dream that undoubtedly came from Julien. He wanted to scream.

He remembered that feeling. Julien was just about to kiss someone

"Only he," he said with an effort. "He knew my sister. Do you remember… what I told you? I mean Celina."

Paphian looked at him understandingly. He did not envy him what he was going through. Although at the same time he had a hard time controlling himself not to smile.

"He likes me!" Oliver added despairingly.

This completed the picture of the bizarre and humor of the whole situation.

"Moment!" Paphian shouted back, rising.

"Moment is too long!" He heard the answer.

"I can't not let him in," Paphian replied a little helplessly, looking at Oliver's torment.

At the same time, Julien kissed Ross...

Oliver inhaled loudly, perhaps too loudly.

Behind the door, Delen and his men looked at each other in surprise. Delen felt a pang in his heart. And unexpected anger.

"What are you doing there?!" He asked.

Paphian rushed to Oliver and put his hand over his mouth. Still, he couldn't suppress a groan, and the distraught Oliver felt the effects of the double desire all over his body. He passed out from the excess of experienced emotions.

Luckily, he didn't feel the effects of Julien's second kiss then, but conveyed a feeling of fulfillment to her...

* * *

Julien moved closer, ignoring what was happening around him, and kissed the barely alive Sel on the blue lips. Her soul, just like after a slap on the cheek, took double everything that her brother had passed on to her. No one in the world, except the healer himself, had a clue that in twins with spiritually connected hearts, the power of the healing gift would affect not only them, but everyone they touch at that moment.

Julien didn't think it might be inappropriate. She liked Sel, whom she always treated as a friend. Until now, she hadn't thought otherwise of him, nor had she thought of Ross. But the gift changed everything. The healer's blood acted like wine. Sel cautiously began to kiss her back, though he didn't even open his eyes. Then, as if the kiss gave him strength with every passing moment, his reciprocity grew more passionate. Finally, Julien broke away from him, which was surprisingly harder for her than for kissing Ross. Only then he opened his eyes.

He stared at the girl in amazement. Julien looked at him conscious, as surprised as he was by his behavior. Though neither of them had said a word about it, both realized that sympathy would not be enough for what had just happened between them. This feeling must have sprouted before. The surprise, however, was not only the disclosure, but the fact that he unexpectedly had an equal bond with someone he had never consciously thought of in this way.

Outside observers watched this scene curious about the further development of events. Their curiosity was satisfied almost immediately. Sel began to change. His face turned from gray slowly to a reddened red, and his eyes shone with a different glow. The lips were no longer blue. In the silence, he suddenly gasped as if he couldn't take a breath for a long time, then began to breathe very quickly. Frightened by his condition, his hands tightened on the sheets, and Julien and Ross fell to him at first frightened, but then a smile and disbelief appeared on their faces almost simultaneously, and then appeared on the faces of the watching women and Len, who shook his head with a laugh for this amazing event.

"What were you doing when I was gone?" Alesei was amazed.

"Wish you came sooner," Sai smiled.

"What did I miss?"

"Kiss of love, man," Len laughed and left to check the area.

The women sat on the bed and gently calmed Sel, shocked by the sudden change and what was still happening to him. He had the impression that someone had given him a life-giving potion straight into his blood, which melted from the mouth all over his body, soothingly warm. At first the changes were sudden, he felt as if his heart was about to burst, all he heard was the rushing of blood and the pounding of a rapidly accelerating pulse. And then, like a receding wave, everything began to soften and fade away...

The most important feeling, however, was, paradoxically, that now he no longer felt pain, only his own free, effortless breathing. He listened to himself in disbelief. Nothing happened. His own body did not refuse to obey him. He wasn't choking. He was still scared, and his heart was pounding as if it was about to pop out of his chest, but nothing bad happened to him. For years, taught to be cautious and restrained, he could hardly control himself not to scream now. Suddenly, the freedom he had obtained made him intoxicated. But because he has always tried to be prudent in action, he has not forgotten where they are now and the danger they face. Therefore, he allowed himself only silent happiness. He hugged Julien and Ross, hugged them tightly against him, then cried out. He was crying against their warmth, hugging them tightly, so tightly as he had never been able to before. Until he calmed down, they held him in their arms.

* * *

Despite the inflamed situation in the castle, the curious guards peeked in to study them as soon as Paphian opened the door. However, what they saw outside of them made the smirks die on their lips. This squad has not yet seen the battlefield in the viceroy's bedroom. Therefore, they were all the more surprised at what they heard before. The brutality with which the treacherous guards were killed would hardly be conducive to the intimate experiences the two suspected. The mere fact that petty Selena might somehow contribute to such a violent death of her captors was beyond their minds.

Delen, pretending tactfully, as the only one, unfortunately, that he did not suspect anything, became interested in the fainted girl.

"I gave her my brother's blood," Paphian whispered to him, deciding that disclosure would be the best solution for this situation. "Heals every wound and puts you in a good mood."

Delen did not comment on what he thought of this rather unusual, but plausible sounding explanation, as he had a brother healer in front of him. And what is his opinion on what this "good mood" could have set a girl in by Paphian actions. He glanced at the bodies of the dead, but now did not consider what he saw. Seeing that the dress was torn, he took off his cloak in concern for the girl and covered her with obvious concern. Paphian felt uncomfortable to see that Oliver was right about the lieutenant's sympathy, and he was grateful that he did not know why the "girl" fainted. Oliver awoke as Delen contemplated how to move him to safety, and seeing him, then feeling the touch of his cloak, instantly recovered.

"I feel much better," he said, leaping to his feet, which ended the lieutenant's dilemma. "I can go wherever you want."

Hiding the real source of confusion, he pretended to be cloaked more tightly because he was constrained by the gazes of the guards watching him. It turned out so well that Paphian wanted to clap him. He bit his lip, however, and ran his hand over the slight stubble to conceal the amusement that Oliver could sense well.

"Are you sure?" Delen asked anxiously, to which Paphian pretended to be still seeing the effects of the destruction in the bedroom, but even that sight had a hard time keeping him calm.

"Yes," Oliver replied, his voice strong, maybe even a little too loud, seeing his behavior out of the corner of his eye.

"Let's go then," Delen decided.

"Wait," Paphian steadied himself and grabbed his arm. "What about my brother?"

"He's safe. It is in the interests of both royal brothers to keep him alive."

"I want to get him out of here!"

Delen looked at him. Through vague suspicions about what was happening in the viceroy's room and loyalty to his brother, he pondered his decision. Finally, he looked at his people and Selena.

The sympathy he felt for the imprisoned Vivan and the fragile Selena won. He smiled. His people too.

"I think we can help you with that," he replied.

CHAPTER 9 — Crazy escape

Returning from the part of the castle reserved for the royal family and the closest royal associates proved much more difficult than arriving. The hidden corridor was the site of the skirmish. In others, members of the guard protected the lives of the surprised nobles who did not side with the viceroy. There was chaos everywhere and there were fights. The corridors quickly became the scene of clashes between the king's supporters and his traitors. Delen was leading the two friends through the confusion, trying to avoid direct contact with the skirmish scene. He and his men surrounded the little woman with their protection, not letting them come near her, though at times this proved impossible. Several times with a well-aimed sling shot in the eye or face, Oliver changed the result of the duel between the guard from Delen's unit and the king's traitors. Once, his effective method of distracting, or rather dissipation, the enemy even helped the lieutenant himself. This was met with his gratitude, expressed in a warm smile, quite different from those Oliver had seen in him before, which made him feel guilty. He no longer wanted to cheat on this nice man who was obviously beginning to have feelings for Selena. So, he was grateful to fate that they were finally in the corridor that connected to the one leading to Vivan's room. It was definitely time to shed her disguise and get Selena out of the way before she caused too much trouble.

They were there after nearly two hours of clashes, which seemed unbelievable, but since they tried to slip away rather unnoticed, and additionally, once or twice, they helped defend this or that man of the king, it was not so strange. It was quiet here. The corridors under the clock tower were empty.

"Weird," Delen muttered. "Stay alert!"

As they reached the corridor leading to the healer, the clock in the tower chimed midnight. The steady, calm blows of the bell were a remarkable contrast to the fighting around them.

The rooms were open. Oliver shuddered to see the beautiful countess still lying on the bed in the viceroy's room. At the sight of her, the guards were clearly sad, because although her lush social life was sometimes the subject of jokes among soldiers, they always had a certain sympathy for her because of her temperament and beauty.

Paphian felt a mounting anxiety. He broke forward in front of the unit, torn by fear, and burst into his brother's room, sword in hand.

After a while it became clear to him and the others that the room and bedroom were empty.

Vivan wasn't there...

* * *

Len got into the cart and sat down heavily in the empty armchair.

"Ramoz is on the left. Moren on the right. The two of them are probably discussing how to get our shit out."

There was silence for a moment. Ross glanced at Sel. As the euphoria of his rapidly recovering health faded, Sel fell silent and retreated into himself. Julien avoided both of them, standing restlessly against the wall, ready to jump or scream if someone spoke to her, so she was left to her thoughts. Each word of Sel sank into Ross's soul, each gesture now had a secondary meaning, bitter and inevitable. Ross looked for signs of a definitive breakup. For now, that Sel was healthy, though he was still not fit, he could be with whomever he wanted, and it was obviously a woman again. But if he could read his mind, he would understand how wrong he was. Sel was far from such decisions, though the kiss caused a stir in his heart, both literally and figuratively. Matters of feelings weren't the most important things for him now, though. He still hasn't gotten used to the sudden change for the better in his health.

There were also reasons too fresh and painful that his two friends, agitated by the unusual situation, seemed to have forgotten.

But he did not forget.

"It's time to prepare."

"Only the three of you don't have a weapon yet," replied Len.

Sai and Lena nodded, as did Valeriea. Alesei was patrolling the area with a sword, crossbow, and dagger at hand. Everything that could be useful was stolen by Ross and the assembled men from customers of the House of Pleasure. Sel was impressed with their preparation.

Len handed Ross a sword and dagger. Julien only chose the latter. Sel chose the crossbow. He was not suitable for direct combat. Not now.

"What's next?" Sai asked. "We hide like rats in the sewers?"

"Not Sai," Sel replied with the smile they had seen so far in a much weaker version. "We smoke out the wild animal before it attacks us."

They hadn't even had time to consider the idea when suddenly the car door slammed open. To the surprised eyes Alesei appeared with a blade to his throat, and behind him stood the leader of the Red Guard himself, the second after Moren's group of thugs in the city. His face, bearing the traces of riotous life, was that of an unrepentant pirate. Rumor had it that he was secretly engaged in slavery on a large scale.

"Well, then you guys are late!" Ramoz roared, not hiding his satisfaction "The beast jumped down your throats!"

Before anyone could react, Julien ran to the window, opened it and, with catlike agility, with the help of a chest of drawers and an unexpected strength, famous mainly for her brother, she pulled herself to the roof. Ramoz's astonished people, who sooner expected that the girl would just pop out, reacted a little too late, which was enough for inexperienced future defenders of the healer. Alesei pulled his hand with the threatening dagger and pulled back from his grip. Ramoz cursed ugly as the hostage quickly climbed the railings in the wake of Julien, and Len closed the door in his face. Sai, Lena and Valeriea started throwing whatever they could get their hands on Ramoz's people through the open window. Julien jumped on the goat. One of Ramoz's men tried to grab her, but at that moment Sel opened the door and punched him in the face with a crossbow. Julien grabbed the reins and urged the harnessed horses. The cart started moving. Ramoz staggered and fell from the small balcony, and Alesei slipped inside the cart through the window, with the help of the women. Ross grabbed Len's bow and quiver, opened the door, and drew the string on the first arrow. Time and time again he fired his arrows just in front of the legs of their pursuers, forcing them to stop abruptly and dodge until they were far enough away.

"Rebecca always said you should be an archer in the royal army, remember?" Len said to him, looking at the bow in his hands. "She had a good eye for people."

Ross smiled sadly, remembering the first time she had mentioned it.

It was not without reason that the inhabitants of the House of Pleasure called her the Mother, although sometimes she could have her own moods and screamed pretty well at the same time. But they knew they could rely on her.

The cart shook violently as the horses reared, neighing. Ross and Len looked to the open door on the other side. Between Julien and Sel, someone stepped out to meet the rushing horses.

They only knew one madman ready to do this.

As he walked, Ross felt a worried handshake from Valeriea. He took that hand tightly, trying to comfort it. Sai and Lena instinctively hid behind Len, as in the recent times when he was working as their home security. Their eyes met for a moment, expressing the same fear.

Alesei cursed ugly.

"Well, well," said Moren, smiling wickedly as his companions aimed their crossbows at those sitting on the coach-box. "And yet we met again..."

* * *

"Maybe they went to the royal chambers," Delen suggested, seeing Paphian's despondency and fury. "Or to the armory."

"This bond of yours," Paphian ignored his words, walking quickly to the surprised Oliver. "She can't tell us where he is?"

Oliver looked around confused. Delen and some of his companions looked at him in surprise.

"Bond?" the lieutenant was surprised. "What bond? What are you talking about?"

Oliver took a breath to control himself, and the nervous Paphian quickly realized his mistake.

"I have a twin sister," Oliver replied tremblingly. "Me and Celina..." he looked significantly at Paphian "we come from a large family."

But Delen continued to stare suspiciously.

"How do you know each other?" He asked, looking at both of them "You didn't say that..."

"There was no occasion to confide," Oliver interrupted quickly, giving Paphian a short, murderous glare.

"Their father once worked on repairing our house," Paphian thought while waiting to save the situation. "I guess it doesn't matter now, right? I want to know where my brother is!" He almost shouted the last words. It wasn't just mock anger.

Delen took the outburst calmly, frowning in thought. Oliver was sure he now recalled all the information Celina had given him about her family. His attention had to be distracted as quickly as possible.

"It does not work like that. I cannot switch to someone else."

"You probably haven't tried," this time more consciously, Paphian remembered in what form he should address.

"He's not my brother. I regret it, but I can't help you," Oliver replied, trying not to get irritated. On the other hand, he understood his uneasiness. "But I think the viceroy has him with him. He's too valuable to be accidentally killed or returned to the hands of a king. He will put him where he can be sure no one is looking for him now. Is there such a place here?"

"He wants to take the throne, right?" Asked the redheaded guard from Delen's unit. "Maybe they are in the Throne Room. Or..." He paused for a moment, seeing that he had attracted everyone's attention. "Maybe he has Vivan held there until he comes back. You know, he'll take the throne, a healer will be his slave... Who would be looking into the Throne Room now?"

The others looked at each other.

"Well," Paphian said to the young guard, his cheeky smile returning to his face. "This is a good idea to start with."

"How can we get there?" Oliver asked Delen.

"To avoid fighting, preferably the Arched Corridor outside the rooms. Otherwise, we will fight our way again."

"Let's go!" Paphian commanded shortly.

The guards checked that their lieutenant agreed with this to be sure, and after a while they all followed, taking Selena under discreet protection again. Delen passed Paphian to show the way. His thoughts, however, did not stop around the girl. She was hiding something, and Paphian with her. He hoped to learn the truth in due time...

* * *

"What did I tell you, Sel?" Moren asked as he gathered everyone in front of the cart. "You were supposed to be on your ass! AT MY PLACE!!"

Sel was silent. He tried his best to look like the old one, that is, terminally ill, though his vitality was almost overwhelming him, and his eyes sparkled with animation. With a little effort, however, and with the make-up still spooky when smeared, it could be done. He made Moren treat him like an opponent again.

"Where's that male slut who helped you get away?" Moren looked around quickly, examining the captured ones. "It's you!" He found Ross with his eyes. "You don't have that makeup on your face, but it's you, you bastard! I recognize you!"

Ross, knowing how those who had exposed themselves to Moren's wrath would end up, remained cautiously silent, looking into his eyes. Moren looked at him closely, looking for a gesture or a word of provocation. For a moment he gasped in disappointment.

"I need an ass," he said defiantly, watching his face. "Before dear brother shows up," he bowed to Julien, who looked at him angrily, "I want to have fun. We already have a place. How much are you taking?" He smiled venomously at his victim. "Ah, I would have forgotten! We're not in the brothel anymore. I don't have to pay you!"

Ross instinctively cut emotions from what Moren was doing, as he always did when the client did not arouse his sympathy, was a boorish man or an exceptional disgusting man. In this profession, personal feelings were not important, only customer satisfaction. And money. Anyone who had the same connection quickly got into trouble, drank themselves, or committed suicide. Although Ross had gained experience in this profession for only three years, he quickly realized that emotions would not help him survive. He looked at Moren with the cold gaze of the old professional, inspiring respect from the others. And the growing fear for his fate.

To keep this calm, he tried not to look at Sel.

Moren slapped him in the face.

Ross tasted his own blood from the split lip, but his expression didn't change. "So what?" His eyes said.

"Don't feel sorry for yourself," he said in a slightly provocative tone, as when he encouraged uncertain customers.

He saw that these words encouraged the bandit to continue beating. He had a feeling this was going to happen since Moren had found him. Such people have had to vent their aggression on someone - one way or another. Otherwise, the pants started to hurt them.

Better to let him get beaten up than to let him take him by force out of revenge on Sel. He would probably survive it somehow. But Sel, or poor, innocent Julien, probably not. It would be a tremendous shock for them, indelible for the rest of their lives.

Moren took a second blow...

"I can see that the fun is in full swing!" Suddenly they heard a familiar voice.

Ramoz and his men turned back for their horses, and now, sitting in their saddles, they slowly moved out into a small clearing where the cart was stopped.

"What the hell do you want?!" Moren hated being interrupted at anything.

The fastest he was able to upset him. Sel knew it perfectly well. Taking advantage of Ramoz's sudden appearance, he slowly approached his surrounded friends.

"Give me the cart!" Ramoz replied carelessly, and his coal-black eyes met all of them with a careful glance. He waved his hand, pointing to the women: "And these two whores," Lena squeezed Sai's hand. "Anyway, have fun as you like."

Sai looked at him with apparent calmness, under which there was a cold fury. Each meeting with him cost them both. And he was never alone. There were several companions.

Unfortunately, Sai didn't know how and, to tell you the truth, she didn't want to give up her emotions, which was what Ross was so good at. The reason for this was simple. So far no one has humiliated and treated their friend exceptionally mean.

But they both do.

Sai wanted Ramoz dead since Lena cried for the first time after spending the night in his company. She especially wanted him to die for that. Fate was almost pushing him into her hands.

Moren confronted Ramoz. They both only had a few people. The fact that the opponent's men were on horses, he didn't care at all. He had crossbows. They looked at each other for a moment.

Then suddenly, as if on command, they burst out laughing, and then their people joined them uncertainly. It was not a sincere laugh, however, but a show. For not a moment they didn't take their eyes off them. Ramoz, always suspicious, which more than once saved his thug life - he also carefully watched the movement behind Moren's back. He saw the opponent's old friend standing behind the back of the bully who had so defended Rebecca - Mother - and whom several whores interceded for when he wanted to kill him. They were afraid that there would be no one to defend them. Now Sel was cutting his bonds quickly with a dagger because the idiot Moren hadn't even bothered to search him. Did he really believe that even the terminally ill would not be able to use the blade when the opportunity arose? Incredible stupidity. He waited this moment for the anticipated game to take on more flavor, until Sel freed Len. When the ties broke, Len slapped a startled Sheron in the face. Ramoz drew his sword and this time his smile was sincere and full of mockery.

To the limit.

"Swords!" He shouted, and his organized people quickly reached for their scabbards. "Kill that fool!" He pointed at Moren.

Sel rushed to sever Ross and Alesea's bonds. Ross and Alesei helped the women to the carriage.

"Len ride!" Alesei shouted, happy that Ramoz and Moren were so engaged in the skirmish that they had almost forgotten them. But it wasn't long before he was able to enjoy it.

"The cart!! Hell, you damned foes!" Cried Ramoz. "Chase them!"

Moren turned pale with rage. Sel slipped out of his hands, taking Julien with him. He didn't even fight him. He couldn't understand because his feelings were too selfish that Sel preferred to take his friends to safety before the final showdown took place. Everyone he cared about now would be far away then, so that the unpredictable Moren could not reach them anymore.

"To the horses!!" Moren yelled to his men until the veins swelled in his temple. "They are mine! And only mine!"

A mad chase has begun.

Len urged the horses on with loud shouts, while Ramoz and his men, followed closely by Moren and his remnants, now united for one purpose, followed him. The wagon creaked and shook in the swiftly curved alleys to the entrance to the garden. There was no way the horses of the pursuers would catch up with the cart at the gate. It was too narrow for that. So, they had to withdraw. They wasted precious moments while the speeding wagon pulled into the road leading to the castle, which the food wagon was driving over in the morning, almost at the same pace. Few fires and torches burned in the nearby market place. Ross took his bow again and, heavy-hearted, aimed at the first of Ramoz's men. He's never killed anyone before. The bow and arrow seemed to be an extension of his body. He released the string. Reliably, as Mother Rebecca felt, the arrow hit the target and hit the heart.

He almost felt the same pain.

Len rode among the assembled people to slow down the chase. Now it was throwing the cart as it maneuvered between the narrow aisles at the few, as yet undressed stalls. People fled in fear, cursing and screaming. It was the middle of the night, but not everyone was asleep, waiting impatiently for dawn.

Safe from his seat on the roof of the little house, Tenan watched as the white car sped toward the city streets, and Moren rode by, almost at the rear wheels. On the other side, Ramoz rode on horseback, cursing the world.

This favored his intentions, so he smiled slightly, his pale eyes brightened.

In the first of the wider streets of Verdom, leading to the square where executions or other celebrations were taking place, a man escaping with his family lost a bag of grain. The sack fell straight into the horse's dung, but that didn't deter the street beggars. They tore it apart and a fierce battle for prey ensued, as a result of which one of them died. The others had left the body, and as the gravediggers were dwindling and the night it was approaching, the body was still there.

Len, who was a great coachman among the people at the marketplace, because he was helped by the lights of fires and torches, as he was leaving the bend, he did not notice the corpse in time in the dark street. He ran over it, crashing bones. The wagon tipped to one side and dropped abruptly.

Two rats screeched along the way.

Frightened by this, the horses reared and, deciding to run away, threw themselves to the side. Len fell inside the car, and then, forced to turn in place, the cart tilted, throwing people around. It rocked dangerously.

Then it fell....

* * *

Delen led his small squad through the Arched Corridor. The crazy architect who designed the entire castle, this time limited himself to white walls and arches, which was a real relief for the eyes. A bit-tired people, except for Oliver, in whose veins still circulated the healer's blood, giving him strength and energy, were disappointed in going outside. Instead of the expected coolness of the night, they found a stuffy air devoid of wind. In the blink of an eye their bodies were covered in sweat.

"Not a single cloud," remarked one of the lieutenant's men resentfully. "Where is the goddamn storm, when is it needed?"

Entering the corridors leading, among others, to the Throne Room, they avoided direct clashes with the viceroy's soldiers as much as possible. However, this was not always the case.

"By the queen's orders, we are to take you and Vivan to safety," Delen explained shortly between each skirmish. "Of course, this also applies to your friends," he looked at Oliver warmly, which made Oliver feel uncomfortable, especially since he encountered a much meaningful Paphian smirk after a while. "Hell, I'm going to obey this order!"

"You got in pretty well," said Paphian.

"It's not easy," Delen remarked, stopping everyone and carefully peering around the bend of the corridor leading to the Throne Room.

Outside and inside the hall swarmed with the viceroy's soldiers. He cursed foully.

"What's up?" Paphian asked shortly, ready to look too, but Delen stopped him.

"Too many for us," he said shortly.

"Really?" Paphian muttered, deftly freeing himself to take a peek.

He returned to them grimly.

"I can't see inside. I don't know if Vivan is there."

"I can check," Oliver said. "No problem."

"How?" Delen was surprised.

"I'll go down from the roof to the windows of the hall and take a look."

Now everyone's attention was focused on him without exception.

"Repeat, sun," said the dark-haired man from Delen's unit. "You said: I'll get off the roof?!"

Oliver nodded. Delen stared at him for a long moment.

"You have amazing talents," he noted. "But it might take too long."

"Long?" Oliver considered the possibility only for a moment, but he was already in his element. "No," he said. "The designer of this castle did not spare on cornices, arches and other ornaments. Be right back."

They did not reflect. Delen opened one of the windows, and the others huddled nearby so as not to miss the beginning of the expedition.

"Take care of yourself," he said, taking Oliver's hand politely to help him climb onto the windowsill.

Bewildered by the lieutenant's ever-increasing interest and the eloquent glances of his men, Oliver blinked rapidly several times, his face flushing. Delen was delighted with the girl's sensitivity. He stared into her blue eyes.

"Selena," he said softly, "come back to us."

And before Oliver could somehow prevent it, he kissed him softly on the lips.

The storm of feelings he felt then he could not even define. But he was sure that he had never experienced anything like this before, and nothing had surprised him more than the discovery of the cause of Moren's mysterious behavior.

Paphian grunted significantly, urging him to hurry, and the moment was gone.

Delen let go of the stunned Oliver as he fought with himself to somehow control himself.

Someone tried to whistle, but stopped in time. Circumstances were not favorable for this.

Feeling his face burn, Oliver gave everyone one last look, meeting friendly looks and smirks. Paphian gave him courage with a gesture. Only he knew more about him than the others. Oliver took a deep breath and left, climbing the carvings and arches like a circus performer, amazing everyone with his lightness and dexterity.

"Hey," the black-haired man whispered loudly behind him. "What about the dress? Does this not bother you?"

The remark met Delen's gloomy gaze.

"Excuse me, Lieutenant," the man stuttered, only a little puzzled by the look. "Bad habits."

* * *

"And how are our affairs?" Asked the viceroy, sitting comfortably on the throne.

He almost felt how wonderful it would be in the future, which had just begun to come true.

"The Queen and her children are gone," replied the Viscount angrily. "The king blocked our way. I couldn't see where they went."

Terlan stood reluctantly, reflecting.

"They didn't leave him. Constance won't do it. They are still in the castle."

"But where?"

"Think you fool!" Shouted the viceroy, striking him suddenly in the forehead with his open hand. "They must be coming here! What about my brother?"

"He locked himself in the room. We're breaking the door. There is a chasm at the bottom. It can only escape us into death."

"Others?"

"We got the Grand Chancellor. He is sitting in the dungeons. We remove the rest as ordered."

"Where's the medic?"

"Recently he was searching the rooms downstairs with his unit. He'll be here soon."

"Stay alert. We follow the plan."

The Viscount bowed and left the hall. The viceroy looked around to make sure all the soldiers were ready. It was time to move and reach for the last asset. Despite some minor complications, his plan worked. He looked at the healer standing under guard. He didn't look very good. But he didn't have to look good. It is important that he was standing on his feet.

"Do you congratulate yourself on your success?" Vivan said softly.

Terlan stood before him in all his glory. Proud and victorious. As he looked at him, he wondered what was it about this man that, despite all attempts to suppress it, he felt the weight of remorse deep within his soul. The fact that his attitude, gaze, mere presence evoked such feelings in him aroused the anger of the viceroy. He didn't want to feel guilty about what he was doing.

It had to be a healer. It was he who influenced his mood.

"Don't try your tricks," he said to him. "You're not changing anything."

Vivan looked at him closely. He didn't understand at first. Then he realized that somewhere in the viceroy's heart there was a struggle with conscience. A fight he had nothing to do with. He did not have the power to influence the mood. However, the knowledge that the viceroy was eatin' up by something cheered him up. Let him think it is because of him...

"We're leaving!" Terlan ordered grimly, eyeing him again.

But like it had happened many times before, he did not cause this fear in the young healer now.

Suddenly, as Terlan turned, Vivan felt an irresistible urge to look at the windows to the left. He sensed a familiar presence.

He glanced at it.

He saw Oliver in disguise, peering into the Throne Room. Fear of being detected made his heart beat for a moment.

Almost immediately, as soon as their eyes met, he looked away.

After a while he felt that the man was gone.

"My lord!" A familiar voice called, and the Court Medic Sedon walked in. "We have Queen Constance!"

He hesitated suddenly, seeing the imprisoned healer and his condition.

"What's he doing here?" He asked nervously. "He was going to be released. That is why I joined you!"

Vivan gave him a grim look. He respected Sedon's knowledge, but apparently the medic was naive to believe the viceroy's words.

"Where she is?!" Asked the viceroy, regaining his former resonance and pride when he heard the news.

"Vivan, I…" Sedon stuttered, clearly puzzled.

"Great medic", thought the Healer contemptuously, losing all respect for him.

"Speak up now!!" The viceroy grabbed the confused man by the shoulders, shaking him. "Or I will order to dehiding you!"

"You need me!" Sedon hissed in response, finally regaining his composure. "I'm the best medic in the kingdom, and there's a plague outside. The deal was clear! Vivan was about to get his freedom!!"

They looked at each other angrily for a moment.

"He'll get it back!" Replied the viceroy through clenched teeth. "On my terms! Get him!"

The obedient soldiers seized the struggling medic.

"You cannot…!" He began angrily.

"Either you tell me immediately where the queen is, or I have my men handcuff you and lead you after me like an obedient mongrel, and then you won't be able to enjoy the abundance you want! You will eat like a dog and sleep like a dog, and for any objection I will beat you like a disobedient dog!"

Sedon trembled with rage and humiliation. But he knew the viceroy's threat was very real.

"She's in the west tower chamber. My people are watching over her," he said finally.

"Alone?"

"Yes."

"It must be a trick," the viceroy thought for a moment. "Watch her!" He ordered the medic, gesturing for the soldiers to release him. "And I'll escort our healer to the door."

"So, you will set him free after all." Relief crossed Sedon's face. "Take the secret exit out of town, as agreed?"

Now even the viceroy's face showed contempt for this man. It only lasted a moment.

"Yes," he replied deftly lying. "I'll take him out."

Vivan sensed a hidden threat in these words. A chill seized him.

* * *

As Oliver went upstairs, he suddenly noticed some movement. A little further away, someone descended on a rope to the chambers one floor below and peered through one of the windows. After a while he gave the signal, hooting as an owl and several other people suddenly appeared on the roof. He heard angry voices through the open window in the Throne Room. He recognized the voice of the Court Medic and heard the Viceroy's threat against him. The damned traitor! A naive fool!

"It could be a trick," the viceroy was saying about the queen's whereabouts, as the mysterious people from the roof slid down the same path as their predecessor on the ropes. One of them noticed him against the wall.

To his surprise, Oliver saw Prince Meron.

They all disappeared inside the chamber below. Oliver looked toward the tower where the queen had been locked up. She was not far from here. And some people were creeping up its walls...

Except that the viceroy is going to get Vivan somewhere first. He will not fall into a trap that they do not know. Cautiously and swiftly, he descended to where the Prince Meron had disappeared. At the sight of him, a large squad hidden in the chamber instinctively drew their swords. He saw several familiar faces besides the prince, including the lieutenant's brother.

"The viceroy won't come here," he said. "He's taking the healer somewhere. He sensed a trick."

"Then we split up," said the prince. "Tell my father I'll follow my uncle. After he deals with the medic, he'll join me."

One of the soldiers bowed and went out the window. The prince and his men waited for the Medic to pass the chamber. He was alone, in accordance with the words of this brave girl. Kirian looked at the window where she had just been standing on the windowsill. She was gone...

* * *

"We saw everything," the black-haired one greeted Oliver with a slight rebuke in his voice.

However, hearing the news the girl had to deliver, he grew serious. Paphian immediately decided that he was following his brother, and while Julien and her companions stood in front of Moren, they emerged from hiding and followed the viceroy down the corridor.

They managed to see him the moment he led Vivan out of the castle through the side passage that led to the servants' corridors that Oliver had been pacing in the morning - though it seemed so long ago now.

It was then that the Viscount and his squad emerged. Oliver felt his anger rise at the sight of him. Murderer of Countess Weren!

"Is it easy for you to kill defenseless women?" He hissed furiously "A murderer and a fool blindly obeying orders! Neither you nor the viceroy will taste the power you so desire!"

Paphian looked at the agitated Oliver, who surprised everyone with his behavior so many times today. Did he hear the cruelty in that voice? No. Only regret and anger. He thought once more of what had really happened in the viceroy's chamber up there. He still didn't believe the boy was behind the massacre. His considerations did not last longer than a moment, while Delen and his men realized that they were facing the beautiful countess's murderer and opponents, so they drew their swords. There was no other way to get to the viceroy. They had to fight it. Delen threw the dagger to the girl, having no better weapon yet, and his squad almost automatically covered her with themselves. Paphian stood at Oliver's side, looking at the pale Viscount. "You're scared," he remarked contemptuously. "And rightly so."

His guess was confirmed by the dark-haired man, who apparently liked every woman he encountered.

"Don't worry, sun," he said to Oliver, "He will pay for the countess's death."

Delen confirmed his words with a slight nod.

When Oliver obtained a sword during the fight and killed the first human in his life, his sister ran away with the others in a white carriage.

Delen clashed with the Viscount and cut off his head. It ended the fight. The remaining traitors died at the hands of his people. Paphian, anxious that this incident would delay his brother's release, wanted to move on when suddenly Oliver dropped his sword and screamed shrilly. His hand snapped completely suddenly, which in the sudden silence of the deserted corridor sounded like a slap on the door and made everyone instinctively twitch in surprise and terror. The other hand, from elbow to wrist, was covered with many deeper or shallower cuts, quickly spilling blood, visible through the torn sleeve of her dress. Several cuts appeared on the face as well. He fell to his knees, turning pale suddenly, a trembling wounded hand trying to hold down with the other. He felt nauseous and fearful for his sister, who surely felt worse now than he did.

He was surrounded by everyone except Paphian, surprised by what had happened. Paphian worried, but not only about what might be happening to Oliver's sister now. Above all he was worried about the fate of his brother, whose life was now in the hands of the viceroy. What are they doing with him now? Where did they take him? He felt sorry for Oliver for his gift of compassion. But the anxiety for brother was stronger.

"Gotta get it dressed," Delen said. "And fix the hand."

"Twins..." one of the soldiers remembered.

"I know that," said another one with deep green eyes and dark hair. "I have twin brothers at home. When one got hit, the other felt it too. But it will pass her soon. The hand will heal without a trace and the wounds will disappear. As if nothing happened. And in my opinion, these wounds look like someone hit the glass. Once my brother ran into people who were carrying the window. What a mess."

Oliver choked back the nausea, now feeling the growing pain of a glass-wounded hand and a throbbing other, broken somewhere above the elbow.

"But so far, she's suffering now," Delen remarked, looking at the girl with compassion and concern. "How long does it usually take?"

"Paphian," Oliver said softly, cutting them off. "Go. I can handle."

Paphian felt a surge of gratitude to Oliver for caring for Vivan despite the suffering he felt. But although he was worried about his brother, he could not leave his friend in need.

"Go," Oliver repeated again. "This man..." He pointed to the green-eyed man who told them about his brothers.

"Marten," green-eyed introduced himself.

Oliver nodded at him.

"He's right," he finished. "It will pass."

"I'm an idiot. I'm still wondering," muttered Paphian quickly, reaching for the bottle and handing it to him.

"I'm not really..." Oliver began, but at his urgent gaze, he took a small sip.

"Stay here," Paphian ordered him. "I have to go."

"Mr. Lieutenant?" The black-haired man asked.

"We're going with him," Delen said quickly. "Sorry, I can't..."

Oliver showed appropriate forbearance.

"Go," he ordered him, trying to soften his tone as much as possible.

Under other circumstances, Paphian would be impressed again with his excellent acting.

"Kertis," Delen pointed to the black-haired man. "Marten. Stay with her until she gets better. Then you will all join us."

Suddenly remembering the previous side effect of the healer blood, Oliver wanted to protest, but Paphian moved on, and Delen and his men bowed and followed him. He felt a wave of heat pour over him.

"It was the blood of a healer, that bottle?" Kertis asked. "I hear it kindles your bowels like fire."

They both looked at the girl more closely.

"You have blushes, sunshine," he remarked after a moment.

Oliver allowed himself an extremely ugly curse in his mind as he felt Kertis's description of how the blood worked accurately coincide with his feelings.

"Will you give me a kiss now?" The soldier asked jokingly.

Oliver rose abruptly and pushed the attacking soldier away with his wounded hand. And then, without waiting for them, he followed Paphian.

On the castle square, the viceroy's soldiers clashed with the royal soldiers, and a few people were just closing the castle gate. At this point, the clashes intensified even more. The young future heir to the throne stood at the side of the mother, already freed by his father, and his brother, who, like son, got out of the trap together with his men. The king made a sign and one of the men blew a horn.

After a long moment, the fight was stopped.

"TERLAN!!!" Cried the king imperiously. "I order you to leave the guardhouse and fight. Don't hide from me!"

Paphian and Delen with the people, not yet in the square when the castle gates were closed, waited with the royal family. Even if they were there at that moment, they did not expect such an unusual treatment with the healer. After a moment, still experiencing mood swings, Oliver and two soldiers appeared next to them.

The viceroy and his companions appeared on the castle square. Terlan regarded his brother with a contemptuous glance and glanced with lecherous delight at the queen standing by his side, who instinctively moved closer to her husband.

"Where's Vivan?" Paphian whispered, turning pale.

"DO YOU THINK," the viceroy said with an ironic smile, looking at his brother, "that after so much effort, I intend to fight with you clean?" He spat at him.

A murmur of scandal passed through the assembled soldiers and civilians who stood on the king's side.

"If you want this crown... YES," replied Heron.

"Well," Terlan looked at him still with the same smirk. "You bring it to me in my teeth!" Saying this, he waved his hand, and at the sign one of his men stepped forward and released a flaming arrow from his bow.

This signal made war cries resound all around, and warriors in foreign colors and armor appeared on the walls and spilling out through the exits. They raised their swords, expressing their readiness to fight.

"Mercenaries," Delen whispered. "I wonder what he promised them for it. Half a kingdom?"

It was evident that they were better equipped than many of the king's men present. The ruler looked at his still smiling brother with his cold eyes. This man was once close to him. The brothers once competed with each other as always, but never had there been so much envy in it. Throughout the years of his early youth, Terlan enjoyed being the latter, swimming in abundance and luxuries without too much effort. But since Constance appeared at the royal court...

Yes, he knew that. He heard rumors, thwarted two attempts on his life that he could not link to his brother for lack of evidence. After two births, Constance did not become disgusted and did not gain weight. She still shone like a star at his side, for they were united not only by the good of the two kingdoms, one of which Meron would once rule, and the neighboring Amalant - where the queen's father still reigned - her brother as soon as he came of age. They were united by their love. And Terlan always envied his beautiful and devoted wife. Lust stirred up his blood and dimmed his mind. From Constance's desire, a will for power sprouted in him, a sudden need to have everything he wanted. He was ready to plunge the world into chaos for his desires, and unfortunately, when they were fulfilled, he would quickly become satisfied with them and abandon them. He would give them away bored and find other entertainment. He would have won the kingdom at any cost to his whims. And he leeched them off until they plunged him into black despair, while on his side looking for other more attractive targets by manipulation. And Constance...? She would be a perfect fulfillment. Until she would break down from despair, disgraced, wounded in body and soul. Then he would probably give her to his soldiers and look for another prey.

For this man...

There was no other way - than death.

A fight broke out. Delen clustered the people together, and they started to break through the chaos together, protecting Paphian and Oliver as best they could. Their goal was the castle gate.

"What about my brother?" Paphian asked during the fighting. "I'm not leaving without him."

"Paphian!" Suddenly they heard a scream.

The viceroy got on the horse that was brought to him and took a strong sword in his hand. He swept the battlefield with the imperious gaze of the god of war.

His gaze met Oliver's. He beckoned to his men, sending them that way, his slightly drooping face, glistening with sweat, contorted from a contemptuous smile. Then his attention turned a bit carelessly to his brother, who was breaking through to him on a white horse. With each passing moment on the brighter daylight, the horse's white coat shone like a star in the square.

It was Kirian who called out, getting through to them with a few other soldiers.

With a few words, he made Paphian's legs bent.

"Your brother was pushed outside by the viceroy's men," he said. "No escort! The viceroy handed him over to the people to appease them. He's counting on people to literally tear him alive. And you know, I'm afraid that's what will happen..."

CHAPTER 10 — Blood on the pavement

It was a massacre...

While the healer was still talking to the viceroy, moments before he was sent to death, Red Rebecca's white carriage dragged frightened horses with the crackle of cracking glass and breaking planks. Confused and frightened animals beat with it against the walls of houses, apart from tremors, causing more damage. Finally, however, they were stopped, and the furious bandits broke into the interior, where everything was shattered and plunged into chaos, and people barely showed signs of life, bewildered by the fall.

Amidst the sheets, overturned furniture, and scattered glass from broken windows, a handful of refugees were just opening their eyes.

"Where is the motherfucker who killed Pereson?!" The bald, scarred man yelled as he burst in first. "You're dead!"

Len, struggling to regain consciousness from a severe blow to the head, was the first to see the semiconscious Ross, who had apparently managed to grab Julien before falling and turn so that she was now lying on top of him, instead of being on the frame of the broken window, where glass shimmered everywhere. However, he was unable to help him in time, unable to shake himself off yet. So he helplessly saw the man pull Julien off Ross as if she were a doll, to get him in his hands. He yanked him out of the tangle of curtains, boards and glass, making the wounded groan, which only gave the bandit more satisfaction.

"You're gonna scream!" He drawled in his face, with the help of his friend, dragging Ross outside.

There was blood on the injured man's back, and Len was almost certain he had seen numerous pieces of glass stuck into the body. As the other bandits entered, and Moren with them, Len tried to get up. He heard the screams of his friend from outside, ruffling his blood at the cruelty and lighting up his thoughts. However, it was not possible to help him. Sheron, one of Moren's closest people, stood in front of him before he could even get up from his knees.

"We have scores to settle," he said.

Len managed to see him prepare to strike as he swung his sword up. In a brief flash he realized it was over and felt sorry that he would not be able to help his friends, as he had always done. He looked into his enemy's eyes fearlessly.

After a while the sharp sword chopped off his head...

"Sel!!!" Moren shouted meanwhile, indifferent to Sheron's actions. "Sel, where are you?!"

He saw Julien. At first he ignored the fact that one of Ramoz's men was dragging her to the exit, and the girl suddenly came to life screaming, grabbing her hand. It was only a few heartbeats later that he realized what he saw and what the consequences are for Oliver.

"Go away!" He hit the bandit in the face, grabbing Julien at the same time. "She belongs to me!"

His men stood by him, restraining the urge to retaliate in the kidnapper and his buddies.

"What about that hand?!" Moren was nervous. "Broken?"

"I think so..." She raised her other arm, with difficulty, strangely heavy and painful, knowing full well that she should not be grateful him for saving. For the time being, he was only the lesser evil.

Moren froze at the sight of the blood.

"Show me," he said shortly, examining the wounds.

There was an elbow full of glass in hand.

"Shit," he cursed. "Oliver feels it too, doesn't he?" She looked at him angry and at the same time amazed at the sudden concern in his voice. "Get her out of here. You have to wrap it up!" He looked at Sheron, who lowered his sword and helped the girl out with unexpected delicacy. Of course, he was also concerned about his well-being, she was sure of that. Now that the first stun has passed, she saw the body of the dead Len. She saw the struggling girls being led outside. Alesei was lying in a mess, dead or alive, she didn't know. Sel was nowhere to be seen. Or Valeriea.

And she didn't see Ross.

Until she and Sheron walked outside of the crushed carriage and among the few Ramoz's people she saw him bleeding, beaten, struggling to stay on his feet. A scarred bald thug was walking towards him, and hit him in the neck with a piece of broken plank.

She screamed shrilly.

Ross fell and didn't move anymore.

She felt warmth spread slowly in her broken arm. Then it melted into the other, and the glass painlessly began to slide out of her body and fall to the ground.

Oliver has met the healer again! They were together!

The bald bandit stood by the dying man with a crooked smile and slowly, deliberately taking his time, raised the broken plank to the second, final blow, while Ramoz, swearing, gave orders to the others, furious about the loss of the carriage.

Suddenly Sel appeared behind him.

He looked terrible. The smudged makeup made him look like a demon among humans, blood from the numerous cuts on his face and hands completed the ghastly work. Julien was frightened by torn clothes and a wild look in his eyes, and a large piece of glass stuck in his leg. She had never seen him so dangerous and so unpredictable. Nobody's ever seen him like this.

Sel fell out the window as the car rocked and rolled to one side, causing it to disappear in a flash among discarded crates, clothes and all the trash on the street. The carriage fell shortly afterwards and it was forgotten. Now he stood up after he regained consciousness, and the blood flowing from his injured leg would have drained his strength, had it not been for the rage that flared inside him after seeing what had been done to Ross. Although he did not know how to wield the sword well, because his previous illness did not allow him to exert himself, although his leg was already failing with every movement that was torn by the glass, the anger repressed in him throughout his life in one moment made him a demon of revenge.

He lunged at his opponent, knocking him to the ground next to the dying Ross and grabbing him by the head hit him so hard and long on the ground until his skull cracked. He jumped up, taking the pole with him and struck the first of the incoming opponents.

Julien heard a thud and the other fell from a sword blow from the hands of an untrained Valeriea.

Valeriea had a lot of luck when the carriage fell, and came out unscathed. It fell onto the sheets, which had slipped off the bed, and the bed itself leaned against the wall diagonally, creating a sort of umbrella above it against the hail of glass and furniture. Nobody noticed her at first under the pile of pillows. She left swaying as Moren followed Julien, intrigued by the sounds of the commotion outside. The sword took the surprised opponent, and her blow, unfortunately for him, was not clean. He was bleeding painfully and for a long time, but she didn't care. Seeing Ross all covered in blood, she felt her heart die with him.

Her friend.

Her confidant.

Ever since he arrived, her life had a purpose. When he was around she could take a lot. And the same to him. When he despaired after learning about Sel's wedding. He comforted her when a drunk client called her an old bitch, and she thought that was what everyone thought of her. Almost a son.

She walked over to him, sword streaked with blood, devastated to see if he was still alive. Terrified that he might suddenly be missing.

Julien screamed again, seeing one of Ramoz's men reach for the short ax from his belt and throw it at Valeriea. The blade bit into the back of her head.

The woman fell without even feeling the full surprise.

Moren stepped forward, concerned about Sel's fate, wreaking havoc on what had just fallen into his hands and seeing that he was wounded. In the name of the friendship he had damaged so many times, he ordered to defend Julien, and he himself came to the aid of the wounded. He persuaded himself that everything that was previously possible could somehow be straightened, set up. Explain. Maybe even forgive. That perhaps the right words and deeds will come by themselves and correct the wrong done, as if it could be corrected as before. He wanted to show that despite everything, Sel could still count on his help in times of need.

Ramoz dismounted from his horse, watching his opponents with a crooked smile. He loved times when his life stood on the edge of a knife. Watching everything, he did not notice the appearance of a new enemy, who came from behind Sheron, who was guarding Julien, and with one almost practiced movement cut his throat, although the sight of blood made him flinch.

Surprised, Julien saw Alesei with an expression in his eyes that she had never seen in him today. Blood soaked from a severed temple into his dark ebony hair and flowed down his neck.

"Another male whore," Rozten, the second of Morena's companions, smiled, seeing Alesei. He never dazzled with his intelligence.

"You killed Darmon?" Alesei croaked, and the sound of his voice so different from the slightly carefree gentle tone Julien knew made her shivers go through her body, despite the warmth from the healer.

"You mean that scout of yours? He sucked. And he squealed like a pig," replied Rozten, drawing his dagger.

Alesei knew who, apart from Tenan, was engaged in punishing and killing. Sadistic Moren chose his victims differently. And his favorite wasn't here.

Rozten's abilities to torture and kill were slim to the strong young man full of anger and regret. Rozten was strong only where his victims were weaker than him and defenseless. In a real fight, he would lose quickly. Like now. Alesei grabbed him and plunged the blade into the stomach, slowly twisting it. Rozten screamed shrilly. For a moment, only a moment, Alesei, who had not yet raised his hand to anyone, savor the scream until it reached the dark ends of his soul, then slit Rozten's throat until blood spurted. Julien closed her eyes as the drops fell on her as well. Justice is at work. For a moment or two she remembered the young man who had smiled at her for the first time at Alesei's side from inside the carriage. He never harassed her. As long as he was, and now she had discovered it at last, with his presence, good word and willingness to act, almost invisible, he moved everyone as she and Sel lost their way into their own affairs. It was he who encouraged Alesei to drive the carriage for the first time. He found a place to stop that Sel accepted. He was like a ghost. He found a stream that Ross had taken water for washing. There were also plenty of other seemingly insignificant things that he discreetly took care of when they were unable to think clearly.

And finally it was him, he went on scouts... from which he never returned.

She couldn't remember if she had a word with him.

They let the corpse fall to the ground.

Sai leaned over the man who, angry with Lena's resistance, unable to achieve his strength, drove her fork-like blade with an extended central spike straight into the heart. Sai took the other similar from him while he was still sitting on murdered friend and stabbed him in the neck.

It couldn't bring Lena back to life.

The surprised little girl waited for the excruciating pain that supposedly accompanied the twins when one of them dies. But it didn't come. They were afraid of it. They sensed it. But, although they were not really tied by family ties, they wanted something to connect them. They believed it was like this, though they misunderstood the reasons for these feelings.

Only an excruciating loss remained.

She stood up slowly, blade in hand, no longer looking at her beloved's unseeing green eyes.

As she turned around, she saw Ramoz opposite Sel and Moren.

The old bandit, sword in hand, was waiting for the fight. She wasn't going to let him fight Sel and endanger her friend, but Ramoz had to pay for his actions. For every tear of Lena. For every wound. Every blood. Every rape. Every terrifying night in his company.

She came from behind. Out of the corner of her eye, she saw that Moren wasn't going to interfere or warn his opponent. She looked at him coldly.

Ramoz sensed someone's presence behind him. He turned, intrigued, and at that moment she raised her hand, plunging the blade into his heart. She pushed him to fall, tore the blade away, and hammered it in again. And again. Again...

"Sai," Alesei stopped her hand, kneeling down beside her. "That's enough."

She waited for the light of life to go out in the bandit forever. Shivering, she stared at him without a single tear, until Alesei pulled her gently away and hugged her. Even then, she didn't cry. She just shivered more. She thought he was trembling too.

Julien wanted to cheer her up. But Moren stood between her and Sel. Apart from him, no one of their persecutors was left alive. The glowing sky clearly showed a street full of blood and corpses, horses prowling between them. Behind her, she heard the growing buzz of human voices - somewhere from the side of the marketplace. In addition, her hands were still healing. Glass fell out of the wounded one, but the wounds had not closed and scarred yet. The broken arm didn't seem to heal yet. She probably needed the presence of a healer himself to fully heal, though it clearly helped Oliver. But Oliver was...

Healer!

DAWN!!

Ross...

She ran to Ross and carefully checked his condition. He was alive. Incredibly, he was still alive. Though he was barely breathing.

"Julien," Sel said softly, glancing at the watchful Moren, torn between his desire to be beside them and being wary of an old friend whom he no longer trusted.

"He will die if the healer doesn't help him," she whispered. "Sel," she lowered her voice, "I think the healer has just been led out the gate..."

The meaning of her words was too clear to all.

"You want to save him," said Moren suddenly, quite calmly and to the point, as he always did when they had agreed a plan together in the past, seeing the pain on Selarion's face. "Save the healer." Before anyone could react, he walked over to one of the abandoned horses and jumped on the saddle. "Time goes by, Sel. Go!" He added and drove away before they shook themselves. He ran towards the marketplace.

"He went for a healer?" Alesei wondered.

Sel felt shivers run down his spine. He looked despairingly at Julien and the unconscious Ross.

In the blink of an eye, he realized that Moren had defended himself against the plague so far, probably having something that had previously belonged to Count Beckert, and that was why he was so confident. He lost his carriage, left unfinished business with him, even abandoned Julien, who was his bargaining chip! He also lost his men. He was sure that in his old friend's sick mind, all the previous events were just a minor complication, and that after all the confusion was over, everything would be back as before. He must have thought they would come to an agreement, he would keep the plan of action from the day before.

Or that he will manage to accomplish his intention. And then even let the world collapse!

Because for a long time his thoughts were constantly on one goal. And only he was of paramount importance. That was all that mattered.

Yesterday, which seemed to go on for eternity, he sent Oliver for a pendant belonging to a healer. He probably hoped that the other would get him, after all, and maybe he wouldn't even learn about his sister's escape and change of plans!

Moren went for what he cared about in the first place.

He went to get Oliver...

A chill ran down his spine. He looked down at his lover's tormented body, feeling excruciating despair. He walked over to him. Ross was pale and didn't even flinch.

He was dying.

Another dear creature was dying because of him. Blinded by his fatal infatuation, he had allowed this degenerate to live for so long. It's because of him that they got here! He knelt beside him to place a kiss on his forehead, and then for a moment placed his hand on the shoulder of the dying man, fighting the tide of self-hatred and tears of despair. For years he had deceived himself like a fool and now his relatives and friends were paying for it.

He allowed his anger to rise again, then looked around and seized the abandoned horse.

"Stay with him," Julien said softly. "You can't help in a different way. You're hurt."

He turned to mount his horse, and at that moment his leg finally gave up. He fell, losing his footing in it, and with sudden astonishment, at last he noticed a broken piece of glass and blood flowing.

He realized that if he took the glass out, it would be much worse. He felt the chills and nausea already as the adrenaline rush passed. Alesei went to him and took off his shirt and belt.

"Don't pull it out," said Alesei in warning. "You're damn lucky it didn't dig any deeper."

"I know," he whispered. "Help me get there."

"You're crazy."

But he had already pulled out the glass and was bandaging his leg, fastening the belt. Sai closed Lena's eyes and took the blades away. She tucked them in the belt, which she also took from the dead Ramoz's man. Then she went to the cart, found the bow and quiver that Ross had used before.

"You know it can kill you?" Alesei added, helping Sel, who was pale as a linen, mount his horse.

"If I don't save him," Sel replied softly, gripping the sword that had been taken from one of the enemies, "then I might die. I have very few reasons to live." He glanced at Julien and Ross, a particularly painful and apologetic glance at the girl.

And Julien, who had lived her whole life with him and knew the enormity of what he had experienced, saw his wife and her friend die, leaned on him when she cried, wiped his sweat when he was sick... She suddenly felt that she was ready to let him make that choice without regret. Like a best friend, she looked at him with warmth and understanding. She nodded in agreement, giving him freedom from feelings that had no chance of survival.

He led the way, and Alesei and Sai mounted their horses and followed him.

She stayed with Ross. She squeezed his hand, pale and limp, as she sat beside him on the cobbled street. She couldn't move it. She rose only a moment later to grab the curtains from the lying carriage and wrap a piece around her swollen, wounded arm. She covered the body of the murdered Valeriea in case Ross woke up. She used the second veil, crying in pain, to dress the boy's wounds even temporarily. She was taking the glass from his back, tugging at the curtain to make a tug of it. She rubbed his neck. Washing with tears of pain and sorrow over the wounded, and over her wounded heart, she treated the more serious cuts as she could. He did not move. He didn't even groan. But as she put a pillow under his head and a blanket pulled out of the chaos left by the carriage - as carefully as she could - as she carefully covered him, covering his wounds, she saw the tears rolling slowly down his face. They came out from under closed lids and marked a path.

She felt regret surge within her.

Ross felt! He was in that shattered body! He had to be! She wouldn't have seen his tears otherwise!

Fear for her brother, the tension of this nightmare day, and terrible despair over herself and the wounded took her heart. She hugged him, crying softly.

In the distance, she could hear the buzz and screams coming from the side of the marketplace. The streets around were quiet and empty. All those who counted on something belonging to the healer and those who, one way or another, passed away, left the extinct city.

Suddenly she heard the clatter of hooves on the cobbles. Someone got off their horse next to them. Slowly she raised her head to see him.

Tenan stood in the light of the awakening day.

His steel-gray eyes had an unusual expression, and for a moment Julien couldn't understand what had surprised her so much. Or rather, she couldn't believe what she saw.

Tenan's eyes filled with sadness. But they quickly changed their expression to show the familiar indifference again, and the girl remembered that no one else had contributed to the death of Milera and their two old servants but only him.

He would probably kill her now.

Tenan crouched down beside them. She dared to meet his eyes. Why would she fear him? He will do what he wants. At least she can show him how to die with dignity.

"I didn't take it for myself," he said in an unexpectedly gentle tone, his voice strangely soft and gentle. "I wanted this for you." He pulled something out of his shirt pocket.

Sparks of silver glow and ruby red glistened in the morning sun. Seeing that the girl wasn't reaching for it, he gently placed the thing on the wounded man's chest. She could see a gold bracelet encased in symbols by his wrist. All she knew was that the symbols were magical. It was it which then caught her attention in their home. A strange bracelet.

"He was wearing this just now," he said. "It's still warm."

She looked at what he offered them and shuddered. She had seen her father do it.

Pendant. Hands holding a ruby.

He looked at her one more time, without mockery, without his usual cold indifference, then got on his horse and rode away.

She grasped the pendant so painfully familiar, so many memories. It was indeed warm. Like the touch on her cheek yesterday.

Healer.

The chain was broken. Whatever Tenan had intentions, one thing had not changed. He ripped it off from a healer neck, probably now surrounded by the crowd, without helping him. He just left him there. His heart was certainly not human. She must have been wrong.

Her hand tightened on the pendant, feeling the warmth spread and relief as the pain began to subside. What's going on now? What will they do with the healer?!

She quickly tied the chain, seized by a terrifying vision.

Then she hung her "hands" around Ross's neck. The ruby glowed red.

Tenan.

He surprised her with this gesture. She reluctantly remembered their occasional encounters since he joined Moren's gang. He was always cold. He wasn't even calculating. Rather indifferent. Without feelings.

Always.

It made her fear his gaze. She saw him looking at her. She thought there was cruelty beneath it. She kicked him at the House of Pleasure.

Whatever the man was thinking about her... one gesture, a few words... couldn't fix anything. She should fear him and avoid him like the plague.

She should hate him.

It was enough that she remembered how he hung Milera. How she struggled in his hands.

He is a monster that, even if he had feelings, was wormy and rotten like his soul.

She fed her eyes with the silhouette fading into the distance on a black horse. May the plague catch him! May he die in torment for the death of a friend, two devoted servants, and who knows how many more people!

She felt a gentle movement. Ross's index finger moved and tightened lightly on hers.

"You are here?" She asked softly.

He tightened his finger again, as if confirming. She lifted his hand and kissed it.

"Don't worry. Help will come," she whispered, fearing that if she raised her voice a little, it would reveal a hidden fear in her heart.

If Sel and his companions don't bring a healer here, Ross will die because the pendant is not enough to help him.

She was afraid to think what was now facing the healer...

Amid the swirling crowd, the healer torn in all directions was almost invisible, but his scream shook even Moren, who stopped his horse. One glance at the whole situation allowed him to say, with some hint of horror, that there was no rescue for the other man.

For a moment, for one brief moment, something like compassion twitched in his soul, because he was a healer, after all. He considered reducing his suffering. He saw what was coming. The sight absorbed his attention so much that he did not even notice Tenan walking away before he went to get the hidden horse, he looked after him thoughtfully. But the thought that Oliver might slip out of his hands won even that human reflex. Moren looked to see if Sel was after him and carefully looked around the castle. Maybe you need to climb there? Of course, even he could do that if he wanted to. You just need to find out where the guards are.

Oliver still had to be in the castle or he would have found his sister and friend long ago. So he went towards the gate.

* * *

Oliver found himself trapped as they tried to open the gate. A handful of defenders fought against the viceroy's soldiers and mercenaries, the latter, seeing a pretty girl, elated to double their efforts. The queen came to help her husband's men. Seeing a brother healer in need, she sent a detachment of her soldiers there. Nobody would believe now that until recently she sat among the ladies of the court gossiping and drinking cold drinks. Stained with blood, she looked like a bloody goddess in her tattered dress and fiery red hair wet with sweat. She was driven by a determination to protect her own children and her beloved, if perhaps too firm, husband. Unfortunately, the dedication of some of her people left her temporarily unprotected. King Heron lost his brother in the crowd at this very moment. Prince Meron and his brother protected each other. Though Meron was protecting his mother, he was not careful enough to protect himself as well. A strong kick from a horse and a collision with a strong animal knocked him off his feet and almost rendered him unconscious. With an effort of will, he regained his composure, hearing the sounds of fighting through the pounding of blood in his ears. He was the future heir to the throne. There his family fought, without which nothing will matter. It gave him strength. He felt a pain in his nose. He stood unsteadily and touched it. He wiped off the blood instinctively.

And then he saw the one who did him that way.

The viceroy on horseback and with his sword made his way to his mother. Lust pushed him to act. He cut off Constance's escape route and with the strong, firm movement of the conqueror, he grabbed her by the hastily braided braid of thick red hair.

"I'll take you with me, Constance," he said in a cold, fearful voice, drawing her head against his saddle. "Even to the grave!"

She struggled desperately against the piercing pain. The young prince went to help his mother. King Heron, finally seeing clearly what was happening in the sea of battle, began to angrily make his way to his brother and wife with his horse. Several of the viceroy's men tried to stop him, but they might as well want to stop an avalanche of stones.

But neither of them would have come to the rescue if it weren't for Oliver. His friends finally managed to lead to the opening of the castle gate, and the Paphian, almost burning with anxiety, made his way to the exit with his sword. Oliver had used years of practice of dodging and sneaking out to people trying to catch him, and he was given a long enough respite to get his bearings. He saw the viceroy dragging the struggling queen. Without thinking, having only a brief moment to lock onto the target, he pulled out his slingshot. The stone fired from it hit the eye. The viceroy cried out in pain and for a moment weakened his grip. The queen managed to pull out almost the entire braid during this time, which her son took advantage of and struck with his sword. Only the end of the braid remained in the hand, tightened by the iron grip, which the viceroy did not enjoy for long.

For another heartbeat or two, the king hesitated to kill his brother before his horse equaled the viceroy's. Right next door, however, he made the final decision and took a strong swing with his sword...

The viceroy's head suddenly lost contact with the body and fell to the pavement, and the body slipped slowly off the horse. The end of the queen's braid was still in his hand...

The viceroy was dead.

This was the end of the great coup.

Deprived of their leader, the viceroy's soldiers partially ceased fighting and surrendered, others got away, but some fought to the end for the lost cause. The mercenaries stopped fighting and began to flock to their leader. Since their murderous toil would no longer be rewarded, it was not worth shedding blood. Now they gathered in the square, surrounded by opponents, biting remarks and crooked smiles, letting them know that they were doing nothing to deal with the dangerous situation in which the viceroy had personally put them, promising a solid reward. After all, their job was to get the job done right. And even better. They were considered the best for a reason. Several of them, who surrounded the defenders of Paphian and the threatened militant Selena with blue eyes, said goodbye as if nothing had happened, promising the girl another meeting in more favorable circumstances, supplementing this promise with rather dirty remarks. Delen wanted to hit them, but Selena held him back.

"You've done enough for me," Oliver said gently, really feeling awkward in his disguise now to the lieutenant's and his squad's apparent sympathy.

These people were convinced that they were defending an extraordinary woman. He would definitely hurt their feelings by revealing the truth now. So he decided to keep it a secret until he parted ways. He wasn't going to ever wear a woman's disguise again. Let Selena remain just a memory. From where he stood, he saw that the royal family was together again. The happy king kissed his wife strongly, glad that nothing happened to her. He thoughtfully looked at her beautiful hair, now moved by the wind, and then he hugged both sons, watching the elder with concern and saying something to him. But most of all, he was overjoyed that the family was complete - safe and sound - except for his broken nose and a few abrasions. Then he finally looked around the castle square, resuming his royal role and considering his next move. Then his eyes fell on the young woman in front of the castle gate, the only one among the men gathered here except the queen. Oliver felt himself blush again. The king nodded appreciatively, but before he could do any more, a shout came from the castle walls:

"PEOPLE! OUR HEALER IS MURDERING AT THE MARKET! TO ARMS!! KILL THE RASCALS!"

Paphian, still standing next to Delen's men after the fight, paled rapidly. Standing at the entrance he could not see the marketplace from here, but a terrible fear filled his heart. The king ordered some of the soldiers to go to the marketplace and the rest to stay with him before the general frenzy and fury took over. The mercenaries, on a short command of the commander, raised their swords with a battle cry, and then, simultaneously hitting their breasts, paid tribute to the king, and then moved towards the gate. The healer was a good given to all people. He was outside the politics of the kingdom. The most precious treasure. And as Vivan Beckert - not even Count Beckert, as he rarely used the title - although his stepfather officially recognized him as his son, he was known for his good heart and willingness to help. People who would kill anyone for gold or some other reward, one for him would be ready to jump into the fire. He was almost sacred.

Crushed by the news, Paphian now thought of one of the conversations he had had with his brother as he ran along the road with Delen's squad. Once, seeing how Vivan without a trace of impatience allows people to accost him, helps with even minor ailments and listens to life stories, he could not stand it and shouted angrily:

"You shouldn't be doing this! People, if only they could, would eat you alive!"

Vivan just smiled then.

What would he say now?!

At the sight of what was happening in the marketplace, his hair bristled on his head. Terrified by the sight of Kirian, his brother and their companions paled with terror. Paphian's words spoken in anger were fulfilled. The words he spoke without giving any meaning to it. People rushed at Vivan like hungry beasts. They tugged, torn clothes to shreds, trying at all costs to get to even a piece of meat, to lick, bite, suck. Even the mercenaries and royal soldiers froze, shocked at the sight of brutal cruelty.

And suddenly something happened that shook them even more.

A few people turned blue and clasped at their hearts. The healer felt looser when the bodies of those closest to him suddenly fell to the ground.

Everyone understood one thing for sure.

This was not the doing of the other scavengers.

In a strange way, a man who was famous for saving human life was responsible for this.

Healer.

He fell where he was standing, and his head hit the ground with an unpleasant knock.

And already some old bag lashed at him with her dirty knife, ready to start a bloody slaughter, when suddenly an arrow caught her...

On the other side of the crowd, a beautiful, delicate girl who some recognized as customers of the House of Pleasure lowered her bow from the saddle of a black horse. Her half-naked companion, with flowing, dark hair, shouted at Paphian and the people standing next to him:

"What are you waiting for?!"

A third of them - also in the saddle like the others - whose face was a grotesque ghost mask, raised his sword and rode into the suddenly confused crowd. People backed away from him in panic, terrified by his appearance. As he hit the first in the crowd, shots rained out. Several mercenaries began firing furiously at the crowd, taking care not to injure the unexpected demonic ally. Sai kept shooting until the quiver was empty. Surprised would-be cannibals scattered to all sides in panic, but neither of them was merciful for this act. One by one they were killed. Men and women. Enraged by their cruelty, the soldiers repaid them bloodily for their wickedness.

Paphian broke through to his brother, passing a pale demon on horseback that left the marketplace towards the castle. The half-naked, black-haired man was already at the wounded man.

"He's alive," he replied, unanswered.

"Let's get him out of here!" Paphian looked with horror at his brother, at his blood and wounds. There was so much blood everywhere. So much blood...

"You won't take him out like that," Kirian said, with whitened lips. "We will arrange transport. We'll take him to the castle!"

"Over my dead body!" Paphian shouted fiercely. "I'm not going back there with him!"

"So, you've killed him," Kirian replied. "There he will have the best care. Perhaps our treacherous medic is still alive!"

"He lives!" One of the king's soldiers shouted. "The king ordered him to be thrown into the dungeon to wait for judgment!"

Kirian looked at Paphian meaningfully. All around, the bloody battles with the survivors were almost over.

"Only he can help him now."

Paphian's face grimaced with rage and despair. He gritted his teeth, unable to speak silently without anger.

"Need a stretcher!" Kirian shouted. "Or a cart!"

A dozen or so people hurried to the castle.

The fights are over. Only a few villains managed to escape the slaughter. There were dead bodies everywhere. Some of them had things that belonged to a healer in their hands. Many had his blood on their hands. With a pained heart and the feeling that he had failed him terribly in his time of need, Paphian embraced his brother as if he were made of the most delicate porcelain in the world. He hugged it to his chest, feeling the tears welling up. In the subtle silence of the morning, as everyone looked at them reverently, crushed, numb with despair, he hugged Vivan like he had never done before - in grief and tears, feeling the weight of a terrible guilt. The brothers should help each other. How many times has Vivan healed his wounds and blows. Without parents knowing. After he got into fights? What did they do to his brother, whose only fault was that he loved people the way they were? Who worried about the fate of others, unknowingly getting involved in their problems? He gave them himself, his gift, taking symbolic fees for it on the advice of his stepfather, who wanted people to respect him in this way. So that they would not surround him from all sides. By accepting at certain fixed hours in the morning, he limited the aspirations of those who would most willingly ask him for help, even in a trivial matter. Of course, these hours were a contractual matter. You could always count on him.

Always.

And how was this kindness rewarded? What was the reward for him?!

"What have they done to you?" He whispered. "WHAT DID YOU DID TO HIM?!" He sobbed in despair. "Look! Look what you did with him?!"

A great deal of regret was building up in his heart. He had failed him. He did not save from this cruelty. He couldn't get him out of this luxurious prison sooner. He couldn't protect him.

When the king's carriage arrived, he was filled with anger and a terrible sense of harm.

"He won't come back to the castle," he said. "I prefer him to die here."

"Paphian," he heard a familiar voice behind him. "I know what you're feeling…"

"YES?!" He turned a little to look at the face of the young prince who had gone out to meet him. "I don't think so. It's your fault he ended up here! You kidnapped him! You allowed it! Only your political games mattered!"

Meron, Duke of Verdom, heard it silently. These accusations met in his heart with a guilt he felt. So he did not raise his voice, he did not punish for his audacity towards the royal person. He knew that he had neglected his friend, some of his fears, how pertinent, had come true today, perhaps attributing it to excessive emotional involvement. And yet he should have listened to him. He should also talk to him more, give him more freedom, and only submit to his father's will. He was a poor guardian and host. A poor friend too.

He sat on a horse, ready to personally escort the healer he had failed. He already knew that he did not want Vivan back to the castle. Vivan deserved to be free after what was prepared for him here, and if he returns now, his father will not let him go again. There was surely another way to keep the royal family safe. He no longer wanted Vivan to be kept in the castle anymore. He couldn't bear it. He would not have made such a decision even if his father had now made him king. Not after what he just saw here.

"Lord Count," Alesei dared to speak. "I know a place where we could bring him. I'm sure my friend won't mind."

Delen's squad surrounded the carriage ready to escort the healer to safety. They were joined by mercenaries gathered in the square. The exception was the king's soldiers waiting for the prince's orders. Delen's men were not subordinate to the prince, but directly to Queen Constance, and in their view continued to accompany Paphian as ordered.

"Do you remember, my lord, the goldsmith's family, with which you visited some time ago?" Alesei spoke quickly, leaning against the cart. "The Rserwer family?"

Paphian nodded his head in agreement, suddenly feeling a spark of anxiety in his heart. Oliver's family.

"Selarion is Oliver's best friend whom you have met. There are traces of plague in the goldsmith's house, but in the merchant's house..." Alesei's voice died for a moment, when, according to rumors he had heard at the House of Pleasure, he imagined Sel's parents' bedroom, it isn't there. He will certainly be honored to have a healer in his home, Lord Count."

"Lead on," Paphian said only. "We'd love to accept your offer."

He looked at his brother, who shifted nervously. They wasted enough time.

He looked around from his seat, but Oliver was nowhere to be seen. Alesei, meanwhile, was instructing the troops in transit.

"Don't go into the bedroom. Don't disturb the dead," he told them at the end, promising himself that as soon as he watched over the fate of Sai, Julien and his dead friends, he would take care of this as well, unless Sel returns. He knew him well enough that he was sure that he would not blame him for such guests.

The carriage rode hurriedly, and with it a large escort with the prince and his men.

"Paphian. I'll join you later," Kirian said through the window to his former companion from Queen's School. "Delena's gone. He went towards the castle during the skirmish and I know why. Selena is gone. I follow them."

His anxiety shared also Paphian, who rightly sensed that something had happened to Oliver. Kirian, without waiting for a reply, broke away from the group, taking the two men with him.

Meanwhile, the hurried procession entered the street, where Rebecca's red carriage had overturned. Almost in the middle of the street, in front of an overturned carriage, among the dead bodies, two people were lying in the street. At the sight of this, two of Julien's friends accelerated to join them.

Freed from the broken carriage, four gray horses stood nearby.

What caught the attention of both the prince and Alesei and Sai shone distinctly purple and silver.

On the wounded's neck shone a healer's pendant...

CHAPTER 11 — Salvation

Voices…

Voices again...

He swoon. He couldn't concentrate longer...

Light. Flashes...

Ache.

"Mother Earth," a voice said softly, a familiar voice.

It was the first time, and just because he was acquainted, he focused on it longer. But that's not possible. After all, he stayed home! He was injured!

"Look at his eyes!"

Something's wrong…?

And finally, a clear, conscious thought. A wave of memories. Nightmare. He could still hear the voices. He didn't recognize the key, just the melody. As if there were more of them. They sounded loud. Too loud. And that hype. That hype! That buzz. This violence. Too much!!!

He's still at the marketplace!!!

This pain...

* * *

"Vivan!" Suddenly Paphian felt his brother's body shake unexpectedly in a strong shock.

For the last hour, he and a tiny girl named Sai, whom the royal medic had taken to help, explaining that his assistant had been killed during the fighting in the castle, and Sedon himself, had patched the healer, sewed and washed with lemon juice and water. Literally. At that time Vivan was lying almost completely naked and unconscious. Pale as linen. What they saw after removing his clothes, or rather what was left of him, shocked them deeply. There was no place on Vivan's body that had not been scratched, beaten, torn with something blunt, and finally - bitten to the blood! These bites worried Sedon more than the cuts. He was afraid of infection, difficult wounds that would not heal easily. But when Paphian asked in a trembling voice if he wanted to burn the wounds, he laughed at the idea. He called it added cruelty and unnecessary stupidity. Working feverishly with them, he did not fail to curse a horse who decided to burn the wound on Vivan's leg after being bitten by a dragon, leaving a terrible scar on his thigh. Everyone in the kingdom knew this story. When Vivan was fifteen, he and his horse were attacked by a dragon on the road to Adelaine. Luckily Vivan slipped out of his mouth then, but the horse did not survive. Count Beckert who accompanied him then and his men killed the beast.

Back then, Vivan was on the verge of dying. A poisonous venom in the wound was suspected. It was nonsense, since these particular varieties of green dragons had no venom in them, but the physician he hastily found apparently didn't know it and didn't want to listen to the locals. People almost beat him up for the suffering he had caused when they found out what his methods were.

But even then… Vivan didn't look as bad as he does now.

When Paphian saw his birthright, he felt like crying. It seemed to be of particular interest, and judging by the amount of scratches, people were eager to just strip it all away.

Vivan shifted nervously again. He shook his body so suddenly that they instinctively flinched, surprised by the movement. Then he did it again. And again. He opened his mouth, gasping for air.

Suddenly, unbelievable, after he had lost so much blood, he raised his hands and began throwing himself, driving himself away in front of something or someone. With all his strength, defending against their touch, pushing back the hands that tried to hold him back and hold him down. By desperately ripping off the dressings that he apparently felt as foreign, perhaps someone's touch.

He did not scream, hardly uttering a voice, but defended himself desperately. Paphian tried to talk to him, to convince him that he was safe now. To calm down. But Vivan, locked in his own nightmare, continued to struggle until Sedon finally ordered him to be held down by force and forcefully poured something into his mouth...

Vivan thrashed in their arms for a moment longer. Even the three of them had a serious problem to keep him. Finally, the apparently sedative drug finally took effect and the body dropped helplessly, though the mind was still in a haze of terror and a sense of helplessness. Paphian watched with pain in his heart as his brother faded and fell asleep. Weakened, dumb and distant from them in thoughts, somewhere in the depths of his own nightmares. Seeing this in a man who so far was always ready to rush to his aid and whose gentle tone of voice calmed many quarrels, it caused despair and fear.

"Talk to him," Sedon told him in a low voice. "Speak now! Let him know that someone close to him is with him."

Tears - unbidden, ran down the face of the usually strong Paphian spirit. In a voice trembling with emotion, he spoke to his brother, trying to break through to his head through the gusts of madness and despair, terrified of what consequences, judging by this attack, could have the cruelty that people had perpetrated on him.

What if Vivan will go insane?

What if they destroyed his mind and he will never be the one he has known all his life?

Sedon and Sai, whose hands were shaking even though she thought she wouldn't feel anything today, went back to work. The medic instructed the girl - seeing that he was dealing not with pure innocence, but with a woman who was clearly no stranger to the sight of a male body - to take care of the healer. And if Sai today would like to thank whatever gods she knew for something, it was precisely because the drug given by Sedon first calmed him down, and then, apparently assisted by his brother's voice or the effect of the drug, put him to sleep. For although she did her best to dress him really gently and skillfully - he would certainly suffer.

She knew the pain he would feel, though it was given her differently.

Finally they finished dressing him, they gently moved him to the bed she had prepared earlier, covering him with a down comforter. The bed and the room belonged to Sel. She was here for the first time. Lots of drawings adorned the walls, but she didn't have time to study them. The linen was previously crumpled. She clearly sensed the characteristic smell known to her from the House of Pleasure.

So it's true that sometimes Sel could do this when he was ill...

For the time being, she and Milera's belongings were hidden in a chest near the bed. She changed the duvet covers. When the healer found himself in the bed in which Sel had made love with Milera so recently, Sai washed the combined tables, brought in haste by the soldiers, of the blood and hair that they had to shave off the healer's head. Paphian sat down next to his brother in an armchair, holding his hand. She was touched by this tenderness, so unusual for her when it comes to men. And so honest. Sedon took one of the sheets on Sel's desk and was writing out care instructions for the wounded, at the same time quietly and in a slightly trembling voice saying them aloud. She listened silently to them. When to administer herbs, when to change dressings, observe wounds, summon him in case of fever, what to watch out for, what to observe... She washed the floor. She scooped up the most blood-dripping cloth - some of what was left of the sheet from Sel's trunk - picked up the bucket and opened the door.

There were a lot of people in the corridor of the pretty good house, mostly soldiers. The closest were Duke Meron and Alesei, next to them were the royal guards, whose task had been to bring the medic from the dungeons and now lead him to them. Everyone waited for the news with anxiety.

She politely instructed them to wait for the physician Sedon to explain, cursing gently to the young prince. In fact, she was so devastated by what she had seen and experienced that she hardly felt like having some polite conversations. Without a word, she thrust a bloody scrap of cloth into Alesei, hoping he would remember what to do with it.

"Forgive me, my dear," the prince said softly, but without embarrassment, "but I'm compelled to give the appropriate orders. The plague is still in town. And I have a family to protect!"

Then he pointed to the bucket in her hand.

"Take the bucket and distribute its contents. Have a bottle ready for me!"

She opened her mouth in silent indignation, feeling her blood rush at the audacity. Alesei put a hand on her shoulder. She shook it off angrily.

"He's bleeding out and you're gonna lick his blood?!" She shouted to the prince and to everyone gathered, giving them an angry glare that everyone now avoided.

"Wasn't that what you were going to do for your friends we picked up on the way?" Replied the young prince, approaching her with a twinkle in his eye and pointing to Alesei. "How is your act different from mine, girl? This is our only sure protection against plague and other diseases. Before wounds and death. You are not the only ones who have loved ones that you want to protect!!!"

She knew he was right.

For Ross, this was the only salvation.

For many others, too.

"There will be another bucket," she replied, worried.

The voice refused to obey her, tearing with emotion. She left in a hurry, looking at no one. Be far away from people. Finally, in the garden behind the house, she found peace. She knelt in mute despair, leaving them guessing how much blood they would get to share, and what else it meant - that many tears, pain and suffering had to endure and will be endured by the healer, when they would be protected by his miraculous gift.

Images swirled in her head. Vivan, desperately defending herself against them, Lena killed by one of those degenerates who, along with Ramoz, so eagerly played with them more than once. Her cry, her wounds. Healer wounds. His mutilated body, torn apart by the crowd, bitten...

People have monsters within themselves. They mask it, hide it in the darkness, in order to free them like rabid dogs and allow themselves to pure cruelty. Then they explain it by necessity or are vulgarly silent. But they always strive to be satisfied again.

* * *

Oliver hadn't really been scared so far. He was surrounded by people who took care of his safety during the fighting. He felt confident with them. But now that they had gone out the gate to rescue Vivan, his courage suddenly vanished in the face of the man who had long since become his worst nightmare. Which he hoped to never see again.

Moren!

He saw him sitting on a horse, watching diligently as they left. He panicked. Even the fear for Vivan could not suppress it. Moren noticed him quickly. He was the only woman in this crowd, and he had seen him in a woman's disguise before. There were too many people to approach him, but he tried it abruptly and fiercely. In the blink of an eye, Oliver realized how close he was to his doom. He turned back. In panic, he began to break through the ranks of soldiers and mercenaries. It was not without a struggle, because if the former simply let him through, the latter, apparently regretting the defeat, which took away the loot and rapes, did not spare him hugs, fierce kisses and attempts to discover the breasts, which were formed by a special corset, cast made of soft material based on the original, which are part of the bizarre furnishings of the House of Pleasures - they were pleasing to the eye under a worn dress. In the blink of an eye, Oliver was in even more trouble, because a healer is a healer, someone else may be running to help him now, since this is such a treat! Furious with this, Moren ran among the cheerful men and tugged a few heads.

Then Delen appeared next to him.

A few certain blows and a cry for help from the soldiers from the square quickly thinned the group, which apparently disregarding the presence of the king, who knows how they would have treated the girl, still feeling an unfulfilled lust for murder and destruction.

Oliver finally broke through. He was in a deplorable condition, but he was glad that the thugs had not been able to look under his skirt. He was so bluntly treated only by Moren. The thought that he was right behind him now made him run until he was back in the servants' corridor, almost at the same time as yesterday, without stopping, even though he wanted to cool down for a while.

He paused around a bend to soothe his heart a little and to control himself enough to start looking for a solution. Glad Delen showed up. May he not die because of this! He could still feel the hideous touch of the mercenaries, a taste of what Moren could do to him if he caught him. Horror wanted so much to control him, to make him lose the ability to think rationally, until he got angry with himself and in anger, he slammed his fists blindly on the walls to somehow remember himself.

The pain of his ragged hands sobered him. Reason returned.

Suddenly he heard quick steps. Someone was running this way!

He covered his mouth with his bloody hand, holding his breath.

The steps stopped.

The someone was listening. He could feel it.

Sudden confusion and the buzz of people's voices at the nearby entrance broke the silence. He could breathe slowly.

"Selena!" He heard the lieutenant's familiar voice, "Selena, where are you? Talk to me!"

But the lieutenant did not enter until now with a few people, perhaps with the servants returning to the castle, who had hidden during the fighting...

"I've found you," he heard a familiar voice suddenly, that voice, and felt the cold stab of steel.

Moren stood beside him, his dagger touching his exposed throat.

Oliver looked into his cold, ruthless eyes. He felt a shudder run through him.

"Coercion is supposed to break everyone," said Moren. "History has come full circle today, don't you think? You're in the dress again... Ready to play."

He brought his face close to his, rubbing his coarse stubble against Oliver's cheek.

"There will be plenty of it, I assure you," he whispered in his ear, "You, me and your sister. At one go. Because she'll feel it too, won't she?"

Blood boiled in Oliver. But the dagger bit lightly into his neck, depriving him of any defense and expression of anger.

"I will only kill you when you beg for it," added Moren softly, feverishly, encouraged by his silence, "You won't do it right away, I know it. You will fight. And she will suffer with you..."

"Why?" He asked in a trembling voice, finally doing it "Why me, Moren?"

The other looked at him thoughtfully, as if he were making the right words.

"Hands off her!" They heard a voice soft, but strongly accentuating the words, and before Moren answered, came another voice: "Or you will taste my dagger..."

Delen's dagger glittered in the gloom, suddenly appearing quickly close to Moren's throat. So close that as soon as the other nervously moved, the blade gently sliced the skin into the blood. But the hand that was holding it still did it firmly.

Involuntarily, Oliver wondered at what point Delen had found them? And how much did he hear? Delen's words made him guess that it couldn't have been more than a moment ago...

Moren smirked and raised both hands in a seemingly surrendered gesture so that the opponent behind his back could see them.

Oliver didn't wait for a better opportunity. He pushed Moren aside to allow himself to escape. He had nothing to defend except a sling, for the sword had been torn from his hand in the crowd. He could not count the blow to the jaw will block Moren, because he had the opportunity to test the hardness of his head many times. Nor did he want to give him an opportunity to hurt or kill the lieutenant. But he knew he would pursue him. It was a better solution than Delen's fight with Moren.

So he started a crazy escape through the familiar corridors.

The push back allowed Moren to dodge the dagger and hit the lieutenant. However, as Oliver had predicted, Moren wasted no time in the skirmish, but instead pursued his victim. He pressed forward, heedless of anything. Adamant. And relentless. Wherever Oliver was in his escape, Moren was almost right behind him. He almost grabbed the torn dress several times. He was right there. One step behind him.

Delen hit him with his sword on the main stairs, wounding his arm.

Moren lost the rest of any semblance of any mental balance. He roared furiously and grabbed the lieutenant who chased him. Delen had more strength than Oliver, but he could barely cope with the murderous embrace. And the sword was thrown from his hand as if he were a newly trained youth.

Despite his resolute resistance, he finally fell down the stairs, losing his balance as he grappled with Moren, powerful and charged with steadfast force. He struck so hard that a loud bang in the temporarily empty corridor. Oliver froze, fearing Moren might have broken Delen's spine, but luckily it didn't. Delen, stunned by the pain, had no more strength to get up, and Moren, overjoyed by this fact, sat down next to him and took his head in his strong hands, ready to smash his skull.

Oliver had come to the first thing he could use as a weapon against his pursuer.

At the top of the stairs was a vase of flowers on a small column. He threw them away in a hurry and quickly found himself near Moren.

He delivered a blow with all his strength.

Moren, guided by his sixth sense, blocked the strike, standing up quickly with his hand outstretched. Then he hit Oliver with the back of his hand. The blow was so strong Oliver felt as if his cheekbone had just snapped. The face caught fire. For one brief moment he thought of Julien, and his blood boiled with anger. He remembered Moren's words at the corner of the corridor. Meanwhile, a dropped vase shattered to pieces. Oliver picked up one of the splinters, cutting his hand on sharp edges, and aimed at Moren. Moren parried that punch, pushed him, knocking him off his feet, then jumped to Delen and struck him a few blows.

They both fell down the stairs.

And then Moren took Delen's head a second time, slapping it against the floor.

Oliver knew Moren liked to hit the head in all sorts of fancy ways. He forced himself to get up quickly, though his ears were buzzing and his face was burning with pain.

This time his blow with the collected fragment cut Moren's head and knocked him off his feet.

"Let's go!" Oliver helped the stunned lieutenant to his feet, glancing fearfully at the stunned bandit. "There will be no second chance!"

"I'll kill him!" Delen narrowed his eyes in pain, but the raised sword in his hand didn't even tremble.

"Excellent," Oliver said sarcastically. "Be like him. Kill the unconscious!"

Delen looked into his eyes. It was evident that he wanted the kindness of an unusual girl.

"I'll call the guards," he said after a short thought, "let them lock him in the dungeons."

Hearing the buzz of voices at the end of the corridor, he started calling the guards while Moren lay still unconscious. Oliver didn't want to be around him anymore. He started walking towards the voices, wishing he would finally leave the castle. The first men, the servants and the guards, had just appeared, and seeing the lying one and the lieutenant of the king's guard quickened their pace.

"Selena," the lieutenant said softly to him, to which Oliver, mentally exhausted, reacted with difficulty, as he should, having had enough for today, "I'll take you to safety."

Moren sprang up suddenly, before the first guards reached him, pushed them away angrily, one of them tearing a dagger from his belt. He got to Delen and Oliver sooner than his head injuries would suggest. He put the dagger to the throat with the lieutenant's back turned to him, pushing his whole body against him and with a quick, strong movement cut his throat.

Surprised, Delen couldn't even make a sound. He raised his hand in a defensive gesture, covering the wound.

Oliver held his breath.

Delen collapsed among the surprised and shocked people.

He was dead.

Moren grabbed the shaken Oliver's gown and turned to find himself behind his back. He brought the dagger to his throat again.

"She belongs to me!" shouted the gathered and coming guards. "Don't come closer, or she will die like your knight!"

Several women cried. The men had their swords ready with an angry expression. Moren slowly backed away, dragging Oliver with him until he found a room, and after a brief peek inside, he pulled the boy in, then closed the door.

"My every plan..." he muttered angrily under his breath. "Take off those hair!" He yelled furiously in Oliver's ear, tugging at the wigs by the hair. "They keep crawling in my mouth!"

But the wig, firmly fixed with numerous hair pins, would not break away. Oliver groaned as he felt a distinct headache as he pulled out his real hair.

"Leave it!" He shouted angrily, and Moren slapped him in the face and twisted the long dark tangles around his arm.

"If they are holding so well," with a strong movement he pulled him to his legs, "let them be useful."

Oliver struggled desperately, still thinking about what might be happening to Julien now. And what will happen to him in a moment... And to her.

"You meant mainly my sister?!" Asked angrily. "So you want to force her? Through me?!"

"You wish it were so, right?" Moren replied with a question, with a strange smirk on his lips. "No, Oli. I wants you. And when it touches her, too," he added, and slapped him in the face again, until Oliver heard ringing in his ears, "it's an added pleasure..."

* * *

Julien cried in anguish. Her face changed more and more. She was swollen and red from blows inflicted not directly on her, but by the power of perfectly perceptible bonds.

She was in the room with Ross, which Alesei only found for them. She locked herself with him for fear of the mercenaries who were lingering around Sel's household for a while until they heard the news of the healer from the court physician. Then they left the house, leaving in it the royal soldiers whom the prince himself had appointed to guard the Beckert brothers. Both were mistakenly convinced that, like Sai, Julien also worked in the House of Pleasure, so for lack of entertainment, they offered her various offers, also thrown through closed doors. Some of them, she did not know, drank some of the healer's blood, which of course increased their sexual urges. She ignored them, concerned with the state of the brother whose fear and pain she felt now constantly.

Alesei visited them for a while, before he dealt with the fate of their dead friends and the destroyed carriage that had now become theirs, that is, his, Sai, and possibly Ross's only home. He brought a cloth wet with the healer's blood. He gave Ross a few drops. He persuaded her too. But the bond made new impact marks appear anyway. They lasted shorter, true, but they were. Fear and pain won over desires she didn't feel now. She was too afraid of what could happen. All she wanted was for Oliver's pain to ease off after using the healer's gift.

She knew everything that was happening to him, and even the power of the healer's extraordinary blood could not suppress it. She could feel his panic.

"Julien?" She heard Ross's weak voice from the bed by the window "Is something wrong with Oliver?"

She looked at him. An hour after giving him the healer's blood, he was finally able to speak and move a bit, but still not much. Apparently, such a severe beating took time to heal. Fatigue was probably doing its job as well. However, there was no doubt that the miracle of bringing him back to life and health was becoming more and more visible with each passing moment.

She didn't answer. She swayed steadily from side to side, listening to her brother's thoughts, trying to figure out what was happening to him now. It put her in a strange trance. As if she was losing herself, losing the contours of her existence, her own identity...

"Come on," Ross whispered, worried about her mood. "Come to me. Don't be alone with this. I want to help you."

"You can't help me with this," she replied quietly despairingly.

She felt the pain. As if someone was tearing her hair out of her head. A groan escaped her breast.

Ross struggled to raise his hand. He was calling for her.

She felt another blow and fear. The inevitable was coming. She wouldn't help him. Wherever he is, whatever awaits him, she will feel it with him.

She looked at Ross. He lowered his hand, unable to make any longer effort, but his eyes looked at her with understanding and sympathy. She ran to him. She slipped under the covers and pressed tightly against him as if he could somehow protect her.

"I'm scared," she whispered.

He searched for her hand. He took it gently.

After a moment she felt the gentle touch of his lips on her forehead.

She snuggled into his feverish body, clutching her hand on his hand.

* * *

A hollow bang on the door thwarted Moren's further intentions. He looked around nervously. His eyes fell on the desk set by the window.

"Let's go!" He picked up Oliver from the floor and forced him to climb onto the window sill to be able to look around this way.

"What are you doing?" Oliver worried at this, while mentally praying that help from behind the door would be in time before Moren did something crazy.

A chasm stretched beyond the window on the side of the garden. A little further, the rocks surrounding the castle began, but it was impossible to get to them from this window. Certainly the mighty son of a pastry chef could not do that. Moren looked at Oliver. He could do that. He climbs like a cat. But he doesn't have to run away. It is him that they go to help.

He realized he was lost.

No.

He won't let them just win! They won't take Oliver from him!

He opened a window that had no bars, for there would be no daredevil who would dare to get here this way.

The door was open with a bang. Guards and onlookers appeared at the threshold. Between them stood Kertis, concerned about the fate of the girl, who had left a despairing Kirian and Marten accompanying him at the lieutenant's body. There was also Alena with her friend from the kitchen and purser Kanel.

Before them, in a ghost mask, Sel stood...

At first, Moren didn't recognize him, and neither did Oliver, who had never seen him like this. Sel looked so different from the people gathered here. The old friend said something to the guards, who had stepped back, lowering their swords, though Kertis was not determined to do so and kept his on the alert, watching Moren, watching his nervous movements. Sel stepped forward with a quick, confident step, without out of breath. Far too sure and too bold for what Moren knew about him.

He felt anxiety overcome him.

He wanted a confrontation with Sel, he even wanted it, dreaming of silencing his troubled thoughts. He imagined that the death of Sel or himself would put an end to strange, disturbing changes in his soul. It will end everything anyway. Something in him will change, break, even destroy, but certainly will not leave it the same as before.

But it was supposed to be on his terms...

"What now?" Sel asked calmly, looking at him "What are you going to do, Moren?"

He couldn't calmly look into the black-inked eyes that looked at his old friend so seriously, with such a strange cool calmness different from Moren's anxiety. He heard his rapid breathing, and his body splashed with sweat.

Sel wants to intimidate him...

Best friend.

Oliver felt Moren pull him slowly over the edge. He was afraid to say a word or make a gesture. At any moment, an unpredictable madman could drag him into the abyss. There was no way to escape.

Oliver wasn't worried about himself. If they fall, death is likely to come quickly. He will die, it is true, but that was not what made him despair.

The violent death of one of the twins reportedly caused unimaginable suffering to the other. Breaking ties was torture, as if the soul was torn apart. It happened that the survivor went insane or committed suicide shortly after the death of his twin.

Oliver had always wanted Julien to be free from his troubles and to live a normal life. And since she had given him the pleasure of kissing from earlier times, he had dreamed of finding a way that would allow them to be intimate at such moments.

He wanted at least she to be happy, since it was not given to him.

His death would not bring her comfort, it would destroy her life.

"She belongs to me," said Moren, strangely calm.

Sel considered. This was not the time for accusations and reproaches, although he would very much like to shout them now. Moren stood on the edge of the windowsill. He held the silent Oliver tightly with one hand, and with the other he held the dagger to his neck. Sometimes his eyes glanced at the crowd of onlookers, checking to see if they knew exactly what they were exposing their kidnapped victim to by some unreasonable act.

Oliver's eyes pleaded him: "Do something," his eyes said.

"You never guessed," so he managed the only words that could change Moren's intentions. "You never even thought of it. Right, Moren?"

The ominous tone in Sel's voice made silence fall.

Knowing that everyone could hear him behind his back did not give him strength. But understanding in Oliver's eyes, yes.

Oliver knew.

"What?" Moren was surprised, as Sel assumed, for a moment forgetting about suicide plans, "what are you talking about now?!"

"I loved you..." Sel whispered to him, putting all his recent feelings into his words.

Moren froze in amazement, experiencing a shock he had probably never experienced in his life. He almost lowered his hand with the dagger, for the first time surprised and devastated by a news so improbable, so shocking that at first he was not only speechless.

He almost felt his heart stop beating from the sensation!

And the tone... The tone Sel used. He did not scream, he did not thrash in great despair.

He said it as he would probably say those words over his grave.

As if Moren had just died.

"Sel..." Moren suddenly felt that nothing but the three of them was important now. As if everything else around had ceased to matter. "You are my friend..." he began to explain gently.

It can't be true!

Sel's mask of death twisted in sudden anger and despair.

"I AM NO LONGER YOUR FRIEND!!!" He shouted, entering his word, his voice full of pain and anger.

Moren stiffened at the scream, felt fear.

For the first time since he chose the path of violence, acting to his liking, he began to fear, as if he had only now discovered that his behavior had exceeded all acceptable limits.

Sel, terminally ill with heart disease according to Moren's knowledge, until recently a friend. The man who, living on the brink of life and death, was the only one who was not afraid of his anger - he stood before him like a judge and a doom demon, not intending to forgive him any guilt. No harm done and no pain inflicted.

It's over.

Suddenly his confidence left him, as if he were indeed standing before the instrument of justice, settling all sins.

He remembered killing Sel's mother...

He wanted to explain to him again that it was for his own good, that she didn't love him anyway, but suddenly all the arguments seemed silly and cruel to him, as if he had woken up from a strange trance.

It was a crime. Ordinary murder. It was true.

He ordered Tenan to kill his father. And Tenan had to obey orders.

And also Milera...

It was good to work with someone else's hands, pretending it was for someone else's good.

He usually chose to kill anyone who separated him from Sel.

With his or someone else's hands.

Like that male whore. The opportunity to get rid of him also came by itself. He killed one of Ramoz's men. He had that explanation on hand, too, should Sel ever ask for it. And Julien was too familiar. She should have been destroyed, not killed. Killing her would destroy Oliver too soon.

And Oliver...

Beautiful, slender, haughty. Mysterious and ambiguous.

He resisted him so much.

And his friendship with Sel made Moren want him even more. They both liked the same man. They had something in common. The three of them could travel the world...

He was the idiot who took these illusions to be true a long time ago! He had long twisted the meanings of words or gestures to suit his desires. He arranged the circumstances according to his own point of view.

He only rearranged the world in his fashion.

Fool!

Blind fool!

He managed a deep sigh. There was something cleansing about that sudden flash of understanding, as if that was what he had been looking for all the time, wanting to confront Sel. He felt a strange peace as he spoke to the dark figure, the shadow of an old friend to whom he so cruelly and ruthlessly destroyed everything that was dear to him for his own selfish gain:

"I understand."

He really understood it all now.

The calm tone of his voice, so different and so long desired by Sel, surprised Oliver. What could it mean?

Life or death?

Moren, still holding him, nodded his head in agreement, and was relieved to see that Sel's eyes flashed with tears at the gesture. He also understood. There was hope for him. He still had strength and heart in him.

He looked at Oliver, his only love. He could see part of his face, dark hair wig. He felt the warmth of his body so dear to him, so longed for, against his body. He wanted to destroy it...? Or maybe keep it forever?

That damned hesitation again!

In a moment he will convince himself that he is doing it because it must be so. Or he will persuade himself another equally stupid, nightmarish argument. Thoughts kept shifting like a poorly set mechanism.

Oliver belonged to him...

Oliver will die because of him...

He pressed his face against his neck, reveling in his scent. The smell of blood and sweat, but above all sweet to his senses, the smell of a loved one. Oliver closed his eyes. Whatever was going to happen now was up to Moren.

This uncertainty was a torment because of the fate of the twin sister.

Death could be a relief...

Moren felt his body begin to fever again. Oliver's warmth turned back into the torch that lit the pyre. Moren's body tensed, and the tense penis began to throb.

Oliver felt he pressing against him and began to tremble.

"Don't be afraid," his tormentor whispered in his ear. "It's all over."

Then he looked at Sel again.

For a while.

There was everything in that look.

He let go of Oliver abruptly, removed his hand with the dagger, and retreated exactly one last step that separated him from death...

His legs buckled under Oliver and he would have involuntarily followed him towards the precipice, had it not been for Sel, who had leapt forward to grant Moren's silent request, grabbed him and pulled him away from the window. Terrified, Oliver clung to him.

"I'll take her," he heard the familiar dark-haired Kertis voice, and a moment later he felt someone trying to pull him away.

"Selena," Kertis said to him, seeing him resist, "your friend is barely standing. He's hurt. Let him go. We will lead you and Alena to a quieter place, with no onlookers."

Oliver looked at his friend fearfully. Only now did he notice that the man had a weird bandage on his leg, soaked with blood, and his whole body showed signs of a struggle. Alena was beginning to say something to him when suddenly Sel moved forward, back onto the windowsill. As if he was going to...

"Stop!" He stopped him abruptly, hugging him tightly. "No, Sel. No!"

He had a terrible feeling that Sel was going to jump out, as sure as his own heartbeat.

He wasn't going to ever let him do that!

The onlookers were still standing, though a few of them left, waiting for the participants of the unusual event to leave the room. One of the soldiers present climbed onto the sill and looked down.

Then he looked at Sel and nodded his head in agreement.

Moren was dead.

* * *

Ross only fell asleep when Julien's breathing became steady and calm. After she cried, hugging him, he was dying of anxiety that something much worse would happen to her than he had ever seen before. He was so concerned about her fate that his condition slowed down in his recovery. He was constantly plagued by fever. As if by force of will he was holding back the saving gift of a healer. After Julien fell asleep, he finally allowed himself some rest.

His dreams were restless. Worry about Julien, about her brother, whom he knew only by sight, but he was worried about her, his recent experiences, and finally the most painful fear about Sel, who had followed Moren, gave him no respite.

Between sleep and fear, regret also rose...

He whispered her name in his sleep.

Once upon a time they just met on one of the narrow streets. She was touched by his fate and his quiet dignity. She had been giving him food or a few coins since she first noticed the beating marks on his body. His mother's drunk friends liked to show, who was the master in the hellhole Ross had to call home. Those who stayed longer for a while were eager to raise him or silenced him in this way when he was little. Five years ago, he was severely beaten for the last time. For beliefs (as Valeriea had generally explained - the only person he knew in this world who was concerned about his welfare). He ran away from home with difficulty and never returned there. Valeriea interceded with Rebecca for him and initially stayed there as a servant after he was able to walk freely. He himself decided about his further fate and enjoyed great interest among customers.

And now Valeriea was dead...

He knew about it. Painfully aware despite great pain, he heard what was happening there with the overturned carriage. He couldn't move, couldn't even speak, but he could still hear. And he wondered for the first time in his life when fate would mercifully take him into the embrace of death, for he was terrified of the thought that in this numbness he might remain helpless and dumb for the rest of his life. He heard the soft, so strange, because sad, voice of Tenan, that killer, right hand in Moren's gang, speaking to Julien. He felt real relief when Julien placed the pendant around his neck and wrapped it warmly. He even heard riders and soldiers approaching, which he was relieved to hear, for he thought he could also hear the wagon creaking from a distance of the undertakers who would probably have enjoyed his misfortune.

And now, in a dream, he was calling her to himself, wanting to see her again. He was tormented by the thought that he couldn't see her anywhere, she wasn't with him, as she had been so far. She taught him so much. They relied on themselves. And now he couldn't find her even in his dreams, as if she had suddenly been erased from his life...

Julien was awakened by his restless movements. She felt better now, and the hits marks disappeared. She knew that whatever she was doing now, her brother was safe, though she felt his sadness. Calmly, as she did sometimes with sick Sel, or to cheer Oliver, she gently stroked a sleeping, feverish Ross on the head until he finally calmed down as if that was what he wanted. The fever dropped and healthy colors appeared on the face.

She also thought about Selarion.

He hated that full name.

She wondered if he was still alive. Moren took almost everything from him. How could their meeting be resolved?

Sel is as calm as if in perpetual sorrow. This was not the last time she had seen him. Those eyes...

She really wanted both of them back. She wanted to hug Oliver and hug him tightly. No matter how much pain and tears it sometimes caused her, she loved her brother with a sad sisterly love, loved the other half of her soul, and felt that he thought the same. And Selarion has always been their friend. A momentary desire and a kiss, the spark between them in her heart she decided to suppress forever. Ross was sincere in his feelings, she was sure, though she wasn't used to his kind of love yet. And Sel, ever since he found out about it, seemed like a man who suddenly saw his eyes. She wanted him to finally start living now. If only fate would allow him to do so...

* * *

Sai sat on her heels by Lena's grave, staring at the fresh soil. Alesei, strengthened by the gift of a healer, as they all began to call blood in a delicate form, finished covering Lena's grave. There was also Valeriea's grave in between, which would surely bring some relief to Ross when he found out she had been laid to rest in Sel's garden. Better not to know that she died of such a terrible blow.

Neither of them would want death if they had a choice.

The day brought with it hot sun and a rapidly approaching storm. It was not the best time to dig graves. Water could wash away fresh soil. Therefore, Alesei collected many stones with the help of soldiers, whom he paid for it and for help in repairing and bringing the carriage to the yard. At the moment they were working there persistently, glad that they had something to do, instead of standing by waiting for something unknown.

Were it not for the healer's blood, Sai and Alesei would have long since given up and lay in the beds in the room next to Ross and Julien. But Alesei did not leave the bodies of his friends to chance. Immediately after he laid stones on the fresh graves, he was going to go to the royal gardens, and even the coming storm could not affect his plans. He felt he couldn't do otherwise.

A friend's body lay somewhere in the gardens.

They entered together the House of Pleasure to earn some extra money on pleasures. Women felt honored when they chose them - it was never the other way around. They loved them and had a good time. And if it was still possible to earn good money...

Then they would go somewhere and finally settle down, settle in cozy houses in a few years, with a warm and alluring wife by side, as they sometimes joked. They liked Sel because, although he could not drink with them, he was a good companion at play, and his silent longing for freedom in the pleasures of life gripped their hearts.

Darmon did not deserve to die. Or that his body was lying in a ditch somewhere now. He was a great companion and faithful friend. He deserved a decent burial.

"You're Alesei, right?" they heard a soft voice suddenly.

He looked a little irritated at the man who dared to interrupt him at such a moment. The soldier looked a little embarrassed at the tense muscles on his exposed belly. The white shirt clung to the body, sweating from the heat and exertion, which also upset a soldier unused to seeing such force. He must have entered the service recently. Alesei might also bet he hasn't plow anyone yet.

"Why do you ask?" Alesei replied in his still hoarse voice, which had not yet returned to its original state.

"You see..." the soldier hesitated. "Others asked to tell you that they were afraid that the dead would drag the living to the grave with them. Such a superstition. The healer is..." he stuttered a bit. "The healer is probably dying. He has got an infection in the wounds, he is delirious with fever. They don't give him..." he fell silent again, apparently unable to bear the thought, "too great a chance. In other words," he began in a different way, sighing deeply, "also take care of the bodies in the bedroom at the end of the corridor, so as not to bring about some misfortune."

Alesei looked at him thoughtfully. The youngster turned red. This must have been his first major assignment. Certainly he had not yet participated in the fighting. Despite his inexperience and terrible shyness, he was accepted into the royal army, probably thanks to acquaintances. He and Darmon weren't so lucky when they applied for it. The sons of vineyard owners, whose estates had fallen into ruin due to poor harvests and high taxes for the king, were not accepted. They had no acquaintances, and they did not want to become mercenaries, because there was all the raff. House of Pleasure wasn't so bad. They were lucky that their bodies seemed quite right to Rebecca the first time she looked at them.

The youngster did not enter Mother Rebecca's house. His innocence so perfectly visible to a trained eye was even amusing, despite the seriousness of the subject of the conversation. Hence, Alesei did not become angry. He smiled slightly, looking at the dark clouds of the oncoming storm. You could see every lightning bolt from here. The thunders grew louder.

"Tell the boys," he said, "I'll bury the bodies as soon as the storm is over."

"But the dead bodies in the house...!" The soldier immediately protested.

Alesei with apparent carelessness pretended to drag on, in fact wanting to give a small display of his well-formed muscles. Judging by the face of the youngster, the effect was achieved.

"I'll only say it one more time," he announced slowly, "I'll bury them after the storm. This is the family of the man the healer is visiting. And if only that is why they deserve a little respect, not a funeral in mud and rain."

"I remember them," the soldier replied softly. "He's the best silk merchant in town. Before the plague, my parents often bought goods here. I saw him several times in the warehouse. Apparently..." he suddenly jammed, remembering something, and glanced nervously at Alesei. "I'll pass it on to them," he changed his tone suddenly.

"What did you want to say?" Alesei asked in a dark voice with a growling hoarseness in the background.

The soldier clearly wanted to leave, but on reflection he replied:

"Apparently, his parents didn't love him. They cared for him, but they really didn't care. They waited for him to die. Everyone around knew about it."

They looked at each other in sudden agreement.

Alesei almost smiled at this thought they both obviously shared.

"A tempting offer..." he replied to the youth's silent suggestion.

The boy smiled and walked away.

Alesei was sure the man had at least some ideas on what to do with the bodies of parents who refused to love their child. He was amazed at the liking for Sel that suggested the idea, but it wasn't the first time that a friend had aroused almost instinctively warm feelings in people when they saw him. Unfortunately, the soldier probably forgot, like his commander and companions, how Sel's parents had died. He remembered. And that's why the smile didn't appear on his lips. The vulgar military jokes were out of place here. When Sel entered the house first, following the story he had heard, he immediately checked the bedroom.

And he did not forget what he saw there...

It was impossible to forget.

* * *

Oliver sat in the corner of his service room, slowly and deliberately pulling out the hairpins that were tucked into the hem of a badly damaged wig. Some of the long hair was pulled out by Moren. If they had remained loose, everyone would have guessed the fraud. But that was not what caused him suffering. While Sel, bathed and disguised, slept in the narrow bed Alena's friends had brought next to him, without unnecessary questions, Oliver remembered Delen's last moments and his own words. If he hadn't stopped him, he would probably be alive. Why did he do it?! Why didn't he let him do that?! Moren was a scoundrel and did not deserve an honest death. He did not deserve the death he had brought on himself. It was too gentle on him...

Hair pins freed the hair, which, in strands, slid down to the shoulders, pricked painfully. Under the midsection he felt the hard crusts of clotted blood, his own blood, and a searing headache. Even so, he continued to remove the wig, not using any of the potions Alena had left for them to soothe their pain.

He deserved the pain. His suffering was nothing compared to what he had prepared for Delen with his paltry attempt at nobility. That's how he felt it. Tears were already streaming down his face, caused by the pain of the torn skin. He did not care about it. Until he couldn't feel any clasp anymore and he was able to take off his wig. His own hair stuck to her with sweat and blood. Her photo was a painful nightmare. Still, he did nothing to relieve himself. Crying in a quiet torment caused not only by the suffering of his body, he slowly drew from his head the proof of deception, a symbol of false identity. He felt like a bandit who chose this disguise to manipulate people for his own ends. A traitor, a bastard of the worst kind. These people stood up for him, helped him.

They trusted him.

He cheated them. He didn't want it to be this way, but it did. Could he look them in the eye and tell the truth? Was he going to tell Kirian that his noble brother had died for a disguiser? He would hurt their feelings and defile Delen's deed. Delen died like a hero, defending a woman. The truth would ridicule his act. It would take his honor.

He couldn't do this to him.

He looked at the wig. There was a lot of his own hair and blood inside. So much so that, fearful of what was left on his head, he took a small mirror and looked at it.

It took his breath away.

First the mad ranger and his companions, then Moren. Much of the hair had been torn out as if it had been pulled in handfuls. There were so many bald, painfully stinging spots that it seemed a miracle that the wig was still on the head. The ones that remained, and there weren't many of them, were covered with scabs.

The sight was terrifying. Now, surely no one would call him a beauty if they saw him. A torn dress, barely clinging to the body, numerous scratches by mercenaries, bruises - they completed the rest.

He didn't know if the sight frightened or saddened him more. He was scared at first, which was natural, but then he thought maybe it was good. Maybe he deserved it? Maybe fate punished him for deceiving people with ambiguous beauty? His appearance was a curse, he was punished...

A knock on the door pulled him out of his gloomy thoughts. He put on a wig, a few hairpins, and with a piece of string, he tied it into a still thick and thick ponytail of dark hair.

Alena was standing outside the door.

"Selena," she worried, seeing his face and taking his hand with concern. "May I come in, honey?"

He nodded in response, admitting her. She closed the door and led him to the chair he had just been sitting in. She stroked his face gently. He could hardly refrain from telling her the truth. He was tired of pretending. Enough of myself in this outfit. Enough of everything.

"I have something unusual," Alena said gently. "I got some healer blood." She pulled out a small bottle with brown contents. "It'll help you and your hurt friend."

He stared at the bottle in fear.

"Don't worry," Alena told him. "They saved him. People wanted to tear him to pieces alive, but they managed to save him from the worst. Suddenly his brother showed up and some people who reportedly work or worked in the best brothel in town! Do you have any idea what was going on in the marketplace? People tore our healer apart like he was a piece of meat!" She said the last words with tears in her eyes, indignant at this brutality. "My brother took him to the Street of Craftsmen to the house of the silk merchant Andilo. Apparently the owners were killed by the same madman who attacked you. Did you know them?"

Oliver was speechless at the news. He nodded his head in agreement. Instinctively, his gaze fell on Sel, and silent compassion seized his thoughts. Moren killed Sel's parents. What else did this monster do?! How many more crimes has he committed that he will learn about?

How could this man still be called anyone's friend?!

"I..." he bit his tongue in time, thinking frantically. He must not fall out of the role, he promised himself. "Celina and I used to go to the merchant's depot when she had a day off. When I visited her, being in the city with my mother, we made use of the hospitality of a goldsmith who lives there. We liked to see the colors of the fabrics and dream about them," he finished quietly.

Mother Earth and all known and unknown gods! His parents, let their souls find solace, could no longer deny anything. They didn't like lies.

Alena accepted the story.

"Here," she handed him the bottle. "A few drops are enough."

She waited while he tasted it. Involuntarily, as he tasted the blood, he thought about how strange human destinies were going. Vivan, whom he had not been able to protect, though he had promised it silently and wished to fulfill that promise but had to save his own life, was now at Selarion's house, a few steps from his own. All his life, Sel dreamed that a healer would help him. And now his dream will come true, and he has even received a little more from life.

He did not know that his friend's heart was healthy and it was also thanks to him... He gently put a few drops of blood into Sel's mouth, watching if he had swallowed it, convinced that it was helping him not only to heal the wound on his leg and numerous smaller and smaller more damage. He wanted his dreams to come true. Due to the healing, calming tea Alena had given earlier, Sel swallowed the gift with difficulty, hardly realizing it. Oliver comforted in her own worries the joy of her friend when she found out that he was cured. Though the source of the healing worried him. Blood. How much was Vivan bleeding? Why was it distributed this way?!

Pleasant warmth and relaxation spread through him like the soothing power of a lotion. It penetrated bones, healed wounds, eliminated bruises. This warmth enveloped his head, as if a healing compress had been placed on it. The pain is gone.

Vivan helped him, though he could not do the same for him.

He felt his eyes sting with tears.

"What about the healer?" He asked softly.

"Unfortunately, apparently it's not good. Sedon will return to the dungeons soon. He said you had to hope, but..." she spread her hands in silent despair. "You have to wait. Hope and be patient. He would visit him again today."

Oliver's heart tightened.

"That's where you met the bastard?" Alena asked. "Apparently he gathered a bunch of people like him. It was known as Moren's Gang."

He just nodded again.

He felt sad, although it was not as strong as it was a moment ago. This was probably due to the gift of the healer.

His blood.

She took his hand in a gesture of comfort.

"Have you heard of the boy called the Cat in town?" She asked to change the subject. He looked at her in surprise. "Apparently he always eluded him and could even walk on a bare wall. No one knew for sure who he was, but the kids in Verdom have had amazing stories about him. He was their hero. I hope he is alive and has not succumbed to the plague."

Involuntarily, and perhaps for the first time since he had escaped death, Oliver smiled slightly. It was weird to hear about himself this way. As if talking about someone complete stranger.

"A little," he replied softly.

"Better?" Alena asked. "Can I help you now?"

"Thank you," he felt his strength growing visibly. "You've already done a lot for me."

Alena got up, getting ready to leave.

He had such a great desire to tell her his secret. But he only managed a slight smile.

"I haven't thanked you for your help yet," she said. "I was lucky you were with me then."

"You don't have to thank."

"Your friend is famous, you know?" Alena tried to hide her embarrassment about unpleasant memories as she said it. "He ran through the attacking healer people like a battering ram. And Kertis told me to say that for the help given to you, he and his companions in the detachment are ready to help him. And if someone would insult him in any way or ridicule him..." she hesitated embarrassed. "He confessed love then..." she paused for a moment to give him time to understand, although it was unnecessary, he guessed what was going on. "This person will be dealing with them," she finished a bit awkwardly.

"Tell him thank you on my and his behalf," Oliver smiled, realizing now why Sel's bed had been placed here without hesitation. There was no threat to Selena's honor.

And that also meant, judging by the words Alena had given him, that his friend might be in trouble here.

You have to leave the lock as soon as possible.

If it were up to him, he would be gone now. But he knew he couldn't do it.

"Selena. There are two more things."

Now, reassured by the soothing warmth, he felt able to continue playing his part. Gloomy thoughts faded. Cheerfulness entered his heart. Soon, he hoped, it would all be over.

The clock in the castle tower struck noon. Alena waited for his final tone to fall, to say with soft sympathy:

"Tomorrow's Delen's funeral. With all honors."

He swallowed nervously. He had to be there. He owed him.

"They ask if you will come..."

"Yes, I will."

"The funeral will be at noon."

"I'll be there. I promise."

Alena sighed.

"Maybe you want me to..."

"No," Oliver replied sadly. "I need a little solitude."

Alena paused for a moment.

"And the second thing?" He asked softly.

"The King would like to thank you for helping to save the Queen. Tomorrow after breakfast, at a special audience to which everyone will be invited. He will generously reward you for your courage. And also some other people who showed it during the fighting. Then there will be a great feast."

Oliver closed his eyes. The last thing he need!

Alena came over and hugged him tightly without warning.

"I know it's a lot for you," she whispered. "But hold on. A bit more. Just a little more."

He felt as if he would hear it more than once...

* * *

Paphian looked at Sedon before he left the room. Several guards were waiting for him outside the door. One of them closed it politely.

Only he and Vivan remained.

The storm had already hung over the merchant's house and the first heavy drops fell on the dry earth and the fresh stone-protected tombstones in the garden. The girl who had helped at the beginning while they treated Vivan didn't move. There must have been someone really close to her in the grave she was sitting in front of. The muscular black-haired man had finished his grim job and was now speaking to her. Paphian couldn't see her face, but he was sure she wasn't listening. Finally, as the thunder fell heavily and the rain broke down for good, the bully picked her up and carried her home. She did not defend herself, she hugged him, her face strangely calm.

The thunder wouldn't wake Vivan. He was so weakened by bouts of high fever and blood loss that he finally gave up. He slept, reassured by the potions Sedon had given him in a horse's dose. His breathing was so quiet that the frightened Paphian checked almost every now and then whether his brother was still alive. He was barely visible under the dressings. They must have tied his hands to the bed, because in fear of deliriums he was tearing the bandages. There were herbal compresses on his eyes. Cracked veins in his eyes made him look like something out of this world. He would have to take them off when Vivan awoke. Bonds and blindness would scare him even more.

Extremely exhausted, he sat down heavily in the chair and took his hand.

Involuntarily, to rest his mind, he looked at the drawings above his head. They belonged to the merchant's son.

A view of the castle from the roof of some building. Entrance to the royal gardens.

Four people at one table. Woman, man, boy and girl.

His family?

A young man with a broad shouldered bull, a swarthy complexion and a mesmerizing gaze. I think it's Moren, that stalker of Oliver.

A view of a town in the valley, strikingly similar to Barnica.

Fair-haired girl of fairly common beauty in a wedding dress. There was another one underneath this drawing, a fragment of it protruding slightly. When he pulled it back, he saw a boy with sharp make-up, dark hair cut back. A theater actor or one of the brothels known here in the city, the House of Pleasure. Apparently, men wear their makeup there.

Whoever Selarion was, whom he remembered only for being sick and therefore having seen him maybe once or twice during his brief stay recently apparently in these drawings he portrayed important places and people in his life.

He looked again at the family at the table. Something was wrong.

The girl was dressed in black with a blurry face without features. The boy was gray. He was all that color, his face was almost invisible. The outline of the figure was also slightly outlined, as if it was about to disappear. The mother wore a purple gown, the father wore plain red.

Epic. And terrifying.

He looked at the drawings more closely, more consciously. The valley where his and Vivan's hometown was dazzled with colors. Dreamland…

There was a shadow on the wall behind Moren. But it was as if black was pouring out of him and seeping into the background. Source of darkness...

The bride looked pure and innocent, which effectively distracted from her hand. In one, she held a human heart, and it looked like she was squeezing too tightly, digging her nails in.

He was already intrigued, so he tilted her portrait aside and examined the boy in makeup.

Apart from the makeup, there was nothing unusual about this portrait.

Touched by a hunch, he tilted the portrait slightly to look at the other side.

There was another drawing there. Some character.

Feeling a bit like a sacrilegist, he took off his drawings and looked at his discovery.

On the other side was a young man. After a moment, recognizing the features, Paphian realized that he was looking at the same boy, but without heavy makeup on the front side. This portrait was devoid of dark features. The perfect image seen through the eyes...

He hastily hung all the drawings back into place. Now he was sure that he had looked into someone else's privacy, and he promised himself that he would not even look at the others, although the author did not make a secret of those, and certainly many people saw it. Then he saw familiar faces.

The drawing showed a couple. A boy of extraordinary beauty and a dark-haired girl. Oliver and Julien. The resemblance was striking. And it also didn't hide dark undertones.

He hadn't heard from him since Kirian went to help his brother. Until now, overwhelmed by what had happened to Vivan, he was ashamed to admit to himself that he had completely forgotten about him.

This brought back memories of Vivan's pendant.

This wounded boy, found at the Julien carriage, had a pendant. How did it fall into his hands?

Was he the one who ripped it off Vivan's neck?! Whoever beat him up would take the pendant too. It didn't. And Julien accompanied him...

The pendant glowed with its own light on this boy's neck. He had never seen anything like this.

There were dead bodies around.

What actually happened there? How did Julien end up on this street?

He got up.

"Lord Count," the soldiers guarding the door bowed.

"You got news about Lieutenant Delen?"

"Not yet, Count."

"Where are the people we took from the street?"

"Here in the guest rooms, Lord Count," the soldier pointed to the doors of two rooms in the corridor to his left. "They are exactly in the first one."

"How's the injured?"

"He already got..." the soldier hesitated. "I saw..."

"You split Vivan's blood?!" The shocked Paphian guessed.

"The prince's orders, sir," replied the soldier softly.

Paphian felt his blood rush in agitation. His jaw clenched.

"Tell him to come to my place as soon as he can get up. And just in case..." He deliberately paused, "keep an eye on them both."

* * *

Paphian learned about Oliver's fate from the merchant, cook Jancey, who had been brought home, and the royal guards accompanying him with a meager supply of food. Oliver's secret friend, whose drawings caught his attention so much, saved his life, and they both stayed in the castle to rest until tomorrow. From what he heard, Oliver was still Selena. Maybe because the next day the king wanted to thank an extraordinary maid for help.

Delen was killed, murdered by Moren.

Paphian felt sorry for Kirian. Delen was a noble man, full of courage. He was convinced to the end that he was defending a woman's life. Oliver must feel devastated by this turn of events. Good thing there is someone with him whom he can trust. The soldiers threw some coarse jokes about Selarion, but he quickly silenced them, reminding them that they were visiting his house, and several of them helped the muscular Alesei to carry parents murdered by the same bandit to the ransacked warehouse. With the approaching evening, the superstitious fear of the dead so intensified among the sentries that Alesei, who left during the storm to look for his friend's body in the gardens as he had decided, and on his return laid it wrapped in linen in the storehouse, had to fulfill their requests, because they were supposedly guided by the good of the healer. Paphian was almost certain that Moren was behind the killings. There were many indications of that. This reminder of the murdered silenced the cheerful comments and jokes.

Still holding Vivan's hand, he worried with every hesitant breath of his brother, so as not to share the fate of his friends and also not to plunge into despair over the loss. With each passing hour, he told himself that it was an hour more, that each moment more was perhaps a moment of hope that Vivan would survive. Because he was still alive. The night would decide his fate. Paphian did not allow anyone to replace him. The whole house was silent, some people were asleep, but he did not want to sleep. Eventually, however, the weariness of his recent adventures took over, and he fell asleep in the armchair, still holding Vivan's hand.

This is how Julien found them, who got out of bed at night, healed and cheered up both by Ross's well-being, who - she was relieved at last - was sleeping the dream of a healthy man, and by the much better mood of his brother, who was resting somewhere in the castle before the next day, apparently also refreshed by the gift of a healer. This time the gift didn't make them both excited, as if they were used to it already. It muted emotions and calmed down, for which she was grateful. Apparently, he acted like this with particularly strong emotions, and they had not lacked these before.

Quietly and delicately, she covered the sleeping warrior in the armchair and took the wrapped hand of the healer with concern.

After a while, she felt him gently return the hug.

She froze. Moved by this gentle gesture, she sat down on the bed and took the healer's hand in both of hers. Much earlier, when she was holding Ross's hand like this, she had the same silent conviction, hoping that she was holding him back with this gesture so that he would not depart for the land of the dead.

"Don't go," she said softly. "Fight."

The healer's hand grasped her firmly. As if he were saying, "Hold me tight."

"I'm holding you," she assured him, seeing the gesture.

The healer's other hand gripped his brother tighter. Paphian opened his eyes, alert to the wounded's every move. He did not dare to arouse hope in himself, but also shook his hand.

Then he looked at Julien, who was gently stroking her dressed hand.

She replied with a calm, sad look.

None of them said a word that night.

CHAPTER 12 — Death changes everything

Sel indulged in bleak thoughts as he lay and peered through the little window above him into the bright and sunny sky after yesterday's storm.

He should be thinking about Moren. It probably should be so. But he couldn't anymore. He cut himself off from him. It was as if someone had finally torn the veil behind which was the true picture of the world. His soul could no longer carry any more. Maybe he couldn't handle it now. Perhaps there will come a time when it will uproot it like a bad weed?

On the other hand, however, he was afraid of the thought of him. Behind Moren and his actions there were evil, great, overwhelming regret and a sense of irreparable loss. He wasn't ready for it. He was afraid that it would be beyond his strength to face it. He didn't want the past to overwhelm him, driving him to lose his mind in despair.

He finally wanted to start living.

Throughout his entire existence, because it would be difficult to call it life, he was preparing for sudden death. Now he could finally discover what it really meant. Although the beginning was bitter, he wanted to finally taste it. He would prefer not to look back anymore. To no longer see anything that reminds him of the past. But he knew it was impossible.

So he tried not to think about Moren. He recalled how he managed to save his friend. He began to dream shyly dreams that they would finally live freely in their friendship and more. Oliver will finally live as normal as he and Julien can. Finally.

He felt remorse for Milera. Not because she met a terrible end. He regretted it. He liked her company. They could talk to each other for hours. And in bed... As for the possibilities, it was pretty good. Milera watched over his well-being, providing him with the company he had missed so much since he had ceased to be close to Moren and had left his friendly House of Pleasure for her sake. He longed for those times, the longing of a sick man who knows that he has little to do in this world. He knew that this year would be his last... It was getting harder and harder for him to live and breathe. He was afraid of the emptiness around him more than before. He knew that he could not count on his parents, so Milera's sympathy and warmth were for him a relief and a shield against loneliness. At the same time, her presence took away from him what he wanted.

That's why he felt guilty now as he thought about it. Because, as much as he liked her, he was relieved in his heart that he was no longer obligated. Had she guessed these feelings? He did not think so. She thought they would love each other with time. It's just that this time was running out and he had recently sensed who he would really rather spend his last moments with...

Was that why she wanted them to have a baby?

What if they were successful after the wedding? What if this murderer killed not one but two lives?

He will never know it...

But he will always wonder where his life was going back then.

The healer survived... But what will happen to him next? How to deal with such cruelty?

He left Ross whom he couldn't help. His bleak thoughts focused on that. That was what his heart feared the most.

What if he died?

"Sel?" he heard Oliver's soft voice. "Are you sleeping?"

He looked at his friend's bed against the wall. Oliver lay dressed in men's clothes, clothes that he had hidden or acquired. He also didn't have a wig, this one hung by the fireplace.

"I wanted to feel like myself again," his friend confessed, seeing his gaze. "Of course I closed the door."

"I guess."

"Alena promised me that she would find a dress for today," Oliver grimaced bitterly. "Everyone is to appear at the king's audience, supposedly to reward me. And then this funeral..." his voice trailed down, still calm and composed, as if resigned to fate. "I must be there."

Sel decided to stand up to him.

And suddenly he felt a completely unexpected surge of panic that squeezed his heart.

He took a sharp breath, as if again, as it had happened not so long ago, he was choking from lack of air.

He was completely irrational with the thought that it was what it was again. He's sick again. And although his mind knew what it was, the thought so shocking, so sudden, had such persuasive power that he believed it.

"Sel!!!" Oliver jumped up from the bed, seeing what was happening. "What about you?! After all, I gave you a few drops of healer blood. Everyone recovers after that! You're healthy, can you hear? Nothing's bothering you anymore!"

He knew it was stupid. He knew he was right. There was a kiss. There was blood. He is healthy. So why does he think otherwise?! Where does this fear come from?!

"You're all right now," Oliver said, trying to speak calmly now. "Nothing. Besides life... like others..."

He helped him sit up. Sel's heart was beating madly in his chest, until even Oliver could feel it under his hand as he placed it there to say:

"It doesn't hurt, does it?"

But the longer the fear in the friend lingered, the more faith in the healer's gift might be weaker in him, despite the evidence. Fear was beginning to overwhelm him as well. He gathered himself up and took Sel's hand to guide it:

"You are not wounded," he moved that hand and his to his leg, also to reassure himself in the belief that where yesterday there was a makeshift dressing, now there is nothing. "You feel?"

Sel's forehead was covered with sweat as well as his entire body. He rested his head on Oliver's shoulder.

"For a moment... I don't know why..."

"I know," Oliver smiled, relieved. "I started to doubt myself. I don't know why either. It's impossible."

They sat in silence for a while, letting their peace slowly return.

"It will probably repeat itself again," Sel remarked quietly, more calmly. "Every now and then I'll wake up in sweat, afraid that I'm suffocating again, I'm sick again..."

"I think so," Oliver replied. "You can always call me then."

Sel smiled sympathetically at his friend.

"Thank you," he said simply.

They were silent for a moment.

"It's a disguise," Sel said again. "It's not curse on you, Oliver. You have a gift. You can impersonate a woman so perfectly that no one can guess the truth. I saw it. The lieutenant died in your defense. But it's probably better that he died not knowing who Selena was. Those people who helped you here would be devastated if they found out the truth. Don't hurt their feelings."

"I'm not going to."

"Then we leave the castle. We will leave Verdom. Forever."

Oliver looked at him. He silently shared his opinion. Nothing stopped them here anymore. Sel stepped back to study him. The friend's hair was very thinning, but the places that had probably been bald yesterday, because they had been torn out, were already covered with a delicate fluff. Soon the hair will be thick and spiky again.

Healer gift.

"When is this audience?" He asked.

"After breakfast."

"Will you still sleep?"

"No. I have to start preparing. Somehow fasten these shag on your head and put this..." he pointed to the chair, where the unusual corset was lying carelessly. "Well, you know... Standard fare," he added with a slight smile.

It no longer felt like a burden. He was driven by a sense of duty and the resilience of a young age. And also the words of a friend.

"Maybe in the meantime you can tell me what happened here?"

"If you reciprocate the same."

"We don't have that much time," smiled Sel.

Oliver looked at him, feeling his chest tighten at the thought of his friend's experience. Sel understood that look and smiled sadly again.

"Much more happened than you suspect. Too much for one morning. And..." He paused for a moment, feeling his eyes start burning dangerously over him, "too much for me yet."

Oliver gently pretended not to see anything.

"I had a good entrance..." So he began his story, standing up. "I drove into the castle in a speeding cart."

Sel looked at him curiously, ready to distract from his gloomy thoughts, hear his story...

* * *

Ross sat up in bed abruptly, with sudden dread.

Valeriea!

She stayed on the street. Probably the gravediggers had already taken her to the stake outside the city.

They burned her!

He spent yesterday in anxiety and fever, and then slept soundly as fast as he had not in a long time. And during this time...

His heart was pounding fast, his head was confused. He jumped up too abruptly. The next thought pushed him out of the room, so he sat up with his feet on the floor. He felt a strange familiar feeling. He's been through this already. This is how he once felt on the first day after a long recovery, when he had gathered enough strength to get up. The difference was that there was no trace of yesterday's ordeal on his body. He touched the back of his neck.

Nothing.

Yet the memory of yesterday's injuries remained in his body, which had thrown him off balance. A strange daze, as if the body had suddenly forgotten how to function properly, how to move an arm or a leg. As if learning it all over again. So when he got up as usual, the world spun.

He needed to calm down and recognize the situation.

He wore clean clothes that smelled familiar. This was what Sel always smelled like when he came in, except for the sweat. Julien, after healed him, changed him and washed him. Now he remembered feeling something in his sleep. He slept so soundly, unbelievable! Oh, that girl has probably never seen a man naked! He felt a little embarrassed about what Julien had seen. His body had scars that did not disappear. They kissed... He wasn't thinking clearly yet, since such things came to his mind. He felt ashamed of it. In fact, apart from Valeriea, who was dressing him when he came to her, beaten up a few years ago, no other woman had ever seen him stripped! It was because, and not because of Julien's innocence, he felt uncomfortable now. He was glad no one saw him now, he would have amused someone for sure. An old man in the oldest profession in the world and he burns with a blush like a young lady! He must control himself! Apparently, his brain had gone crazy!

Julien left, leaving him a piece of paper on the table and a jug of water, cup, towel and bowl. He got up more carefully this time, feeling weird like an old man, but it helped. The body understood what to do. He walked slowly the few steps to the table. The balance was almost back.

The card contained a short piece of information. Julien went to a healer. Well, she met his brother once. He stayed with them for several days. Sel mentioned it.

The hand almost touched his neck. He felt the pendant. He looked at it a little dazed.

Elaborately shaped hands encircled a ruby.

Yesterday he almost died.

When he thought about it, he concluded that just yesterday death had been eager to reach out for him several times. She almost made it last time.

The gravedigger cursed him? Why are curses so eager to come true? Faster than good wishes. Why, when he cursed everyone who beat him, especially the latter, Ramsey, who believed that by beating him would turn him back to the right path for a man, the curse would not come true?

Because evil feels good near another evil, as his mother used to say.

Well, he's not going anywhere yet. Not yet.

They probably think he stole the pendant. Probably Count Beckert doesn't believe Julien's words. Their story is so unusual, so much happened that night.

The murderer fell in love with an innocent girl and deliberately tore the pendant from the healer's neck, who must have been torn by the crowds.

Sick love does not deserve admiration.

Thanks to this - he was sure of it, though it filled him with bitterness - he was still alive.

It was so close. He could die or be crippled.

He tugged on the chain. The clasp should come off when you tug it, as it did for Tenan.

Nothing happened.

He pulled again.

Nothing again.

He reached up to the nape of his neck and ran his fingers for the clasp. Then he examined the chain carefully, more and more amazed.

There was no clasp. The chain was a uniform whole.

So he tried to put it over his head.

Like being pulled by extraordinary force, the chain was pulling his hands towards his neck, preventing him from doing so!

"It's impossible!" He whispered, feeling panic overwhelm him.

After several tries, he quit and found another way. He wanted to take off the pendant itself.

None of this.

Ruby could not be removed from his neck by any means available.

He sat down in the chair, stunned by this phenomenon.

"What am I going to tell them now?" He asked himself.

They may not believe it too. That's for sure.

He looked around, trying to collect his thoughts.

It was Sel's house.

He had never entered its threshold before.

The discovery of this fact made all other thoughts fade for a moment. Sel's house. He would not have known about it if he had not seen some familiar drawings on the wall. Sel sketched people in the marketplace. Stunned by the discovery, Ross recognized these sketches as a baker, a vegetable stall, and even one of the customers, who probably no one suspected of having contacts with "porcelain women" from the House of Pleasure. He felt his heart beat faster. He was at Sel's house! He hadn't expected to ever be here. He didn't even dream about it. There was no room for him here. He wasn't allowed to be here. Sel started a new life without him. And now he was in this house, feeling as if he had entered a forbidden temple. The thought made he feel excitement. He felt dizzy, happy and anxious at the same time. He was at Sel's house! He was touching things that he must have touched. He was wearing his clothes! And this house! This house was nothing like the ones he remembered. This was the room in the house that Valeriea was supposed to have. Calm, without ornaments. No dirt.

"Valeriea," he whispered, with tears in his eyes. "Do you see it, in the place where you are now?"

He continued in that intoxication and sadness until his emotions faded, savoring a moment that might never happen again. Slowly his thoughts returned to reality. The thought of Valeriea brought his attention now to the fate of her body. He had to find out what happened to him.

He left the room.

"I'm Ross," he thought it would be better for him to get some information from the guard outside a little closer. "I'm looking for my friends."

Unfortunately, his gesture, although completely devoid of ambiguity, completely natural, was met with unfavorable reception. In addition, the pendant on his neck even aroused suspicion.

"I don't hang out with a fagot and a thief, Ross," the guard pronounced his name underlining it with mockery. Fortunately for you, and the healer's misfortune, we are not to disturb you until Count Paphian comes to us. Then you have to go in there. Believe me, I will take you there for sure.

"No doubt," Ross replied coldly, angry at being treated like this.

His old survival instinct had made him vigilant again, since that was how he was being treated.

"Perfect. So get your ass up to the room. I have a more important task than watching over you."

"Interesting," Ross approached the other, prepared not to let him off his behavior. "You say you don't hang out with fagots and yet you thought about my ass. Wasn't that what your words were?"

The guard gasped in mounting anger, and perhaps the conversation would have been sharper had it not been for Alesei's appearance.

"What do you guys coo about?" He asked in a seemingly cheerful tone. His eyes, however, watched the situation carefully.

The guard calmed down. It would be foolishness and indiscretion to argue when the healer is in such a serious condition. In addition, he was well aware that it was really his fault. So he let go of the tone. He had a job to do.

"Don't waste your time," he muttered, resuming his original pose.

Ross was still glare at him as Alesei approached them.

"Problems?" He asked briefly.

"Yes," Ross said softly. "Once again someone sees only what he wants to see."

The guard pretended not to hear it.

"How bad is it?" Alesei asked, pointing to the door to the room with a healer inside to ease the tension.

The guard's expressive gaze was enough for the answer.

"I'm glad you're alive," Alesei quietly turned to Ross. "I missed a friend to talk to. Everyone acts as if they are in a tomb."

Ross smiled. Alesei had not sought contact with him before, they hardly spoke to each other. It was Darmon who was always outgoing and knew almost everyone at the House of Pleasure.

Alesei seemed to be afraid of men of a different orientation, although he never showed any hostility. The muscular young man sensed the irony in Ross's smile.

"Death changes people," he said, a hint of sadness.

Now Ross fully understood the meaning of his earlier words. Alesei must have felt lonely after losing his best friend. Just like him after losing Valeriea.

"I just wanted to know what happened to Valeriea's body," he whispered without looking at anyone. "And what is happening to you..."

The guard felt uncomfortable hearing these words. Now he really understood how he misbehaved.

"I buried her yesterday in Sel's garden," explained Alesei. "Just like Len and Lena. And Darmon this morning..." he paused for a moment, then added softly. "And how will I bury Sel's parents if he doesn't come back by noon."

Both men did not know what to say to that. Ross felt relieved and regretted at the same time, and he looked down, hiding bitterness. These people didn't treat Sel as they should. And they would never let him into their wonderful house himself, he was almost sure. Standing in the corridor right next to the door behind which the healer lay, he also felt a fear that this unknown man, famous for his good heart and kindness, would soon share the fate of his dead friends and the world would lose a significant part of its goodness. His hand found the pendant itself, as if summoned by him. Evil spread with impunity. Good was losing strength. Valeriea, the best woman he knew, was dead. And Len, always ready to help friends. Darmon. Lena, the other half of Sai's soul...

"Don't you get the feeling that evil feels good here?" Alesei asked him, looking thoughtfully at the door, unconsciously sharing his feelings. "It kills with impunity with plague and sword. It hurts. And waiting for more. It waits for everyone who has even a spark of goodness to die."

Ross looked at him, feeling cold and uneasy. As if a shadow engulfed his soul.

Cruelty.

Envy.

Intolerance.

Hostility.

Anger.

"Stop it," he said, trying to be calm, though the gloomy mood had spread to all of them after the question.

"Why? Am I wrong?"

"Evil cannot win."

"It already won, Ross."

"The plague will make all of us dead, sooner or later," the guard added grimly.

Ross looked at them both in horror.

"What is going on with you?" He asked in a fearful whisper. "Alesei," he grabbed his friend's hand, "evil will never win. Can't win!"

Suddenly the ruby glowed with a warm gentle glow that surprised the men. Ross felt a warmth seep through it, giving him strength, not physical, but one that was beginning to radiate in his soul, warming his heart. Alesei stared at him in surprise.

"What the hell? What are you doing?!"

Ross was surprised too, but he felt no fear. The words he had spoken, heard so many times that they had almost become banal, suddenly regained their former meaning. He saw that the same reassurance also filled Alesei, as if life had suddenly shone again unexpectedly. The warmth ran through the pendant to his heart and ran down his hand, then it kept going, and he felt the connection. He released Alesei. The guard looked at him.

"Just like when Count Vivan stood by my side," he observed. "Same feeling. As if suddenly a man could move mountains, and comfort would warm the heart like the warmest quilt on a winter night."

Rubin went out, but the impression remained. Ross was beginning to wonder what that actually meant to him when he suddenly felt a hand on his shoulder.

"We started this relationship badly," the guard said calmly. "I'm Nils. And you can go to the garden with your friend. Everyone knows Count Paphian's orders. I don't have to babysit you all the time."

Ross shook the hand that was now extended to him without hesitation, feeling relieved.

"I thought you would like it," he replied with a smile.

"It seems," said Nils, pointing to the pendant, "that it belongs to you now. The count will not be pleased."

Ross looked at both men calmly, knowing they were waiting for an explanation of this phenomenon. He replied, at that moment convinced that there was a lot of truth to it:

"It doesn't belong to me. It's filled with good, like a goblet with wine. Still partly belongs to the healer."

He said goodbye to Nils, following his friend.

"So, the pendant has no healing power, but it lifts people up, as the healer himself always did?" Asked Alesei on the way.

"It has, but not much. I'm not sure about the rest."

"It kept you alive."

"I think so."

Alesei stood on the stairs not far from the next guards and looked at Ross intently.

"I'm serious. It's the only reason you're still alive, Ross. You were dying. I saw it."

Ross swallowed nervously.

"I believe you."

But he thought a little differently. Before the pendant fell into his hands, he fought to live. He really wanted to live.

The pendant supported his efforts.

Looking at Alesei, he suddenly remembered his earlier words.

"Would you really like to still know me?" he asked with hope.

Alesei looked at him a bit surprised.

"I do..." He hesitated a little, smiling nervously. "Don't get it wrong. I would like to be your true friend."

"How else would I understand it?" Ross smiled gently, feeling the hidden meaning between the words.

"Don't smile like that," Alesei said a little irritated. "I mean, I don't mean..." He paused for a long time, which made Ross's smile widen involuntarily, and his emotion squeezed his throat. "Stop grinning!" He scolded him, terribly embarrassed by this situation. "You're not like those effeminate jerks from the House, and even if... I would be proud if you would accept my friendship. Really."

Ross was silent for a moment. He felt the guards glance at them, listening. He knew too well what they could do when they were out of sight. There will be no end to smiles. Stupid jokes probably won't either. Though it might not have mattered much, these people here will soon be forgotten. However, he knew that similar situations would always happen. There will always be someone willing to joke and look for what is not there, and Alesei was not a very patient man. Dermon knew this and he was slowing his efforts.

On the other hand... What if Sel doesn't come back? Or he will come back, but will want to stay with him because he should, not because he wants to?

Will he endure lurking loneliness?

"Friendship with me will not be easy, Alesei," he observed mildly. "There will always be people who will take you for my lover. Are you ready for it? Are you ready to make friends with a male miss?" He used one of the milder terms.

Alesei hesitated, and after that Ross realized he hadn't thought about it. However, it didn't take long.

"You are a brave man who does not hesitate to help friends in need. You helped Sel and Julien, though you knew what Moren could do to you. You turned back for Valeriea and us after you found out what Reniel was up to, though you might have run away. You persuaded us to go get Oliver and help the healer. You faced Moren. I don't care what they say about us."

Ross sighed softly.

Alesei held out his hand to seal his friendship. The only thing left to do was to shake it.

"Well... I told you you're not like a woman," Alesei grinned as he felt his shake.

"Is that a compliment?"

"Just getting started."

When they saw the garden moodily lit by the morning sun, still full of dew, they both stopped for a moment.

"A beautiful place," Ross said softly, and seeing the tombstones heaped up and Sai kneeling, he added, "Valeriea has always dreamed of such a garden."

"Will you help me?" Alesei asked just as softly, as if he didn't want to disturb the peace of this place, "I think I'll have to bury Sel's parents."

"Yes," Ross said seriously, looking at the graves. "Of course I will help you."

As they approached, Ross gently touched the girl's shoulder. At first, she was surprised by his presence, and then, delighted and touched, she stood up and hugged him tightly, as she had done so often in the House of Pleasure when she sought consolation. He was one of the few men she knew who she wasn't afraid of getting hurt. She did not cry. As if she no longer had tears in her.

He felt the familiar warmth of the pendant in the shape of hands holding a ruby...

* * *

"Does that mean I'm dying?" Vivan thought, the first conscious thought of the day.

He remembered the girl holding his hand at night before he fell asleep. He remembered that his brother was with him, though it seemed unbelievable.

He remembered the attack.

And what was before it. Reason lost to the nightmare. He felt them again. Again, he felt as if he was being pulled by people.

And they die because of him...

Then the attack passed. Before he fell asleep, he heard the excited voices of Paphian and the girl. And Sedon's voice.

"I killed those people," he whispered to them, but wasn't sure they heard.

All he could see was darkness.

Now he is awake but different. It was brighter. He felt and heard with his whole being. He was lying on something soft.

Everything hurt. It pulled, it throb, but it was bearable. He felt like he had drunk too much wine. He was sluggish.

He couldn't move. His hands were strangely numb. He moved his tongue.

"Wait," he heard the same gentle girl's voice, then felt a soft, damp cloth against his lips and a few drops of water dampening his throat.

She must have waited until he swallowed, then gave him more.

His throat stopped burning him with fire.

"Better?" She asked gently.

He nodded his head slightly, feeling the pain of the movement. He heard loud sighs.

"Vivan," Paphian's voice came closer. "Can you hear me?"

"Yes," he wanted to answer, but there was a strange squawk from his mouth, unlike his voice.

Then he felt himself falling into drowsiness. And he pondered his question again before he slipped into a dream that might as well have meant death. He might not wake up anymore. Why is there no strength to do more than that? Why does it have to end this way? He would like to at least say goodbye.

Unless he didn't deserve it.

Death…

…It could be it…

* * *

"Are you sure all is keeping everything right?" Oliver asked anxiously. "I don't want to fail at the end."

"It's perfect," Sel replied calmly. "If I hadn't seen you all my life…" He broke off suddenly.

The word "life" suddenly made him think, one thought would make him turn pale and tears glistened in his eyes. He realized he was only about to break down, and the thought encouraged him to fight himself. Oliver was aware of his condition as well.

"You don't have to come with me," he remarked softly. "I won't be alone. I can handle. After all, Kirian is waiting outside the door. Take a break."

"I won't be left alone with my own thoughts, Oliver," Sel replied warningly. "I don't want to be alone. Not now."

"So why not go home now..."

"What would it look like?"

"They would understand."

Sel sighed heavily.

"I know that I'm not support as a friend now..."

"Stop it. I understand everything…"

He raised his hand.

"Wait!" He thought for a moment. "I don't understand this. I've always been able to control myself."

Oliver looked at him meaningfully.

"Have you always had such experiences behind you?"

Sel didn't answer, but his friend knew he was right.

"Half of what you've experienced could be shared by several people," he added.

"You're doing it."

"My parents weren't murdered, Sel."

"I don't care!" The young man exploded unexpectedly, to which Oliver stopped abruptly, though he wanted to go on. He waited for the continuation.

"I can't be alone, Oliver," Sel calmed down from that outburst very quickly, too quickly. His former mastery of his emotions had worked.

"The wall you set up for self-control is starting to crack," Oliver remarked softly. "It won't take long. Don't give us any trouble!"

"I can handle. At least now."

Oliver regarded him with concern. His wig was arranged in an elegant bun, his face was almost invisible, except for his eyes that were supposed to stand out. Alena found him a black dress, modest and with a delicate neckline, which lacked a lot of a clever corset, but it perfectly emphasized the waist he marked. Oliver was Selena - a girl of delicate beauty, dark, curly hair, dark-rimmed eyes and long eyelashes, an almost flawless complexion and a figure that would be envied by more than one girl. He could even put a bag on, and it would still look good, Sel said silently when he saw it fully "made". Behind this perfect mask, however, was the soul of a boy who was ready for adventures without hesitation. The gift of a healer cheered him up. But it didn't work right for Sel. There were too many repressed feelings in him.

"We'll only be as long as necessary," a disguised friend promised.

"I know."

Oliver moved away from him. He closed his eyes.

For a moment he stood there, mentally preparing for the next events, imagining himself returning to town and saying hello to Julien. The thought of his sister made him smile.

They will see each other again soon.

"Ready?" He glanced over his shoulder at Sel, who looked almost normal today, with no makeup and new clothes on. Not counting the signs of nightmarish transitions on the face.

Sel stood eagerly beside him, offering him his arm. Then he took the knob on the door.

"Let's start," he said with a sad smile. "I wonder myself how they will thank you."

Oliver also smiled as Sel opened the door.

Nearby, in the corridor, amidst the hurried servants and soldiers, and the seemingly ubiquitous purser whose shouts and orders were heard everywhere, stood a few men in the uniform of the queen's personal guard - that is, what was left of Lieutenant Delen's unit. A black sash was tied around their chest as a sign of mourning. They were greeted with friendliness and respect around them. Redhead, Kertis, Marten, four others whose names he has yet to recognize, Oliver, and finally Kirian, Delen's brother. So few... Kirian had dark circles under his eyes and looked exhausted. He loved his brother very much. Even the healer's blood, which he must have drunk like the others because there was not even a trace of injury on him, hadn't suppressed his grief. Oliver's heart ached. Remorse overwhelmed him. Maybe he should rethink his decision?

But will it bring someone back to life? Fix something?

The soldiers' eyes fell on him, and they all expressed the same admiration and appreciation for Selena's beauty. Even Kirian looked at Oliver warmly. Oliver blushed at the stares and pressed himself tighter against Sel leading him.

"You look beautiful, Selena," Kirian said, taking his hand to kiss it.

This gesture finally confirmed Oliver's decision. They will never know the truth.

"Probably the gift of a healer," he replied softly, touched by his appearance.

He smiled sadly at him.

"Selena," Kertis said. "Honey, the queen calls you to her place before the audience. She want to thank you personally before all this great fanfare begins. We are to escort you to her chambers."

Oliver looked at Sel in faint surprise.

"Not bad," said the friend. "There will be a lot of stories at home."

He couldn't disagree with him.

"Hey darling!" Said some teenager suddenly, looking at Sel. "I'm here! Now love me!"

Oliver held his breath. Sel bit his lip as Kertis chased the whippersnapper who quickly cut and run.

"Leave him!" Sel called after him. "It's not worth it."

"I warned you that I will beat anyone who says a fool," Kertis said as he returned, "Selena's friends are our friends."

Sel bowed slightly to thank him and the others.

"You didn't tell the servants that," Marten pointed out to Kertis.

"Or the dishwashers," Kertis observed dryly. "But then I'll make up for the shortcomings in the kitchen."

"Don't bother," Sel told him calmly. "After the funeral, Selena and I return to my house."

"Alena made it clear to us," Kirian said, gesturing for them to be on their way. "What then, Selena? Will you be back on duty?"

Oliver paused, and after a while they all did the same.

Feeling a strange weight on his heart, he replied:

"I'm not going back to the castle anymore. I'm leaving Verdom."

They looked at him in silence for a moment and he could see the regret on their faces.

"But you wanted to say goodbye to us, sun?" Kertis finally asked.

"Of course," Oliver replied, looking at them all in turn, finally leaving Kirian, whose sight made him feel sorry for the murdered Delen, "I wouldn't have left without it."

Kirian nodded understandingly.

"We have to go," he said softly. "There will be time for that. Now the queen is waiting for you."

They set off in a gloomy mood, which was not yet improved by the fact that they were now passing the places of dramatic events. They passed through a corridor to the left of which was the room Moren had dragged Oliver into. Then they went to the doorway where Delen was murdered. Kirian paled. There was still a blood stain on the floor, even though it had probably been washed and polished many times. Its faint shadow was visible when they blocked the light from nearby windows. Blood showed in these shadows. Then they went up the stairs where the fight took place. On a table carved with griffin paws stood a new vase and a beautifully decorated bouquet of black tulips. Oliver paused to touch them.

Yesterday's day in morning light seemed like a bad dream...

"Come on," Sel whispered in his ear, "Just a little more..."

He looked at him, unable to express his mixed feelings now. Sel smiled reassuringly.

"Yes," Oliver replied. "We have to go."

* * *

After greeting and obligatory courtesies, Queen Constance approached a delicate young woman in black standing before her. Sel and the guards lined up a few paces back, the watchful castle guard keeping an eye on them - suspicious of yesterday's events. The queen's chamber still bore some traces of struggle - the paintings on the walls had sword cuts, the curtains were torn. Apparently, other things mattered more to the queen than the tidying up of her rooms, though good progress had already been made, and servants were moving frantically in the bedroom visible through the open door.

"My dear," said the beautiful queen, whose beauty intimidated all men, including Oliver hidden under a female disguise, who blushed again. "Can I see the item that helped save me from disgrace?"

Oliver, a bit hesitantly, pulled his reliable slingshot from a hidden pocket in his dress. The guards watched the move closely, and the lieutenant's recent soldiers barely concealed meaningful smirks. Even Sel pretended to clear his throat. This was his friend as he knew it! Here was Selena, whom the guards had met.

Slingshot in audience with the Queen!

"You have great strength of spirit in you," the queen remarked, examining the object and at the same time tactfully pretending not to notice the movement it caused, though a smile lurked on her full lips. "I would like such an extraordinary woman to always stand by my side. I would feel much safer then."

Inadvertently, Oliver opened his mouth in amazement, accepting his secret weapon from the Queen's hands. He himself admitted to himself that he had not considered such a proposal. And yet, when going here, he should at least consider this possibility.

Sel looked at him, wondering how he could get out of this situation without offending the queen. He was sure Oliver would refuse. In fact, there is only one way left for him to do it to his best advantage. Kertis, on the other hand, remembering the earlier conversation, exchanged concerned glances with the others. It was obvious to him what Selena had to do now if she didn't want to lose her head.

"Your Majesty..." Oliver looked down, seriously considering what he would say. "Please, let me tell you something that prevents me from accepting such a generous offer."

The Queen, curious and somewhat disappointed, nodded politely.

"Well. You can talk."

"I would prefer it to be held in private, if I may ask for it, Lady."

The Queen was genuinely intrigued by the mystery.

"Get out!" She ordered the guards and the servants.

"My friends..." Oliver glanced over his shoulder at them, which surprised them immensely. Everyone except Sel, who already knew what was going on.

Expressing her astonishment with a raised eyebrow, the queen asked them out too.

After everyone had left the chambers, Oliver stepped so close to the queen that he could feel the gust of her breath, approached her ear trembling, then said softly:

"I'm not a woman. I'm a man."

Then, without waiting for the Queen's further reactions to his words, he gently and discreetly lifted the pinned wig, revealing a fragment of the tuft.

"If you ask for it, my lady," he said calmly, though his heart was hammering, "I offer other evidence to confirm my words..."

* * *

The royal audience gathered a real crowd. In the first words, the king thanked everyone for their loyalty and courage. Then it finally became clear what had been the subject of rumors and conjecture since the end of the attack. With true regret, King Heron bade farewell to his most faithful and devoted soldier, Captain Jenue Gereme, who died in the fight, breaking the king from a trap and dragging one of the viceroy's soldiers with him. They both fell straight out of the tower window into the abyss. Unfortunately, it was not possible to collect the bodies and bury them with due respect. This risk could result in more casualties. So the king entrusted his captain to the memory of his ancestors and to the protection of Mother Earth, not hiding his emotions. Then he called a woman who helped him to protect the one close to his heart. Seeing Selena quivering in front of him, the king broke with all the proceedings contained in the numerous audience protocols and went to meet her, which caused a real stir among the gathered and made Oliver extremely embarrassed by such a distinction.

"Selena Calis," the ruler turned to him. "Our maid?"

For the first time in a long time, Oliver heard his false name. The name of the murdered Celina. His fake sister.

"A woman who stood out in the fight in the courtyard with such courage should not take her eyes off the king," said the king, seeing his confusion. "Look at me."

Oliver looked up quickly and boldly, which pleased a king who disliked excessive servitude. From behind him he could see the king's sons watching the scene with interest and Queen Constance on her throne who watched everything with mild amusement. Her eyes examined the entire figure of Oliver's disguised over and over again, as if she still did not believe what he had revealed to her in deep secret.

"Perfect!" The king said, seeing his reaction. "A brave girl who is not afraid of anything!"

Several people started clapping at this remark, and after a while everyone joined. Sel smiled slightly as he watched the queen's behavior.

"So," the king became serious. "What kind of reward can we offer her for this?"

Oliver felt a twinge of fear. He had known the king for a long time and knew that he was rarely seen in a good mood, but that he often fell into anger, often turning into an attack of rage. He was a man of changeable moods. Though he undoubtedly loved his wife above all else and his sons were his pride, he was sometimes too impulsive with others. Refusing to accept his gift could even end badly for him. Although she could also meet with another appreciation for Selena's courage. He was sure that he was in greater danger of the former, because he would most certainly offend the king in front of everyone present. He looked quickly and pleadingly at the queen, who of course took matters into her own hands.

"Sire," she said to her husband in an official form. "Giving in to the request of the girl who miraculously escaped death and had a really hard time behind her, I would like to ask you to give her gold and jewels, or one of the lesser assets of your brother's henchmen, because she wants to rest in peace and leave our castle. I would also like to remind you that her sister was murdered here on the orders of the viceroy, so that the conspiracy to remove you from the throne would not be exposed, my king. So let her experience peace in the family circle."

The king looked at his beloved, now standing two steps behind him and waiting for an answer. She could see the feelings on his face. She saw him struggle with himself, whether to get angry because she had interfered with his intentions, or to be understanding and sympathetic. Finally, to the relief of the crowd, he opted for the latter.

"Okay then," he said. "May it be as requested by my beloved queen," he smiled, which gave his mesmerizing gaze a softer expression.

"I just want to ask you for one more, Selena," added the queen, walking up to her husband and nodding to thank him for granting her request. "Consider your decision. Your courage, cleverness, and skill would surely be of use to the kingdom. There may come a time when we will need you. Promise you will think about it. The gates of the castle will remain open to you."

"All right, Your Majesty," Oliver said, not daring to meet the queen's eyes.

Then he was dismissed and the next heroes of yesterday were rewarded. Of course, the defense of the healer was also mentioned. After the queen's guardsmen were honored for their special courage and after a proper reward, the audience ended. However, to Selarion's amazement, the king and queen summoned him to their presence when they all went to the feast and began preparations for the ceremonial funeral of those killed in the fighting.

"We already know," said the queen, "that you are now the sole owner of the Rserwer estate, and that you also suffered painful losses in yesterday's events. We are informed that a wounded healer and his brother have found refuge in your home. We have provided them with all possible conditions, but we count on you to ensure that they are properly looked after on our behalf. If you need anything else for this to happen, please let us know. Of course, we made sure that you and your friends, whose courage was also noticed, would not lack anything. However, I would like to warn you. Near your home, our soldiers noticed a suspicious movement. Perhaps someone will try to get to a healer. So when he is able, he must leave town," she ordered.

"Yes, Your Majesty. I understand perfectly."

"I would like to entrust you and your friends with an important mission. Go with him. Don't give us your departure date or any other details. As I said, you won't miss anything if you take care of it. We will secure your assets. The escort would be too conspicuous after leaving town, it would expose you to attack. A small group is more likely to slip away unnoticed."

Sel looked at Oliver, whom he had left by his side.

"You mean there will be no protection?" Oliver asked, amazed.

"It's for the best."

Sel thought for a moment. He should not question the royal decisions, although he would have a lot to say about it. The healer deserved more attention.

His protection should be of the utmost importance to the king himself.

The queen's gaze met his, and he saw the same hesitation in her eyes.

So it was the king's decision...

"This sword," said Prince Meron, joining the others and drawing a sword with a hilt carved into a unicorn to Sel, "It is for his protector who has already shown courage."

"I can't accept it," Sel replied, moved by this unexpected gift. "Then I just ran past him. My friends stayed to come to his aid. I rushed to the rescue of..." He looked at Oliver. "Selena."

"We know what happened," replied the queen. "Yesterday evening your friend Alesei told this to the commander of our unit, which we sent with the cook to your house. We received the report at dawn today. You went out to help the healer and you were attacked. Several of you have reached the destination. You have come to the aid of the healer selflessly. Therefore, from now on, you and your friends will be the team to protect him. As a sign of our gratitude, each of you will receive such a sword. And you will give the healer a letter from us assuring his inviolability." She looked at him warmly. "Compared to the life you have led so far, the new future looks more interesting. I'm not wrong, right?"

Sel stared at the beautiful queen as if she had just opened the gates to a new, maybe even a bit dangerous, but very interesting life. Words ran out. Apparently, she learned a lot about him.

He was offered a future he had never dared to dream of before.

The Queen smirked and looked at Oliver.

"Don't forget us, Selena," she said, her eyes sparkling.

Her smile made the men almost take their breath away. Oliver blushed slightly, bowing a bit clumsily.

"Time to sort things out," the king said, letting him know the meeting was over.

The whole family, assisted by guards, solemnly left the audience hall.

Sel and his friend looked after them in a faint daze. Everything was back to normal. The king was on the throne again, the castle was clearing the traces of the struggle.

But what did it change in the fate of the kingdom this time?

Changes were to take place, as evidenced by a different position of the royal family towards their subjects. More accommodating to people. Awards, privileges. Everything announced today in the audience hall was a harbinger of change. Formerly distant from humans, now the king and queen have come closer, appreciating the courage and sacrifice for them and their friends.

Just… Was it a deliberate action, planned and calculated? Did the royal family really learn something about the subjects of yesterday's events and will they want to correct their mistakes - or at least they will not make new ones and learn to live in harmony with the kingdom?

Was it really the best decision to send the healer with a group of amateurs?

"Are you thinking the same as me?" Oliver asked, watching the retreating royal entourage.

"The healer did his job," Sel said dryly, thus confirming Oliver's assumptions, "He almost gave his own life. He was detained against his will for a month and did everything to keep the royal family healthy. They probably also have a bottle of his blood somewhere similar to yours, but much bigger. Enough to hope that they would survive the plague and live long years, if used wisely. They no longer need him, so he may go away."

"It must have been our king's decision, right?" Oliver asked softly, "The Queen is not like him."

"I think so too."

"She didn't tell him about me."

Sel looked at him closely, but not surprised.

"Interesting," he remarked thoughtfully.

Oliver returned his gaze calmly.

＊ ＊ ＊

Delen's funeral was even more pompous than might have been expected as it was linked to Captain Gereme's funeral. The young, promising lieutenant who would one day take his place was buried with all honors. There was solemn singing of mourners and crying of women. The lieutenant's body and the symbolic coffin of the captain were buried in the royal gardens with all precautions taken towards the royal family. Everyone who could and did not have other duties participated in it. Everyone liked the lieutenant.

Captain Gereme was appreciated for his devotion, but was widely considered quite rude to others. The exception was the royal family, which he loved as his own. However, both were said goodbye with regret.

Sel watched the funeral ceremony as an outsider, unconnected with most of the events at the castle. He watched the participants.

He saw the sincere grief among the queen's guards and the tears of Kirian as his brother's body was placed in the tomb. Oliver's sadness that let tears run down his face. Many other soldiers and many women said goodbye to the young lieutenant in mournful silence. There were also those like the soldiers who were under the captain's command yesterday, who sadly bid him farewell too.

But there were others too.

They hid smiles, talked mysteriously to each other, and sneaked glances at each other.

The death of the viceroy did not close all matters.

He was glad to take Oliver from this snake habitat.

After the ceremony, the guards decided to escort their friends to Selarion's house, and unfortunately, to Oliver's quiet despair, it could not be prevented. They had good intentions that had to be respected. He knew about it. Kirian wanted to personally see to it that Selena got there safely. He also obtained the queen's permission that he and his men would keep watch, taking turns with the soldiers appointed by the king in the merchant's residence until their friends left Verdom. He also managed to plan his trip in such a way as to escort the travelers to the first stop before night and return to the castle at dawn. It was his idea, which met with the full approval of the Queen and Prince Meron, which only confirmed the conjectures of friends that from the beginning she did not agree with her husband on this matter, and Prince Meron even offered his company to make sure that at least on the first day Vivan will be properly protected. Unfortunately, as a potential heir to the throne, he regretfully had to abandon this idea.

The square and the marketplace were terrifying. Despite how many people and horses had already passed this way, the stain of blood was still visible where the tormented healer had fallen. Other traces and bodies of those who were trampled or killed have already disappeared. The marketplace was empty and completely devastated. There was no trace of the stalls standing before, except for a few boards and some mud.

The place became as dead and empty as the city itself.

Silence followed them everywhere.

The streets were deserted. Mute.

Looking at this, Sel and Oliver wondered how the castle's inhabitants could still celebrate the king's victory in peace. Lead a normal life. Make plans. What exactly did the king and his beautiful queen still want to reign over?

Will the old normality ever return? Especially now that the plague has left the city unnoticed. Certainly there were those it had not reached and who had decided to flee without waiting, but here and now it seemed as if it had taken the world in her possession forever and ever.

Verdom has become a city of death.

Listening to Kirian's words about his plans along the way, just to distract from the gloomy sights, Oliver fumed at him in his mind. However, the truth was that he could not interfere in any way. It was out of the question to be exposed, which he understood would also be unpleasant to Queen Constance.

He had to endure to the end.

Julien will understand that for sure. And Sel will take care of the rest.

He also involuntarily began to think about what he would find.

He did not know his friends from the House of Pleasure. They were a part of Selarion's life that he had never known before. Except for an unplanned visit to this place when he was forced to do so, he had never been there for obvious reasons. But he saw these people on his rooftops. Sometimes he watched them, fascinated by the atmosphere of freedom and decadence. People could have fun there. Colorful as butterflies, the inhabitants of the House of Pleasure, unaware that he is watching them, lived a completely ordinary life during the day, having their joys and problems, like everyone else in the city. They led two lives. Maybe he will recognize one of them? He remembered a beautiful girl with fragile beauty and white skin, hair as black as ebony and her friend with a phenomenal look. He had seen them once in the window of the House and then in disguise at the marketplace. Once or twice the thought flashed through his mind that if it had been in any way possible, had it not been for Julien, not for Moren, he would have been there. They seemed delicate, without spoilage. Natural.

And sad.

They made him long for normality.

Maybe Sel's friends will know what happened to them?

As long as he can talk to them normally. What will they say when they see him like this?

At least he would finally see Julien. And Vivan.

CHAPTER 13 — Meeting

The brother of the healer insistently asked about him. Ross was afraid of this meeting. He felt that it would not be very pleasant for him.

"I can testify that I saw the ruby in action and felt its influence," said guard Nils, trying to cheer him up.

Ross shook his head as no.

"It's useless."

"Let's get it over with," said Alesei shortly, opening the door.

He was not going to leave his friend to face trouble alone.

They saw a room in partial shade, with ink-colored curtains letting some sun in through a small slit. Two figures stood by the large double bed.

But on it...

On the bed was a covered with bandages, deathly pale figure with only a part of the face and neck uncovered.

The table in front of them had a distinct dark stain on its countertop.

Only after a while Ross, shaking off the gloomy sight, noticed Sel's drawings above the injured man's head. He didn't look at them, however, too shocked by what he had just seen. Regret gripped his heart. There was no gift for the healer to heal quickly. He owed his life to his blood. He wished he could help the healer like this. He wouldn't hesitate for a moment.

Paphian slowly approached them in gloomy silence. Julien stayed with the wounded man, sitting in the armchair. However, she was ready to come to Ross' help in case of trouble.

He could see her concern. It made him even more nervous.

"Perfect likeness," the young count whispered to himself, looking at Ross. Before he began to think about his words, he added aloud: "Your friend is great at drawing," he pointed behind himself, "He has a real talent."

"Sel drew me?" Ross was surprised and touched at the same time, but still not looking at the drawings. It had to wait now.

"He will be very happy about your appreciation, Count," he bowed politely as Valerie had taught him, avoiding the gaze that might have been considered a kind of insolence and arrogance in a lesser person.

He waited impatiently for the continuation.

"You are...?"

"Ross Hope, and this is my friend Alesei Nilos."

"Count Paphian Beckert, as you probably already know," said Paphian in a serious tone, extending his hand in greeting, determined to begin this conversation in a manly way.

To his amazement, the man who came with his brother's pendant around his neck did not extend his hand.

"I'm not sure, sir," he said hesitantly, "if you will regret this gesture in a moment. I can't... return the pendant. Neither your brother nor you." His face twisted in genuine regret as he looked down at the bed. "Unfortunately, that's impossible."

As predicted by friends, Paphian did not like this answer.

"What's that supposed to mean?!" Asked ominously, his hand involuntarily rested on the helve of the sword at his belt. "Do you want money?! My brother's blood?! Do you want this?!"

Ross replied calmly, though his heart was pounding fast.

"I can't take it off. It doesn't allow me to do so," he hastily demonstrated, and the astonished Paphian gave him a murderous glare, almost ignoring the clearly visible resistance of the unusual ruby to parting with the new owner." It obviously wants to stay with me..."

"Guard!" Paphian shouted, falling into a rage, at which the door opened immediately and Nils appeared anxiously. "Tell the captain that I want these people imprisoned for theft!" He pointed the finger of new friends, especially targeting Ross, who expected a similar reaction.

"Ross," in order not to shout over the wounded, Julien approached them. "What are you doing?!"

"It's not me," he replied with apparent composure.

Alesei stepped closer to him. As assured, the guard tried to explain something, but Paphian was not inclined to listen to the explanations.

"I demand!" He put a clear emphasis on the word, which made Ross hold his breath for a moment, but this time he staunchly returned his gaze, accepting the challenge.

"There's only one way for me to do it," Ross said through gritted teeth. "Order to cut off my head or do it yourself!"

"It can be arranged." Paphian brought his face closer to his.

"I showed that I can't take it off!" Ross tried not to scream because of the wounded healer and out of respect for him, but he was angry at the outright injustice. At the same time, he wondered why the pendant was not working now when he really needed it to ease the situation. Apparently he was going to find a solution himself. Or he just didn't know how to influence it to get the help he needed.

"You used magic to bind it to you!"

"Nonsense!" He snorted nervous laughter at such absurdity. "I'm "porcelain" (this name came from the makeup that men of different orientation had to wear in a brothel and became a common, rather contemptuous term for them in the kingdom) from the House of Pleasure. Where's the place for magic here?!"

"You just need to read."

This was not the time to discuss whether reading skills would be enough to be proficient at this level of magic like a spell that his healer brother had suspected him of being. So Ross cautiously silenced that remark.

"Paphian," quite consciously, although he did not know what prompted him to do so, he switched to this form, although he risked with it. "Look!" And although he completely did not understand what was happening to him, because the hand itself seemed to grab Paphian's hand, he decided to succumb to this mysterious impulse, allowing Paphian to put his hand on the pendant.

He felt a familiar, soothing warmth envelop him, and the ruby began to glow again.

"I've seen it before..." whispered Paphian.

Gradually, his features softened, and everyone felt the tension drop from them.

"Please," Ross whispered urgently. "Believe me. I don't understand how it happened... I didn't mean to hurt you."

Paphian withdrew his hand thoughtfully.

Three friends waited anxiously for his decision. The guard as well, curious about the further development of events.

Julien believed that Ross was definitely not cheating now. It would be so unlike man she knew.

Paphian returned to the bed where his brother was lying. He looked at Vivan.

He was asleep. A peaceful, measured dream. Completely different from the hour before when he was thrashing in the net of his nightmares.

He always felt good among kind people.

He reached over his head, taking the drawings he cared about. He was beginning to understand...

Ross noticed that Paphian hurriedly put the picture of the girl down on the table, instead offering him his portrait in the House of Pleasure outfit. It was not only him who was speechless for a moment out of amazement at the similarity. Alesei clicked admiringly.

"It's you, isn't it?" Paphian asked.

Without waiting for an answer, he hastily flipped the portrait around.

On the other side, Ross saw the real himself... at the same time as Sel must have seen him.

So all this time...?

He felt his throat tighten with emotion. Julien sighed softly, finding it final confirmation of her guess. Alesei smiled at his thoughts, but made sure that none of those present noticed it.

"Do you have a similar feeling for this man as he does for you?" Paphian asked softly, trying to make the question sound perfectly at ease.

He felt a bit confused that it was a love between two men with which he had never had a chance to meet. But who it was about made it by no means not less real.

Ross, feeling everyone's eyes on him, just nodded.

"The murderer who gave it to you," Paphian turned to Julien, "said he wanted it for you. With such a valuable thing, he gave it without hesitation to the girl he had affection for. Apparently it was real. And my brother..." his voice failed him with these words, "he has a great love for people."

He looked at Ross.

"This jewel has followed those who love others. My brother wore it all the time. He never parted with it. He marked it with his gift. Apparently it has its own rules now. You have received a precious gift. Handle it carefully. For I'm sure that it is in good hands."

"Could you..." Ross handed him back, still touched by the truth he had discovered. "It belongs to Sel..."

"True," Paphian smiled, collecting the drawings. "He wouldn't be pleased if they disappeared.

"On the other portrait," said Alesei, "is his wife."

Paphian looked at the drawing of the girl.

"She was murdered," the strong-arm man explained. "They were a marriage of convenience."

Julien lifted her head and looked at him, tears welling up.

"You haven't seen...?"

The last picture of her friend was for her the sight of her body with the noose around her neck, in a pool of her own blood from a broken head, right in front of her and Oliver's house.

"I'm sorry," said Alesei. "The gravediggers must have picked up the body earlier."

Everyone was silent for a moment, pondering the fate of the unfortunate Milera. Ross stared at the drawing full of conflicting emotions. They coincided with her portrait, equally ambiguous in its expression, contrasting the beauty of the bride with the almost cruel grip of her hand on her heart. There were feelings mixed with sadness and regret that perhaps shouldn't have been.

Julien returned to the bed thoughtfully. She looked at the drawings she had never looked at before, absorbed in other matters.

Then she leaned over the healer and carefully removed a few drawings.

"They are our friends," she said to Paphian, showing them to him. "They died yesterday."

There was Len in the drawings - at the entrance door to the House of Pleasure. Then Sai and Lena, sleeping on the bed, palms clasped together in the empty space between them where Sel had previously lay. Valerie brushing Lena's hair. Alesei and Darmon are clearly pleased with each other, of course in the company of women. Sel displayed their appearance masterfully, so faithfully that emotion touched the hearts of the watchers, overwhelmed with emotion and sadness. Paphian realized that he was slowly becoming a part of them. These people were very connected - almost like a family. Their mutual friend, whose talent the king himself should see, must have been very attached to them - more than to his own family, who apparently did not treat him properly.

Suddenly Ross, touched by a grim thought, returned the drawing he was holding to Julien, whispering:

"I'll never forgive myself for this."

Then, without waiting for Paphian's permission, he suddenly left the room. They heard the clatter of his shoes in the corridor before they gradually died away...

"What is he doing?" Paphian asked in surprise.

"It was he who persuaded us to go to the healer to help," replied Alesei, thus generalizing yesterday's decisions. "He blames himself for what happened. He's wrong. It wasn't his fault. We had enemies. They are already dead," he concluded gloomily.

Julien looked at the shaded window.

Ross must have gone to the garden.

* * *

While Oliver and Sel were getting ready to depart with the guards, Alesei and Ross, with the help of some soldiers, buried Sel's murdered parents. The ceremony was short and almost everyone attended, except a few sentry and the Beckert brothers. Sai, who had somehow put her in order after Ross's reassuring and giving will to live touch, showed up at the funeral for her friend's sake. She looked like a sad queen of the elves, and men whom her friends had feared a bit after yesterday's gift of a healer treated her instinctively as if she were her, even though there were some of her recent clients. With her quiet dignity and delicate beauty, she evoked involuntary respect in them. They yielded to her, showing their good manners with impeccable demeanor. Julien was recognized by several as the goldsmith's daughter, so she was also safe, and sadly this and that shook his head when he heard from others about the fate of her parents.

Paphian watched the ceremony from the window, encouraged not only by the action of the pendant, but also by the condition of his brother, who was clearly improving as the day passed, although his brother's heart was afraid of still premature happiness. He removed the bandages from his eyes and he and Julien changed others. Then they were amazed to find that a few minor wounds and scrapes had simply disappeared. More hours passed, during which Vivan slept with no bad dreams. Still, there was a real fear for his life. He was very weak. Paphian thought of the coming night and feared it. It has been known for a long time that every disease intensifies at night and that what good day brought, night could destroy irretrievably. No one knew why this was so, but it was widely said that apart from the plague, death had always liked the night. So he was afraid of his sprouting hope.

Pleasantly surprised, after the ceremony, Alesei immediately went to tell Ross, who was dragged by the girls to Sai's room, which she shared with Alesei from the beginning, so as not to be alone. Ross, begged by the women, had to comb them to cheer up their rather gloomy mood. Sai talked Julien into it, saying that Ross learned it from Valeriea and was very skillful about it. He and Lena had often asked him to do this before. Red Rebecca and many of the House girls did the same. There Alesei found a new friend and his unusual ruby that warms people's hearts. He wanted to tell him the good news. The carriage was almost repaired and repainted, but a brown color, for it had been too conspicuous previously. Inside, things had been put back together, reattached, and everything from ceiling to floor gleamed with cleanliness. He was also given back the money he had borrowed. The soldiers told him that the king covered all the costs and paid them handsomely.

"Sel's got pretty good up there," Alesei winked at his friends.

The cook cooked the most delicious broth that everyone had eaten so far, and this also significantly influenced the mood of the people gathered in this house, and overshadowed the sad ceremony. Then Paphian invited his new friends to Sel's room, because their company was clearly good for his brother, who had a small room screen built for a bit of privacy. They sat down at the table and quietly talked about recent events.

This, finally, peaceful atmosphere was interrupted after some time by the arrival of Queen Constance's guardsmen and their two long-awaited friends...

* * *

In a narrow street, a small group greeted the guards stationed here, and soon after that, Alesei was called, who was respected by his strength and charisma. He went out to meet Sai, and they both welcomed Sel in a warm way, and they introduced Oliver, showing no prudence of any sign of amusement, though they were still surprised to see him in a female costume. However, they were both impressed at how perfectly he pretended to be a girl in every detail.

According to them, he looked tired, which wasn't too much of a surprise that day. Their friend, on the other hand, had never looked this good before, though his eyes still had traces of recent events. He jumped off his horse lightly for them, pleased with his new, unusual for him fitness.

"I'm not used to it yet," he told them with an uncertain smile.

Sai hugged him and touched his hair, soft and thick, dark blond, glad that she can no longer see this ghastly make-up on his face, and his hair is back in a natural color, which until now was poorly presented during his illness. Though still thin, it seemed he was going to start to improve quickly. He returned the hug gently, sadly. For a moment they met each other's eyes, sharing the same thoughts. Alesei was glad that his friend's handshake had become stronger. He smiled knowingly at Sai, seeing Sel clearly looking for someone with his eyes.

"And Julien?" Sel asked in his and Oliver's names, though he wasn't the only one he wanted to ask about. His heart was already pounding uneasily when he still couldn't see the familiar face.

"He's waiting inside," Sai replied, beckoning to him with a gesture while the guards dispersed to make their way through.

In a new reflex, he turned to take Oliver-Selena by the arm, as befits him.

He saw his friend's anxiety.

"I'm sure it's okay," he said softly.

"There she is," Oliver replied, his voice hushed, taking advantage of the guards' inattention, "I'd know if it were otherwise."

Over his shoulder, Sel looked back to where the soldiers were now. Between them, you could see the rest of the street, where the goldsmith's house stood, and one of the windows of the house was still open. Like then…

He saw a stain of dried blood on the pavement…

Everyone, involuntarily, also looked in that direction.

Only his friends knew what the regret in his eyes meant.

"She was gone," Alesei explained quietly, as before, "I'm sorry."

Sel turned away without a word, dragging Oliver and Sai home with him.

Julien waited for them with her heart pounding. Alesei was a bit ahead of everyone.

"She's in a black dress," he said, aware that the house was full of guards.

So, prepared for what she would see, she went out to meet them.

She hugged Sel.

They stood there for a moment, and she could feel his trembling. He allowed himself to cool down a little in her arms. Then she pulled away and kissed him lightly on the cheek. He was so tense that he hardly smiled at the tenderness. She was glad he would have reason for a little joy in a moment.

"Is he lives?" He asked barely audible.

Knowing who it was, she nodded gently, which made him visibly relax. He released Oliver in the gown, keeping his eyes on him, and went up the stairs. The soldiers were still nearby.

Julien looked at her brother.

She had purposely avoided the first greeting with him, choosing Sel first. Now she let a smile of relief and happiness brighten her face, then hastily grabbed his hand.

"Come!" She exclaimed, and before the curious cool off with this behavior, they ran upstairs after Sel, they passed him and found themselves in the room where Sai and Alesei were staying, just as she had agreed with Ross earlier. There, when she closed the door, they could finally feel freely, and there the brother's grip was tighter than it should be for a woman. Just as it would seem strange to outsiders that the seemingly petite Selena lifts her sister and turns around with her in undisguised joy. Then Oliver snuggled into his sister's arms, enjoying the feeling of unity and peace. They shared the same joy of meeting, the same thoughts and concerns.

Same relief.

* * *

At the top of the stairs, Sel paused.

He slowly gathered himself up.

Everyone went somewhere, only he heard a movement upstairs.

Ross was there.

But there were also them. Locked in a room, murdered. Speechless.

He felt their presence throughout his existence, knowing nothing of the funeral.

"You can't talk anymore," he whispered, but the thought didn't help him. It did not take away the fear of them.

It's like they still have power over his life! He would see them again. True, already dead. He imagined his mother's dead gaze, reproachfully asking him, "Why am I dead, and not you?". "Why did you do this to us, son?" Father will ask with his pained eyes.

He felt his confidence draining away from him, as if he were losing his strength. It was as if he had to fight for his existence again, to prove that he was worth the life that was given him.

"Ross," he whispered pleadingly.

He didn't know why he was calling him. Ross was probably recovering slowly in one of the rooms upstairs and couldn't come to him. He has to go to him. In his anguish, he had forgotten his joyful surprise to see his friends alive and well. The world was becoming just as it had left it.

"I have to," he whispered to himself. "If I want to live, I have to move on."

The thought inspired him with new strength. He set off, unaware that hidden from his sight Sai and Alesei waited with fear for him to gather himself and enter the familiar corridor.

The guard Nils silently indicated the door to the room next to him. Sel passed his parents' room, avoiding even a glance at him, and entered another one - this time wide open.

Ross was standing at the window. The sun, still high in the sky, illuminated his short, dark brown hair. His face expressed fear, hope and happiness at the same time, not hidden under the make-up he was forced to wear at the House of Pleasure.

Sel, with unspeakable relief, embraced him without saying a word...

* * *

The sun had gone down when Vivan opened his eyes for the first time in a long time.

It felt as if it was floating on water. The pain washed over him, but it was no longer unbearable. The world around him was animated and he heard voices, but they were not too insistent. Rather soothing. A dark shape stood before him.

He could barely make out its contours.

"I'm glad that I finally met you," he heard brother's voice. "You draw perfectly well."

With the feeling that he was still drifting somewhere, he didn't understand the answer.

"Paphian," he said softly.

They didn't hear him. He wasn't surprised. He wasn't sure if he really said anything.

He thought a moment had passed when he heard Paphian's voice. It must be much later. He could no longer hear the voices in the room.

"Vivan? You are with me?"

He opened his eyes and saw him above him. His brother's face lit up with relief.

"You still have bloodshot eyes, but that will pass," he assured him gently.

He was sitting with him on the bed. After a moment, Vivan felt his hand.

"Do you remember me?"

He nodded slightly.

Paphian breathed a sigh of relief.

"You definitely want to drink," he suddenly blurted out, only to regain shape after a moment. "Here," he felt the cool water, which he tasted greedily. "Take it slow. You'll get the rest in a minute."

He shook his hand in a reassuring gesture, as if to reassure him that everything would be all right now. But the tears that glistened in his eyes contradicted it.

"Sorry," he looked away, and Vivan realized for the first time that he must look really bad if his brother couldn't hold back tears.

Unable to speak, he returned his handshake as hard as he could to show him it wasn't that bad.

"I'll be here all the time," Paphian assured him. "Hold your ground. I'm with you. We're all with you in this house."

He did not release his hand.

It was like life.

* * *

Over the following days and nights, Vivan wandered away and returned. Sedon visited him every morning.

"Death pulls him by one trouser leg and you pull the other," he once heard him say to Paphian.

He's got an infection. The medic was nervous, he cursed the people who bitten the healer and jerked their teeth. He eluded him. He could feel it. He had a fever, he was losing the idea of where and with whom he was. Paphian was hopeful when he saw him conscious. And he was almost out of his mind when it seemed to him that Vivan was weakening. He alternately asked or argued with the medic. He also saw women. They bravely bandaged him, tried to put water or a few spoons of soup into his mouth. Once he vomited on a girl of oriental beauty.

"He doesn't know what he wants!" Sedon was upset during the third visit, when Paphian accused him of inept acting. "He doesn't know if he wants to die or live!"

"Who would like to live after something like this?" A gentle male voice asked softly. "This is the grace of your dead viceroy!"

"Ross, don't interfere!" Paphian raised his voice at him.

"Be careful who you talk to!" Sedon clearly turned to the one, called by Paphian Ross. "Be careful with your words!"

"Nobody will order me…!"

"Your friends may need my services someday. Just like you!"

After the silence that followed, Vivan understood that the man had relented.

During the night he was awakened by commotion and the sound of breaking glass.

"Relax," Paphian said to him, under whose eyes he saw clear shadows. "You are safe with us."

He was not alone. In the room there was another young man with dark blond hair, who drew his sword quickly while Paphian was still uttering these words. Carefully, Paphian glanced out the window as he stood by the wall.

"And?" The other asked.

Before Paphian could answer, the door swung open. Through the screen still standing, Vivan could not see the visitor's face.

"We caught two people who tried to get home through an empty store," he heard. "In the morning we will drive them to the dungeons. We closed them in the warehouse. Some people are still patrolling the garden and its surroundings. Be cautious!"

As he closed the door, the man muttered softly:

"This is the second time."

"Sel!" Paphian warned him with a gesture.

Named by his name, he glanced quickly at Vivan. He smiled at him.

"Don't worry. Get well calmly."

He really wanted to touch Paphian and make him feel better. But all he could do was force his hand to lift a little.

He saw their expressions of disbelief and secret joy before he dozed off again...

* * *

He had survived the entire Sedona visit in the morning. The medic agreed with Paphian's opinion that there was an improvement. However, he advised caution in pinning faith on it. He was also worried about his brother's condition. At the urging of the medic, Paphian went to lie down in the next room, and his place was taken by a muscular bully with shoulder-length, curly dark hair and another with hair the color of chocolate Vivan liked... with his pendant around his neck.

They both introduced themselves to him. The bully's name was Alesei and the other was Ross, whose voice he had heard before. They made a very nice impression.

"I was hoping," Ross began as he sat down on the bed beside him, "I could talk to you."

He reached for the pendant. To Vivan's amazement, he couldn't take it off of himself. It was as if the pendant would not allow it.

He concentrated on the memories with an effort.

Ross wasn't the one who took it from him. He would never forget those eyes for the rest of his life. Cold. Without emotions.

Now Ross looked at Alesei as if to say "See? I told you it would be like that."

What happened? Why did he sense the change? As if in the room apart from them there was some consciousness...

"He doesn't want to leave me," Ross said, "And what he's doing..."

He told him about how the pendant ended up with him and how it affects others and himself. It calms down, soothes manners, drives out bad dreams.

"I got up three times the first night," he said. "Sai..." he stopped, apparently not wanting to say anything more, to continue after a while "Selena," he smiled knowingly, "says that you met at the castle. Sel..." he thought. "He still feels like he is suffocating sometimes. Completely unexpectedly. He was sick for a long time. Now there are no such attacks. At least for now."

"Tell me what we called that pendant," said Alesei.

"Well," Ross smiled slightly. "We called it the Jewel of Hope. It's not a name that fully reflects its gift, but..." he thought for a moment. "I hope you will forgive me. I don't know how this happened. I didn't want to take it from you. But since he is with me now, chasing away bad dreams, I thought maybe it would bring you relief as well," he said, gently taking his bandaged hand.

What happened a moment later was one great nightmare...

Vivan first saw a girl of oriental beauty. In front of the mirror. Her naked body. Torment on the face. A cruel, pirate-like type who took her by force on the table. Her scream, her pain. Through the terrible vision, he saw Ross' face gasp, and instantly realized that he was seeing the same. Then another girl. She was screaming on the bed and Ross and the other one, named Sel was trying to help her. Beaten up. Close to losing her mind.

Oliver. In the viceroy's chamber.

"I decide myself what to do!" He heard the angry voice of the guard who was leaning over him, then fought with his own companions to finally pounce on him, trying to tear off his dress. Then he suddenly sees Oliver's eyes as the guard struggles with him, grimacing in cold fury, his face splattered with blood, he feels his hand under the fabric of his dress, and suddenly sees the uncovered truth transform that face - at first incredulous, then changing in a face of unimaginable cruelty...

Then Sel.

"I'm not worth living for you!" He shouted to a woman similar to him.

It's his mother.

He feels his anguish in these words and the strength of this despair that drives him.

Tears run down Ross's face, but there's something else too. As if the hair was changing...

She can see him now. The mother stands in the doorway to the room and encourages her lover to beat him with a poker and Ross defends himself...

"Stop!" Ross suddenly shouted. "Stop it! Please stop it!"

His hair is clearly whitening in one place. One streak turns completely white after a while. Snow white.

It's a Gem! It glowed with a red glow. Ross was losing his strength. His thoughts scattered. He couldn't take it.

Shocked, Alesei calls out to his friends.

"Help!" Vivan tells him, and these is the first word he hears from his lips, in a hoarse voice so unlike his old voice.

Alesei helps him sit up. Vivan touches Ross's forehead and calms his mind, warms his heart with encouragement, repairs the damage done by the jewel. Out of the corner of his eye, he sees that the room is filling up with people, but he pays no attention. The most important thing now is to help other people.

Then he reaches for the jewel, puts his hand on it, and mentally speaks to it, "I know, it's terrible what happened to them."

Suddenly the visions disappear.

The jewel glowed with a soft glow, and Vivan felt relieved over him, and his thoughts began to calm down. The memory of the terrible visions is blurring. The sensations soften. The mind takes a proper distance from them. It will not be the way it was. It won't come back anymore... It's passing... It's been over...

"It has an awareness," Vivan whispered softly, looking at the jewel. "I gave it to it..."

Ross released him. Vivan wished he could clear his memory and the jewel. It will stay in them forever. He always saw something happened in his mind. Like when a woman broke her arm, allegedly hitting a door. He saw her husband mistreating her...

He has always seen: how, when, what, by whom...

Always.

He never told anyone about it. Except for the mother. They might have found him too sensitive, too little masculine, but the truth was, he just couldn't take it anymore. Because he knew the bitter truth.

They thought it was just what they saw with their own eyes.

But it was also about what they had NOT seen...

Now Ross knows his secret.

Ross shakily stood up, hands pressed together. Instinctively defending himself against the healer's next touch, his fingers tightened on the gem. He hasn't understood yet. He was convinced it was the healer's fault. He was horrified by what he saw. In shock, he did not think clearly. Not looking at anyone, not hearing his friends calling for him, he yanked himself out of their hands and left the room.

"Stop him," Vivan whispered, feeling his head dizzy, slowly losing consciousness again.

Alesei repeated his words, someone went. Paphian was close to the bed. With care, they both laid him gently back into the sheets.

"Vivan, what happened?" Asked the worried brother.

"They only held out for a moment..." said Alesei, and he wanted to say more, but suddenly he stopped talking as he saw what was happening to the healer.

He lost the sense of reality. He was loosing time and place. He was drifting off.

"Don't go," whispered Paphian, seeing what was happening. "Look at me. Vivan!"

It took a lot of effort. He focused on his face.

"Tell them to call Sedon," Paphian said frantically to Alesei. "Let them hurry up!"

Alesei did not discuss. After a while, he was gone.

"What have you done?!" Paphian asked frantically. "Did you treat him? Of which? What happened?!"

"He saw..." Vivan whispered, his throat burning with fire, and Paphian hurriedly reached for the cup of water.

But he didn't have time to tell him anything more, because suddenly they heard the voice of the soldier from the threshold:

"Count, Ross ran out of the house. They had to wait for such an opportunity. They kidnapped him. They threw the noose around his neck and pulled after the horse."

Vivan saw his brother's face suddenly disappear into the darkness...

* * *

"He hasn't deteriorated," Sedon said as he finished examining the healer. "In fact, I believe there has been a significant breakthrough in his illness. He'll slowly recover, though I've never really seen anything like this. He seems to be motivated to live by helping others." Vivan felt the medic bend over him, his scent became more intense, he felt his sweat and stale clothes. "After all has been done to you, Vivan?!" You really still want to do this?!

He opened his eyes with difficulty.

Paphian, Sedon, and almost the entire group he had met were standing nearby. Sel was missing. And Ross...

The voice failed him again. He tried to ask, but his throat felt rusty and old. Paphian leaned over to his mouth.

"He asks what about Ross," he explained to everyone and smiled at his brother with a long-unseen gleam in his eye. "You probably will never change."

They didn't seem concerned or worried, and after a while Vivan found out why.

"Your brother sent me to the captain," Alesei began to say. "I told him what I had and heard confusion from outside. They threw a noose around Ross's neck and tugged on the horse. There were three of them. Selena ran with us, I mean with me and Sel who joined, but she was out of sight so I thought we were alone ahead as our guards were a bit late. And he... she," he corrected hastily, "She chased them across the rooftops. Wish you could have seen it. She discovered where they wanted to go and cut their way. They couldn't go too fast, they clearly didn't want Ross to drag himself on the ground. Maybe they were afraid of losing the jewel. It saved him. When we ran over, Selena knocked them down with a few well-aimed slingshots. They fell off their horses. I caught one and the other. I beat them up a little. So did Sel. The soldiers did the rest. I brought Ross. He is lying in his bed and Sel is mothering him. He'll be fine. He sleeps."

Paphian smiled at Vivan with brotherly tenderness.

"Don't scare me anymore," he said softly.

He had to answer with the slightest shadow of a smile, and he tried hard to do it because everyone relaxed, even Sedon, whom he didn't want to talk to. Other memories and previously hidden feelings came back slowly.

Even though they seemed calm now, he could see a hidden fear on their faces. A sense of danger.

It was a bold attack, which meant that the thieves were getting impatient.

They were not safe here...

* * *

"My care for you is coming to an end," Sedon said to Vivan the next morning after the examination.

"Some of the milder injuries have disappeared, the scalp is already healed, as I can see, the hair is growing back, although it is certainly not the latest fashion at the royal court. The eyes are not like demon eyes. You do it yourself, right?" As Vivan nodded his head in agreement, sitting on the edge of the bed, the medic continued his argument. "You heal faster than anyone else in your case."

Vivan looked at him meaningfully. Were there cases like his? He did not think so. Sedon was confused under that gaze with the accusation hidden in it.

"I know," he replied. "I should be punished for treason. But apart from you, I'm the only good medic in this city, and I dare say my skill saved my miserable life. After all, when the healer is released from his hands, the king cannot deprive himself of his protection, and although he has the protection of your blood, never enough of careful. I was sentenced to life in the castle, arrested in decent, but not so luxurious conditions, under constant guard. I'm a useful prisoner, Vivan. It is not in the interests of the kingdom to kill me," he added with a hint of irony.

He was silent for a moment, glancing at the guard standing in the open door. They were to take him to the castle. Behind them, you could hear the healer brother talking to the captain of the guard and his new brothel friends, the way Sedon always thought of them contemptuously. Whores and thieves - this is the new companionship of the healer. Of course, talking in front of the medic was not about something important, although he already knew that after yesterday's attack on this mouthy "porcelain" they were planning something.

Seeing the healer's scrutinizing gaze, he commanded himself to rest. Vivan could read body language and sensed hidden thoughts.

He was clearly getting back into shape in this area as well. You had to be careful with it.

"I regret one thing," he said, while Paphian returned to the room and sat down next to him in the armchair. "Honestly, or at least that's what you should believe me, I regret what happened to you. I believed him. He assured me that it was not in his interest that get hurt you. After all, you are a real miracle for the entire kingdom!" in the tone of his voice both brothers still heard a clear disbelief that it was possible to do this with a healer. "You are a gift to humanity! You cure any disease, no matter how serious or hopeless it may be. How could you be so foolish as to waste such a treasure in this way?!"

Vivan didn't take his eyes off him, trying to make his gaze reflect his feelings after these words: contempt, regret, anger.

Sedon was no fool. He got it.

"Yes," he replied. "I know what you want to say. For me, for the king, for those scavengers even - you are only a useful tool. That's all we care about. That's what you think, right?" He sighed resignedly. "I've never been able to express my feelings well. I guess that's why I'm still a bachelor for example," he smiled slightly at both of them, but they didn't reciprocate. "I was a fool, it's true. But I never stopped admiring your gift. And your stubbornness. Heal others, even though they do not always reward you with due gratitude! People should worship you! They should bow to your waist for what you do for them! Instead, they carelessly destroy the most precious gift they could have received.

The medic looked at him with seriousness and respect. There was a genuine honesty in that look. Vivan's gaze softened.

The man smiled at the change. He bowed politely and with dignity.

"Bye, Vivan," he also nodded politely to Paphian, "I will go to see the man who, twenty years after his birth, waited for your gift to cure him. And he freed mourning from this house."

He bowed to them once more, and after a while they heard him talking to Sel.

* * *

After lunch, the discreet preparations that Paphian had begun with the captain of the guard were completed. Equipment and provisions were prepared. It was checked if the carriage was really in working order and ready to go. Everyone was carrying weapons now. The women also wore trousers under their dresses. Seemingly, life at home continued as it did so far. Ross was forbidden to leave under any pretext. The soldiers who, after yesterday's action, found out about the great efficiency of Alesei and Sel during the fight, treated them with greater respect and friendliness, while Selena, whose bravery some of them had managed to convince in the castle square during the fights, had now almost divine reverence. Oliver took it calmly, slowly accepting that it was part of his second life, which by a completely unplanned twist of fate was already becoming a legend.

Even the circumstances of Moren's death were told otherwise. Apparently, Selena buried the body of the infatuated gang leader in the garden, and Sel helped her by crying over his lover. They both did not like this version, which sounds so romantic in the stories about the circumstances of the assassination of the king. It was not possible to get Moren's body out of the deep abyss. The realization that he was still lying there unburied influenced Oliver's imagination, who on the first night thought Moren was standing at the window again. His fear also had a strong influence on Sel, still struggling to shake off the recent events. Only Ross's help put an end to the anxiety.

Finally, Oliver decided to go to Vivan's.

Seeing him, he paled with terror. Some of the dressings have already been taken off. The barely visible bite marks healed quickly. The crooked regrowth of hair was still not that thick, but judging from what Julien had told him, it had hardly been there before, so it was certainly something to be enjoyed now. In those few days after the tragic events, Vivan lost a lot of weight. His cheeks were sunken, and there were deep shadows beneath his shining - probably from fever - eyes. He looked like a skeleton covered in leather. Only the eyebrows with a dense, wide arch still stood out in his face, giving it an expression of an almost odd ferocity right now.

And smile. He was still the same.

"Hey," he greeted him, sitting on the edge of the bed.

He was still moving as the disguise required him. He was constantly watched by guards who liked his extraordinary beauty.

"Do you remember me?"

The answer was easy to read in Vivan's face. Paphian smiled to himself.

"You're probably wondering," Oliver began in a low voice, "why am I just coming here now? You see..." he paused for a moment, "I felt that I let you down," he wanted to say it in the right form. "I said that you are not alone here, remember? I didn't want to," the guards surely thought Selena was just deeply moved now, but he tried not to think about them. "That you would find out there was Paphian in the castle, because if something was wrong... Sorry, Vivan," and then he whispered softly for only a healer to hear it. "I failed you. I didn't help you. I'm sorry."

Vivan held out his hand. The hand he had clasped tightly on the cross during the attack, now glistening faintly against his neck. The people, mad with lust, almost skinned him. Sedon used whatever methods were available to him to prevent contamination. Otherwise, it would have to be amputated. He was a really brilliant medic. Unfortunately, the hand, even after healed, largely thanks to Vivan's gift, although functional, it was to be scarred forever. He carefully tightened his grip on Oliver's hand and pulled him close enough to whisper in his ear, hiding him behind the screen:

"You didn't let me down. Do not apologize."

"You know about...?" Oliver whispered back to him.

He felt Vivan nodding, still holding him close. It was good to feel his closeness again. He felt so much like someone close to him. Father... Mother... The tears glistened in his eyes. The memories, pushed back into the shadows, stung the very heart.

"You could have died," he whispered in pain.

Vivan embraced him and let Oliver settle in his arms. In his hometown, people often wanted him to hug them. Whether they were children or adults. Everyone at some point in their life, standing at the corner, sought close contact with him. It didn't matter if it was a little girl or an experienced warrior. They needed him. This desire broke pride or embarrassment. Something in him... his openness to people always made the walls fall and no one around thought this gesture as funny or not very masculine. Sometimes it was a bit strange when a stranger gave him a big hug. And then he walked away, clearly in this spirit, as if he needed it. Vivan had taken it as quite natural for a long time.

Now he felt Oliver's hidden emotions as if he were touching them. Oliver became accustomed to the regained freedom after the death of his pursuer. At the same time, he was frustrated by the thought that he was stuck in this disguise, while next to him there is an extremely beautiful girl, whom he had even been afraid to dream about, and everything was going wrong in his life again. Though he was relieved to know Vivan didn't blame him for anything, he didn't stop blaming himself.

Thanks to his touch, he came to agreement with his conscience and gained some peace.

Ross showed up after Oliver left. The snow-white strand of his hair gave him charm, but at the same time gave his appearance a certain maturity, as did the bitterness at the corner of his mouth.

"Tell me," he whispered, "will we ever be able to shake hands again? I don't like to be afraid forever. I prefer to meet fear."

"I know," Vivan thought. "I saw it. I saw how you started to defend yourself against this bastard."

"I wasn't prepared," he replied softly. His voice was still torn from the scream, and sometimes he was still wailing, "It won't happen again."

So Ross held out his hand without hesitation.

"Show me," he said.

They shook hands, though at first Ross twitched nervously, remembering what had happened before. Vivan admired his courage nonetheless.

They both breathed a sigh of relief. The jewel was silent. Vivan, ready to shut his and Ross's mind to it, relaxed.

"Why did they beat you?" He asked with concern.

Ross clenched his jaws.

"Because I was different," he replied. "Different in every way."

There was no division of people into skin color, religion or preferences in Vivan's mind. Only for good or bad hearts and deeds and justice. He knew what Ross was talking about. But he could never understand it.

"What happened to your mother?"

"She went on a journey with her fancy man after my escape from home. I haven't seen her again. She didn't even come to ask if I was alive after… She wasn't even looking for me."

Vivan remembered the vision she had beguiled her lover to beat her son.

He closed his bad feelings from himself.

"You know," Ross whispered. "After what happened… I understand them better… My friends… Knowing more, I can help them better. I feel it."

"The jewel and you are one," Vivan explained to him. "You learn from each other."

"Will I have these visions?"

"Only if you let it."

"You got them. Always, right?"

"Yes."

Ross looked at him with understanding and sadness.

"It's not easy for you. This is why they say you cry. And some thought that..." He broke off and smiled at his thoughts.

"That...?"

Ross looked at him with a twinkle in his eye.

"That you are like me," he replied.

They were both smiling now.

Before evening, Paphian brought another guest to his brother.

"You may remember Captain Teron Winn from our personal guard," he introduced him. "He has something important to tell you."

Vivan nodded.

"I remember, but not as captain," he replied.

"I'm the captain of the troops of the Prince of Meron," replied Teron. "I was promoted after the death in the fight of the previous captain.

The young captain seemed unsentimental and determined. Vivan met him while at the castle. He often accompanied the prince alongside the former captain. His dark hair was almost as black as ebony. Just like the eyes. He had thick black eyelashes and eyebrows which made him look a bit harsh. The impression faded as soon as you got to know him better.

"Lord Count," Teron said to him, "I asked your brother for this visit in order to have the best understanding of your health. I can see it's better than I thought. That's why I have to warn you. We are planning to leave this house as soon as possible. Everyone is ready to go on the road at my signal without hesitation. My advice is to put on your clothes and have a gun on hand. You, Lord Count and one of your friends, are no longer safe here, as you may have guessed from yesterday's events. Our enemies, the wild gangs that are moving in more and more numbers, becoming more and more organized. We know they already have a common leader. Keeping waiting increases the risk. With the consent of the prince, due to the circumstances, there were some changes. The journey will take two days. During this time, we will guide you to your destination. Originally, protection in the form of the Queen's Guard was supposed to be for only one day. And officially," here he lowered his voice even more, although he spoke softly from the beginning, sitting close to Vivan, "it will still be so... Let's hope we can leave the city safely."

There was only one thing left for him.

"I understand," he replied. "I'll be ready."

CHAPTER 14 — Say my name

Night.

All windows are covered. The weapons were kept with them.

Every room was guarded by the guards. They were patrolling the garden. They hid in a fabric depot and a deserted, plundered silk merchant's shop. The captain had dispatched scouts to research the situation and waited now for their return. He wanted to know what was happening on the route of the planned escape from the city. Vivan, whose door to the room was now constantly open, got dressed after a long effort and help from his brother.

"Vivan," said Paphian, standing behind the curtain of the window, partially hidden in the shadows as only one candle was lit. "Tell me, are you able to repeat what you did in the market if necessary?"

Vivan went numb with horror. He felt a familiar chill sweep over him.

"You're not talking about what I think," he replied hollowly.

Paphian sat down beside him. He looked fearfully into his brother's eyes.

"That's what I'm talking about."

Vivan felt as if he had just been punched in the stomach.

"You just asked? As it would be brewing tea?" He asked in a whisper, unable, this time under the influence of agitation, to get his voice out.

"Don't say you regret it..."

"You should know best what I think about it!"

"These people would tear you to pieces without hesitation. Death for you or them! For once, you have not thought about how others feel, but have taken care of your own skin! Can you do it now?!"

"It's murder, Paphian."

"What they wanted to do with you in the marketplace would be murder! Have you forgotten what they did to you?!"

"Never..." Vivan whispered, instinctively closing his thoughts from the dark...

The silence that followed his words overwhelmed Paphian's heart. Always, for the rest of his life, he will blame himself for what happened. He will never forget what he saw. He will never fade in his memory. Still as he thought about it, regret and anger made him want to hurt himself, feel his suffering, on his knees to beg him to forgive him for the tardiness that led to that situation. Because if sooner... If he did... But he knew Vivan didn't want him to fall to his knees before him. He doesn't want to be begged for forgiveness. As soon as possible, he wants to forget about it or at least go on, living with this burden, away from those events.

How could you get away from it?! As if he was not thrashing almost every night in the clutches of that nightmare, and he woke up drenched in sweat and trembling, sometimes struggling to restrain himself from assuming the embryonic position, so as not to fail in despairing in despair. But Vivan was strong. He believed that he would come out of this, that he would still manage to live normally. He saw it in him. He drew this faith from the hope that when he returned home, to his relatives and friends, he would be able to control the nightmare and calm down.

For his sake, Paphian believed it just as strongly.

"I wish..." he began calmerly, "talk about it differently. I understand how you feel..."

"No, you don't understand!" his brother contradicted him violently, "nobody will understand! Each of you will get over it sooner or later. You will move away from these memories and start living. And I will not be surprised! I would have done the same in your shoes! I would give anything to go on what you are striving for now!"

"You can do it! Just give yourself some time, Vivan!"

"Damn it!" Vivan clenched his fists as if trying to contain the emotions that began to tear at him. "You know nothing, Paphian!"

It would be hard to disagree with him.

"You always give people health and life," Paphian tried differently. "You took them there. I have no idea how, but you did it. To save life, Vivan. Your life."

Vivan was silent, so Paphian continued his speech:

"I know. It hurts you had to do this. It's clear. After all, you are a healer..."

Vivan, still not looking at him, was mentally touching painful memories. Their despair, their fear of death. They burst into his soul, tore him from within with their grief, plea, and accusation. Before they finally fell silent forever, they left him with painful wounds, their sense of harm and injustice. These memories made him angry and despair. He only defended himself...

Anger.

They murdered him. Cruel and without feeling, they were tearing him to shreds.

And they had have the cheek to accuse him?!

They had the right to invade his soul punishing him for their death?!

"They deserved to die," Paphian voiced aloud his subconscious thoughts, seeing the change in his brother's face. "I forbid you to feel sorry for these degenerates! They deserved it."

Anger and grief ruffled Vivan's body. Paphian rarely saw him angry, but whenever he did, something really important had to happen, upsetting Vivan. As it happened now.

"Now they want to do something wrong to you again," he argued. "Who knows? It could end up worse now than it did then. This time they can kill you. You, Ross, who will most likely be cut off this time to get the Jewel in their hands. They'll kill us all to get you, Vivan!"

Vivan met his eyes. Go ahead, firmly, with determination.

Paphian knew that if he mentioned himself and others whose fate was connected with them, he would surely convince his brother, who always cared about the welfare of his relatives.

"I'll do it again," Vivan replied ominously, without hesitating.

"Finally!" Paphian rejoiced in spirit. "You finally felt what you should feel, brother."

* * *

More hours passed. The sent soldiers returned home.

Silence. Single shadows. They watched the house. There were several intruders. There are also a few at the West Gate. Nothing special.

"Apparently they thought it was too early to attack today. Maybe they know what condition the healer is in? They think we're unlikely to want to leave town today," the captain said when he arrived at the brothers'. "Well. We'll stay tonight, but beware. Be ready. We will leave at noon or at dawn. These plans had better be a little chaotic. Let them have a few surprises."

* * *

"Sel, I'd like to see Julien," Oliver said.

"Now? At night?"

"She's awake."

Long taught that Oliver knew his sister's thoughts and moods, Sel was not surprised at the remark. He looked at Oliver's dark dress.

"What about Sai?"

"Sai?" Oliver feigned surprise. "What can be?"

Sel was not fooled by his friend's seemingly carefree reply. He saw his eyes follow the beautiful girl when it seemed to him that no one was looking at him. Oliver caught his eye.

"Am I doing something wrong?"

"Why?"

"I'm not going to..." Oliver stopped abruptly and gestured to his disguise. "Look at me. Who am I now?"

"She knows the truth."

"And she knows me and Julien... These thoughts have no future, Sel. Not in my case."

He spoke the last words bitterly.

"Have you never broke this bond up?" Sel asked curiously. "Or close yours minds to each other?"

"Broke up?" Oliver laughed bitterly. "Forgot what supposedly happens to the twins then?!"

Sel paused in silent sympathy.

"When Julien is asleep, if she has peaceful dreams, I don't hear her. Or sometimes when she takes offense at me, she can…" Oliver paused suddenly, seized with a quiet hope.

"Can she distance herself from you?" Sel became interested in it. "How long?"

"Then she usually gets mad at me."

"And she really wants it," Sel added calmly, analyzing his thoughts aloud. "How long?"

"We cannot live without each other for a long time..."

"Oliver..."

"Maybe an hour. But that doesn't mean..." He looked at Sel, who smiled significantly. "Stop it! It does not mean anything!"

"Not for Sai," Sel said silently.

He thought warmly about his friend. Though she was more secretive now, as if she wished no one could see her despair in her heart, she continued talking to others. She looked for solace in being with friends, and quickly became fond of the slightly impulsive Julien. She knew her brother was eyeing her discreetly. She knew why Oliver kept his distance. It was obvious. But she obviously liked him very much, and was always warm and understanding towards him. Her gaze pierced with the strength of her sad gaze, as if she was staring at him through a woman's disguise.

He caught her gaze once.

"He's lonely," she said, seeing he caught her. Oliver took Julien somewhere then, they stayed for a while. "Lonely among people. Locked in the cage of his own heart. As I."

"If she can, you can too," he said to his friend now.

"Maybe you better check out what Ross is doing, okay?" Oliver retorted with a hint of anger, though his heart suddenly began to pound, fueled by unexpected hope.

Julien explained to him what was happening between Sel and Ross. Oliver wondered if Ross knew about the hidden love Sel had for Moren. He did not think so. However, he valued the young man for tactful behavior towards his friend. Thanks to Julien, he could see how much Ross tried not to impose on him. His feelings betrayed subtle gestures only visible to those who knew about them. Admittedly, the soldiers were making fun of him and Alesei, but Ross's discretion prevented even the care of Sel, concerned about him, from giving rise to gossip. There was no evidence that they had anything in common. Sel was reserved, more silent and introverted. It was obvious that he wanted to keep his distance and have time to recover from the tragic events. Instinctively, even if the soldiers saw something like Nils, or suspected like the rest of them, out of respect for a man who had been through so much, they did not talk about it among themselves.

Sel had no intention of being angry at these words, although they surprised him a little. He guessed Julien had told him something about it. Probably so that his brother's actions did not accidentally spoil the relationship between him and Ross, by misunderstanding the situation.

"I'll go," he said. "But then you will look at your sister, as you said."

Oliver looked at him and saw the understanding in his friend's eyes. Ever since he returned home, Sel has tried to be seen always steady. Steady to a fault. Despite the conversation they had at the castle, he was still trying to hold onto the wall he had built himself.

"Okay," he replied a little hesitantly.

To his surprise, Julien was not in the room with Sai.

"She went to Ross," the girl explained. "She said she needed something urgent to discuss with him."

Oliver got scared. Sai was alone and he felt extremely awkward. The disguise suddenly felt particularly grotesque when his sister was gone. He felt terrible about it. A man who disguises himself as a woman usually causes laughter and pity. Suddenly the reason he was doing this struck him as absurd.

Because here was a beautiful girl with a phenomenal, eye-catching face, delicate, flawless. Her hair, pinned up partially, streaked her face as if she wanted to hide underneath it. Her silhouette seemed just perfect to him. She was dressed in a dress that accentuated her waist. He was wearing a similar style himself. Even the belt with the Queen's sword seemed to fit her perfectly. Several candles lit her, the glow of which seemed to emphasize her beauty even more.

Oliver was ashamed of his appearance.

He will never look as perfect as she does. He didn't want this.

He never wanted a woman like Sai to see him in this disguise.

"Are you leaving?" she asked, seeing that he was withdrawing. "Stay. Talk to me."

She walked over to him. She looked at him right into his soul, as if he wasn't wearing that hideous makeup that was supposed to soften the contours of his face.

He hated himself for this look.

"You rarely have the opportunity to talk freely," said Sai. "Stay. Julien will probably be back soon."

He felt no amusement in his sister's mood flowing through him. She didn't laugh at his confusion. She seemed strangely calm, relaxed, as if after a pleasant bath. As if she was getting ready to go to sleep.

Sai looked at him gently. She held out her hand.

"Come."

"Why did she go to Ross?"

He could not find a clear answer in his sister's feelings. Worse, those feelings were beginning to reach him incomplete, as if she didn't want him to really know the cause. Like when she really wanted him not to know what she was thinking.

"She wanted to talk to him. I don't know what about."

He went deeper into the room. His proximity to Sai was like wine for him. It hit the head. Confused thoughts.

"I'll be back later," he said hesitantly because Sai stood close to him. He could smell the faint scent of soap and herbs. "You need to get some sleep before the trip."

He felt his face flush as she said, "sleep."

Suddenly he heard a clear message from his sister in his head. She made a decision. She passed on all her sisterly love to him. She calmed him so that he would not be afraid.

Not be afraid? What is she planning?!

He had never heard her thoughts like that. As if she strengthened them. She gives utter to it.

"Oliver," he heard her soft voice in his head. "I'm closing the gate!"

What's that supposed to mean...?!

And suddenly she fell silent.

He gasped for air. Worried, Sai grabbed his arm.

"What happened?" She asked, leading him to the only bed in the room.

He still knew Julien was here. But nothing else. He couldn't hear her thoughts. He couldn't guess her mood, he couldn't feel her emotions. She cut off. She was alive. He felt it without a doubt.

But he stopped hearing and feeling her in all sorts of ways. As if only a narrow line remained, connecting her to him, instead of a rushing stream.

Ross. Stone of Hope. How did they do it?!

"Oliver," Sai gently forced him to look at her. "What's happening?"

She said his name...?

Shocked by this sudden silence, as if something had been taken from him, he gasped:

"She closed the gate."

Sai gently stroked his face.

At first, he didn't even notice her proximity to him. He listened to the faint signal Julien had left him. He didn't recognize her feelings. He couldn't sense them. So she was talking about it! She closed the gate, but opened the gate. She couldn't cut herself off completely.

"We are alone," Sai whispered suddenly.

He looked at her understanding.

They planned it. Julien went to see Ross, who somehow helped her. He reassured her. He brought her into a state of relaxation.

She did it so that Oliver could be alone with Sai.

Doesn't she understand how ridiculous this is?! He is Selena now. He is sitting next to Sai in that dress with a disgusting corset underneath, painted over his face like a fairground jester, with a goofy wig hiding his real hair!

There is nothing natural about him now. He is a misfit of strange, ambiguous beauty, maddened by the mad sadist, kissed by the now dead lieutenant.

She is a misfit in a black dress pretending to be a girl. Hiding his true form.

Throughout his life, he was constantly running away from someone, hiding, avoiding close contacts. Now he is also hiding. His whole life is an escape. He will never be able to know love. Disguiser. Twin.

Misfit.

Sai moved closer and kissed him softly.

Time seems to have stopped.

Oliver's heart suddenly somersaulted.

The leap from one sensation to another almost took his breath away. Kiss. He had never felt it alone before. Sai parted his mouth with her lips, digged deeper, bolder, feeling no resistance from him. At first it crossed his mind that Julien must feel it. But he didn't know what she thought about it. When Sai moved away, ending the kiss, he was inextricably linked with his sister all his life, he was looking for her automatically, looking for traces of her impressions from this unusual event, putting her feelings above his own.

He didn't find her. There was an unprecedented silence.

Julien wasn't here.

They were left alone.

Sai was looking at him gently, thoughtfully. It was more difficult than she expected. The bond made Oliver confused when he was about to get close to someone. It was not only the shyness of a young man inexperienced in these matters. It was more complicated than she had imagined.

It remained to rely on your own desires.

She had her own desires? Only yours? She was like half of one existence detached from the other, despairing with longing and the desire for contact.

She was almost like him.

They separated him and Julien from his previous life. It's normal to feel lost. In him, she saw the desires of every man in the presence of the alluring woman he wanted to feel. And at the same time, he resisted them out of fear of the feelings of his inseparable sister.

Once or twice in her life, Julien had succumbed to some desires. He did not allow himself to do so. Not being able to succumb to desires when you are so emotionally developed, so vulnerable, could once have had tragic consequences for them. The Raven twins, who worked in the House of Pleasure, reconciled their work with emotions. They went to bed with their clients at the same time. Never apart. This was the case until one of them fell in love with her client with reciprocity. Love was tearing their soul apart because both, despite the fact that one of them was no longer accepting clients, were going through what the other was doing with hers. For one, it was a constant torture. For the other, the relationship of two lovers was a torment, because it evoked a hidden longing in her.

Unanimously, seeing no other option, they committed suicide.

"We're alone," she whispered in his ear.

She gently kissed his neck. He was very tense. He slowly succumbed to her caresses. She heard his muffled groan.

"Sai..." he whispered, "what are you doing? I should... It should have been different."

She smiled to herself mentally. Oliver wanted to adore her. Like any boy who just went out with his dream girl. He wanted them to get to know each other better first. So there are still such noble men? Oliver was no different in that respect. It flattered her, and her feelings for the nice boy deepened even more.

It was already very nice. She wanted to introduce him to a deeper experience, and then his eyes accidentally fell on the gown-shaped breasts of the unusual corset he was wearing.

The mood was broken.

Oliver remembered who he was now and how grotesque the whole situation must be. She felt he slipping away from her. Everything was in ruins.

"Look at me," she said firmly, turning his face to hers, "Oliver..."

"No!" He almost shouted. "It's you, look at me! Look! I'm a misfit!"

She put a finger to his lips, gesturing that they should be quieter. There were guards in the corridor.

She took his face in her hands. Yet that unfortunate disguise! What was it all doing to this boy's soul?

"I see you," she said seriously, looking him straight in the eye.

She didn't let him get away. She kissed him again, putting a lot of affection into it, touched by his fate.

"Look at me," she repeated after a moment. "Just look at me. Focus. Understand?"

She looked into his eyes. Only there. She knew he was following her eyes. That he was waiting for her to start looking at him. She won't look. They can't get rid of this disguise. She closed the door, but there was always the possibility that the captain would give the signal to leave immediately. Oliver had to stay in this disguise. To everyone but his friends, he was only Selena. She also couldn't undress. Not completely. It didn't make them get closer.

"And if..." she whispered in his ear. "Julien won't be able to do it again? Or one of us will die? Do you want to regret until you die that you weren't really with me today?"

"I want to be myself with you," he replied softly.

She got up. She snuffed out almost all the candles, leaving one behind. They plunged into twilight. She put aside the murderous weapon she had kept, the fork-shaped blades with an elongated center.

"They have my name," she explained to him.

Then she put down the sword. He looked at it, torn by emotions. Then she went back to him, put her forehead to his. His makeup was not visible in the dim light, only his inked eyes stood out in his face. He reached for the wig.

"No!" She shouted softly, but it didn't change his intention.

Dark curls landed on the floor. She ran a hand through his own matted, soft and short hairs. He looked more like himself now.

"Oliver..." she whispered.

"Repeat it again," he asked softly. "Say my name again..."

"Oliver," she repeated fondly.

She felt him tremble. She showered him with caresses and kisses. He answered them a bit clumsily, he lacked the skill she had, but he put a lot of affection into it. She guided his hands over her breasts, hidden under her blouse, wishing they could afford more. Her heart was racing. They had difficulty controlling themselves to be quieter. She rebuked him gently, touching her hand to his lips. He surrendered to her. She made sure that he only looked at her, only touched her. He wandered over her body, kissed her, but she wouldn't let him look below. Without the wig, he felt more freely, more himself. The blood rushed in his ears. He only heard their soft voices and their breathing and that hum. Julien didn't hear. She was not there. She gave him a moment of freedom. Emotion and excitement ignited his previously suppressed feelings. Sai made sure that the fire did not completely engulf him, but what he now received seemed to him the most beautiful fulfillment.

Sai felt the warmth not only warm body, but envelop heart numb with grief.

She felt a tear on her cheek, which she wiped hastily so that he would not be scared again. She had impressions it was the first time she was doing it all. As if Ramoz and his evil gang and the House of Pleasure had happened a long time ago, or even to entirely someone else whom she no longer wanted to remember. Only Oliver mattered. Here and now.

She fondly found his pants under his dress and slipped them off. She took off her own, also hidden ones, along with the underwear and semi-consciously kicked them under the bed. Then she literally sat Oliver down, twisted the fabric of her black dress without any respect.

She could hardly make herself not look, but she knew perfectly well what she would see. Instead, she lifted her gown to sit on his lap, facing him. Remembering that he didn't know what to expect, she slowed down and pushed him slowly into her...

He flinched. She covered his mouth with her hand so that he wouldn't scream or even groan. His breathing became fast, choppy. It wasn't going to take long. She adjusted to his pace. She snuggled against his shoulder so as not to moan herself, losing herself in the pleasure that had happened to her only with Lena. She would never have thought it would happen to her with a man.

He hid his face in her hair, shivering all over his body on fulfillment, trying to calm his breath and his maddened heart. She felt her face wet with sweat and tears.

A wave of tenderness overwhelmed her that she had never expected before.

"Are you alive?" She asked playfully, feeling her heart beating with fear. What if now that it's all over he changes? Will he push her or say something to hurt? He had no idea how much she gave herself to him. How much she trusted him.

"As if," he replied with a hint of merriment between one deep breath and the other. "And you?"

She looked into his eyes. She saw no falsehood in them. There was no cruelty in them. Only tenderness.

"Sai," he said softly. "We are crazy. No," he corrected immediately cheerfully, "You're crazy!"

"I?" She asked, trembling slightly, still unsure.

He hugged her to him.

He pressed his face against her hair. She felt he was trembling again. She hugged him tightly and allowed him to hold her in his arms. It meant more than any words.

* * *

Ross looked at Julien asleep on his bed.

"And I'll never understand that," Alesei said softly to him, reaching for the water to refill himself. "A beautiful girl is sleeping in your bed now, and you won't even budge?! I don't believe."

"A beautiful, INNOCENT girl is sleeping in the bed now, Alesei," Ross corrected him. "And hold your tongue, if you please. It scares her terribly."

"Did you notice that too?" Alesei smiled. "Although at first she was embarrassed every now and then. Well, but after you kissed..."

Ross glared at him. Alesei made a face at him.

"Yeah... Nothing happened."

He looked at his friend curiously. Ross thought about something, but his face was unreadable. It was only after Alesei had finished his last remaining water that he said softly:

"It was not that bad."

Alesei raised his eyebrows but skipped the teasing when he saw his friend's expression. He saw sadness and despondency. It certainly wasn't Julien.

He glanced at the Jewel of Hope, which, since Julien had come to them with her unusual request, had been glowing faintly but clearly. Jewel watched over the girl's mood.

"You're getting better at it," he said, pointing at the necklace. "How do you know what who needs?"

"I just know," said his friend softly.

He could hear the sadness in his tone as well. He knew its cause.

"You think Oliver and Sai are just kissing right now, how does this innocent girl think?" He asked half jokingly, to ward off the mood.

After the change in Ross's face, he figured that not only had he failed, it had actually made him worse.

"Maybe he'll come yet?" He cast a supposition as gently as he could.

Ross nodded his head as no.

"Maybe you could...?"

"And Julien?" Ross asked softly. Without me, her delicate balance will be imbalanced. She will open the gate again. She may do it too soon."

"Will you stay awake until dawn?"

"I don't have to. I'll take a nap next to her. In a moment."

Alesei looked at him seriously.

"And yet you are waiting for him..."

Ross didn't answer. Alesei went back to his bed, carelessly putting his boots on the clean quilt. He put his hands behind his head. He wanted to keep his friend company, but sleep quickly overwhelmed him. Ross glanced at him.

He was left alone with his thoughts.

"Why am I doing this?" He wondered. "I'm waiting for him to come to me again. And then it turns out that when he is ready, he will choose someone else."

He felt a gentle warmth envelop his heart. The gem sensed his mood.

"Yes, I know," he whispered to it. "I need to stay calm."

His mood could ruin everything too. Maintaining inner balance was necessary to shut Julien's mind to Oliver. The best solution was to fall asleep. It was maybe three hours until dawn. But no one could sleep soundly that night.

He heard a soft knock.

Guardian or Paphian, he thought, not giving himself any special hopes. Alesei grunted to go to the door, instinctively touching the sword that he was not parting with. After a while he was asleep again.

He could fall asleep instantly and anywhere that was reasonably comfortable.

So Ross went to open it.

Sel was standing in the corridor. Ross froze in surprise and hidden joy. Right behind him, he saw two guards talking in low voices.

"Can I go in?" Sel asked seriously.

"Invite the other ladies," one of the guards told them. "I think they are very scared because they locked themselves in the room."

"Gentlemen," Ross feigned scandal, letting Sel in. "What comes to your mind at this time?"

"The same what you guys. The same what you," replied the other guard as Sel entered the room. "But you already have one."

They heard laughter behind the door, already hastily closing.

Ross could feel Sel's presence behind him, silent there.

So he turned to him. What now? What should he say or do? Sel approached and Ross stepped back until he felt his back lean against the door. He had nowhere to run.

Behind them he heard the soft conversation of the guards.

"Jokers," he said with an uncertain smile to break the silence.

Sel looked at him in an unreadable way. As if he was considering something in his mind.

He leaned one hand on the door, next to Ross's shoulder. Close. He was heading towards his goal. He wrestled with himself.

Then he kissed him.

Ross had expected the kiss to be imperious and ruthless. It will crush his mouth. He was fooled by the way Sel went about it.

Instead, he was gentle, passionate, full of longing. He almost took his breath away. He succumbed to him because he would not have been able to do otherwise.

"I can't stop thinking about you," Sel whispered in his ear. "I should despair, drown in a sea of tears. Instead, I picture myself back with you and everything seems more bearable."

Ross froze. He could feel the blood starting to circulate faster through him. How the body, against reason, wants to follow the desire.

"Sel..." he began to talk, but at the same moment Sel pushed him gently to open the door.

He looked at him quickly and left.

Ross stumbled slightly over to the table. Sel filled his mind. He could still hear his words in his head.

"Ross," Julien whispered softly, standing up. "I can't keep it without you. You're distracted. Sorry. I know what happened, but..."

Hurriedly, though still dazed by the happiness, he walked over and kissed her forehead.

"It's okay," he whispered.

"Sorry, it's the first and last time. I'll find another way."

He smiled at her, filled with warm feelings.

"We'd better go to sleep."

They lay down on the bed close to each other. She put her head on his shoulder.

They let the emotions subside.

"Give him some time," she whispered.

"Yes, I know," he replied, closing his eyes.

The thought of what was going to happen during the day crossed her mind, and for a moment she felt anxious. But she did not let it control her.

Ross succumbed to the Jewel and fell asleep. She listened quietly to his breathing, free from the presence of her brother in her mind, beside the man she trusted. It was strange to feel such a void and good at the same time. It was good to take a break from the bond to miss it again.

* * *

Someone knocked on the door.

Behind them was a young boy with whom Alesei was talking about Sel's parents.

"Here's our favorite bully!" exclaimed the boy, happy at his sight, "dressed and ready to fight!"

Alesei made a face at him.

"We're leaving," he said.

"As soon as we have a snack."

Alesei looked at him.

"Have you been drinking?" He asked.

"No," the boy replied in a more serious tone, glancing deeper into the room. "Ooh!" He smiled ambiguously. "I didn't expect that. The guys were betting she'd be in your bed."

Too late, Alesei covered his sleeping friends, giving the young guard a rather cloudy smile.

"Aren't you scared?" it was more a statement than a question.

"A little," the boy replied sincerely. "But it's better to laugh than to be afraid."

"You're crazy."

"That's right," the boy replied. "I feel good with it!"

Alesei smiled as the other walked away. And then suddenly came understanding.

"What is her name?!" He shouted after the boy.

He didn't have to wait long. As he had suspected, the young man stopped and looked at him in surprise. But he got over it quickly.

"Klarisse," he replied softly.

Alesei made another face at him.

* * *

Vivan swung his legs to the floor. It seemed to him, that his boots weighed at least as much as a cart full of potatoes. Even dressing up was a huge effort for him. But today he was pleased to find that the effort paid off. It was enough to take the first, if a bit shaky, steps, then the second and third, for the body to get used to the movement and gravity. Paphian stood by him, ready to support him at any moment.

"I can do it," he told him though, feeling the blood circulate faster inside him.

The ground swirled slightly and spots appeared before his eyes. Paphian caught him quickly.

"Slowly," he said. "Aren't you asking too much of yourself?"

"I don't want to be a burden to you."

"You didn't have to get up."

"No?" Vivan wondered, feeling the sweat beating on him from the effort.

"If it cheers you up, I'm impressed that you managed to get to your feet so quickly."

"You need more from me today."

Paphian looked at him seriously. They didn't just talk about his fitness.

"We know that you should still lie down," he replied gently. "You're not so weak anymore, and completely useless. You survived a miracle, and had it not been for the fact that you were in danger here, I would not have let you get up today. You are not a burden to us. Come on, that's enough. Come back. Don't expect too much of yourself at once."

He had to agree with him. His legs trembled with the effort. He sat down on the bed with relief.

"Hey," Sel appeared in the doorway. "Can I go in? I brought breakfast. Jancey outdid himself today."

Vivan looked at him sympathetically. Sel cheered silently to see the healer looked better.

"And I crash a party," Alesei appeared right behind him. "And I brought the others. You will eat with us because I don't give you a choice anyway."

Vivan smiled at the remark, which the open-minded Alesei liked very much. The healer did not exalt himself and was really sympathetic, he was told. He liked him more and more. And his brother, knowing how meetings with kind people affect Vivan's health, did not protest, although he might prefer to spend these moments alone with his brother. It was evident that he was ready to endure much for Vivan, though he was a little lonely wolf. Not particularly caring about the procedural customary order on the table, Alesei began setting the plates he had brought until the women exchanged meaningful glances. They took it over quickly. He did not protest. He preferred to watch it with a satisfied cat smile.

Vivan watched his new friends with warmth in his heart.

There have been some seemingly invisible changes. From the fact that the group had apparently gotten close to the guards, to whom funny remarks were made (reciprocally), to the relationship between some of them. Oliver, though still in female attire, was more casual. He looked at Sai once or twice, and you could clearly see the warmth in that look, although he was very careful that the guards did not see it. When Oliver saw that he saw it, he became tense for a moment, but quickly relaxed nevertheless as he noticed a faint, warm smile of approval on the healer's face. Sai did not owe him. She engaged him to make preparations to gently brush his hands under the guise of arranging bread or fruit, or look him in the eyes for a moment. Ross seemed to be radiating some kind of inner light, and it was not the jewel that betrayed him, but his eyes. He and Sel avoided the gaze, but half-consciously their bodies were attracting each other. Julien stood between them aware of this inner tension, treated by both of them as a younger sister, which seemed to suit her. All these people addressed Vivan with kindness, as to an old friend, as to Paphian. Looking at it from the side, you might assume that everyone has known each other here for years. And although there was not much merriment between them, because everyone was more or less aware of what was going to happen soon, there was no shortage of a friendly and warm atmosphere. When he got up to sit at the table, they waited tensely to see how he could cover that distance, everyone tense to jump to his aid immediately. Alesei did not allow Paphian to sit forgotten for a moment, amusing himself in the spirit of his poor attempt to make him understand that he was a little tired of it.

Vivan was worried about these people. He loved them with all his heart.

* * *

"We're operating as planned," said the captain.

Everyone, except Vivan, knew what this meant and what their assigned duties were. From that moment on, the civilians were under the same regime as the soldiers from the detachment. In an empty warehouse, they showed up for the last briefing. The Beckert brothers were the only ones who did not join the general discipline. Vivan sat down on the empty table where Sel's mother's body had previously been. Paphian stood at his side. The guards - all but the young son of the current captain of the royal guard at the castle who accompanied them - had already participated in the fighting, mainly in the recent riots. They worked perfectly there. Queen Constance's guards stood beside them, showing impeccable posture. Kirian, Marten, Kertis and the others looked ready for the worst. Sashes mourning the murdered lieutenant were still hung on their uniforms. However, there have been some changes. They all wore veils and light armor, and on their heads helmets with the emblem of the kingdom. Since they had almost established themselves as defenders of the Beckert brothers from the beginning, their unit was not only the one closest to the carriage. In the midst of their ranks - as had been established in the interviews in which Vivan did not take part due to his health - they hid Ross, and one of them, similar in shape and with a strand of hair dyed white, took his place. Ross stood out in the ranks of the bonnet and helmet guards. He looked as good as if there was always his place here. The women looked at each other knowingly, and Alesei gave a nudge to Sel who was staring at this new image of his beloved. Everyone, except the healer, wore light armor. The women had their hair up. Oliver used almost the same number of hairpins and pins as its predecessor for his bun.

The captain hurried down the ranks. He mentally considered the weaknesses of his people. Then civilians.

Sel said he watched his old friend Moren during training. He knew better than he did when to strike, he was well aware of his opponent's movements. His weakness was his lack of practice. So far, as a heart patient, he has not trained at all. These few critical days must have been enough for him for the time being.

Alesei had a teacher in his hometown as long as the family could afford it. He was clearly a diligent student.

Paphian trained at home. He was good, so if he was lucky, he would be even better. Only now had he been able to use his skills, and he had already shown that he could do a lot - or so the guards said.

Vivan was said to have been able to fight with a sword, but at the moment he was too weak for that.

Sai has learned to wield her unusual weapons enough not to hurt herself. Both for the sword donated by the royal family and the weapon she named after her, she would still have to train, but there was no time for that.

Selena... In her case, she was extremely accurate, which she showed with her slingshot. Additionally, she knew how to wield a dagger, but worse with a sword.

Julien. A weak point. She could improvise, use anything that could be a weapon. She couldn't wield a sword or shoot. So far there has been no occasion.

Ross...

"Do it again," he paused, seeing her instinctively reach where the Jewel was hidden under his uniform. "And you bring death yourself."

Scolded, he withdrew his hand.

Ross fired well with almost any weapon. He could not fight with a sword, although he showed great potential in this direction.

Overall, without diminishing them, the captain believed that these people, in critical conditions, completely incongruous with their previous experiences, showed during their crazy mission to save the healer extraordinary courage, determination and will to fight. They were luckier than they thought, despite their losses, and in a short time had to learn what others had to work for many days. He admired how well they coped with their opponents, and their teamwork was both a core asset and a weak point. Knowing how much they cared about each other, the enemy might have tried to take advantage of it. Or come across an impenetrable obstacle.

They had to face another danger.

"Remember," he said to everyone. "Among those there are people who wanted to tear the healer alive without hesitation. Without thinking, they will kill you to get what they want. You cannot pity them. They've already shown that they are capable of anything," he looked significantly at Ross, reminding him and everyone else of the recent incident. "Kill them. Otherwise they will kill your friends. They will make the healer's fate worse than death. These aren't people anymore. They proved what they can do at the marketplace. So don't hesitate!"

He waited a moment for the words to sink well into their souls.

Then he turned to the people whom the royal family had appointed as guardians of the healer.

"Say goodbye to the dead in your hearts. Take care of each other. Take care of a healer."

Let's go!

Ross was reluctant to leave. As he faced the next challenge, he felt fear begin to tighten his throat. He didn't want the others to see it. The guards, sensing his behavior, let them all ahead. Sel looked back.

We'll be fine, Kertis patted him consolingly on the shoulder. Go.

Reluctantly, he went to get his horse, glancing at Alesei, who was also looking for his friend.

"What's the matter with him?" Kirian asked. We have to move.

"Lieutenant," Kertis said quietly to Kirian, who had been promoted after Delen's death, but his former colleagues, under military discipline, somehow couldn't speak by name now. "From what I've heard, this guy has reason to be scared. He had been close to death several times."

"Just like us," remarked the lieutenant a bit irritated by this weakness.

"But we were not tortured. Guardian say he has scars all over his body."

Kirian said nothing about the remark, surprised at the images his imagination gave him. He returned to the warehouse. He was relieved to see that Ross was not tearing, as he was inclined to suspect him, but simply standing, clenching his fists and trying to calm down.

"Sorry, Lieutenant," he said quickly, seeing Kirian. "I'm leaving already."

Kirian regarded him calmly. What would Delen do in this situation?

"We don't leave our people in need," he said.

Ross was silent.

"I promise you, I'll do anything to protect you."

Ross nodded his head thoughtfully.

"But if you have to choose whether to save me or a healer, you will choose him," he replied, trying not to sound blunt and accusing, but like a simple statement.

"You know the answer," replied the lieutenant calmly.

Ross smirked.

"Then promise me you won't let me suffer," he pleaded. "I don't want my friends to see this. Promise it."

Kirian looked at him seriously.

"I promise," he replied.

* * *

"Take care of yourself," Oliver whispered softly. "You can always take shelter in the carriage."

Sai smiled slightly.

"Stay low," she told him. "Remember! Whatever happens."

"I hate it," he said to the remark.

She studied him, unable to find the right words of comfort. There were no such. Oliver was responsible, as always before, not only for his own life, which he was well aware of, although he would have preferred to do otherwise. He had risked himself too many times. The bond limited his behavior and noble motives.

He lifted the gown so as not to step on it and climbed the steps into the secured, reinforced and shuttered carriage.

Then he met Kirian's gaze.

Kirian saw his conversation with Sai.

Certainly the guards told him that Selena and Sai were sleeping together in the room today.

He saw his strange look.

"I'll have to leave it like that," he sighed into his thoughts.

Even Selena had to have the right to make her own choices. And difficult decisions.

* * *

Ross looked at the young soldier who was now pretending to be him. Oliver was just talking to him inside the carriage, handing him something.

He wished their eyes would meet for a moment before leaving. The soldier's name was Ethan. They met while discussing the strategy.

He was risking his life by pretending to be him.

Finally he looked.

Unable to reveal anything, the two men nodded at each other. Then Ethan bolted the shutter.

"Good luck," Ross said in mind. "I will defend you as you would defend me."

Kirian lined them up around the carriage. The openings in the shutters were to facilitate shooting a bow or crossbow from the inside. They didn't let Ross see his friends' faces.

Alesei lined up in the back. Sel next to him. The guards staked their positions.

From this point he could not see Sai on the other side of the carriage. He felt fear and even the fact that he was riding a horse for the first time did not distract him from it.

He checked that the sword was at hand and the crossbow was easy to pull out. Apart from him, everyone was making final preparations for the journey, waiting for the signal. He heard his own rapid breathing. He felt hot in his mask and his new disguise.

Everything is in its place as it should be.

Everything is…

"Let's go!" Captain Teron called.

Nothing bad happened to them in the narrow street the captain feared. Nobody chatted on them. But when they pulled out onto the street leading to the West Gate, they noticed the first observers. Then the first shots fired at them, several of which stabbed the walls of the carriage. They rushed the horses.

The insane cavalcade had to cross half a seemingly deserted city. Arrows from bows and crossbows announced that it would not be that easy. After repair, the carriage made turns with greater ease, and the coachman did not spare his whip, shooting it over the four gray horses. Blood rushed to the refugees' heads.

The closer they got to the city gates, the thicker the shots were. Along the way, archers were set up in certain sections, especially where the passage narrowed. The captain was giving orders, changing paths abruptly, weaving between streets, losing shooters and small groups of bullies armed with various weapons. In this way, many times the guards and guardsmen managed to avoid death. They had to make a difference. Some streets were deliberately barricaded. Fortunately, the Verdom was so vast that you could run almost anywhere in several directions, and the barricades usually lined the sections leading to the Gate.

"Stick together!" The captain roared from time to time as they turned.

The riders, speeding fast, did not have time to fire, often dodging in narrow streets where you had to react quickly so as not to be crushed by the carriage. Paphian alternated with Ethan's defense of the coachman, leaning out to fire his crossbow. In the back, Oliver fired at the chasers through an opening in the door.

Once, Sel almost got hit by a fist-sized stone thrown at him from the roof.

Two guards were slightly injured.

Halfway to the goal, Alesei noticed that behind them there were much better armed riders who quickly closed the gap between them. Apparently they had caught in the riots.

"Turn back!" The captain shouted once again, steering the horse to the right, a dozen or so meters ahead of the carriage.

The coachman obeyed, knowing the way out of the map, knowing about this maneuver earlier.

If the refugees were able to see the whole situation from above, however, they would see that as the road neared the West Gate, the enemy ranks steadily tightening on almost all sides, and a trap awaiting them at their destination. People hungry for the healer's blood chased them on the roofs closer and closer, tightening their pursuit like a noose around the condemned man's neck. Maybe they didn't know when the healer would want to leave town. But that didn't mean they weren't prepared for it.

That was all they had left when they lost everything they could care about.

"Good job!" the captain praised everyone. "We are not far away! On my signal!"

They discussed it several times. A few people from both teams would lead the rest. Everything had been going well so far, though the coachman, with his wildly bulging eyes and flowing hair, performed miracles to avoid death. Were it not for Paphian, he would have died at the beginning of the road.

Several flaming arrows fell to the ground in front of them. Fortunately, that didn't scare the horses.

The West Gate was already visible in all its glory. As well as about twenty people standing underneath it. Alesei looked around. The riders were no match for the refugees. Their horses were gaunt.

The opponents were weaker than they first believed.

The captain raised his hand.

"Now!" He shouted.

The whole group made a wide arc on a street marked earlier on the map.

And she rode to the North Gate, leaving behind her pursuers and the prepared trap.

The road along the walls led them straight to their destination. The horses galloped through the deserted city, one last tapping of their hooves on the pavement of Verdom. The North Gate was open. It was through it that day and night the gravediggers traveled to the place where the bodies of the dead were burnt in a small valley. Nobody closed it for a long time. There was no one to watch her anymore. The times when life would awaken in the city was yet to come. The fugitives passed through the gate, unstoppable by anyone, and headed west at the fork to find the merchants' road leading all the way to the vast Teryn Mountains, visible from here, where the healer town was located.

The carriage swayed on the rough road, leaving behind the royal city and smoke from the valley of death.

Only when the first trees began to obscure the city and the carriage disappeared into the thicket of vegetation did they dare to slow down to ease the horses, but they did not stop for a moment until the road leading up to the mountains appeared. They were already far from the city then.

"Did you hear what they say about our mountains?" Paphian asked all of them after the first euphoria had passed.

Vivan smiled mysteriously.

"Apparently dragons live there! The youth from the guard squad called."

"People die there sometimes without a trace," said another.

"And the women are hot like a fire in there," he had to add his, as always incorrect Kertis.

Paphian smirked as he looked at everyone. Then he looked at his brother.

"That's only part of the truth," Vivan said.

There was a new tone in his voice. As if he was letting them understand that everything they had gone through so far is just the beginning of what was yet to happen...

CHAPTER 15 — Journey

They rode in silence, listening carefully. The road now led straight to the village, looking deserted from a distance. Unfortunately, the terrain gradually changed, there were more and more hills, rocks and ravines. With a carriage, they had no choice. They realized that they were thus even more exposed to danger, but on the other hand, they hoped that thanks to an armed escort they would be able to avoid a possible attack.

It was only here, in the open air, that the soldiers and the accompanying civilians realized how exposed they were. Most of them never left the city, and it's no wonder that fear began to creep into their hearts.

"You fell silent like at a funeral," Alesei muttered to his friends and closest guards.

"What's the name of this village?" Ross asked to Marten who was riding close him.

"Adelaine. All in all, it is slowly becoming a town. A few years ago it was a small settlement."

Sel looked around curiously. Vast meadows and fields, forests on hills, play of light and shadow as the clouds moved across the sky. It was all new and fascinating to him. The world stretched out in front of him a multicolored rug that he would probably never see. It consumed him as a drafter of unprecedented talent, and as a man who had been kept in isolation all his life, allowing him only a peek at the beauty. Ross allowed himself a smile under the mask hiding his face. Sel looked so much like himself now when he was drawing at Home. He took his drawings, hiding them and the accessories in the saddle bag. Ross hadn't told him yet that he had seen his portrait. He was counting on Sel to mention it himself sometime.

He was glad that Sel waited for the moment when he could finally see the world beyond the walls.

He must know now how much he would lose.

"Shall we stop there for a stop?" Asked the son of the new captain of the king's guard.

"Did you forget the plague, kid?" Alesei snapped.

"For your information," the boy said to him. "My name is Bedal. Yes," he added thoughtfully, "I forgot. It's so easy here. It's so beautiful."

"Soon you will see the dead and take your words back," Alesei muttered. "Get used to it. It will be a common sight."

The expression of quiet delight faded from Sel's face as he listened, and Bedal quickly darkened.

The calm mood vanished somewhere. Ross turned his attention back to looking for signs of life. He only heard a dog barking. No sounds of the usual bustle around houses, no squeaking of carts. People's exhortations...

"Be careful," Marten said to all of them, "Death changes everything."

Adelaine was empty. Only the screeching of horses and the creak of a carriage echoed through the streets.

They encountered the first dead bodies while driving between the buildings. On the side of the road, behind the walls, lay two young people. The girl had her boy's head on her lap. After his death, she must have waited for her turn. She didn't want to leave him. Or maybe she died of exhaustion and hunger?

Others were hiding in the gates. Mostly alone. An old woman was lying by the closed fountain. A man was lying beside the road with vomit marks on his face and clothes. Perhaps he choked.

There was a stench all around. They all hid their faces as they followed the guards.

The captain rode up to the carriage and rapped on the closed shutters.

"Don't open the windows! Don't go outside!"

"Got it," they heard Ethan's muffled voice.

Bedal nervously touched the uniform at chest height, beneath which he carried a small gift vial.

Alesei approached Sai.

The dog was sitting next to an overturned wagon, which no longer had horses. Among the scattered little possessions lay a mother and a baby, both dead. Mother smashed her head. The blood had soaked down the dry, dusty road long ago. The baby died with the mother. The emaciated dog looked after both of them, although there was no one to watch anymore.

Alesei called him softly. The dog barked indecisively. He was definitely hungry and already a little weak. The young man stopped his horse and dismounted. He grabbed the first bowl he spotted and poured some water from his water bag.

"We're not stopping," the captain said sternly, but no one listened.

The coachman stopped the carriage. The soldiers stopped their horses. The dog walked hesitantly to the bowl and began slurpping the water.

"Come, brother," Alesei said to him. "You can do nothing."

"Maybe we should bury them?" Sai guessed.

"Only them?" Asked the captain seriously, looking into her eyes. "Are those also?" He pointed to the surroundings.

She was not afraid of his gaze.

"Listen," he said to everyone, "I know what you're thinking now. But don't forget that we want to cross this road as little visible as possible. Besides, which of you will guarantee me that you will not infect the healer by acting kindly towards these people? I'm listen."

The silence that followed his words was enough for his reply.

"Remember that," he said more gently. "I'm sorry. These people will stay where they are."

That said, he moved on. After a while, the others joined him. Alesei was the last to ride with one hand on the saddle in front of him. Sai smiled sadly at him.

And once again she looked back, at the mother and child.

Ross turned around as well, letting the others pass.

And then, with his heart clenched in grief and anger, he saw the crows who had already been surrounded by the dead, abandoned by the faithful dog. They were already getting closer. Their sharp-beaked heads crooked. They looked out. When they are gone, the birds, still uncertain in the presence of humans, will quickly find their way into their eyes.

He couldn't stop looking. He wanted to go on them and kill them all, but that wouldn't change anything.

Others would come.

"Don't look," he heard Sel's soft voice suddenly turn, alarmed at his behavior.

"It was crying alone in here... until it died," Ross said softly.

Sel felt chills run down his spine at the words. They influenced his imagination so much.

And then Ross felt calm overwhelm him. The gem worked. It calmed their thoughts. So he turned back in silence. He allowed himself to help when he wanted to. Manipulated the Jewel of Hope.

For the first time, Sel looked at him as if with different eyes. So overwhelmed by his misfortune, he did not notice that there was a man living next to him, whose life was also not the easiest. Ross has always had the strength of spirit, and it made Sel forget what he had heard about him, forget about the scars he had seen. Ross was not giving up. But after that nightmare of meeting the healer, when his hair turned white, something happened inside him. Seemingly everything was as it used to be. Now Sel suddenly anxiously noticed that Ross wanted others to think nothing had changed, not to worry about him.

Perhaps that's why the gem won't leave him. Because it needs him.

Because it's worse than they might have suspected.

"I must save him," he thought.

* * *

Paphian sat talking to the coachman through the ajar door. The inside of the carriage was stuffy. It was not one of the hot days of the ending summer, but it could still take its toll. Using his disguise, Oliver fanned himself with one of Red Rebecca's surviving fans. He felt hot in his tight corset and armor. Too hot, actually. He looked through the slit in the shutter at Sai riding next to him. At least they had a gust of wind there.

"I'll open the window upstairs," Ethan offered, seeing his torment.

The window in the roof was assembled while the carriage was being converted. But even that had brought Oliver little relief.

Vivan was asleep. Julien soaked the cloth and walked over to her brother.

"Lift your hair," she said, and as he did, she put a cloth around the nape of his neck. Then she soaked the other one, wrung it out, and held it to his forehead. He looked at her with gratitude and relief.

"Poor thing," she whispered softly.

The carriage stopped suddenly. They heard the captain giving orders. And strange grunts. Ethan jumped to his feet and walked over to Paphian.

"What's happening?" He asked.

Paphian glanced at him. Although at first glance he resembled Ross, especially thanks to the streak of white in his hair, he had a different disposition from him. In fact, there was something about this man that turned him off at first sight. Some fake. He was seemingly nice to everyone, but something was wrong with him. And Vivan, who could read a lot in people, treated him kindly but coolly. He could rely on his opinion on such matters, so he was on guard against Ethan.

"There are two carts with animals on the road," the coachman explained.

Paphian opened the door wide. He and Ehtan both leaned out curiously.

They were well beyond Adelaine by now. The sun was setting, and according to the captain's plan, they were about to look for a place to stop.

There were indeed two colorfully painted carriages in the middle of the track.

"These are the Cars of the Wonderful Circus of Curiosities," explained Kirian after a moment. "A plague has caught them."

"There," Kertis pointed out, when they all appeared to look at the carriages, "the tied animals escaped," he pointed to the railing of one of the broken harnesses and strings. "I wonder what it was this time. I remember visiting the city last year. They showed truly extraordinary plays. And there were also more carts."

"Probably that's the only left of them," one of the guards muttered.

There were strange grunts and scratches from inside one of the carriages. The dog barked nervously at this, but fell silent at Alesei's gesture.

Ross led the horse forward and gasped at what he saw there. There were dead people in front of the carriages - two men. On the carriage, partially over the wheel, was a woman and a fat man, also dead. He could see the arms and legs of probably two boys on the roof. It did not scare him that all these people were dead, but the way they died, and the horses tied to the carriages.

Horses and people were bitten. Of the four horses, there was almost nothing left but bones and bloodstains where flies had gathered. People had partially bitten off limbs, parts of the face. In the light of the setting sun, the sight of blood and bodies torn by wild animals was even more macabre. Julien instinctively clung to Oliver in disguise, who was studying the face of one of the boys lying on the roof.

"The fat one is the circus owner, Sampan," explained Kertis. "That's what he told himself to be called. Nobody knew his real name. It's his wife..." He stepped back, too shocked to speak, feeling the vomit build up inside him.

"Maybe you shouldn't watch this?" Kirian looked gently at the women, directing his words to Selena.

Oliver could still see that expression in him, that look when he saw him with Sai. He didn't look at her at all, as if he were doing it on purpose.

"We'll be fine," he replied softly, embracing Julien with a female gesture, given the circumstances.

Vivan watched the carriages from the doorway. He was gathering strength.

"Since the kids are upstairs," remarked one of the guards, whose name they haven't known yet. "Then what did they die for?"

The captain studied the boy's face, along with the twins and Kertis.

"This one died of the plague," Oliver remarked, seeing the traces of mush on the boy's face and the dirty wagon.

Alesei rode up the other side and climbed up to see better. He went white slightly in the face.

"And?" The captain asked.

Without looking at Oliver and Julien, Alesei explained:

The other one stabbed his heart with a knife. They were twins."

Sai looked quickly at Oliver, and Julien nestled her face against his shoulder. Everyone who knew Selena and Julien were cousins, as it was impossible to hide the resemblance, looked at them with sympathy. Sel was one of the few who immediately understood the horror of this information. Others took more time for this.

When the brother died, the other one could not stand separation from him, so he took his own life. From the boy's appearance to everyone, they weren't more than eight or nine years old.

Moments passed while everyone pondered what they had just learned about the twin bond.

They understood how serious a burden it could be. What a burden to those born with her.

Sai was looking at Oliver. Being in front of everyone, hidden under the mask of the girl, he hugged his sister so tightly and desperately as if he was trying to shield her from everything, hide from cruelty and curiosity. Sel, not wanting the soldiers to suspect a closer relationship between Selena and Julien (they thought they were cousins so far), looked significantly at the captain.

"What are we going to do with them?"

His eyesight meant: "Do something. Stop it. Let them breathe!" Teron understood him perfectly.

"Let's get them together," he ordered. "Be careful. Do not touch them directly with your hands. We'll make a pile. We'll burn them. They can't stay as in the road as some carcasses. And then we will continue at night to the town of Umbriel. There, in its vicinity, we will stop for the night.

"What about the animals on the carriage?" Alesei pointed to the carriage, from which murmurs and scratches were coming all the time. "We'll let them out, right?"

Bedal looked nervously at the shaking carriage, as did the others.

"And who knows," muttered Kertis, "what a beast sitting there."

"I would be in favor of leaving it as it is," Marten said hesitantly, trying to calm his horse.

"Leave your head!" Kiran said sharply to him. "Who's going to the roof with me? I can see the handle. There is a window."

"I'll go," said Paphian.

They both entered and knelt by the window. The others watched with interest, even Julien, wanting to distract from her gloomy thoughts. Sel looked at Oliver with concern. The friend's face was like a mask. He glanced at Ross. Though only the eyes and part of the face were visible, he saw fear in them. He was also looking at Oliver. He saw the painful understanding appear in his lover's eyes, reaching deeper than what appeared in the minds of others. He approached him.

"What happened?" He asked softly.

Without looking at him, Ross replied:

"I haven't thought about the consequences so far..."

There was a meaning in the words that Sel knew instantly, knowing the twins. He remembered the night. He remembered seeing Julien on Ross's bed and Oliver had been with Sai at the time.

"Sel," Ross spoke softly only he could hear. "What have I done?!"

"You wanted to help him," he tried to console him.

Meanwhile, Paphian opened the window and he and Kirian looked inside, from where the murmurs clearly grew louder.

"What is there?!" Cried Bedal.

Ross fell silent with a foreboding feeling.

Paphian and Kirian exchanged knowing smiles.

"Two white tigers," replied Kirian. Damn hungry two white tigers!"

"Then we'd better leave them there like I said," Marten replied.

"Vivan." Paphian looked at his brother with sparkle in his eyes. "Can you help it? Calm them down. You have no idea how beautiful they are!"

Vivan smiled involuntarily at the expression on Paphian's face. Like a child who has just been given a beloved toy.

Of course he could influence animals like that. They won't attack anyone here.

He sat down on the steps of the carriage.

"Let them out," he said confidently and calmly.

The tone of his voice calmed everyone down. They knew that nothing bad would happen to them.

* * *

As intended, they stopped outside the city for the night. The Captain and Kirian discussed whether setting the cars on fire was indeed the best move, having passed unnoticed so far. But they knew they couldn't have done otherwise in this case. Knowing that these people would have stayed like that the next day, especially these unfortunate two boys, was enough for them to justify their actions. The remaining soldiers set up a makeshift camp. From where they chose to stay during the day, they could see the city, now plunged into darkness. There were no torches, not even the smallest light. In the moonlight, the outlines of walls and structures could be seen, with no sign of life. It didn't bode well.

"Where's your new arrival?" Alesei asked Paphian. "Tell these mascots to stay away from my dog."

"They went hunting," Paphian replied rather carelessly, looking at the dog that was eating next to the new master with enthusiasm. "They can't attack anyone here, but they can't stop eating either. A hungry tiger is a bad tiger."

"Just like men," Sai said as she passed by.

He looked after her involuntarily, contemplating her beauty. Alesei smiled under his breath.

"Aren't you afraid they'll hunt people?"

"Vivan forbade them to do so," Paphian replied confidently. "As long as people don't attack us."

"He can really do that?"

"You haven't seen anything yet," said Paphian, sitting down next to him. "Now that he is finally free, he will show what his power is."

"He showed," Alesei replied quieterly, glancing at the carriage. "From this side I didn't know him so far."

Paphian felt the eyes of the listening soldiers on him.

They waited for his answer.

He didn't know what exactly to say to them. The healer killed people with his power. He was forced to do so. He himself didn't know he could do it.

Every answer that came to mind did not fully explain what must have been going on in his brother's heart to lead him to such an act of violence.

"We're going on patrol to the city," Bedal stood beside them, breaking the gloomy silence.

"Are you coming?" Asked Alesei.

"I'd rather check with my own eyes," he replied.

"Hey!" One of his companions said grudgingly.

Bedal smiled at him, softening his words.

"Watch your skin," Alesei said sympathetically to him. "I don't want CLARISSA to cry her eyes out for you."

Bedal was scared when the girl's name was mentioned and his friends threw more or less dirty jokes at him.

"Thanks," he said sarcastically to the bully.

Alesei grinned at him, then quickly turned serious.

"Take care of yourself, kid."

Bedal rolled his eyes.

"Bedal," he reminded him as he departed. "My name is Bedal, ALESEI!"

Alesei looked at him thoughtfully. Ross sat on the other side of him, unfolding his makeshift bedding.

"New friendship?" He asked with a smile.

"He reminds me of him," said Alesei. "He fucking reminds me of him."

Ross looked at him with understanding and sadness.

"We'll still see them in others," he remarked, the tone of his voice echoing the soft longing in his heart. "I just hope it won't hurt that much one day."

Paphian was tactfully silent until they both turned to other matters again. He felt sorry for their painful losses.

"I'll be right back," Ross said. "I want a word with Ethan."

Torn by curiosity, they looked after him. Ethan stood in front of the carriage, talking to his fellow officers. Ross politely asked them for a moment.

"I want to thank you," he said to Ethan. "You exposed yourself today because of me. I'm glad you're okay."

Ethan looked at him oddly.

"First," he said. "It was the lieutenant's order. Second, just because I look like you doesn't mean we're the same, okay? And one more thing. I'm also glad that this whole farce is over. If I had died pretending to be a nancy-boy, I would have disgraced my family's good name."

Ross felt like he was being slapped in the cheek and spit in the face.

Alesei jumped to his feet. The dog, concerned about his behavior, began to bark.

"Ethan," one of the disguised man's colleagues said. "You're such an asshole!"

A commotion arose that attracted Kirian's attention. Paphian grabbed Ross before he attacked his double.

"What is going on here?" Kirian asked.

Then Vivan appeared at the door of the carriage.

He slowly descended the stairs and stood in front of the group. Suddenly, touched by a strange thought triggered by Paphian's earlier conversation with Alesei, everyone fell silent. Even the dog calmed down.

Vivan approached Ethan and looked him straight in the eye.

For the first time since they had met him, they felt uncomfortable. They saw him calm. Serious. Even sometimes cheerful. And angry. But they had never seen such a look from him before. The association of this very look with the sudden, mysterious death of people at the marketplace aroused in them a previously unknown respect for the healer. Ethan tried unsuccessfully to show that it made no impression on him.

"Why are you insulting him?" Vivan asked in his melodious voice.

There was something about him. Something they haven't seen before. After the nightmare he was weak and broken, but now, the more strength he grew, the greater his inner strength became, which they had not had the opportunity to recognize before.

Never again...

Paphian looked at his brother, whom he suddenly saw as if from a different angle. It wasn't the Vivan he knew. This one seemed stronger than he was.

Ethan huddled slightly under the healer's scrutinizing gaze.

"Vivan, I'd be fine," Ross said softly, freeing himself from Paphian's grasp. "Do you think that since I'm a fagot," he looked coldly at Ethan, "you can treat me with kid gloves or insult me?! To hell with you!"

He pushed through the crowd, ignoring even Sel's gaze, and stood just outside the edge of the camp, staring at the outlines of the city. For in spite of his anger, he was afraid to distance himself from his friends again.

"I wish," Vivan said coldly to Ethan, "that you treat my friends with respect."

They had never heard such a tone from a healer before. There was clearly a threat in it.

"I'm sorry, Count," Ethan softened.

But Vivan, able to read a lot between the lines in people's hearts, sensed the lie in the apology. He couldn't change Ethan's mind and make him tolerate. It was not his intention. He did not drive the will of the people. He just wanted them to learn to understand. And Ethan was still far from there.

He walked away to talk to Ross, not giving the other a glance anymore. People prudently moved out of his way.

Several of them began scolding Ethan, and Kirian called him to the side.

Alesei and Paphian looked at the people talking beyond the edge of the camp.

"Your brother can be dangerous," said Alesei.

Paphian silenced this remark. He smiled thoughtfully.

* * *

Oliver sat on a clothes chest, pretending to watch the view outside the window. He also saw the city. He saw Ross heading that way and Vivan joined him shortly after. But to tell you the truth, he wasn't really interested in it now. Like Julien, now pouring boiling water over the herbs in several cups.

Oliver defended himself against thoughts of Sai and last night. During the day, the journey and the heat distracted him from his memories.

The night reminded him of everything.

He defended himself unsuccessfully, knowing as always that Julien was feeling his thoughts.

He remembered kisses.

Touch of Sai on his skin.

"Oliver," he heard her voice say his name. His real name.

He felt a thrill of excitement involuntarily. He concentrated to suppress his desires, though he painfully wanted to be entitled to the memories of that night.

Perhaps the only night of this kind in his life.

"What if Julien fails to do it again?" He heard Sai's voice once more.

His eyes burned. Pressing tears.

He was avoiding her. He was avoiding Sai even now. He wasn't looking. He did not speak.

But he couldn't forget.

"Please," Julien whispered softly, handing him the cup. "They are supposed to calm down."

He smelled the herbs. Melissa...

She sat down next to him, with her back turned.

"You feel sorry for me?" She asked.

"You know I don't."

"I know," she said. "Though sometimes I'd rather not know..."

"Forgive me for bothering you with my thoughts!"

"That's not what I mean!"

"At least pretend," his voice broke. "I'd like some privacy."

He felt her grief and pain at those words. He hurt her.

"Julien..." He turned to embrace her. "I'm sorry. It isn't your fault."

He pressed his face against her back.

She felt his tear. Maybe she could give him more freedom, but the thought of her brother making love to a woman was strange and obnoxious to her. She shouldn't, didn't want to share those feelings with him. She couldn't. Instead, she understood his longing. She felt how much pleasure this fulfill was. The thought carried at the same time joy at his happiness and a sense of disgust, as if she had entered into her parents' bedroom while they were making love.

How to distance them from each other so that they can live normally?

If Vivan could make her close the gate of her mind effortlessly. Or he found another way. Ross could help her, but he would have to be around all the time.

She looked at her brother and saw the same in his tear-filled eyes.

Hope.

* * *

"Let's give the city a wide berth," said the commander of the patrol sent to the city.

They returned deep in the night. Like the white tigers that lay down beside the carriage, causing the discontent of a dog that crouches closer to its new master. Alesei pretended to be asleep while listening to the conversation. Opening his eyes slightly, he saw Ross was faking it.

"What did you see?" The captain asked.

A watchful Kirian stood beside him.

"Well, then," they heard Kertis hesitate in his voice. A reconnaissance unit consisting of both groups of soldiers was commanded by him. "Lieutenant. Red Rebecca, the one from the brothel..."

"Yes?" Kirian cut off any further explanation, probably because of his friends pretending to be asleep.

"Well, apart from that cart, she had another one that was less fancy," Kertis said. "It used to be in it... Anyway," he said hurriedly, "This carriage is now in Umbriel. Lieutenant," Kertis's voice sounded angrily. "I met it because it had such decorations and there was some paint left... The horses were taken and ate. They, that is, city dwellers. Because they hang out there. Like rats."

"Did you talk to someone?"

"No, sir," Kertis said suddenly firmly, "we won't talk to anyone there. Let's give them a wide berth."

"What happened?"

There was a moment of silence.

"Bedal?" The captain asked, looking forward to an answer.

"They locked them in that carriage," the young soldier explained, his voice breaking. "Those from the House of Pleasure. They burned them alive in the middle of the square!"

Alesei heard muffled sobs. Ross sat down with Sel next to him.

"We agreed," Ross explained, his voice breaking. "We were to meet in the city of the healer."

"No one could have foreseen this Ross," Sel said softly.

Alesei felt anger and regret overwhelm him. He enumerated the names of the murdered in his mind. Among them was the woman who helped Oliver dress up as Selena. Ross was sobbing softly.

CHAPTER 16 — Last evening

In a gloomy mood, a group of wanderers prepared for the morning. The news about what happened to the fugitives from the House of Pleasure has already reached everyone. Changing their original intentions, a completely compact group went back to the fork in the road to avoid the cruel city in a wide arc. It was only when they were in the mountains, and the road began to wind between the hills and valleys, providing great views and artistic impressions that the mood improved significantly.

But the recent inhabitants of the House of Pleasure and their friends were still grieved. They lost a lot to appear here. They paid a dear price for their new life.

Ross was silent during the trip. Even a gesture of goodwill from Ethan, who handed him Oliver's gift of copy of the Jewel of Hope, hadn't helped. Oliver lent it to Ethan before leaving, explaining it with the elaboration of the details, as those who watched them in the city knew well that the white-haired man wore a Jewel around his neck. He explained the possession of the pendant with a gift from the goldsmith's son. Ethan was afraid to hand him over to Selena because she was with the Healer now, without saying it directly. So he asked Ross for help, quite awkwardly trying to blur the memory of his previous behavior.

Two white tigers, majestically and with feline grace, walked on both sides of Paphian's horse, without disturbing the dog, which had gotten so used to them that it was already running freely next to them and the riders.

Depressed Sai rode her horse. Her thoughts circled around Oliver, whom she missed painfully. He hadn't spoken a word with her since they left. He was avoiding her, not looking for her eyes. She knew he was being cautious about his disguise, but she hoped that with just one gesture he would reassure her of his devotion. As time passed, however, she began to get used to the idea that this was clearly not the case. It was only a temporary relief from his suffering. Just like it has happened to her with other men in the past. And though it seemed so real at the time, in reality she was probably under a delusion. That hurts.

So she was a whore to meet his needs. A lonely, loss-torn whore who helped become a lost young man a man.

These were bitter thoughts.

Sel looked around, contemplating the sights. Only he looked up to see the peaks. And that's why, at one point, he was the first to notice the unusual phenomenon.

"Dragons," he muttered, drawing Ross's thoughtful attention. "There are dragons!" He pointed to the valley on the left, above which flew several large-winged creatures of different colors. In the silence around him, everyone whose eyes followed his gesture heard strange noises, never before heard.

"They are huge!" Kirian remarked, quickly taking the telescope out of the saddlebag. "Oh, Mother Earth!" He shouted in delight as he took a closer look at them. "They are beautiful!"

He handed the telescope to the others so that they could judge the beauty of the unusual creatures for themselves.

"They are dangerous?" Bedal asked worriedly.

"Certainly," replied one of his companions, who had introduced himself to Alesei yesterday as Renal.

"Hopefully they're not hungry," said Nils wryly.

Sel looked at Ross. Before they moved on, he gave him a warm smile. They had too little time to quietly exchange even a few words with each other without witnesses. He reached out a hand and placed it on top of his. Seeing his despondency, he sincerely wanted to hug him tightly. But he felt that Ross did not want the gesture now. He called to be alone with his thoughts.

* * *

The captain ordered a stop for a meal and a little rest at noon. Unaccustomed to horse riding, they took this rest with relief to relieve their sore muscles. Soon, however, the concern for the further journey on horseback was forgotten when the healer removed the pain by touching. So they all sat down together to eat the supplies, not lighting a fire, so as not to draw attention to themselves. The soldiers asked Paphian to tell them a bit about dragons, so he gladly shared his knowledge.

The future was also discussed. The guards and soldiers were to return to the capital - unless the situation in the city required their longer stay. The few people appointed as watchmen may not be a defense of the only hope for many.

Vivan looked much better now. Unfortunately, he did not sleep well through the night, due to persistent pain forced to finally take the medications that Sedon had prepared for him. He hated them because they made him strangely numb and hard to move. The injured body healed quickly, but it would take some time for it to recover completely. The hair grew completely, however, so Julien trimmed it during the stop to make it grow evenly. The scars that disfigured his body paled almost as pale as Ross's, but their number and the realization of how they had happened filled everyone's hearts with pain. He did not complain, although the sight of his reflection in the mirror from the carriage was at first a shock to him. He also did not talk about the nightmares and the growing fear of leaving the carriage he was trying to fight. But those who traveled with him knew this. It was clear that the healer was already dreaming of returning to his own home.

In one thing, he never lost his enthusiasm. If he could help in any way, he did it right away, no matter how sore someone was or if it was just sore muscles or abrasions. The moods also began to improve after a friendly meal. Despite the sad events, everyone began to hope that now it would only get better. Even Ross perked up after eating with his friends, and the Jewel, unstoppable by him, warmed his heart again and filled the hearts of others.

For Oliver and Julien, who feared harassing a healer for their cause after a bad night, their continued journey was only disturbing. Vivan, who quickly noticed the depression of siblings, figured out the cause of the condition. He apologized to them for their negligence on this matter due to their exhaustion. Just by touching their heads with his warm hands, he made what Julien had managed to do for several hours with Ross' help now remain permanent. The narrow bond that could not be completely severed remained, minds given a distance that allowed them to freely close their thoughts when they were to be a mystery. The feeling of the mutual presence and state of mind also remained, but Vivan had locked up the effects of trauma or other sensations forever, limiting them only to the awareness that they had occurred. From that moment on, if one of them was going to cut himself, the other only knew it, nothing else.

"The only thing I did was that," he told them, "you are a twin pair. I don't know what I could do for two boys or girls. They never came to me for help."

"If this bond was sometimes a nightmare for us," Oliver said grimly, "I'd rather not know what it is to them."

In his heart he felt a strange emptiness and at the same time joyful elation. It was like the night he was with Sai again. This strange silence in thoughts, everything as if separated, as if through the wall. It was a strange feeling after many years that he and Julien had lived so closely together. His whole life was suddenly forgotten, his decisions, choices made for the sake of his sister.

He didn't have to be so careful anymore.

He can't get it yet.

But he could already feel his strength growing, some joy, the sound of blood in his ears. And one thought, one name fueled this feeling, it burst his soul, entailed changes that he had never hoped to experience.

Vivan tactfully stepped out of the carriage, leaving them alone, but Julien, who knew, though she couldn't be that close, what might be going on in her brother's heart, because she had known him forever, didn't want to stay any longer. She wanted to enjoy this strange change that was to accompany her forever from today. Peace seized her. The healer contributed to this. She was grateful to him for that. Without his support, she would probably soon be overcome by terror and loss. There were no such feelings within her. Instead, she felt a sense of security, love and peace in her heart. Like when her parents gave her something she really wanted, hugging her with love. The warmth she felt in her heart made her want to share her quiet joy with someone close to her, and let her brother feel it without her participation. She knew only one person who became not only her friend, but also became close to her, associating with her family. She came out of the carriage to find him, and despite the fact that she was talking to Sel, about whom she had slightly different feelings, she approached Ross, cuddling up to him, as when she was tormented and he was lying badly wounded in bed yet ready to help her in her time of need. Reliably, just like her brother, Ross hugged her tightly without asking any questions, waiting for herself to explain her behavior to him. Sel felt a pang in his heart. There was a time when he was so close to Julien. Now he felt that there was still an invisible obstacle between them. And while he understood why, the feeling didn't make him feel any better.

Ross closed his eyes. He remembered the moments when Julien cried and screamed because Oliver was getting hurt. Now he was relieved to feel at peace within her, as if some important change had taken place. But he waited patiently. Whatever she wanted to share with him, she had to do it herself. He had learned long ago not to put pressure on such matters, and recent events have taught him to be cautious.

His patience was soon rewarded.

"We can live now," she said softly. "Ross, we can live normally!"

He hugged her tightly, thus showing his joy. Over his shoulder, she also looked at Sel, who took a moment to fully understand what she was talking about. He smiled at her with emotion.

She smiled back at him and her eyes glistened with tears.

But then she turned her head so as not to look at him anymore, not to think, not to disturb with the desires he evoked in her, though she had thought she had withdrawn from such thoughts about him before. She didn't want to destroy what was between them three. She did not want misunderstandings and unnecessary dreams. They were going to be gone forever, as was the strength of the bond she had with Oliver. They must have become the past...

"What's the matter, Julien?" she heard Sai's alarmed voice suddenly, "You argued with..." she quickly reflected before pronouncing the proper name: "Selena?"

Julien gently released herself from Ross's embrace and looked at her new friend. She smiled reassuringly. She couldn't say it the way she wanted it for the sake of the soldiers, as several of them were peering at the scene curiously, muttering to each other. She heard scraps of comments about threesomes and foursomes. She also noticed some meaningful smiles. It didn't bother her. These were just innocent jokes.

Explaining what had happened might have elicited a reaction in Sai that was better not shown.

"No, I didn't argue," she said cheerfully. "She better explain it to you."

Sai, encouraged by her gesture, went to the carriage.

Oliver stood beside the front door, invisible to all. She stood in front of him, scrutinizing his face, intrigued and somewhat worried nonetheless.

He loved that look that always reached into his true self.

He kissed her, no longer hiding the long-repressed longing that seemed to drag on for eternity.

Stunned by his spontaneity, she succumbed to this kiss, fearing at the same time that they would be discovered. She would have preferred to close the door immediately and let him shower her with his caresses, which he clearly wanted to do. His eyes sparkled. His heart was beating hard under her hand as she struggled to hold him back, also fighting her own desire.

"Now you're crazy," she whispered in his ear, feeling her body tremble under his touch. "Someone might have looked in here!"

"I'm sorry," he said completely insincere, with a gleam of cheerfulness in his eyes, "I'm sorry." He repeated after a moment, becoming serious and releasing from his embrace with a great effort of will. "I'm sorry that I had been silent so far Sai. You do not even know…"

She covered his mouth with her hand.

He knew what she meant by that. He had to be careful. But it was becoming almost painful.

"What happened?" She asked to calm their thoughts a bit, which were followed by again defiant hands and thirsty lips. They barely managed to stop it.

For a moment he did not know how to express his thoughts in words, so as not to scream for joy without hugging her to his heart. Right now, he hated his disguise as never before.

She waited impatiently.

"Julien," he whispered finally in her ear, brushing her neck as she did so, making it hard to focus on his words, "and I... closed the gate. I can..."

There was so much in that one word of the broken sentence. The very thought of what they might endure ignited their senses like fire. At the same time, it aroused so many emotions in Oliver that he was losing his voice. She fully understood his happiness. She hugged him tightly, and he pressed his head against her shoulder, soothed by her closeness, extinguishing the fire of desire that quickly faded away, muffled by other feelings and, unfortunately, a necessity that he hated.

"Forever?" She asked softly.

He nodded his head in agreement.

She had to suppress other feelings. They couldn't do that. They couldn't be together now. They both knew it bitterly.

"Sai," Oliver whispered. "All my life... I've been hiding."

"I know."

He trembled in her arms. She felt sorry for him. She could only guess how hard it had been for him.

"We'll find a way," she said. "Hold on. Just a little more. I promise."

He was silent. Still glancing to see if anyone was coming, she held him in her arms until he finally calmed down.

It was all she could do for him now. Though she wanted so much more.

She released him slowly.

The latter parted their hands.

She left, leaving him alone.

Soon they were on the road again. Vivan grew gloomy with every hour he approached his goal. His companions knew perfectly well the reason for this mood. Julien tried to cheer him up with a good meal and a warm word. Oliver tried to involve him in the conversation, but Vivan was reluctant to do so. His gloomy mood slowly began to affect his brother and friends, and finally Paphian, unable to bear it any longer, asked to stop.

He briefly explained to the captain the reason.

"You didn't have to!" Vivan said nervously, "Whether we come home an hour later or not, it won't change anything."

"I'll get Ross," Paphian told him shortly. "Maybe he…"

"Damn it all!" Vivan interrupted him, upset, until everyone around him looked in his direction in surprise. "Don't call him! I have the right to be afraid!"

"He's right," said Ross, who had just appeared in the doorway.

Vivan looked at him gratefully.

"I want to help you," Paphian explained to them both. "I can't watch you get tired."

"Then don't look!" Ross said as he approached them. "Say the word and we'll stay overnight," he said to Vivan.

"What will this change?"

"It'll give you more time."

"For what? To prepare?!"

"Let's say that," Ross replied. "Or maybe to get drunk."

"What?!" Paphian was surprised, sure that he had misheard, expressing with this question also the feelings of listening siblings.

"Get some sleep," Ross began to calmly explain, gesturing the words with a feminine gesture. "So get drunk. Drink yourself silly. Drink to death..."

"I know what that means," interrupted Paphian nervously.

Ross looked at Vivan with a slight smile.

"Think," he told him with a twinkle in his eye. "When was the last time you had fun?"

"You mean fun and dancing? I do not feel like it…"

"No, dear," this time Ross was starting to wake up to the spirit of his recent personality, as Sel was watching outside, noticing with a smile. "Wine and singing. Good company. A sea of possibilities! Crazy night…"

Vivan looked at him as if he were crazy.

"I don't know ..." he replied hesitantly, but Ross already knew from his expression that he had hit the nail on the head.

So he reached into the cupboard where the food and drink were kept in the carriage and then, deliberately making some noise and drawing Julien into it, prepared cups and wine. Sitting down next to Vivan, he quickly invited Paphian and Sel to join him. Sel called to Alesei, along with the dog, who followed him, and he signaled the soldiers. Seeing what was going on, the captain and Kirian determined who was to be on guard and who was allowed to play, and then sat down as well.

"Listen," Ross said, pouring the wine first, starting with the healer first, "We're both terribly stiff..."

"Right!" Said Alesei cheerfully, always willing to spend a pleasant evening, thus arousing quiet laughter in those present.

Ross stopped him with a gesture.

"I will not make you dance with me..." a few voices commented these words in a joke. "You have to get drunk with me!" Ross finished eagerly.

The mood was getting better and better, the closer it got to the pleasant evening. Sel eyed the Jewel on Ross's neck suspiciously. He was glowing slightly, at which he smiled indulgently as he watched the situation unfold.

To avoid possible ambiguous jokes, Ross added quickly, lifting his cup, "Get drunk with us!" And he tapped Vivan's cup with it, then held it out towards those present. They eagerly accepted the toast and drank the first contents to the bottom.

Vivan, already succumbing to the mood of the moment, followed suit.

"My dears!" Ross, feeling completely in control of the situation, stood in front of everyone with a mysterious smile. "We're not going anywhere today!"

All gathered and the soldiers outside raised their cups in honor of these words...

Much later, when the evening was in full swing and Vivan sat in a much better mood chatting between Alesei and Oliver, Paphian managed to pull Ross unnoticed, who had drunk much less than he had tried to show. The jewel was not shining again.

"Thank you," he said honestly, "that was a really great idea!"

Ross looked at him with a mixture of cheerfulness and seriousness. In the light of the small fire, his white strand of hair gleamed with its own light.

"We all need moments like this," he replied. "Otherwise life would have crushed us like a huge stone."

Paphian looked around the camp. Vivan, with a slight smile, was just listening to Captain Teron's story. Kirian visibly relaxed. Oliver was slightly confused about the courtesies of Kertis and Marten, who were clearly sympathetic to Selena. Julien was talking to Sai about something with a mysterious smile. Everyone was petting a dog passing between them, which Alesei still carelessly called simply a dog. From time to time that evening, various offers were made from all over the camp regarding a name for the dog, most of them evoking merriment and opportunities for jokes. There was no doubt that the dog's name was a leitmotif that fueled the mood when other topics were missing even for a moment. Bedal had the most offers, and today he was excellent company for Alesei. The latter, however, also did not forget about his friend and raised a toast to Ross as the perfect host for the evening, which everyone eagerly picked up on. Even Ethan joined the toast a little reluctantly, and Nils got everyone to stand by.

Ross thanked the appreciation with a nod and the shadow of a smile. Paphian noticed tears in his eyes, dictated by strong emotion. He waited for everything to settle down. Only then did he ask curiously:

"Do you have any part in this game?" He pointed significantly at the Jewel.

"No," Ross said calmly, "They don't need my help."

One of the tigers returned to the camp from his trip and rubbed carelessly against his new master's leg, demanding a proper greeting.

"Hello, Reeba," Paphian stroked the female with a caressing gesture. "Have you eaten you bully-girl?"

The pet's purr must have been enough for him to answer. Reeba left and lay down with royal dignity between the wheels of the carriage.

"I miss it," Ross said suddenly.

Paphian followed his gaze. Ross was currently looking at Sel, who was just talking to Alesei. The healer's brother felt a bit awkward. He understood what this might be about. But he still hadn't gotten used to that kind of feeling in men. But he was well on his way to doing so the longer he was with his new friends.

"Tell him," he replied, trying to sound completely natural. "I guess this will be the right time."

"I wish it was. You don't even know how much." Ross sighed dreamily. "Until recently, there wasn't a day to…"

"I'm begging you!" Paphian interrupted him playfully, terrified of what he might hear.

Ross laughed honestly for the first time in a long time at the look on his face.

"Right," he replied, winking at him significantly. "The tongue always turns to the aching tooth."

Now they both smiled. One of them was somewhat relieved, which did not escape the other, who accepted it with indulgence.

"Do you miss that house?" Paphian asked after a moment.

He had never known the representatives of the oldest profession in the world. He was able to cope without their services. He was curious about the answer, knowing in advance that he would have denied himself immediately. He certainly wouldn't miss a place where he would sell his body for money.

Ross was silent for a long moment. Paphian wondered if he had offended him by the question.

"I miss those people," replied his new friend at last, seriously, "Valeriea, Rebecca, Lena. Even behind that bum Len. True, you didn't even meet him..." His voice broke for a moment. He cleared his throat nervously. "They were better for me than my mother," he continued calmly, but sadly, " Rebecca said: "Ross, I'm sick of people in this business. You don't have to..." He broke off suddenly, taken over by the sudden memory "But I wanted..." he added softly, "I wanted to do what I had to defend so much at house. I wanted to forget about it!"

"Did you have to sell yourself?"

"It was stupid, I know," Ross said with a sigh. "But I had no future with the House of Pleasure. I just wanted to get some money. Valeriea also had some savings. We had plans. We wanted to leave."

"And Sel?"

"Sel?!" Ross looked at Paphian with a hint of surprise and regret. "Sel got married to Milera! If it weren't for Moren, he would probably still be with her... until his or her death. There was no room for me there anymore."

"It probably wasn't an easy decision," said Paphian.

"No..." Ross sighed heavily. "Sel probably doesn't want to offend me, but now that he has a second life, he doesn't dream of having a relationship with an ex-male whore. He's thrashing and doesn't know how to tell me. I think so."

"So he is a fucking idiot," summed up Paphian with a hint of anger. "I, if I could understand... had..." he waved his hand to somehow define it, having the most sincere intentions, "someone like you in my life," he paused to give more meaning to the words, which he wanted to say now: "I wouldn't let him go," he concluded gravely.

He could feel Ross's eyes on him. After a while he dared to meet his eyes, wondering if he would be mocked or misunderstood now.

But Ross looked at him as if he had never expected such words from him. He clearly didn't know what to say to that, it moved him so much.

Paphian smiled in mind. Ross was not acting as expected of him. He had a certain dignity and intuition that always told him how to behave so as not to become exaggerated or ridiculous under the careful observation of others. Even now, he tried to control his emotions.

"Thank you," he finally said in a choked voice.

Paphian nodded silently to him.

* * *

Dawn greeted them cool but sunny. Fortunately, some of the soldiers assigned to watch kept the fire burning throughout the night. Both commanders got up in good shape - taking their duties seriously, they did not indulge themselves too much last night. Only a few of the soldiers muttered dissatisfiedly as they stood up. Bedal awoke a coachman named Peer. His hair was even more disheveled than before, and his eyes drifted uneasily around the camp.

"Something's going to happen today," he said to the boy. "I feel it."

"We'll be right there," the boy protested at these words, but Peer shook his head.

Peer always seemed a little crazy. A year ago, his hair had started to turn gray at the temples, though he was not yet thirty. However, he was a good soldier and his companions got used to his unusual behavior. He involuntarily aroused sympathy.

"We were doing too well," he said mysteriously, leaving Bedal to his fate to look after the horses.

"What's up?" Nils asked. "Mad-eyed saw something in the forest?" he joked. "Trolls considered him their own, when he went aside and wanted to marry him with a female?"

"He has a feeling," Bedal said seriously. "And you know he usually is right. Like the last time he told us Ross was going to get in trouble and then they kidnapped him after the horse."

Nils looked serious immediately.

"What did he say this time?"

Bedal passed on Peer's words. Since the coachman's hunches were legendary among his companions, Nils knew they had to be treated with due care.

"Let's be careful," he said. "Tell Alesei and the others to be especially vigilant today."

Alesei became a kind of link between the soldiers and the healer's guards, because they saw him most often, especially at the beginning when they helped him in the first days. They also became the best friends with him, so far, especially Bedal, so the boy without hesitation went to the still sleeping bully, following the instructions of his older friend.

Alarmed by Peer's anxiety, the companions of the expedition carefully prepared for the further journey. Patrols were sent ahead. They were about four hours from Barnica. They had never met wanderers on their way, but now Kirian assumed that such an encounter would take place today. Only the tigers seemed calm, walking on either side of the carriage, as if they were taking care of it.

Vivan, though the anxiety had spread to him as well, woke up in a much better mood after yesterday evening. It was not even disturbed by the feeling that he would have to take on new responsibilities on the spot. It was, after all, a part of his life with which he felt inseparable. Knowing that he had friends around him comforted him, but it did not take away the fear that was already hidden in his heart. As they continued on, he reminded himself silently whenever he felt his fear begin to choke him again. Those who are probably waiting for him in Barnica are not the same as those barbarians from the marketplace in Verdomza! They are completely different people and must remember this. He known many of them throughout his life. There will be no second attack.

Besides, he's not alone now.

But no matter how often he told himself this, the fear would not leave him, and every accidental glance at his scarred hands reminded him of human cruelty...

* * *

The next day was not so hot and the weather slowly started to change. Clouds accumulated more and more, hanging low in the air, covering the tops of the mountains. It got colder. It started to rain. The captain was not thrilled with this state of affairs, and neither was the lieutenant of the guards. Such weather made visibility much more difficult, the road was blurred, sometimes mud was formed, mountain streams turned into brooks, people and animals were immediately soaked, and the rain distorted or even drowned out the sounds of the area. Fortunately, the route led higher now, hiding the travelers in the woods. In the valleys, the march would probably become more difficult.

At last the sight of a town in the valley spread out before them.

Or rather, it would have happened had it not been for the rain and fog that blocked the view almost completely from them, preventing them from enjoying its splendor. They saw neither the bay nor the houses well, let alone the peaks of the mountains there.

It was a strange and unusual experience for the travelers to finally reach this far, almost to the end of their journey. So much had happened before they got here.

Here they finally encountered patrols. Fortunately, their concerns about the possible danger in the forest turned out to be unfounded. It was not the forest that they would fear.

The town made them uneasy.

When they finally found themselves on the straight stretch of road that led directly to the town, they felt a growing tension. They were there.

Even from here, the recently built walls looked a bit ominous. Maybe it was the lack of sun, or maybe their mood... but the truth was, they hadn't been pleased with their arrival. Even the siblings looked at Barnica with caution.

Vivan was so tense he could barely remain calm. In fact, he already preferred them to arrive, he wanted to know what would happen next. Is something bad ahead of him or not?

He wanted to get over it.

Ross discreetly instructed the Jewel to act appropriately.

Everyone slowly felt that it was better to get there as soon as possible than to remain tense. They moved on vigorously.

Kirian, with a hunch, glanced at Ross, but the Jewel hidden beneath his uniform did not reveal its glow. But he was sure it was because of him that they had made that decision. Moments earlier, he remembered the marketplace and the bloody healer. The fear that the situation might happen again was strong, he was almost choking him. And then suddenly, as if in spite of himself, he abandoned these thoughts to move resolutely forward. It smelled like magical manipulation. Ross didn't show anything, cleverly avoiding suspicion. So the lieutenant had to stay with his guesses. In fact, he even felt grateful that the man had mobilized them.

Enough of procrastinating the inevitable.

"Ross," Sel said suddenly, drawing his partner's attention to it. "Whatever I was doing with my life, you were always in my mind."

After these words, he took a folded piece of paper from his breast pocket and handed it to him. Seeing the fragments of the drawing, Ross felt his heart speed up with barely hidden joy. He unfolded it carefully.

He held in his hands the portraits of himself that he had first seen in Sel's bedroom.

With tremor he pressed the drawing to his chest for a moment and handed it back saying:

"I was hoping you would say something like that."

* * *

Oliver looked at Sai through the patterns in the shutters of the carriage.

"How do I do that?" He whispered. "How? Aunt Semerald will be dead when she sees me. We don't have a chance to let her know sooner."

"Leave it to me," Julien replied softly. "I'll say that she is your and my father's cousin, daughter of Celina's father."

"This is getting sewn with too thick threads, Julien," he warned her nervously. "It was a miracle that the lie that we are cousins has gone through."

"Do you see any other way out? They'll get out of here eventually. This is the queen's personal guard and royal guards."

"What if it becomes too dangerous for Vivan for them to leave?"

"Sai talked about it with Sel."

"With Sel? What does she have to do with it?"

"Sel will say he has to go away to cool down and collect his thoughts. He will not tell the truth even to Ross. Then Selena is asked to ask him to take her with him and drive her back to her family. And Oliver will be coming home."

Oliver was silent, staring at the stretch of road.

"Sel is the Queen's appointed guardian of Vivan."

"Vivan will understand that."

"It will break Ross's heart."

Julien sighed heavily.

"The breakup must be real. Then I'll tell him the truth."

"What if Sel really thinks that?"

"He's going to tell me," Julien replied thoughtfully.

However, she felt that the conversation was starting to weigh on her for the sake of Ross. You cannot manipulate someone's feelings in this way.

"Oliver will be too much like Selena," he added thoughtfully. "Give it up. I'd rather wait until they leave."

She smiled warmly at him. He thought about everything. She was relieved that because of Ross and the dangers it involved, they would not implement this plan. She was sure he was thinking the same. She didn't have to hear his thoughts to know that. She had known him all her life.

"I got used to it so easily," he said. "That silence in my head..."

"Well, yes," she said sarcastically. "You're glad I'm not sitting there anymore..."

"I can feel you," he interrupted defensively. "I still think you're closer..."

She looked at him.

"Me too," she said with a little sadness.

"You regret?" He asked with fear in his heart.

She smiled fondly at him.

"No," she said.

He knew she had done it for him… like then, at night. He only hoped that someday he would also find happiness and understand fully what their decision had given them.

He wouldn't have done otherwise.

* * *

"Well," said Kirian seriously. "It's time to start!"

"Open the gate!" The captain exclaimed loudly, and all the wanderers with him felt that a turning point in their lives was happening now.

"Who's asking for it?" A deep voice asked from the walls.

"Asylas," Paphian said with a smile to his brother, who returned the smile nervously, listening for the continuation from inside the carriage.

"Healer brother," the captain replied thoughtfully, and shrugged at the lieutenant's questioning gaze. "It doesn't hurt to try."

"Yeah…" came a doubtful tone from above, "probably together with my mother!"

Paphian decided it was time to show up. He squeezed his brother's hand and left. Peer glared at him as if he suspected he had lost his mind by showing himself now.

"She said she didn't want to see you anymore!" He shouted cheerfully.

There was a clear commotion from above that lasted a while. Behind the smile, Paphian tried to hide his tension.

"Help?" Ross asked.

"Wait," Paphian replied. "First we'll see how things turn out."

"We open it!" They heard a loud answer and after a while the gate opened slowly.

The dog started barking. Several figures hurried over to them. One of them had a long, thick beard and long rust-colored hair. However, this was not what interested travelers who had never been to Barnica. The bearded man was accompanied by two elves, and the presence of elves in Verdome was so rare that it was always of interest. It was no different here. Apart from them, a few more lives were hiding on the walls.

"Lord Count!" The bearded man shouted a bit nervously, peering suspiciously at two white tigers "What a surprise! We are very pleased," he looked around at the soldiers with a quick glance. "They're an escort, I understand!"

"Dear Asylas," said Paphian to him, "please meet the queen's guards and the royal guards and their commanders - Teron and Kirian." They both bowed slightly. "And my friends, too," he pointed to Alesei, Sai, and Sel, also accidentally embracing with it Ethan, who was still with a strand of white hair and in civilian clothes sitting on his horse next to them. Ross, hidden under the hood and helmet, was slightly ahead of them. After the morning discussion, the captain decided that the switch was to continue, as it may have significance for other plans in the future. Another thing was that the paint Ethan had used on his hair did not wash off, which was concealed by Ross with a contemptuous smirk with a hint of satisfaction. Whether he wanted it or not, Ethan was still going to be Ross. With all the consequences.

Of course, Ross knew a way to remove it, but since the captain decided it might be useful...

"Yes, yes," Asylas replied nervously, glancing nervously back. "Asylas. Blacksmith. And these are Washeba and Silent, noble forest elves."

Washeba smiled a little provocatively at the men. Her red hair was pulled back into a braid. Silent did not change his expression.

Some of the men, including Alesei, immediately responded to the smile with theirs. The second elf was treated with reserve.

"I beg you, my lord," said Asylas nervously, though without the servility, "people will think you're carrying there," he pointed to the carriage, "the healer himself!"

Paphian looked at him meaningfully.

"Can not be!" The blacksmith was surprised. "But then he can't go in like this! You have to hide him!"

"You, give me your coat," he said to the girl. "Fast. We're about to arouse interest! And also during the day!" He looked at the sky. "Well, but maybe this rain... We will lead him home by a safe way, and you..." he thought for a moment. "Well!" He waved his hand. "Go! Ladies will see you and they will be disappointed and then they will leave!"

Paphian followed Asylas into the carriage. The blacksmith greeted the healer quickly and warmly.

"Can you go?" Paphian asked his brother with concern.

"I have to try," Vivan replied.

Paphian walked up to him and hugged him tightly.

"See you at home, brother," he told him with a feeling that hid both brotherly love and guilt and compassion.

Vivan returned the hug, feeling his brother's condition improve. The pain was gone.

"See you later," he whispered, touched.

He put on his coat and hid his face under the hood. Hurriedly, he walked over to say goodbye to the twins.

"Go with him," Julien suddenly told Oliver. "Go. You will warn our aunt!"

They both looked at her somewhat distractedly.

"She's right," said Vivan at last. "Go with me, Selena."

"Hurry up!" Asylas was nervous.

Oliver hugged his sister.

"I'll see you soon," she whispered to him. "Don't worry. It'll be fine."

He saw her comforting smile.

Selena's decision caused some anxiety among the guards. However, they did not have time to make any decisions. They could not accompany Vivan. They had uniforms.

"I'll go with you," said Alesei.

"Too big," with a sonorous tone said Silent unexpectedly.

"And I?" Sai asked him quickly.

Without hesitating, he nodded his head in agreement. Sai jumped off the horse and was next to them. Oliver's heart somersaulted again, this time with joy. He managed to exchange a brief glance with the healer.

The group quickly moved away from the travelers and disappeared through the gate.

Paphian locked himself with Julien inside the carriage. Comforting himself and her at the same time, he took her hand and squeezed it tightly. She looked into his eyes with concern.

"Let's go!" The captain commanded.

Peer snapped his whip at the show and the carriage followed through the gate following the troops accompanying him.

Filled with curiosity and fear, the cart finally reached their destination.

The city was filled with crowds of people...

THE END

ACKNOWLEDGEMENTS

This book would not have been written without a few important people whom I would like to thank.

First of all, Agnieszka - without her faith in this story I couldn't do it. It's like I always say: Frodo wouldn't have gone anywhere if it wasn't for Sam.

Renata - whose critical remarks and humor made me stand upright.

Mrs. Aneta, the publisher of the Healer, for the light in the tunnel, and Mrs. Katarzyna - for her wonderful cover.

Magdalena - the writer - for steadfastness and constant support.

And two people whose place gave me the atmosphere and the necessary balance in my life, which was as necessary to me then as the water in the desert. Thanks to the atmosphere prevailing in them, several scenes were created that "remembered" those moments in the pages of the book. A good spirit who is always willing to support the Healer - Damian. And to Daniel - briefly. I know how he hates comments.

Thank you all.

Table of contents

Printed in Poland
by Amazon Fulfillment
Poland Sp. z o.o., Wrocław